M'len and the pilot had not noticed me. I stepped silently into the hall, planning to cross the marble floor unannounced.

I had made perhaps a third of the distance when an hand came down firmly from behind me on my left shoulder.

Reflexively I dropped and kicked out. I felt my foot connect with something hard. Crouching free, I pulled my hair back from my face.

My would-be attacker was on his knees, clutching his diaphragm.

M'lennin and the pilot were leaning on each other, laughing hysterically. I saw the overturned chairs and spilled fruit on the floor, and the menial robot clicking irritably as it scurried to set things right.

"I would introduce you two," gasped the Liaison through tears of laughter, "but I see you have already met."

# RETURNING CREATION

## JANET MORRIS

A BAEN BOOK

Distributed in Canada by PaperJacks Ltd., a Licensee
of the trademarks of Simon & Schuster, Inc.

RETURNING CREATION

This is a work of fiction. All the characters and events portrayed in this book are fictional, and any resemblance to real people or incidents is purely coincidental.

A Baen Book

In Canada distributed by PaperJacks Ltd.
330 Steelcase Road, Markham, Ontario.

First Baen printing, October 1984

ISBN: 0-671-55915-X

Cover art by Victoria Poyser

Printed in Canada

Distributed by
SIMON & SCHUSTER
MASS MERCHANDISE SALES COMPANY
1230 Avenue of the Americas
New York, N.Y. 10020

# I.
## Chaldra of the Mother

I am Estri Hadrath diet Estrazi, former Well-Keepress of Astria on the planet Silistra. I have begun three times to tell this story, and three times I have been interrupted. This, then, the fourth attempt, will surely prove successful.

Perhaps you have heard of Silistra, the planet that was catalyst to the sexual revolution in the year twenty-two thousand, seven hundred and four Bipedal Federate Standard Time, or of the Silistran serums that lengthen life and restore vitality in virtually any bipedal life form, or perhaps you have at some time contracted the services of a Silistran telepath, or a precognitive, or a deep reader. It is possible that you have in your own home the scintillating, indestructible web-cloth woven by our domestic arachnids, or have seen holograms of our golachits, those intelligent builder-beatles who exude from their mouths a translucent, superhard substance called *gol* and create from this gol, under the guidance of the chit-guards, the formidable and resplendent structures in which we live and work.

And perhaps you have seen no web-cloth, no gol, never been ill, and are not interested in sex. If so, you may never have heard of Silistra.

I carry Silistra in my mind's eye, here under this alien sun. In my mind alone can I look out the east window of my beloved exercise hall in Well Astria and see the sun's rising burst upon the jewellike towers and keeps of the Inner Well and a thousand rainbows arc and dance in the greening sky.

I was Well-Keepress. Seven thousand people thrived under the aegis of my Well. I was sought and celebrated for my beauty and lineage, for I was great-granddaughter to Astria Barina diet Hadrath, the Well-Keepress who seduced M'Glarenn, Liaison First for the Bipedal Federation, and who changed the sexual habits of bipeds on one hundred and forty-eight worlds. I was high-couch in the greatest house of pleasure in the civilized stars. I commanded a great price.

Any being who was capable of desiring me, I could fulfill. I was fluent in the language and customs of fifty worlds. I had more than a passing acquaintance with the other ninety-eight. I was reasonably happy, happier than I knew.

I must speak briefly of chaldra and chaldric chains, for it is chaldra that brought me here, to this strange and frightening world, so far from all that I hold dear.

It is a Silistran saying that we are all bound, the least of us no more than the greatest, and a Silistran would have it no other way. The bonds of which the saying speaks are bonds of the spirit, of responsibility and duty and custom, and these are called chaldra. Upon the body of each Silistran, proudly displayed in twisted belts called chalds, are worn thin, supple, many-colored chaldric chains of precious metals. A Silistran without chaldra is a person bereft of purpose and self-respect, a pariah in our society. Indeed, all too often such unfortunate individuals, when unable to acquire ennobling chaldra, choose to take on the chaldra of the soil—by their death gaining that which was denied to them in life.

There is high-chaldra and low-chaldra. One example of high-chaldra is the chaldra of reproduction, of begetting one child (no easy task among Silistrans), which is symbolized by the bronze chain before the chaldra is met, and the golden chain after the child has been produced. Another is the chaldra of the mother and father, the task set by the parent of the same sex, symbolized by the red chain before completion and the blue when the task is done. The chaldra to the Stand of Well is high also, and the chain is always silver. Low-chaldra may be bonds of choice, such as the chaldra of couch-bound between a man and a woman, recognized by the pinkish titrium chain; or of skill, such as the black-iron Slayer's chain; or of vocation or avocation, as the Day-keeper's slate-colored chain or the golachit breeder's brown. There are over two hundred chaldric chains, if one counts both high and low.

I still wear my chald of eighteen intertwined chains. Once it lay snugly across my navel, but I have lost much weight in this dreadful place, and now it slaps annoyingly about my lower abdomen and I labor at the senseless tasks set me by my inscrutable masters.

I was marked from birth for this end, and all saw it, but none understood. I was born out of couch-bond to Well-Keepress Hadrath Banin diet Inderi by an out-worlder known only as Estrazi. My mother carried me thrice the normal term and died bearing me on the twenty-five thousandth anniversary of Well Astria.

How much my mother knew of my fate is still

open to conjecture, but until I received her legacy, and another, on my three hundredth birthday, I thought myself little different, if more favored, than my couch-sisters. The other bequest came in the form of a letter from my great-grandmother Astria, to be opened upon the three hundredth anniversary of my birth.

My great-grandmother's letter, which I received in the office of Rathad, my dead mother's half-brother and adviser to my Well, had my full name upon it and the date, Macara fourth seventh, 25,693, and was written eight hundred and forty years before I was born.

The letter lay between us on the table of thala-wood that I had shipped down from the northern forests as a gift to my mother's brother almost a full year ago. A silver cube, bright and shiny, lay beside the envelope, yellow with age, upon the night sky of the thala. The reflection deep within the wood seemed to go on forever.

Musicians tuning, laughing, limbering through their scales mixed with kitchen clank and the gol-master's hoarse calls as, outside the window, he set the golachits to their building. I did not rise from my seat to watch them at work in the Inner Well amid the bustle of the Well as it is rising, as I might have on another day. Nor did the smells of the morning meal, of baking bread and roasting meat, entice me. My appetite had disappeared with Rathad's summons. My recalcitrant precognitive gift had given me no warning, nor any information as to why, on this, the one day of the year on which I habitually secluded myself, seeing and speaking to no one, he had sent for me although my dreams were then and still are troubled, full of stars small enough to hold in one hand and seven men in a seven-cornered room who glow as no men should. The one who brought me here says that some day I'll understand my dreams, and I believe him. But then, as now, I had only troubled nights.

On that day, long ago, Rathad had sent a messenger to summon me from my solitude. I had run the entire distance to Rathad's keep, filled with foreboding, leaving the messenger in the exercise hall staring, undismissed, openmouthed at my undignified haste.

When I'd reached the mirrored doors and burst through them, I was badly winded. Rathad did not so much as raise his grizzled head to me in greeting, but waved me to the dark carved chair, silent, staring fixedly at the two objects on the table between us.

My breathing was no longer labored when Rathad, his fingers upon the silver cube, raised his eyes to mine.

"Daughter of my sister," he said, "have you, perhaps, some foreknowledge of these things before me, that you have arrived here so swiftly?"

I shook my head no, and his jibe passed unanswered, though at any other time I would have berated him for disturbing me at my exercises and for teasing me about my psychic retardation—one of my breeding and my standing should have been a foreseer of note by now.

He sighed. "One can only hope that the foreseeing abilities of your mother, and, it seems, your great-grandmother"—his hand was on the envelope—"may someday manifest in you. You have no idea, then, why I sent for you today, or even why you showed such uncharacteristic haste in presenting yourself to me?"

"None at all." I did not care for the amused condescension in his voice. I am, as you may have guessed, a very weak foreseer; then, as now, this was irksome: "Did you call me to discuss my psychic debilities? If so," I said, rising, "I will return to my day's undertakings."

"Will you indeed? I doubt it. Now, sit back down. Good. It would be a sad thing, Estri, if you let our personal differences prevent you from receiving this message from your mother, and this ... ah, shall we say, unusual communication from the Foundress of the Well herself." He was leaning back in his chair, fondling his chald, a smile playing around his lips.

"What do you mean, Rathad? Do not toy with me." Rathad, and men like Rathad, were a blight upon my happiness, always trying to mold me, to guide me, to shape me to their vision of what a Silistran Well-Keepress should be.

"I mean but what I say, Well-Keepress. This," he said, picking up the silver cube, each side of which was the length of my middle finger, "is a recording device, popular in the days of my youth. When your mother knew herself pregnant with you, she came to me with it and asked that I deliver it to you at this time. She knew she would not survive your birth."

I heard the bitterness in his voice. It was common knowledge that Rathad considered his sister's self-sacrifice ill-conceived, and had urged her to abort me. Because it was his chaldra to do so, he had brought me up. I am sure he would rather have drowned me upon the day of my birth, so great was his love for my mother, Hadrath. Should I return to the Well of my birth and tell him what I now know or show him what I have become, he might try it yet.

"And this," he continued, fingering the yellowed envelope, "this comes to us through the kindness of Day-Keeper Ristran, who attests to its authenticity, and bids me to tell you it has lain in the

Hall of Records these eight hundred and forty years, awaiting your maturity.

"I have not opened either of them, nor do I have any information as to their contents. I have my suppositions, of course, the validity of which we will ascertain here together." Again that deeply seasoned face smiled at me. Rathad's smile has always made me nervous. It is the smile of the predator upon a new kill. If he had been a woman, he would have been dangerous to me, probably attempted to usurp my position. Since he was not, we had a wary understanding: he attempted to turn me to his purpose, and I to stymie him. It was a game which I thought then was very serious. Since then, I have learned what is serious and what is merely annoying. I will have much to say to Rathad, should I have the opportunity.

That day, however, I had no benefit of hindsight. I was full of the insolence of a young high-couch, the budding of my maturity. I made a face at my uncle, who ignored the impropriety.

His hand closed about the silver cube, and he shook it. A dull rattle came from it. "As is often the case with such containers, there is something within." He placed the cube carefully beside the envelope and folded his hands on the desk as if meditating on the two objects before him.

I knew he expected me to burble questions, to thank him, or perhaps to reach eagerly for the envelope or the cube. Suspecting a trap, I did none of those. I sat as quietly as he.

Finally he said, "Which one, which will you explore first, Estri?" and reached out to fondle the cube.

Having won the waiting game, I grabbed for the silver shape so fast I brushed his retreating hand. He had not made clear to me the significance of the letter, except that it was old and that it had been in the possession of the Day-Keepers, those among us who study the past and keep its legacy. In any case, I, who had never seen my mother's face or heard her voice, had in my hands that which she had meant for her daughter to hold. Emotion roared through me like the Falls of Santha. My hands shook and my tongue attached itself to the roof of my dry mouth.

I held it, turning the metal cube in my fingers. My mother's name rang in my head. I searched for my voice but, as my wits occasionally do, it had deserted me.

Bereft of words, I examined the silver cube. On it were two small circular insets, and above them a larger triangular one, all on one side of the object. The other sides were, as far as I could determine, featureless. I was afraid, suddenly, that I might somehow damage it before its long-held secrets could be revealed. And this fear brought back to me the gift of speech: "How does it work?"

"Hold the cube with the circles uppermost."

I did so.

"Farther away from you. Now, press once firmly upon the triangle."

I did this also, and a rectangular section halfway down the cube's surface slid back, and then from the opening extruded a dished bar, metal on all sides but the one facing me, which was composed of two lenses recessed in a metal frame.

"Put the eyepiece against your eyes so that the metal bar between is in contact with the bone at the bridge of your nose. Now, press the left-hand circle, once only."

I held the expanded cube before my eyes. It was contoured so that it rested against the bones of my face snugly, letting in no light.

"Carefully!" I heard Rathad say, though all I could see before me was a dark milky distance, an artificial distance. And I was discomfited: this object that I held in my hand was an article of off-world manufacture, a creation of the off-worlders, a machine-thing. Though I had made "friends" among the off-worlders and learned to use their toys, I prided myself on being a scandalous young rebel. My mother, I had always been told, had had a better sense of propriety. That she would send me an off-worlders' toy as her gift across the years was an act of questionable fitness. It occurred to me that this point had not been lost on her brother, my uncle, Rathad, and I smiled.

Then I pressed the left-hand circle.

For a moment, nothing happened. Then I saw her.

My mother was standing before a window set into umber gol, the same shade as Rathad's keep. Her dress was the simple wide-sleeved white and silver of the Keepress, chald-belted, and flowing translucent to the floor. Her belly seemed a trifle rounded, but her breasts were high and firm, the nipples standing well up. I thought her much more beautiful than I. Her skin was the rare Silistran white, transparent and delicate. Her eyes were the gray-green of the predawn sky. Her hair was the color of the finest northern thala—black, blue, and glistening silver. She was smaller than I, wider-boned. Otherwise we were much alike. Her nose was as mine, deliciously straight, chiseled, and haughty. I could see her nostrils flaring as she breathed. Her mouth, also, was like mine, full, sensuous, with a touch of cruelty at each indented corner. Her cheekbones were high and wide, her chin tiny yet firm, with the subtlest hint of a cleft in its middle. But for the size and coloring, her stamp was heavy upon me.

The woman in the little box—that is, the image

of my mother preserved therein—stepped forward.
She raised a fine-boned hand to her forehead.

And then, for the first time in my life, I heard
my mother's voice.

It was musical and breathy: "Little one, spark of
life that kicks and twists inside me, now that the
moment is here, I do not know how to say what I
must. Since you have received this, my life has
been well-bartered." My mother cleared her throat,
rubbing her belly absently with her hands.

"I have some fear that Rathad and others may
press guilt upon you. Let me assure you, by my
own mouth, that you were conceived in love, with
full understanding of the consequences, and, values weighed, that my life for yours is little to give.

"Oh, Estri—for that is the name you will bear—at
this time in my life, when I most wish to be warm
and loving, to give you all of motherhood and
sustaining purpose in a few short moments, I find
myself cold with fear and stiff with self-conscious-
ness. How will you see me, daughter? I did not
desert you willingly. The arrangements for your
upbringing have been well attended to, your social
and economic position secured. But what is it to
be without the touch of a mother's hand, the com-
forting circle of her arms, in those difficult times
of youth?" My mother's face seemed suddenly to
twist; she half-turned as if someone else had entered the room or spoken, and I saw a temper such
as I'd often been told by Rathad that only I, of my
entire line, had ever dared display.

Then she turned back and her face was composed and elegant once again: "No recording can
give you that which has been denied by fate and
need. If you can bear me no ill will for the frailty
of my flesh, I will know it, for I have demanded of
my eternal spirit that it watch over you all your

days. I have no doubt that this will be so." She stopped, swallowed hard, blinking.

"That is the worst of it, I think," continued my mother.

"Now that there is understanding between us, child unborn, I would speak to you of your father, and what was between us, your parents. Though we were couch-met, it was as if I had known him for a thousand forevers. Our races are only semi-compatible, hence the long term which I will carry you, and my projected death at your birth. The benefits to the issue of such a union far outweigh the debits. You will live twice, perhaps three times the normal Silistran span. Were you slow maturing, little one? You now know the reason. Within you lie dormant abilities far beyond the ken of those around you, and in time you will come to know them.

"We are as children to your father's people, and he did me great honor in choosing me to bear his get. . . ." Again she paused as if searching for composure.

I remember thinking that this was exactly the sort of mother I'd longed to have, the perfect mother, full of grace, and I remember blinking, with my eyes pressed to the little device so tightly that my lashes brushed the lenses recessed there.

Then my mother continued: "All of which brings me to the chaldra I would put upon you: it is my wish, and that of your sire also, that you seek him and meet with him, be it here on Silistra or upon the planet of his origin. Little help can I give you in your task, for there is a testing in its accomplishment, but be sure that there is reason greater than any you could dream in our request. The time is short, and I must hurry." She looked down for a moment at something off the screen.

"You will soon see the evening of your conception.

What prompted me to record our coupling, I do not know, unless it was the meeting that preceded our union. But it is the only ... likeness of your father ... available. And it is ... something more. You will understand, when you view it, why you have not received this until, in your own blossoming maturity, you have become wise in the ways of men.

"When the record is ended, put your hand beneath the cube, and receive the ring of your father. The ring is the key. Keep it on your person, even in sleep, until you rest within your father's house. It will identify you and keep you safe among his people, should your search take you so far."

She smiled, a smile I will never forget.

"It is, child of my heart, a great sadness to me that our meeting and parting be so close together. Remember, Estri, I love you and am with you ever. Tasa, Estri Hadrath diet Estrazi."

The grayed screen flickered, became what could only have been the magnificent bedchamber of my mother, the Keepress.

And then I saw her there, upon the silver covers of the couch, her skin glistening with sweat. Her breasts rose and fell with her impassioned breathing, nipples flushed and erect. She leaned back on stiff arms, naked, her marvelous long legs outstretched, slightly spread, her feet beneath the iridescent coverlet.

The room was candlelit, and the light flickered and glowed about her.

"Come, then, barbarian god," she taunted, teeth flashing, "come and take me, if you can. Put that deathly seed of yours where it will do the most good." She laughed low, and tossed her head. Her hair fell curling across her left breast.

"You must petition me more prettily than that, well woman, before I fill your belly." The second voice was deep, undeniably commanding, full of strange sibilances. "Surely you cannot expect to do so little, and receive so much. Show me the skills that have made you high-couch here. Or, perhaps, you do not truly possess them?"

With a leap from the darkness, he was on her, one knee beside each of her breasts, his hand still upon her throat. He turned his head to her left shoulder, and his face, eyes heavy-lidded in his heat, was clearly defined.

He was indeed and truly my father. His eyes and hair were the color of molten bronze, his skin but scant tones lighter. His body was light-boned for his mass, and the muscles on his frame rippled in long flat slabs as he crouched above her.

That was the first time I ever saw one of the glowing ones in the flesh. Even then, filled with conflicting emotions over what I saw before me and the impropriety of being a voyeur at one's own conception, it wasn't lost on me that his skin and his person resembled the glowing seven in my dreams. But I also knew, even then, that this man was none of those, that this was a purer being than any my dreams had shown me.

I watched my father take my mother, and I have never seen a woman so diabolically aroused, so freed from the bonds of mind. He brought her, leaping to his hand, to the edge of climax three times before he allowed her to attempt to please him. Finally, acquiescing to her desperate pleas, he lay back and allowed her to work her skills on him. Their multilingual love-abuse encompassed all that I knew and went beyond.

Once he pulled her head from his lap, and holding her arched back by the hair, said in archaic Silistran, "You are truly worthy to be high-couch," and thrust her head back down.

When he was ready, he lifted her into the air

and set her down upon him as one might lift a young child of no significant weight. If she had been beneath him, the violence of that final coupling surely would have crushed the life from her there and then.

The last thing I saw was my mother nestled in the crook of his arm, her tears rolling down his shoulder, to settle in the hollow in his throat.

The screen went blank and something inside me wilted: I knew what I had been looking for, among the men I had encountered, and even why I had turned on occasion to off-worlders in hopes of finding it. No such man existed among Silistrans as this one who was my father; no such man existed among the off-worlders I had met. A Silistran woman has a duty to find her soul's mate, and mine had long seemed impossible to discharge: even without knowing it, I had judged every man I met against the standard my flesh knew—the standard of my father—and all men had failed that test. It was possible, I thought then, that I would never find him, never find one like him, never discharge the chaldra of the mother, never beget one child as was my responsibility. But I should have trusted my mother better.

Nonplussed, feeling ultimately lonely and completely deserted by a mother I'd never had, I started to lift the cube from my face, only at the last moment remembering my mother's instructions.

Just in time, my hand shot out to catch the ring as it fell from the opening bottom of the cube.

I did not look at it, but pushed the cube across the table to Rathad, who'd been quiet this long while and was waiting, watching me, with an odd look on his face.

My uncle asked for my permission to view the cube and with a nod, I gave it. I could not speak. The room swam before my eyes. I leaned back in

the carven thala chair, the ring clutched unex-
amined in my fist, to let my tears flow while my
mother's brother viewed the cube.

I had not cried for some years, and as the moisture of my grief and joy poured out of me and
filled my lap, my confusion was washed away with
those unaccustomed tears.

For the first time in my life I was sure in my
purpose: I knew what I must do. I raised my head
to tell Rathad, but he was still sunk deep within
Hadrath's record.

Dispassionately I deep-read him, knowing that
he could not feel the touch of my mind while so
engrossed in my mother's story. If foreseeing is my
weakest skill, deep-reading is my strongest. I can,
in moments, and without trancing, acquire from
any sentient being an accurate estimate of his basic nature, motivation, and any deep-seated emotion he is feeling. I did so. I was pleased with what
I saw. Rathad would be less troublesome to me in
the near future. He was deeply moved and full of
remorse. Whether or not he had treated me fairly,
he now felt that he had not, and that was sufficient.

If he had caught me shamelessly deep-reading
him, however, I would have lost all that, through
my mother, I had gained. I withdrew almost
immediately.

My father's ring was still clenched in my right
fist. So much was happening, my head was so full
of plans, I had not even looked at it.

I brought my fist to eye level and slowly opened
my stiff fingers. I had been clutching it so tightly
that the blood had been forced from my hand.

My father's ring lay face up on my cold, wet
palm. The metal was a pale yellow in color, perhaps gold. It was very large and heavy. I could
have fit two fingers within its circle. I remembered the hand that had worn the ring, and I

shivered. Within the bezel was set a glowing black stone, as large as a titrium half-well coin, and in the black stone itself were a thousand white points of light, scattered in a seemingly random pattern. As I looked closer, I determined that these were not characteristic markings of the black stone, but tiny inset gems, some as small as a pore on the skin, some slightly larger. One of the bigger stones was not white, but a brooding blood color. This was set in the upper-right corner. If this random patterning could be said to resemble a spiral, then the red stone was far out on the northeastmost arm. I had never seen such a ring. The craftsmanship was exquisite. I turned it. The sides were covered with raised script, but it was no language with which I was familiar.

I slipped my first and middle fingers within the band and closed my hand into a fist once more. I wished there was a way to make it smaller, but I knew I would not so deface it. I put my right hand within my left, and both in my lap. I would have to find another way to wear my father's ring. I considered the possibilities until I heard Rathad place the cube back upon the table.

His face was ashen white and his eyes bleary. He leaned his elbows upon the table and supported his chin with one hand. In the other he held the letter. He extended it to me. I shook my head and made no move to take it.

"Not yet," I said. "That which has waited so long can wait a while longer. Summon a runner. I will leave with Santh tomorrow morning. There is much to do before the next sun's rise. If Ristran is still here, I will meet with him in my keep, and we will take our mid-meal there together." Ristran was a high Day-Keeper, one of the few who held the administrative rank of dharener, and a hide council member—he could make my departure much easier than it might otherwise be. He could also, if he chose, make my quest a short and easy one: the high officials were the keepers of a body of secret knowledge that not even I, a Well-Keepress, had access to; they had their own leader, the dharen, a mythical personage who may or may not, as they claim, be the same dharen who led Silistra out of darkness after the war so long ago. Whatever the truth of the dharen's age, he is Silistra's spiritual leader and his servants, the dhareners and the lesser Day-Keepers, are a law higher than the Well Laws, the supreme authority among us.

"If not," I continued in my most authoritative tone, "then I will do the same with the highest-ranking Day-Keeper you can produce by that time. I will also need the toilet women to help me prepare. Send a chalder also to Jana's room, for she will be high-couch while I am gone." Jana and I thought al-ke on most social and political issues; she had met her chaldra of reproduction, and I liked and respected her. She would enjoy being high-couch, but not so much that she would be unwilling to relinquish the position when the time came.

"Impossible," Rathad snapped. His face had regained its normal color.

"Which?" I asked.

"All of it, Estri. You cannot leave the Well until the chaldric priorities have been determined, if at all. How many chains do you wear? Are all of them meaningless when compared to this adventure? Such tasks are usually carried out before major responsibilities are assumed. The Day-Keepers must decide. I have never heard of a three-hundred-year-old woman, of responsibility and position, romping off to do the chaldra of the mother. Perhaps thay will allow it, but not until the papers have been filed, the purifications done, the ceremonies complete. It will take time." His voice was very loud, his face red.

"It will not," I said calmly, "take longer than a day. It will probably take less. All these objections you make are the prattle of an old man. I have the chaldra of the mother to perform. It takes precedence over all mundane matters. As for the Day-Keepers 'allowing' it, how not?" I said blithely. "The dhareners are always complaining that we don't 'rise to our full potential.' That's why I want Ristran, so that none of you old men can bind me up with your paperwork and your time until I, too, am old and frightened of my shadow as it falls on the Inner Well."

"And your chald," Rathad continued as if I had not spoken. "You cannot go without another strand being added. We cannot allow the Well-Keepress to go jaunting off to an undisclosed destination with her chald in need of an additional strand. It must be made, wound, prayed upon. The chalder will never be able to produce one for you in a matter of hours, should he wish to, which he will not. You cannot possibly leave before Detarsa fourth seventh. It will take the full pass to arrange things. I do not agree with you about Jana. There are those more deserving of such an honor." He rubbed his hand across his face. "But if you insist upon her, she must be readied to take on your duties. All these things take time. It is now the last of Macara. Give me these twenty-eight days, and when the pass is done, I will not obstruct you. Truly, I do not obstruct you now, but simply remind you of the forms to which you must attend. Perhaps the Day-Keepers will uphold you. The circumstances here are very unusual. But whatever comes to be, you must meet your fate with an eye to the traditions of this Well, and with dignity and grace."

"I know you mean well, Rathad, and that you would not obstruct me," I said, though I was not as sure as I pretended—Rathad was like a collar around my neck. But he was also my mother's brother, and he too had looked into the silver cube and seen her there. So I pressed the advantage I knew I had, then and there: "I ask you again to attend to these things for me. Only summon for me Ristran, the dharener, or some other high Day-Keeper, the chalder, and the others that I need. I feel certain that this matter can be arranged in a way acceptable to all concerned. If I am wrong, then I have but taken mid-meal with the Day-Keeper, and discussed certain matters with the high-chalder. I will take Santh to the Liaison First's tomorrow, whatever the outcome, so I will need the fitter and the toilet women. I will let the subject of Jana rest for the present, but the rest must be done." I smiled my most winning smile.

"Estri," Rathad rubbed his cheeks with his palms in exasperation, "you are not listening to me—oh, the words, perhaps, but not the sense of what I am saying. This is dangerous. Your . . . father . . . what kind of creature might he be? What kind of peril are you hastening toward? You are Well-Keepress—"

"That is who I am," I agreed with equanimity. "And the Well-Keepress is ready for a meal: parr and eggs, fresh fruit, cheese, and wine. Perhaps enough for three, for the high-chalder might also be hungry. Do hurry, for midday is close upon us."

Shaking his head, a smile playing across his lips, Rathad strode to the mirrored doors with a swirl of his iridescent web-cloth robe. I heard his muffled voice giving instructions to the runner just outside. I sighed with relief. I had been unsure I could persuade him.

When he reentered, he did not sit again behind the table, but came to lean against it by my side, so close that I could see every white curling hair that poked its way through the straps of his thonged sandal.

"There remains this second . . . bequest, if that is the proper word, from your great-grandmother, Estri." He handed me the old yellowed envelope once again, and this time I took it.

I broke the seal and withdrew the sheet within. The hand was sure and strong. There was no greeting.

It said: *"The woman I seek, whose name the envelope bears, is all of a color, the color of the spring sun rising, with hair of molten bronze that brushes the ground. In my vision it seemed that this woman and I were of a kind. I will never know. To her I say: 'Guard Astria, for you may lose it, and more. Beware one who is not as he seems. Stray not into the port city of Baniev. And lastly, look well about you, for your father's daughter's brother seeks you.'*

*"If you succeed, you will be lauded, even as I am lauded, for you will accomplish more than you attempt. Be strong, for the father will surely help his daughter."*

It was signed "Astria Barina diet Hadrath."

I read it twice. A woman from the distant past had looked forward to this day and seen me: for *I* have a glowing tinge to my skin, not so bright as my father's, perhaps, but there—and bronze hair that in those days brushed the ground. She'd parted the veil of years to speak to me. And what had she said? Lose Astria? Never. The Well named after my great-grandmother was my heritage.

I read the letter again, and the riddle there became no clearer. It seemed that every hair on my body stood away from my flesh. It is said that obscurity is the cloak of the forereader. My great-grandmother had drawn that cloak close about her on the writing of this message. That it was meant for me, and no other, was beyond doubt. But no one is as he seems; I had no intention of visiting Baniev, far up the coast; and I had no brother. Her encouragement made even less sense. My search was of personal import only, and my mother had said it was a testing, so no help from my father would be forthcoming.

I had no fear for Astria, I told myself. The Well was in the same hands that had guided it these three hundred years. But I would take care.

I shook my head and handed the perplexing oracle to Rathad.

I felt most discomforted, yet I was glad my great-grandmother's message had reached me. It would be a stout lever with which to pry the Day-Keepers from their conventions.

"What sense do you make of it, Estri?" said Rathad, frowning at the letter in his hands.

"Very little," I replied, "but I will look more sharply about me, and you must see the affairs of the Well with great care."

"Doubtless there is a hidden meaning," he mused.

"Doubtless," I agreed. "But perhaps it is too well-hidden."

"I would take all pains to avoid Baniev, were I you," he continued.

"I will avoid," I announced, "not only Baniev, but Baniese also, and products bearing that city's stamp."

"Has it occurred to you," my mother's brother asked, "that much time has passed since Hadrath's death, and the father you seek may be no longer among the living?"

"It occurred to me," I admitted. "But the message of my mother said he awaits me, and it was she who chose the point in time at which I would assume the chaldra. If he is dead, it is by accident and not by age or infirmity. I must seek him. Who knows how long the bronze people live? Not I."

Rathad grunted and sucked his teeth. "I yield." He sighed. "If it was known that you would take this chaldra and make this journey eight hundred and forty years ago, then, by the Day-Keepers' Clock, you must make it, and I must give you whatever help I can."

He reached behind him for the silver cube, and handed it and the letter, which he placed carefully within the envelope, from his pale hands into my copper ones.

"Run, child," said he, bending to kiss my cheek, "or you will keep the Day-Keeper waiting."

# II.
## The Liaisons, First and Second

When I could restrain Santh's need to hunt no longer, I found a resting place in the shade of two large boulders, removed the surcingle from about his black-furred girth, and let him loose.

The hulion lowered his black-maned, leonine head, blinked his slit-pupiled eyes, and butted me from his path only half-playfully. Though Santh's intelligence might well rival a man's, his instincts ruled him: it was time for the hulion to hunt, and hunt he must. For my sake, he had refrained from nature's call as long as he could.

With a great leap and a snap of his mighty wings, he was off, bounding and gliding, silent, deadly. Four bounds took him from my view. There is nothing on Silistra to compare with the speed of a hulion at the hunt.

While I waited for him to return, cool and comfortable in the late-morning shadows, my back against the larger boulder, I reviewed the events that had brought me here to the trail that would lead, by nightfall, to the house of the Liaison First, M'lennin, my former couchmate.

My mid-meal with Ristran, the dharener, had
produced some surprises and a satisfactory outcome. The Day-Keepers are a mysterious, solitary
lot, and rarely frequent the Wells; a dharener such
as Ristran, who oversees the comportment of lesser
Day-Keepers, makes a habit of inscrutability, the
better to keep the underlings of his hierarchy at a
distance. As for the rest of us Silistrans—to us
dhareners are fabled creatures, rarely seen and
seldom met. If I had not been Well-Keepress, I
never could have secured an audience with one.

I had supposed, somewhat naively, that Ristran's
primary interest would be the objects of antiquity
I possessed. It was my father's ring, the cube and
the letter, I was certain, that had moved him to
rearrange his affairs and see me so readily. I have
always been Well-Keepress, or Well-Keepress in
training, or Well-Keepress to be—sometimes I underestimate the effect my station has on men. In
the matter of my meeting with the dharener, I was
taken completely by surprise: I hadn't thought of
our encounter as one between a man and a woman.

Yet I read his desire when we touched hands in
greeting, and the fantasy deep within his mind
was an easy one for me to fulfill. I pleasured him
while he lay back on the amber cushions, matching my actions to the picture I had pulled from his
subconscious. Dealing intimately with men on a
daily basis, I have found that, as with women, in
matters of sexuality, neither intelligence nor spiri-
tuality serve to mitigate or transform lust. We are,
and will always remain, procreative creatures, and
the urge in Silistrans is so strong that none can
deny it and remain either sane or healthy: only
wizened, self-destructive souls pretend otherwise.

Ristran, it turned out, was eminently sane and
completely healthy, unabashed in thought and competent in deed. The fantasy his mind whispered to

mine was not unlike that of a brin-brewer or a
golachit-master, but he was wise enough to know
that this was normal, although I had never couched
a spiritual master before and was at first expecting something more arcane than I might find any
evening among the customers who frequent Well
Astria.

In such a situation, where I was the supplicant
in the real world and he the powerful one who
could grant the favor I'd come there seeking, his
desire to take pleasure while giving nothing back
by spilling seed where it could not take root was
not as scandalous as it would have been on a Well
couch, where a man and woman unite in hopes of
creating new life.

Thus I delivered him his dream without protest,
and the taste of him was thick and overly sweet,
the taste of a man long denied.

It had been so quickly done that the food upon
the low thala table was still warm when we seated
ourselves to eat.

We struck a bargain that benefited us both. I
would leave the cube and letter with the Liaison,
who would deliver the originals into Ristran's
hands, taking with me in their stead the copies
which I knew M'lennin's star technology could
provide. In exchange for these priceless artifacts,
Ristran waived all formalities and ceremonies usually associated with the assumption of chaldra—
including the need for a new, virgin chald—and
upheld me in the face of the chalder's wrath when
we went together to the chalder's shop to expedite
the matter.

The chalder, although clearly resentful at having the dignities of his office preempted, did as the
high Day-Keeper instructed. After a perfunctory
blessing, my old chald was cut from me by the
chalder's hand, the red chain woven into the al-

ready existing belt, and certain alterations made in the chald's construction. These were the addition of a hidden lock, and a tiny key which slipped into a compartment in the lock itself when not in use. Thus I could remove the chald at will, rather than wearing it soldered about my waist. Before I snapped the lock shut, I had drawn the width of the chald through the band of my father's ring, in this fashion securing the ring on my person.

When we left the chalder, Ristran, his hand on my waist, offered additional assistance: since even the dharener had been unable to decipher the script on the ring or identify the race of people to which my father belonged, he suggested that I travel to Arlet, where he would provide me with an expert in off-world culture and language in such a way that secrecy might be maintained.

Thinking only that the Day-Keeper had now made it impossible for my uncle, Rathad, to prevent my departure, I accepted, only afterward realizing that Arlet lies uncomfortably close to Baniev, that port city which I had intended to avoid.

But by the time I had recollected by geography, Ristran was long gone, and I was already making my way across the plain that separated the Liaison's keep from Well Astria.

Previous to my departure, with the help of the two toilet women, I had made what I considered the supreme sacrifice: I had cut my ankle-length bronze mane. It had been my trademark. I could do little about my skin tone, but it had become fashion in Well Astria (and to a lesser extent in Port Astrin, our dependent city) for the women to spend long hours beneath the sun, gilding themselves with oils and ointments so that their skin might glow golden in the manner of Well-Keepress Estri.

With my hair now so shorn that it barely reached

to my buttocks and confined in a thick braid down my back, I could be any Astrian well woman of high position. My chald was thicker than most, but whatever degree of anonymity I could foster would serve me. I wore a soft tas-skin jerkin, cream-colored and sueded, and matching knee boots to protect my legs on the trail. Above my chald was another belt, of thick parr-hide, from which hung a full coin pouch and double-bladed hunting knife.

I felt fierce and strong, and very free. I had not realized how heavy the cares of the Well had been until I laid them aside.

I took the surcingle I had removed from Santh and wedged it between the boulders. In its laced pockets were the cube and letter, dried meat and fruits, and a waterskin.

The shadows were rapidly disappearing as the sun reached its zenith and I was thirsty, as well as anxious to be on my way. I called Santh silently, with all the mind-force I had.

His answering mind-picture was clear and sharp: I could clearly see his black wedge-shaped head, tufted ears laid back, yellow eyes slitted from the sun, mighty fangs bared in a silent roar. He had heard me and was on his way.

M'lennin, the outworlder who had been my couchmate, had found Santh and his sister abandoned by the Falls of Santha. What had happened to their mother was impossible to determine. Santh had been small enough to cuddle in my arms when the Liaison gave him to me as a couch gift. His shoulders now were the height of my own, though I stand upon two legs and he upon four. The intelligence of the hulion has never been studied, for they are rare and seldom thrive outside their native mountainous home, but I guess it be at least as great as our own. However, they are not tool-makers. Somewhere back in antiquity Santh's ancestors had chosen not to compete with the hairless bipeds of the plains and valleys. They live their own way, isolated, primal, high in the crags of the Sabembe range.

In some ways the hulion and Silistran are much alike. M'lennin calls us of Silistra anachronistic, haughty primitives. We, like the hulion, insist upon our freedom and individuality. Silistra once trod the path of technological culture. In our prehistory lies a long and bloody story of wars, of great and powerful governments, of taxation and oppression, of madness and suicide. At length the people rose up and dismantled the machines that had come to rule them, and the parasitic bureaucracy that served those machines.

M'lennin would argue that it was the men, not the machines, we sought to dismantle, to neuter and to render impotent—M'lennin, a M'ksakkan from beyond the sky, does not understand the role of women in our culture, nor is he comfortable with the Law Within.

It is a Silistran saying that the law lies within the man, and that no amount of coercion from without can alter that law. The hulions, also, obey the law within. Santh is no more mine than I am his. It may be that in Santh's mind, I am his charge and in his care. Whatever the truth of it—if there is only a single truth to be had in this or any case—we serve each other, Santh and I, with respect, admiration, and more than a little love.

Soon after I had mind-called Santh, I saw a spot in the azure sky, far to the west. I stood, shielding my eyes, to watch him come.

The tiny black spot rapidly became a speck, rising high into the air, gliding, stooping, disappearing from sight, then rising again. Soon I could see his wings, snapping out straight at the height of his arc, beating the air to ease his descent, then the coiled crouch and spring as his powerful hind-quarters thrust him almost instantaneously back into the air, with those mighty wings pulled close to his sleek black back.

A bound away, I saw that he carried something in his jaws. When he furled his pinions and padded to my side, he dropped the mangled carcass at my feet and lay proudly beside it, growling softly in his throat. I could not tell what animal that bloodied corpse had been. Only a few tatters of red-brown fur remained, and the head had been bitten cleanly off at the shoulder. Its hooves were cloven and black, its four legs long and spindly. I thought it some subspecies of bondrex, the nimble plains grazers—but which, I could not tell.

I stepped over it, carefully approaching the hulion, who had just mauled a man-sized animal and might still be imbued with kill-fever. "Santh," I said softly, slowly extending my hand toward his head to scratch behind his ears.

The great hulion stretched his neck appreciatively as I scratched beneath his ear and began licking the blood from his outstretched paws with his coarse tongue.

"Thank you, Santh," I said as I bent to cut a strip of the still-warm flesh from a half-gnawed haunch. It would have been an insult not to eat of his kill, though I had neglected to bring a fire-maker, and I am not fond of raw meat.

Santh rolled onto his side and watched me eat through slitted, yellow eyes. I cut another piece and chewed it noisily, exclaiming my praise through a half-filled mouth. The blood ran down my arms and stained my tas-skin jerkin. I made great show and ate little. The meat was tough, stringy, and tasteless.

I got down a third thin strip, wiped my bloodied

knife on my boot, and returned it to its parr-hide sheath.

Then I got the surcingle from between the boulders and stood over Santh's drowsy head.

"Get up, lazy one," I demanded, prodding him with my foot and pointing to the surcingle. "We must make M'lennin's by nightfall."

Complaining loudly, Santh stretched and rose. I threw one end of the web-weave band over his back, between his shoulder and forewing and, grabbing the dangling end from beneath his belly, hitched it tight. Having secured the cube and letter from harm by this means, I relaxed again. Whatever might happen on the trail, Santh would bring the cube and letter to M'lennin. Although the danger of the open plain is slight, and with such a companion slighter still, I had been uneasy in Santh's absence. Silistrans have only one natural enemy: other Silistrans. I had seen no one since we had set out before sun's rising, but one fears the enemy one doesn't see. With Santh at my side, I feared nothing.

We set out again, I at my easiest jog and Santh padding beside. He would have allowed me to ride him, but my legs were strong under me. I had not had time for my usual exercise this day, or yesterday, and I needed to work the kinks from my muscles.

Santh paced me patiently until I felt loose and pleasantly tired. Then we rested and shared the contents of my waterskin. When I had replaced it in its pocket and laced the flap securely, Santh nudged me toward his back with his wedge-shaped head. He was becoming impatient with the slowness of our pace. I laughed and scrambled up onto his back, placing my feet and hands in the surcingle loops provided for that purpose.

When I was securely mounted, he got carefully

to his feet and broke into an easy lope that ate up the distance. His approval was a purr in his throat.

Now we sped across the green and yellow flatlands toward the foothills where the Liaison First had built his angular, ugly complex. Jitkaws swooped and darted in the green-blue sky. It was a clear afternoon, and the west wind carried the smell of new awakening, for it was Detarsa first first—that is, the first day of the first seven-day set of the pass Detarsa, our fifth month from winter solstice. Yesterday had been Macara fourth seventh; that is, the last day of the last set of the pass Macara. We have on Silistra a fourteen-month revolution, each month containing twenty-eight days. Our year is eight days less than the standard B.F. year of four hundred days. Our day is forty minutes shy of the Bipedal Federate Standard day of thirty hours, but we divide it into twenty-eight "enths," or "bells." Each enth, or bell, contains seventy-five iths.

I had not been conscious of the problem relating times until I had spent a year as M'lennin's couchmate. This questionable custom is not a chaldric matter, but courtesy to the outworlder Liaison, and had been originated by Well-Keepress Astria. I had found it very difficult to live with M'lennin, in his strange home of clicking machines and canned and frozen food, where time and date are Bipedal Federate Standard, and nothing Silistran. M'lennin prides himself on his retention of off-world customs, and holds us, I am afraid, in sour contempt. He would have us mechanize and modernize and become like all the other Federate worlds. Much money comes to Silistra, but little goes back to the star-worlds. This is a great problem, in his mind. I think matters are as they should be. If Silistra became as all the other star-

worlds, if we were not unique, what would we
have to offer them?

Such were my thoughts as Santh bore me effort-
lessly toward M'lennin's star-steel fortress. Within
its walls was the help I needed. It was well within
the Liaison's power to analyze the data contained
in my mother's tape and make me the copies I
desired. Since each major Well had its own Liaison,
and these kept in constant contact with each other,
I could also benefit from his assistance in arrang-
ing my stay in Well Arlet. Doubtless, too, he could
provide me speedy and anonymous passage up the
coast. Perhaps his computer complex would be
able to pinpoint my father's race and planet, and I
would not need to go to Arlet at all.

There was, however, one problem in obtaining
this invaluable assistance from my former couch-
mate, and this problem was more and more in my
mind as the hulking geometric Keep of the Liaison
First loomed larger and larger on the horizon. I
would have to *ask*. I, who had so many times
derided M'lennin for his all-consuming technological passion, who had declared my independence
from communicators and computers, now found
myself in the ignominious position of needing those
very machines which I had so loudly decried.

Dusk was fast approaching. The lights, keyed by
an electronic sensor, were ablaze in M'lennin's
outer court. Still I had found no way to approach
him that would allow me to retain my dignity.
Perhaps I would have to admit that, indeed, his
toys were good for something after all.

Stopping Santh with a touch, I dismounted and
walked by his side through the electric eyes that
sentried the outer gate. Now M'lennin knew I had
arrived.

Suddenly nervous, I dallied in the empty court,
hoping in these last few moments that some inspi-

ration would come to me. I scratched Santh under his massive chin, and he butted me with his head toward the door. He knew where he was. He had been raised his first year here. The hulion was anxious to be indoors with his sister, Sithantha. I sighed. It would be unpleasant, but the time called the move. I must set aside my pride and principles and my personal feelings for M'lennin. I wished it were not he whom I must petition for aid. He would take much satisfaction from my plight.

Santh growled restlessly. I ran up the three broad steps to the star-steel door and pressed my hand against its glowing red panel. The door slid silently aside to admit us. With Santh at my heels, I stepped into the reception hall. The door slid back into place.

We had taken only three or four steps along the hallway when I heard the clatter of running feet and M'lennin careened down the steps directly in front of me, almost colliding with Santha.

The Liaison First to Silistra was gasping for breath, his black-and-gold dress tunic rumpled, his face contorted. He reached out a hand as if to steady me, his pale face full of the furrows of concern.

And then I understood:

"Time has improved our relationship, M'len." I grinned at him. "I had not imagined you so anxious to see me."

"The blood! Estri! I thought, that is . . ." He took his hand from my shoulder and ran it through his blond beard. His blue eyes were keen and icy.

"I thought you were hurt," he began again, looking pointedly at my bloodstained garment. "I see I was mistaken."

"Only a fresh meal I took with Santh on the trail." I reached out to take his fine-boned, freckled hand. "It is good to see you, Liaison. What have the winds blown you?"

When I got no response, I dropped his hand and stripped the surcingle from Santh, slinging it over my left shoulder. The hulion, sniffing loudly, his head to the ground, disappeared around the first corner to our right. I let him go.

M'lennin just stood there, watching Santh. His back was to me. "He is immense," the Liaison said at last, and his voice was strained. "Twice the size of his sister."

"Males are often bigger than females," I reminded him.

"But not always," he said, turning to face me. M'lennin and I are the same height. "Time has been easy on you," he observed.

"And you also," I lied. I could see new lines upon his boyish face and silver in his flaxen hair.

"Not as easy as it could be, if you people weren't so damned stubborn . . . and so greedy."

It was the Silistran serums, those that extend and improve life, of which he spoke. The withholding of these drugs had long been a bone of contention between us. The M'ksakkans insist on thinking we withhold them for mundane advantage, as if we could, if we wished, provide the universe with this unsynthesizable elixir of life.

I moved to join him where he had seated himself on the bottommost of the three steps that led up into the keep proper. A discussion of the serums, their rarity, and the opposition among the high Day-Keepers to handing them out on a wholesale basis to races which were, in the dhareners eyes, still children, would only lead to an argument which neither of us could win. So I changed the subject:

"You did not answer me," I reminded him, "when I asked of your affairs. I assume you have been profitably engaged? We have not seen you in Astria

for more time than is customary." I had not seen
M'lennin since the end of the couch-bond.

He shrugged. "You seemed to want it that way,"
he said softly in M'ksakkan, examining his booted
feet. "Should I have come after you in your whore—
in your Well? When we parted, you wanted nothing more from me . . . nothing that I could give, at
least. Nor has there been any amendment to the
trade arrangements. They've remained unaltered
since you took up control of your Well." His eyes
met mine. "Did you come here to try me again? I
doubt your luck will be better now than it was then."

M'lennin had not changed. He was bitter, still,
that he had not brought child upon me in the year
I had spent with him, and hurt that his feelings for
me were more than I could return. He had also
thought that by becoming intimate with me he could
change the stance of our dhareners, use me to
facilitate the acquisition of the serums by his people.

For all of these reasons, M'lennin had wanted
me to himself, and had managed to acquire me for
a year. When the year was over, I left with no
regret. It had not been so for M'lennin. During
that year he had tried to manipulate the trade
balance in the Well through me. He had not
succeeded. I had thwarted his plans in more ways
than one. M'lennin was used to getting his way. I,
also, like control of my situation. There was much
discord between us.

I did not answer.

"If not my glorious body," he asked again, this
time in Silistran, "then what brings you here? And
why alone? How will the Well fare without its
Keepress?"

"I came," said I, snatching the opening, "because
I have taken up the chaldra of the mother. It must
be done without aid from the Well. I have the
Day-Keepers' leave to pursue this end. I would

have your help. These things," I said as I handed him the cube and letter, "were my lever with Ristran. He will pick them up from you. I need copies, computer evaluation, anything that will help me discharge this chaldra."

M'lennin turned the cube in his hands.

"How did you come by this?" His voice was sharp with curiosity and again he slipped into his mother tongue. "There shouldn't be anything like this viewer in Astria, unless it came through us . . . and not this type, certainly—it's on the Restricted Items list. So if you didn't get it through us, then where?"

The M'ksakkans jealously guarded their access to our culture. These outworld rules and restrictions were beyond my comprehension and I remembered a time when I was forever falling afoul of them. The last thing I wanted, now, was to upset M'lennin. So I said soothingly: "It is old, before your time and mine. . . ."

"Before *your* time?" he interrupted, incredulous.

"From my mother's time," I replied as if it were something a child should have known, as if I had not been shaken by the revelation of its existence so recently. "In my mother's time we had looser standards. We had surveillance devices in the Well. My mother made the tape, and it was held for me. On it is the record of my conception. It shows my father. The chaldra involves—" I stopped, for he had raised his hand.

"Estri, I have guests in the dining hall. This is a long and complicated story, it seems, and dinner lies cooling on the plates. I'll give you what I can in the way of aid. Perhaps you'll see your way clear to help me, also. Will you stay the night with me, Well-Keepress?" This last was a formal request, spoken in Silistran.

I nodded. I could see no way around it, though I knew he would exact his price.

"Have you something else I might wear? And I would wash the trail dust from me before I meet your guests." I plucked at my bloodstained tas jerkin.

He got to his feet, lifting me from the step.

"All your things are still here, in the room you had. I'll walk you there, and you can explain to me about this new chaldra you've taken up." He smiled, guiding me down the corridor, his hand at the small of my back. "It *is* an interesting twist—you coming here for such specialized assistance. I might just enjoy aiding you." He chuckled.

We stopped at the door to his sleeping quarters, and I waited while he locked the cube and letter in his private vault and called the house computer to alter the dinner plan. It clicked disapprovingly.

I leaned against the blue wall in that blue room that I had thought never to see again. Caught up tight in the weave of some strong time skein, I felt helpless.

M'lennin must have been thinking the M'ksakkan equivalent of the same thought, for he made no move to leave. Instead, he lit his pipe and, half-sitting on the carved desk there, watched me ruminatively, puffing the mild aromatic smoke.

"Who are these guests we keep waiting?" I asked, to remind him.

"The new Liaison Second, bound to Arlet, and his pilot. We Liaisons would rather fly than walk."

"What?" I clutched my chald. *Arlet!* Still tighter wove the weave. "What happened to the previous Liaison Second?"

"He died of . . . natural . . . causes. He was an *old* man," said M'lennin in that manner that implied that every outworlder who died thus was a man we Silistrans could have saved. Then he eyed me curiously: "Did you know him? You seem upset."

"No," I whispered, "but I must go to Arlet from here." Now I knew why I had felt the need to hurry here and I silently cursed my recalcitrant precognitive gift for being so weak that its every message was obscure.

"To Arlet? In connection with the chaldra?" he asked.

"I must meet with a Day-Keeper there. I had thought to take residence in Well Arlet, but under another name. There is some need for secrecy. I have much to discuss with you, M'len, and little time."

He waved me out of the room, and followed, palming the door shut. We hurried down the corridor, past three doors on the left. Before the fourth he stopped.

"Perhaps we can settle this here, and you'll not have to journey to Arlet. The new Liaison Second, Khaf-Re Dellin, and his pilot must stay here a few days. Dellin is young, and painfully unfamiliar with Silistra—just between us, he's here for political reasons on M'ksakka that unfortunately overrode little considerations such as competency. The old Liaison's death was sudden, and Dellin is being shoved into this thing ... ah ... unprepared. He needs more than briefing and language tapes before taking on the second-greatest Well on Silistra. It's my task to orient him before he settles into his responsibilities." He grinned snidely. "I may ask your help with him. Who knows Silistrans better than the Well-Keepress of Astria?" Leaning against the wall, M'lennin fingered his beard.

"Tomorrow," he continued, for I had not replied, "as early as sun's rise, if you wish, we shall see what can be learned from the letter and viewer. There is ample time to arrange your passage with Dellin, if we decide it's prudent. Tonight we eat and enjoy each other's company, and Dellin will meet the high-couch of Silistra." He rubbed his hands together. "This is really most opportune."

"But I would start—"

"No," he interrupted me firmly. "No chaldra, no business, no predictions. Not tonight. Tonight you see to my aid and comfort, tomorrow I to yours—a fair trade." He touched the red block beside the door, it glowed, and the panel slid soundlessly aside.

"You will find it unchanged," said he, and waved me within.

It was true. The room that had been mine two years ago was exactly as I had left it. I shivered as I entered. M'lennin followed, and the door closed behind us.

I stood in the midst of all the off-world opulence imaginable. Thrah-skins from Torth covered the floor, multicolored and luminous, their pile ankle-deep. The curtains were wine plush, heavy-napped and glowing, like tiers of strung rubies, woven on the looms of Pleiatus. The Pleitu are the master weavers of the known galaxy, and their magnificent dyes are their greatest secret. The table and two chairs were carved from the white bone of the wistwa, giant seabeast of Oguast. The windows behind the tables, framed by those blood-red curtains, were quartz crystal slabs from M'lennin's home planet, M'ksakka. The only thing Silistran-made was the couch itself. It was double to my own thala well-couch, crafted by Astria's own masters.

It was unsettling to realize that in over a year my room had remained undisturbed: there was no dust on the wistwa table, no wrinkle in the resplendent silken hangings from Kost. It was as if he had made a shrine of this place. It felt wrong; I did not like it.

I liked less the look on the Liaison's face. I turned from him and knelt before the low chest beneath the windows. In it were the clothes I had brought with me long ago from Astria. I stripped off the jerkin and threw it aside.

The M'ksakkan's predatory silence screamed its message: men may be different, depending on their origin among the stars—now I think they are more different than once I did—but for a M'ksakkan man to have tried for a year to beget a child upon a woman and failed was a loss of face that M'lennin could not forget or deny, though it was not his fault. . . .

I freed my hair, and it fell around me.

Rummaging in the chest, I finally found what I sought—a comb and two gold clips, and a length of embroidered Koster silk to cover my nakedness.

These I laid beside me on the pile rug. I sat on my heels, nude, and with the comb I went to work on my ratted hair. Through the curtain of its strands I saw M'lennin's booted feet appear in front of me.

"M'len—" I started to say just before his hand twisted in my hair and pushed my head hard to the floor between my knees. I felt with my hands for him, but he caught them with his and twisted them up behind my back.

"Did you think I would give you the chance?" he growled as he used me so brutally I cried out. "Think I'd wait while you read my mind and manipulated me, while you witched me again? No, no. *This* time you'll take what I see fit to give you—my way."

It did not last long. This was one of M'lennin's problems, but one for which, at that moment, I was exceedingly grateful. When a man like M'lennin seeks to debase a Silistran woman, using sex, he cannot win: his civilized nature fights him more than any woman could. But an insult it was, and one I would not soon forget, to have one's rear passage invaded as if one were a man or a goat or a sheep, with no regard to the fertility of either of us.

When he let me go, I rolled over and looked up at him. I would have, had he wished it, made love to him. He had not wished it—nor had he wished to succeed with me, even in that. It had been painful, and clumsy, and abortive—the more so because I could not move to ease him.

He stood above me, already buckling his gold-studded belt, looking dissatisfied and frustrated.

Rolling to my back, I said, "I know the way to the dining hall. I will meet you there."

For a moment I thought he would speak. Instead, he turned on his heel and in three strides was out of the room, slapping the lock without looking back.

"Have I hurt you so deeply, M'len?" I asked softly of the empty room. It appeared that I had. I explored myself with my hand and, finding no blood, rolled to my feet.

As I made my way into the adjoining washroom, I picked from the pile of silk my bone comb. In the shower I attacked my ratted hair section by section. When it was tangle-free, I lathered my body and leaned back, letting the steaming spray run long over my aching buttocks.

Then I flipped the knob that controlled the shower's temperature, holding my breath as the icy needles struck.

The cold was invigorating, but it did not cool my inner heat. I was still much aroused. I smiled to myself, thinking of M'len. I hadn't thought him capable of even such misdirected ferocity. That was my mistake. It lies waiting in all men. I had made the novice's error of allowing my conception of the man to blind me to his needs.

No one is perfect, I decided as I padded on squishing feet back into the apartment. It had turned out the better for my surprise. By surrendering control of the situation, I might have gained an edge— M'lennin's sort was full of guilt. And if the edge was there, perhaps I could exploit it.

I stood on the Torth pelt wringing my hair dry. The smell of the room, of star steel and damp clean body, of my own need, excited me: I was on my own, out of the Well, not couch-bound to anyone or constrained by any duties other than the unstructured mandate to discharge the chaldra of the mother. I could hardly wait to meet M'lennin's dinner guests and set out for Arlet, to meet my fate.

Finally I was dripped dry enough to dress. I wound the Koster silk, all embroidered in gem tones, around my body and, clipping two ends at the neck and the others at my hip, drew it taut over my breasts and hips. Then I regarded myself in the mirror behind the couch. My skin gleamed from the needle spray of the shower. I tingled all over. My image reassured me. Even with my hair still damp, and parted simply, I looked well. There were no toilet maids to dress me here. I would have to get used to caring for my own needs. I reached back and took the curling mass of my hair where it fell over my hips and squeezed once more. The drops ran down my legs and dripped on the rug.

I inspected my reflection once again. Good enough, I thought, and tossed the bone comb on the couch. The rust silk set me off to my best advantage. There was, however, something missing. Thoughtfully, I disengaged the clip that held the two ends of the silk strap together at my right hip. I lifted the ends and stuffed them through my chald, so that they were higher on my thigh. I fingered my father's ring for a moment. Better. I turned, slowly, full around. Much better.

As I made my way to the dining hall, my anticipation heightened. My hungers had sorted themselves out. I was more than ready to eat, and the smell of roast parr and fried grintafish made my mouth water.

M'lennin's back was toward me, and he was engaged in animated conversation with one of his visitors, the one whom I took to be the pilot, for his hair was cut close to the head, and he wore a tight-fitting brown uniform, that of his vocation.

This small dark man was almost hidden behind a pile of Silistran fruit of every conceivable variety. I stood in the doorway scanning the room, as is my wont. All the food upon the table was Silistran. M'lennin never ate local produce. There was a whole parr, its skin shining with glaze, its square snout propped up in the air by the narne fruit between its teeth. There was a side of denter, with roast tuns, a starchy dark-skinned tuber, for garnish. The table, as long as my body and half again as wide, was overflowing with meats and vegetables and fruits. There were four large decanters, two of an amber liquid which I took to be brin, for it bubbled and frothed, and two darker, almost certainly kifra wines. It was an impressive spread, and would have fed forty, rather than four. M'lennin was consistent, at least, in his excess.

M'len and the pilot had not noticed me. I stepped silently into the hall, planning to cross the marble floor unannounced.

I had made perhaps a third of the distance when a hand came down firmly from behind me on my left shoulder.

Reflexively I dropped and kicked out. I felt my foot connect with something hard. Crouching free, I pulled my hair back from my face.

My would-be attacker was on his knees, clutching his diaphragm.

M'lennin and the pilot were leaning on each other, laughing hysterically. I saw the overturned chairs and spilled fruit on the floor, and the menial robot clicking irritably as it scurried to set things right.

"I would introduce you two," gasped the Liaison through tears of laughter, "but I see you have already met."

My adversary raised his head to me, steadying himself with one hand on the floor as he rose.

I, too, got to my feet.

My hands on my hips, I regarded him. I did not think the situation humorous. I have had much training from the Slayers. My teacher, Rin diet Tron, would say I have many moves. I would say I have a few, though I am no match for a Silistran Slayer.

"My apologies, lady," said my attacker. He was a good head taller than I, dark-complexioned, with a great mass of black hair. Under straight, pronounced brows his eyes were gray, frank, open. A smile played at the corners of his mouth. I thought him very attractive, though overly muscled. I had brought him down through luck, and he knew it. He weighed perhaps thrice what I carried. He rubbed his middle.

"I am Estri," said I, extending my hand palm up. I would not exchange apologies with him. I smiled and nodded my head.

"Khaf-Re Dellin," said he. His voice was pleasant, low and rich. His large hand, palm down, enveloped mine. The back of his hand was fleeced with black silky hair. He wore a white, collared shirt, and the black shorts I knew were part of the Liaison dress code, though M'len always wore pants and boots.

His eyes held mine and we stood there, palms touching, longer than was appropriate. Neither of us spoke. I searched for something to say, but I was mute. Instead I disengaged my hand and turned to M'lennin.

"You had better teach him some manners before he goes to Arlet," I advised in a low voice.

"It looks like you'll do it for me," M'lennin said in M'ksakkan, giving me a piercing stare. He stepped between us and put his arm around Dellin's shoulder. He had to reach up to do it. The Liaison First said something to the Liaison Second in a voice too low for me to catch his meaning.

"Seat yourself, Keepress," M'lennin suggested. I did so, choosing a spot before the platter of parr and wincing when my bottom settled on the padded bench.

M'len, standing over me, grinned and reached under the table. When his hand reappeared, it held a cushion. I placed it beneath me and sat down again, this time gingerly.

The Liaison First took his armchair at the narrow end of the table. The pilot sat across from me. He introduced himself as Dalf Tragett, of Beten, a B.F. planet in the adjacent quadrant. I had had Betenese in Astria. They are tiny powerhouses, brilliant and sensitive. The Betenese are among the best mathematical minds in the B.F., much sought as astrogators. We exchanged suitable pleasantries and I asked after two captains I knew from his home town. He was flattered, surprised at my interest, and we chatted.

Dellin did not take his place at the table, but continued his inspection of the tapestries that hung from the gray walls of the huge and lofty dining hall, that inspection which my entrance had interrupted.

I was piqued.

M'lennin was openly amused. He leaned back in his steel and sueded armchair, sipping brin. As host, he should have served us, but he did not.

I rose to serve the pilot, and turned to face M'len, letting my hair fall over my shoulder so the Betenese could not see my face. I stuck my tongue out at the Liaison First, and he choked on his frothy mouthful.

"Brin is a lightly intoxicating drink, brewed from grain called binnirin, which grows both wild and cultivated all over Silistra and is one of our staple crops," said I, handing a crystal glass of amber liquid to the pilot. He sipped it hesitantly, then nodded and took a larger swallow.

"It will not, of course," I continued, "intoxicate a Beten, unless one of such prodigious appetites were to drink, perhaps, a whole barrel."

We both laughed. I poured another tall foaming glass and carried it across the hall to Dellin, who was dutifully inspecting a Torth sculptured panel. Looking back over my shoulder, I saw M'len handing a pipe to the pilot.

"Liaison," said I, a safe distance from Dellin's broad back, "will you taste brin?"

He turned and looked past me toward the table. We were well out of earshot, if we kept our voices down.

"Keepress," said he, extending his hand for the glass, "I'll taste whatever you recommend to me," and his eyes were frank and appreciative.

I tossed my head, letting some of my nearly dry hair fall over my breast. The curling ends rested on my naked thigh.

"My couch-price," I breathed, "is fifty gold dippars, in Astria. Here, however, I am at the Liaison First's disposal. Should you make an arrangement with him, I shall have no choice but to honor it."

A cloud crossed Dellin's face. Had I misread him?

"I'd prefer to give you that choice," Dellin said in awkward Silistran, his voice low and angry. "Any arrangements I make *about* you, I'll make *with* you—not with M'lennin. I want nothing not freely given. Understand, lady?"

I saw then that M'lennin was right, that Dellin had much to learn of Silistra.

"I understand that you must call me Estri, if we are to become friends, as M'len hopes we will, and as might be advantageous to us both if you are to become Liaison in Arlet. But you must understand that I cannot," I explained, "give you what is not mine to give."

He stared at me uncomprehendingly, leaning his shoulder against the Torth panel, sipping his brin so that I could not see the expression on his face.

"You are incredibly beautiful . . . Estri," he tried again.

"Surely worth fifty gold dippars, then?" I asked.

First he seemed nonplussed, then angry, then frustrated, and at last amused: "Doubtless," he confirmed gamely. "But that's hardly the point, is it? I mean—we're meeting socially, this isn't a Well . . . You're not . . . what's the proper term? . . . working here, are you?" All of this was in M'ksak-kan, rattled off so fast I had a hard time translating it after so long away from the tongue.

"I cannot lower my price, my value, my status, by lying with a man like some binnirin farmer's daughter, for nothing. Do you understand? On Silistra, such things are not done. If you would have me this night, you must pay my couch-price to M'len, or strike with him some bargain." I smiled reassuringly. "You have much to learn before you go to Arlet."

"Check." He raked his fingers through the harsh

mass of his hair, shaking his head slowly from side to side, and handed me the half-full glass of brin and said with an uncertain half-smile, "I'll be right back."

I took his glass and tried to suppress my amusement as he strode to M'lennin's side. My former couchmate would be very annoyed, but he had little choice. M'len could not, in his position of mentor to Dellin, refuse him. I had no choice at all, but it happened that I wanted the Liaison Second. I would, in any case, have had to abide by M'len's decision, even if Dellin had been old and ugly. Had he been the least attractive man on Silistra, I would have answered him the same. But he was not.

I watched covertly as Dellin bent over M'lennin. M'lennin rubbed the back of his neck and played with his glass. The Liaison Second nodded, and the Liaison First smiled, though the smile seemed a trifle strained from where I leaned against the Torth sculpture at one end of the long, narrow, high-ceilinged gray room.

It was good to watch Khaf-Re Dellin move, I decided as he came toward me, graceful, fluid, catlike on the balls of his feet. He did not swagger or strut, but moved with sinuous, unconscious ease that I had seldom seen among the outworlders. In his hand he held a second glass of amber brin.

When he reached me, he took the half-glass from my hands and gave me the full one, looking down at me with a bemused expression on his strong-boned face.

"My lack of familiarity with Silistran customs is too obvious to be denied, but only a fool wouldn't want to learn what he could from you." He reached out and touched my hair, then my neck.

"You struck, then," I guessed, "a satisfactory agreement with M'len?" I read his path, as it is

said, by precipitating the question and watching
his mind react.

"You are mine, as the Liaison put it, to command until sun's rise. I command you, then, to tell
me now if you would prefer to avoid my . . .
attentions." His face was but inches from mine;
his narrowed eyes searched mine.

"Avoid it!" I laughed. "Does the musician avoid
his instrument? Does the singer avoid the song?
Such is my chan-tera; my study, my vocation, my
way of life!" I turned my face to his. He took a kiss
from me. I tasted my own blood as his lips pressed
down upon mine. His hands were on my buttocks.

After a time he pushed me from him and held
me at arm's length, his fingers digging into my
shoulders.

"That's not a direct answer, Estri. And I think I
deserve one. Let's try again: Do *you* want *me?*" His
grip on my arms did not relax.

"Do you *want* me to want you, Liaison Dellin?
Your mouth says one thing, your touch another," I
replied.

For that question, the Liaison Second had no
answer. His face showed no expression as he let go
of me and headed for the table, but he slapped my
buttocks as he passed, saying only, "We have de-
layed the meal overlong."

The pilot and the Liaison First stared at us until
we were seated behind the roast parr. M'lennin
was drumming his fingers on the tabletop and on
his face was the look of a man who had tasted
kifra gone sour.

"Where are you from?" I asked to break the
awkward silence, passing Dellin his plate, upon
which I had placed three thick strips of parr, juicy
with blood.

"M'ksakka is where I grew up," said he, accepting the cream sauce I passed him. He spooned

some on the stewed narne he had chosen from a large bowl of mixed fruit, "but I was born on Itabe, of a M'ksakkan father and Itabic mother. Why?"

"Curiosity. You remind me of M'len in some ways," I said, shooting a look at the Liaison First. "He has never truly gotten used to Silistra. I think perhaps he is afraid that it is all just a dream and one day he will awaken and find himself Liaison to a mining colony on Centaus. They instill a strange brand of morality on M'ksakka," I added, serving the ruby kifra wine.

"Not as strange a brew as is found in Astria," growled M'lennin. "I might prefer Centaus, were I given the choice." He popped a chunk of grintafish, crispy and brown, into his mouth. "I hear the food on Centaus is incomparable."

We all laughed. Centaus was a bare, airless rock. The colony was underground, its food hydroponically grown.

"And there is no blasted chaldra to drive a man mad," M'len added. "Nor chaldless outlaws, nor highborn ladies of the evening. Just men making a good living, who have no compunction about doing so." He drained his wineglass and refilled it. "Planet of dizzy whores," he grumbled.

Dellin had one hand between my thighs beneath the table. With the other he forked a bit of mashed tun into his mouth.

"I see nothing wrong with Silistran food. In fact, I rather like it," said the Betenese pilot, emptying one decanter of kifra and starting upon the second. The Beten was quietly getting very drunk.

"Has Estri told you, Khaf-Re, that she intends to make her way to Arlet on a mission of great chaldric importance," said M'lennin bitterly.

I choked on a bit of narne. I had wanted to tell

Dellin in my own way, at a more opportune moment.

The Liaison Second squeezed my thigh. He put down his fork and looked at me.

"Perhaps," said he, "if I can get a pass's advance on my salary, the Well-Keepress of Astria will allow me to deliver her to Arlet?" He was grinning.

"Certainly, if that is the case, she would allow it," I answered, straight-faced.

"Done," snarled M'lennin around a mouthful of denter. "Although—*if* the Liaison Second will allow the Liaison First to advise him—there are other women on Silistra, many more reasonably priced. One should taste the vintage before stocking the cellar."

"That's one bottle I'd buy unopened," mumbled Dalf Tragett, the pilot.

"Thank you, Master Astrogator," I acknowledged, but, as I did so, the Beten slumped forward on the table. Kifra is smooth and deceptively delicate, but it is potent.

"Tell me about these chaldless outlaws," Dellin asked M'lennin as the button-bristled tubular menial robot blinked its way to the table with a pot of steaming rana grasped in its jointed metal tentacle.

While I served the sobering rust-colored brew to the three of us, M'lennin launched into a tirade concerning the ungrateful malcontents that harried tourists and waylaid star-goods caravans. It annoyed him terribly that the chaldless seldom bothered Silistrans. The pilot snored loudly. I thought he would sleep until sun's rise.

M'lennin ran dry of words as I served the fruited binnirin cake, and we ate it in silence. The Liaison First then pulled out a large-bowled ragony pipe and filled it carefully from his parr-hide pouch.

I knew what he had filled it with, the moment he lit it, from the weed's yellow smoke and acrid odor. We would smoke danne, the rare and costly psychotropic herb that grows high on the Sebenbe range. Three puffs would put an out-worlder such as Dellin out of commission for hours.

I leaned against Dellin's shoulder and whispered a warning in his ear. He nodded, and when M'len passed him the pipe, he inhaled only a tiny amount and blew it out almost immediately, then passed it to me.

I dragged deep and held the smoke. I felt my limbs tingle and the colors in the room brighten. I handed the pipe back to the Liaison First, leaning across Dellin's lap. My breast brushed his hip and burned at the heat. Inherent sensuality is greatly intensified by danne. I looked up at Dellin; his face was beaded with sweat.

I got up, putting my arm around the unsteady out-worlder's waist.

"Your room or mine?" he murmured, nuzzling my neck.

"Mine," I said, maneuvering Dellin toward the door.

"Tasa," said the Liaison First indistinctly from his armed sueded chair. I doubted M'lennin would make it to his couch this night.

"Tasa," I replied, steering Dellin around the corner.

The danne had been of exceptional strength, I decided as I helped the out-worlder down the corridor which seemed to extend for miles.

And it had been: I stepped square on Santh's tufted tail where he lay stretched out beside Sithantha across the threshold to my apartment. The hulion growled softly, opened one eye, and regarded me balefully. Supporting Dellin with one arm as best I could, I leaned over the two hulions stretched out on my threshold and slapped the lockplate.

"Step carefully," I warned Dellin.

He shook his head, rubbed his eyes, and removed my arm from his waist, staring at Santh and Sithantha.

"I," said he, "am in worse shape than I thought."

"No, they are there."

"They?" He looked straight at me, making a valiant effort to focus on my face.

"The hulions. Step over them."

"Hulions. Certainly."

Somehow I managed to get him into the shower. When the cold water struck his clothed body, he howled and grabbed for me. I evaded him, laughing, while the stinging spray did its work.

Sputtering and muttering, he stumbled out of the stall and stood dripping, hands on his hips, much sobered.

"Come strip me, woman," he said forcefully, then began chuckling: "I don't believe I said that, but, damn it all, M'len says that's what you like . . ." He raked black hair from his eyes. "Is it? What you like, I mean? At least give me a point for trying to adapt—"

By then I was doing as he bid me, and doing some things he didn't yet know enough to bid me do.

Dellin took me there on the pile of sopping clothes, intoxicated by danne and, perhaps, by his first Silistran couching.

Then he stripped me of the Koster silk and regarded me.

"Does this come off?" he said, hooking a finger between the chald and my naked body. He closed the chald in his fist.

"No," I lied.

"Good," he grunted, and dragged me by the chald

across the floor and up on my Astrian couch. "Now that I've got the hang of this, you're in for one marathon surprise, lady."

He was superb, and I told him so, over and over, as he used me. He had the skill of taking a woman out of herself, and I was truly lost to him. Only in the pre-dawn did I have a chance to deliver to him an Astrian lovemaking, and even in that he was a creative partner.

Then we slept, and I missed my appointment at sun's rise with M'lennin.

Dellin wakened me with his renewed interest, and afterward I lay on my back in the crook of his arm, staring at the lofty ceiling, thinking that if M'len had been like this, things would have been very different between us—and perhaps between Silistra and the star folk. Even then, I was not without influence. But M'len was nothing like Dellin, which served only to prove that everywhere, even beyond the sky, things are the same.

When the midmorning light streamed through the crystal windows, Dellin kissed my temple. "Tell me about life in the Well," he said in an odd voice.

I extended my right leg as high as I could in the air, pointing my toes. I studied the play of shadow along my inner thigh. I sighed: "You wish to know what a fine girl like me is doing in a place like this, do you not?"

"It's not the place," said he, fondling my breast, "but the situation—or predicament, or whatever. Yes, I suppose that *is* what I want to know," he admitted.

I wiggled my toes.

"I understand," he continued, "the economics of Silistra. I realize that each Well is autonomous, and that each Well-area has its Liaison, acting independently of the others. I can even accept that I shall be one. I've been a good boy—studied my tapes and committed the four major Silistran languages to memory. I've looked at all the available data on your time theory and your Day-Keepers and your genetic manipulation, though there's precious little of it—you people are so close-mouthed it approaches racial paranoia. I understand your concern with your low birthrate, your unwillingness to use drugs to alter your natural-selection system, a system that puts the woman in a centralized location of sexual activity until that precious and unpredictable egg drops and is fertilized. I can even swallow that bit about only the egg knowing the right sperm, and that a Silistran woman ovulates only upon the presentation of desirable sperm, and then only two or three times in her life. I find the concept of shipping your best psychics off to the Day-Keepers—so they'll mate only with other psychics—hard to take. It must be even harder for Silistran men. And the costs of access to the Well! How do you avoid pricing yourselves out of the local market? How about the fine physical specimens who can't get up the couch-price?" He was up on one elbow, staring down into my face.

I said nothing.

"Why do Silistran women commit themselves into public usage, and then, when pregnant, become willingly the property of the men who impregnate them, giving to those men title to all they have gained in their years in the Wells?"

"Why not?" I retorted. "You will never understand Silistra if you take the facets of our culture out of context. That is M'lennin's mistake. Chaldra. All is chaldra. There is great chaldra attached to the Wells—"

"I had a tape on chaldra," he interrupted. "It didn't explain the Wells."

I sighed. The sun was getting higher, and I had to find M'lennin.

"I shall try to show you, then. A girl, when she reaches puberty, takes a number of examinations. Her scores on these, she submits to the Wells. From this information on her physical, psychical, and mental potential, the Wells either accept or reject the girl. Astria has first choice, Arlet second, and so on. Astria will take a highly intelligent girl with a strong fore-reader index, if she is attractive; Arlet will take a high hormonal index, for they specialize in exotic sex. Each Well has a character. It is a great honor to be an Astrian girl, and wear the silver chain with white interwoven. Once a girl is accepted by a Well, the security of her family is assured. They are gifted by the Well and benefited in many ways. The girl's earnings are invested by the Well, and we are very good with money. A woman goes out of Astria with a great fortune. She is also educated continually and thoroughly. She learns comparative cultures, the known languages of the galaxy, musics, dances, a large number of required subjects, and others of her choice. She learns the ways of love. She becomes cultured and sophisticated. She has opportunities to mate with some of the most powerful and brilliant men in the known galaxy. Should a woman, given a choice between such a life and the lot of the farm girl on the plains, choose to churn bondrex milk and slop parr? And meet perhaps a hundred men in her life? Should she risk bearing the unfulfilled chaldra of reproduction to her grave? The chances of an isolated Silistran woman conceiving are sixty to one.

"As for the men," I continued, "I believe our men are content. Only four percent of Astrian women conceive by off-worlders. A man need not have money to partake of the Well if he is Silistran. There are games once a set, and festivals once a pass, where the men may earn silver and gold well tokens. These games range from physical to psychical, and any man with a talent or skill may gain entrance to the Well in this manner. Men love the gamble as they love wealth. A man knows that should he bring child on a girl in the Well, he will acquire not only a sensual, beautiful woman, but the money to enjoy her at his leisure in luxurious surroundings. If he can impregnate two, then two women and two fortunes are his. The men control much on Silistra. Both the dependent and independent cities draw great revenue from the Wells and the traffic they bring. Our traders, merchants, Slayers, hunters, weavers, and more, prosper from the Wells. Thousands of years ago the Day-Keepers and the forereaders determined the social structure of Silistra, building upon the ruins of past mistakes. It has endured."

"Are you angry?" he asked, tracing my lips with his finger.

"No," said I, "but I have said this say many times."

"What if a woman falls in love with a man without him having impregnated her?" he asked thoughtfully.

"There is the pressure of chaldra to consider," I reminded him. "Perhaps she would stay in the Well until she conceived, and petition that the father's right to her body be waived. If the Well accepted this, they would pay the father double the birth-price, and the woman would, once having repaid the Well, be free to leave and go to her lover. The Well would gift them and absorb the loss. I have never heard of a woman leaving the Well without conceiving. She goes to the Well to become pregnant. Why would she leave without fulfilling her purpose?"

"You have not conceived," said he, "but you have left the Well."

"Oh," I replied blithely. "I have taken on the chaldra of the mother; to find my father. I seek him. I have no man whom I love. The skein of the time weave bears me to Arlet. My father was an off-worlder who did not want my mother, nor the birth-price, nor me. He spread his seed and disappeared. If a man does not want the woman, the Well buys her back, and the profit to the father is high. But he did not wish it. I was raised by the Well, for my mother died at my birth. Women who have been in the Well and have not conceived are given such children to raise when they can no longer take the couch. We care for our own."

"I'm half-caste, also," said Dellin. The way he said it make me think the fact had caused him some pain. He sat up and swung his legs over the edge of the couch.

"Anything I can do to help you discharge this chaldra, whatever I can, I'll do—just ask. Remember, once I'm installed in Arlet, I won't be without resources. What race was your father's?"

"That," I said, "is what I am here to find out. Come with me if you wish, while M'lennin and I attempt to unravel the riddle."

He nodded and pulled me to him again. I begged off, and we showered and I dressed. In my short white sleeveless s'kim, which tied behind at back, waist, and hips, I walked him, naked, to his own room, where he pulled on black shorts and sandals, and we went searching for food and M'lennin.

# III.
# The Context Within Which
# the Act Is Viewed

Dellin and I never made it to the kitchen.

The door to M'lennin's main room was open, its expanse dimly lit. M'len was there, among his clicking, whirring machines, each of which blinked a thousand varicolored eyes and spun its wheels and flickered its indicators back and forth across the lighted maws of its meters, singing to itself and its fellows in machine song.

M'lennin waved us within and we came up behind him where he sat before a bank of controls. Somehow he had devised to project the contents of the cube onto the right-hand screen that covered the wall before us. My mother's image was just fading into gray.

As we watched my father take my mother, double life-size, Dellin sat catty-corner on the console and pulled me against him.

"He's got the moves, eh, Dellin?" said M'len with a touch of the prurience that makes M'ksakkans less attractive than many of the other races to Silistran women.

"Quiet; I'm studying," retorted Dellin.

I said nothing. My night with the Liaison Second faded into perspective as I watched. Had I conceived with Dellin, I would have felt the egg enter my tube. With such a man as the one on the screen before me, I would surely conceive. I pulled a bit away from Dellin's encircling arm.

"One needn't be a deep-reader to know what you're thinking," he whispered in my ear.

M'len pushed a button, and the scene froze. He touched another and another, and the left-hand portion of the screen lit up with columns of words and percentiles and numbers decimal.

"There you see it, Estri," said the Liaison First.

"No, I do not," I answered. "Explain it to me."

He went through the list item by item, causing the screen to superimpose physiological, skeletal, and neurological models on my father's image as he did so. It was a very complicated analysis, and some of the M'ksakkan technical terminology he used was not in my vocabulary.

"So you see," he summed up, "what we have here is a 1.0000 to infinity bipedal standard air-breather. The archetypal man. The bipedal standard is a composite of all the divergent characteristics of the four-hundred-odd races of the hundred and forty-eight planets of the Bipedal Federate group. There is no such thing as a living 'standard biped.' Or there was never known to be one. Now we see such a man before us. The absolute man. The only one I have ever heard of. I can't place him for you, Estri. There should be no such being."

My heart sank. "May I see the skeleton again, please?" I asked.

Studying it, I noticed some of my own peculiarities there: cervical ribs, excessively thin, flat bones. I counted the vertebrae. He, as I, had two more than was the Silistran norm.

"All right, M'len," Dellin said finally, "this isn't getting us anywhere."

Perhaps Dellin had felt my despair from my body—an almost imperceptible slump, a nearly inaudible intake of breath, a subtle shifting of my weight—or perhaps, I thought, looking at him sidelong, he had actually sensed it. Then, I discounted this last possibility, but it was the first intimation I had that Dellin was not psychically crippled, as were other M'ksakkans.

But as the Liaison First tapped his console and the lights came on while the projections on the screen faded, Dellin's next question wiped my own from my mind:

"How about the languages?" the Liaison Second asked the Liaison First. "Did you catalog?"

M'lennin, twisting dials and sliding faders while watching two lit meters, handed Dellin a fax sheet without turning from his machines.

"All dead languages," mused Dellin. "Even the Silistran is archaic. And there are snatches of three argot-dialects which the computer banks can't identify. Yet the women seemed to have no trouble understanding him. Could she have gotten the meaning of his words from his mind?" he asked, looking at me.

They are superstitious about our mind-skills, these outworlders who are deaf and blind to what cannot be touched or perceived with the senses they recognize—taste, touch, sight, hearing, and smell. Even *time* is not truly a sense to them, just a process in which they are helpless, like leaves in the wind. M'lennin, when I first came to him, was sure I was a spy for the Day-Keepers, looting his mind of all its devious treasures. Would that I had had the talent, or even half of what skills were my birthright.

"Perhaps she could have," I replied carefully—we

didn't wish the M'ksakkans to know just what we could and could not do; it was well, our dhareners said, that they be afraid to lie to us, lest we find them out. "Although I could not have. My mother, I am told, was an exceptional telepath, but not enough of a deep-reader to go to the Day-Keepers." I did not succeed totally in banning all bitterness from my response. There are some on Silistra to whom the human mind is an open book; in those days, I was not one, though there is a chance, I'm now told, that I may yet become one.

"What a pity," said M'len sarcastically, his chin propped on his fist. The console hissed and burped up a small flat oblong and two sheets of the orange, rubbery fax. Then: "Do you want stills?"

I nodded, and he ran his hands over the coder again.

The machine spit two palm-sized color holos into his waiting fingers. Then, turning from the console, the Liaison First handed me the fax, stills, and a black flat oblong, which he explained was a modern version of the silver cube.

After he had instructed me as to its operation and questioned me to make sure I understood, I said, "I must leave now, M'len."

"I expected that you'd want to go today when I realized how little I could make of this. Dalf is at the hover, ready when you are. Take care, Estri. I like this whole business less and less, the more I know." My reading was that M'lennin was genuinely concerned.

Then the Liaison First extended his hand palm up to the Liaison Second: "Everything is ready for you in Arlet. They're expecting you. You have the call codes if you need me. Tasa, Liaison."

"Tasa," Dellin and I said in unison. We had been delicately dismissed.

"How long will it take to get to Arlet in the

hover?" I asked Dellin as I grabbed up my belongings and stuffed them in my old parr-hide sack. I would leave nothing behind this time.

"A set, at least," said Dellin.

"A set!" I cried. "I could walk there in that time."

"Ah, but it will be infinitely more pleasurable to fly," said he.

"I must get to Arlet," I objected.

"You will," he assured me as we made our way across M'lennin's stone court to the egg-shaped, creamy metal hover. "But you must teach me about Silistra on the way."

We climbed up the ramp and I found I had to duck my head in the low entryway. Inside the hover was a very tiny space, filled with more hateful blinking gadgets and three contoured seats. I chose the back one, away from the window. I do not like to fly. One must give over too much of one's destiny to the caprice of circuits and steel.

The Beten pilot waved hospitably: "Welcome aboard, folks. After last night, you can bet this is going to be the smoothest trip I can manage." With a rueful grin, he turned back to his work.

"Just make it the slowest," Dellin told him.

I was not pleased with Dellin. I knew he could have had me in Arlet before next sun's rise and he knew that I knew it. Therefore, I did not speak to him.

Leaning back against the seat, I closed my eyes, hungry, irritable, and tired, and feeling guilty about having snuck off without saying farewell to Santh. But the hulion would have insisted on following me to Arlet, and one cannot be inconspicuous with a giant hulion at one's heels. I had been lucky to get away without him. The last thing I remember hearing was the pilot bringing his engines to life: I was asleep before the hover gained the air.

And the dream I had then was one of the most prophetic I had ever had until then; if only I had realized that fact, things might now be different.

The dream itself was different from any I'd known: in it were no seven bronze-glowing men, no seven-starred chamber, no tiny sun to hold in the palm of my hand. I dreamed I was in a strange checkerboard land, where all of time-space was jammed together like some impossible collage. A piece of winter laid half atop a chunk of primal sea, which bubbled over an unseen edge into a volcano that vomited fire and ash onto a plain covered with waving grain, while hailstones fell bouncing into a triangle of rain forest that grew in the midst of desert dunes, and a single great bronze figure stood laughing, towering over the scene, legs astraddle. He pointed at me with a finger, and I saw that his finger was adorned with my father's ring. I fell down on my knees and cried in fear, but the giant only laughed and snapped his fingers. Instantly I was imprisoned in a block of transparent ice.

I awoke sweating, to find Dellin shaking my shoulder.

"You were moaning and crying. Are you all right?"

"Yes . . . now," I said, knuckling the sleep from my eyes. My stomach churned, and my face and eyes stung from lack of restful sleep. "I had the strangest dream. About the ring." I sat up, wide-awake. "I forgot to show M'len the ring! I am such a fool, it's a wonder I can feed myself," I groaned.

"Easy, Estri." He brushed my hair from my eyes. "We are going to set down for a meal. I thought you might prefer eating in the open air to taking lunch cooped up in here." He patted my arm and took his seat next to the Betenese pilot.

My head was spinning: how *could* I have forgot-

ten to show M'len the ring, which might be the key
to finding my father? Then I remembered the contents of my dream and the man in it and began
trying to analyze my dream in the Silistran fashion,
a fruitless task that nevertheless absorbed my attention so that I forgot to worry about the imminent landing—landing and takeoff were the most
dangerous moments in such aircraft.

The landing was accomplished without incident,
and I found that my spirits lightened as soon as I
had solid ground beneath my feet.

Dalf, the pilot, carried out a basket filled with
good Silistran fruit, cheese, honeyed binnirin bread,
and the inevitable brin. Dellin made pleasant small
talk with his pilot while I ate in silence, seemingly
determined not to discuss the ring or my dream.

So be it! After all, he was not a Silistran, only an
ignorant outworlder; he and I had nothing in common but mutual lust. It was foolish of me to expect more from him than from any other M'ksakkan,
I told myself, and whiled away the time examining the glade around us.

When there was nothing in the basket but crumbs,
seeds, and cores, the diminutive Betenese disappeared into the hover. Returning with two large
bladders of drink, the pilot handed one to Dellin
and retired with the other to the shade of a giant
wisper tree.

"Let's go exploring," Dellin suggested with wicked
innuendo, shouldering the bladder and helping me
up.

Brushing the crumbs from my white s'kim, I
took his arm. My irritation was fading. A full belly
and the warm sun of Silistra do wonders for the
temper.

We walked far through the thick brush and trees.
Above our heads, jitkaws flitted and the black
harths cawed and the large-eyed, bush-tailed krits

scurried in the high branches. It was a beautiful day. I pointed out flora and fauna to Dellin as we went, so that he might see pictures for the words he had hypno-learned. Wandering past the glade, we found ourselves in a deeper forest of dappled light and moist cushioned sound, then came upon a sunken meadow.

I sat beneath a fan-leaved wisper tree, leaning my back against the cool velvet bark, motioning Dellin to join me. He squatted cross-legged and pulled the bladder from his shoulder. Uncorking it, he tipped it to his lips, swallowed, then handed the skin to me.

"I don't know the name of this, but it is good," said he, wiping his mouth on the back of his hand.

"It is fermented narne, from that round red fruit you ate last night," I told him when I'd tasted it. "It is called the same whether food or drink. The drink is always potent," I warned.

"Tell me about your dream," he suggested, moving to share the support of the tree trunk with me.

I did so. He listened, his arm around me, his nose in my hair.

"Let me see this ring," he said thoughtfully when I had finished.

I reached down under my s'kim and took the tiny key from its hiding place and removed the chald from my body and held the ring, still strung on my chald, out to him.

"I thought you said it did not come off," said he, referring to the chald.

"They do not, as a rule." I smiled. "I would not be without my chald, even in sleep."

He was holding the ring close to his face and the ends of my chald, looped through its band, dangled in his lap. Again and again, Dellin turned the ring, peering for a long time into its stone. Then he handed it back to me.

"It reminds me of something," he mused aloud as I refastened the chald around my waist, replaced the tiny key in its housing, and smoothed my white s'kim down around my thighs. "Something about it that I should connect. I can't quite grab ahold of the connection, though I'm sure I *have* seen something that relates to it, somehow—and recently."

"Think," I urged, staring at him. "Think hard. It is supremely important."

He raised his free hand and dropped it in his lap. I waited. Finally he shook his head.

"Sorry," he sighed. "Perhaps later on. My mind is on other things." He grinned broadly.

"Not now," I snapped. I had an uncomfortable chill.

"Now," said he, taking me by the hair. "Fight me," he advised. "I need the practice, for Arlet."

I did, until I felt myself fighting my own desire.

Then I lay on my back under the wisper tree and struggled futilely, deliciously, and with much art.

I was very close when I opened my eyes and saw them staring down at us. Dellin's mouth was on mine, and he was deep in his pleasure. I tried to warn him, but it was too late.

Hands dragged us apart. Hands forced me to my belly on the leaves and bound my wrists to my ankles, right to right and left to left. There, under the tree, a number of them took their turns with me. I caught a glimpse of Dellin trussed and helpless, watching, while two of them held him. The two men that held Dellin wore no visible chalds.

The chaldless outlaws took much glee in my debasement: a well-woman, such as I obviously was, was a sort of woman normally unattainable to men of genetic and social defect such as these. And I, disgusted and in fear for my life, forgot all my high-couch skills and fought them like a hulion.

Eventually I lost count of them, and my mind went elsewhere and I endured them until the last rolled away and pulled up his laced pants.

In that moment I gathered my wits about me and, feigning unconsciousness, raced through the mind-clearing ritual and called Santh with all the power I had. Then one of them was shaking me by the hair, and I did not get the hulion's answer.

A filthy bearded face loomed before my eyes. The teeth in that face were yellow and broken, and the breath from that mouth was fetid. I tried to turn my head away, but he jerked me back.

"High lady, do I offend you?" he rasped.

I spit at him, hitting him square in the eye.

He jerked my head back by the hair until I thought my neck would snap. I cried out in pain.

"My Well will pay a ransom for me," I gasped. He loosened his hold, and we eyed each other. Over his shoulder I could see Dellin, bloodied, down on his belly on the ground, naked. I groaned inwardly.

"No. We know who you are," my tormenter informed me. "Yes, we do." His eyes were filmy and glazed. "We know that man, Liaison to Arlet, and you, high-couch girl. And we know because a little fellow we met on the trail was kind enough to tell us before he died. Terrible accident, that. Boom! Right, Tark? Boom!"

A straw-haired, hulking youth nodded and turned toward us, his right leg dragging. Kneeling at my tormenter's side, he touched my dirt-smeared breast with a scabby finger.

"Pret-ty fi-ire," said the youth, slowly and deliberately. Then he giggled and hunkered back on his heels. "Pret-ty fi-ire, Morkel."

I shuddered as I realized the extent of our difficulties. Poor Dalf. I counted the chaldless. I could see eleven ragged, filthy men. The civilized little Betenese pilot would have had no chance.

"Your couch-mate does not please us," Morkel, the torturer, said. "You tell him, lady, to do what we say, and maybe then we won't kill you. If you're nice—very nice—us'll keep you, and you be happy to be alive, you will, high-couch slut. You tell him that Jorna and Trinard like boys like him. You tell him, lady, to do good by my friends Jorna and Trinard." He caressed my cheek with a horny paw, pushing his bristly cheek against mine. "Or off we'll cut something . . . maybe slow, maybe fast . . . something we be sure he wants to keep, and then we feeds it to you. You's all man-eaters, you high-couch sluts, we knows . . . ." He was consumed in laughter at that.

Pushing himself away from me, the degenerate rolled on the ground, kicking his legs in the air and chortling: "And then we *feeds* it to her," over and over, pointing at me.

The rest of the band of defectives took up the cry, giggling and guffawing, dancing around one another as the two I assumed to be Jorna and Trinard dragged Dellin to within an arm's length of me. His arms and legs were still bound, and there was another thick hemp rope around his neck.

I searched the sky for a growing black speck, a stooping spot, the blur of wings—some sign of Santh. I saw nothing. I turned pleading eyes to Dellin. He was struggling furiously, his face transformed with impotent rage. He looked upon me, unseeing.

Morkel jerked me to my knees and pushed me, his foot in the small of my back, toward Dellin. I fell forward, my face so close to his that I could see the blood and sweat mix on his skin. He was cut above the eye, and more blood ran from the right corner of his mouth. His eyes were wild.

"Please," I whispered in M'ksakkan. "Do what they want. They'll torture us to death if you don't. I called Santh." I begged him. "We need just a little time. It's not the act, but the context in which the act is viewed. It isn't that terrible a thing, what they want—not terrible enough to die for. . . ."

Dellin shook his head and spit blood. "No chance. They'll kill me afterward anyway." His voice was toneless. His eyes implored me to understand.

I could not think of anything else to say to him. M'ksakkan virtue is a convoluted matter; men do not lie with men in their society. Death and life, however, seemed simple and straightforward at that point in time. If I could, I would have done for him what the degenerates required. We stared at each other in silence.

Then a foot struck me in the kidneys, and I bit my lip.

"You better tell him good, lady," someone said.

"Please, Khaf-Re, if not for yourself, then for me. Santh will surely come, in time, and save us. If you lose your manhood here, and then the hulion rescues us, what good will your life be to you? Of what value is such a sacrifice? Buy me the time, please," I nearly sobbed. I had never before used his given name.

I craned my head to see the sky. Still nothing.

Looking back at Dellin, I let my tears stream unchecked. His face swam before my eyes.

Yet he seemed unmoved: he stared at me and said nothing.

Morkel stepped between us and hunkered over Dellin.

"You ready to put on a show for us, star-man?"

He giggled. The Liaison Second of Arlet did not respond.

Morkel picked me up roughly and set me on my knees between himself and the bloody, hulking Tark. The men had formed a circle around the prostrated Dellin and the two men Jorna and Trinard.

"You watch," said Morkel to me, grasping me by the throat. When the two men forced Dellin's mouth open, he kept his head, and hence his own imperiled sexual organs. He cried out once when they used him as if he were a woman. I sympathized with him.

When the show was over, the two men dragged him to his feet and pushed him, stumbling and naked, to my side, where they knotted the end of the rope that dangled from his neck around my throat and forced us both to lie down. My hands were rebound behind my back. Our feet were rope-wrapped, and they left us, facing each other, bound together.

They seemed almost to forget about us as they prepared a fire and cooked a meal of stolen stores from the hover.

Dellin did not speak to me. I watched the sky. I nudged him, but he turned his head away. I kissed him once on the shoulder; he shivered, but that was all. The day passed slowly into dusk, and our tormentors, drunk and sated, snored under the peaceful wisper trees.

I must have dozed. When I awoke, it was pitch dark and a sliver of the moon was rising in the velvet night.

I heard a rustle near me, then a soft sound as of gnashing teeth. I raised my head. At first, I could see nothing. Still I stared, straining, into the dark. Gradually I began to be able to make out the shapes, dark against dark, of the men sleeping on the little rise above us.

Once again I heard the rustle, this time farther away. Sniffing deeply, I could barely detect a musky smell.

And then I saw him, silhouetted by the feeble moonlight between the trees. It was a hulion, surely the hulion. His head was held high and he was shaking something in his mouth. Back and forth he shook it. Then, with a great toss of his mighty head, sent the thing flying into the midst of the sleeping men. I heard a grumble, a shout, and two figures rose up, their knives glinting.

The battle was short. I heard growls and snarls and shouts, and I saw Santh throw one man so far that the sound of his landing was lost in the commotion the other man was making, screaming to his fellows for aid. But no one moved among the still forms at the campsite on the rise to assist him.

Santh followed his prey into the trees. I was so filled with pride and trepidation that I could hardly speak. I nudged Dellin, who, by the sound of his breathing, still slept.

He did not wake until I nudged him again, harder. Then he tried to move his arms, as if he were stretching in a soft M'ksakkan bed, and finally came alert, realizing where he was.

"Santh is here," I whispered, still afraid that, somehow, some of our captors still lived.

"Santh? The big cat? Then it's over; those slime are all kitty-food? Where is he? I want to thank him personally," said Dellin loudly, struggling to sit up. "Move your feet here. Good. That's good. Hold it."

We could, by placing our mutually bound feet between us, sit facing each other.

"Hey!" Dellin shouted.

"Sssh," I pleaded.

"Why?" His tone was flat and cold. "I thought you said your pussycat was here. Either I'm saved, or I'm not. Either way, I'd like to know."

*"Hey!"* he called out again. "Hey, retards! Slimesacks! Here I am, sweeties!"

None stirred in the camp. But if they had, I realized then, it would not have bothered Dellin: he was intent on death or salvation, with no particular preference. We Silistrans do not consider this a mark of valor in a man.

"Could he have killed them all so quietly that I slept through it?" he asked wonderingly.

"Easily," I gloated, "especially considering how deeply you sleep."

"Has he ever tasted man flesh before?"

"No, he has not."

"Then maybe we've got worse problems than the defectives . . . what do you call them? . . . chaldless." His voice was deeper now, and troubled.

"What do you mean?" I asked, puzzled. "We are surely saved."

"Saved by what—for what? What if the hulion, in its blood rage, forgets he likes you? Humans probably taste pretty much alike. What if he decides to eat us, too? We're bound and helpless—"

"Santh would never hurt me," I assured him with more confidence than I felt. I had not thought of that.

Just then, Santh bounded out of the darkness and laid a large wet form at my feet. He snuffled my hair with his nose. I trembled.

"Good Santh," I said in my most approving voice.

The great hulion sat with his front legs tucked between his rear, his fur touching my leg, waiting for me to taste his gift. His huge eyes shone like two golden full moons out of the night.

"Santh, find a knife," I commanded, sending to

the great beast's mind a picture of the object I
wanted.

He sighed explosively and slunk off into the
darkness.

"Well"—Dellin let out a deep breath—"at least
he won't devour us immediately. Do you think he
understood you?"

I nodded, forgetting that Dellin could not see
such a slight gesture in the dim light cast by the
small sliver of moon now directly overhead.

Only when Santh returned and laid the knife he
carried in his mouth between us did I realize that
I, also, had been holding my breath.

Dellin bent to the ground and took the knife in
his own teeth. It was not long before our feet were
free. The Liaison Second crawled behind me and
sawed through the ropes that imprisoned my hands.
Then I took it and cut him loose.

Santh sat guarding his fresh kill, purring softly
in his throat, watching us through eyes that were
luminous—now red, now gold, now green, depending upon the angle at which they caught the
moonlight.

Rubbing my wrists, I approached the hulion
slowly and carefully: though I knew beyond doubt
that Santh was my friend, though I could feel his
goodwill in my mind and my heart, some of the
M'ksakkan poison of distrust and doubt had seeped
into me with Dellin's words.

But when I came up to him, hand extended,
Santh—who surely felt the disquiet in my mind
and chose to overlook it—merely lowered his massive head that I might scratch behind his tufted
ears. Feeling chagrin and vowing to myself that
never again would I allow Dellin or any of his
outworld brethren to shake my faith in things I
knew to be true, I dug my thumb deep into Santh's
inner ear and then let him lick the wax, stroking

and fondling him as he lapped his favorite treat
from my fingertips.

Meanwhile Dellin, exploring amid the camp of
our assailants, had found a torch; now he lit it. In
the flicker, he waved me to him.

Santh growled as I started up the gentle incline
and nudged the body at his feet with his nose.

"No, Santh; I love you, but I have no stomach
for such a meal," I said. The hulion snorted
disapprovingly.

At Dellin's side, in the glow of the torch, I inspected the carnage Santh had wreaked among
the chaldless. None of the men had any throat left,
nor had they stomachs. Some were mangled beyond
recognition.

I went to my knees and vomited quietly. Finally,
when my stomach stopped convulsing, I wiped my
mouth with clean grass and then, still on my hands
and knees, found myself unable to rise: my limbs
were trembling uncontrollably. While my life had
hung in the balance, I had been clear-headed and
dispassionate; now, safe, I was consumed with fear,
and with anger at the Liaison's thoughts, which
came to me as clear as the chimes sound sunrise in
the Inner Well and which were much less welcome.

"Are you hurt?" Dellin was saying as he knelt
beside me, his hand on my bowed back. A softer
voice, his mind's, condemned me as if I had been
in league with the chaldless who had assaulted us,
asking if my composure during that horrendous
episode had masked an enjoyment, if this was not
the reality of which our earlier loveplay had been
just a poor shadow.

I raised my head and looked at him. "How not,
outworlder? Can one have such an experience and
remain untouched? When two people share such a
point in time, when the wind from the abyss roars
around them and they live to remember, cannot

there by trust? No, I did not get pleasure from them. I see the question in your mind and it pains me that it is there."

He swore softly in his own lanugage, then added: "You can't damn me for something I only thought, something I had more sense than to say—or can you? I heard you people were difficult, but surely a man has the right to the privacy of his own rumination."

I just watched him. His mind told me his right-eous indignation was a show, but not what lay beneath it.

Then, running a splayed hand through his hair, he said, "All right, maybe I wondered—*wonder*—about that: your behavior gives me cause. You like rough trade, you Silistran women—I didn't really believe it until I met one. I've been told all that rot about needing sufficient stimulation to ovulate, but that's tape-learned; this is field education . . . what M'len wanted to make sure I got from you." He grinned ruefully, as if it had all been staged for his benefit.

I almost slapped him. "I like *life*—I am not afraid of it, but deeply unwilling to lose it. You are a . . ." I almost said "offworld barbarian" but thought better of it; instead, I gave him the benefit of the doubt: ". . . man; submission is not in your genes—perhaps not within your ability to comprehend. Those chaldless ones did me a favor: they bound me, and I am grateful for that: I had no alternative but to submit. Had they not bound me, I would have served them anyway, for my life's sake. But I did not have to suffer that greater humiliation. I am grateful for that. Although every woman in her primal self may desire a man who can at least overcome her defenses, because of the quality of these nearly subhuman chaldless and my terror, I felt very little. I am also grateful for that. And I live,

embassy posting, and that's certain. I may not be
. . . suited . . . for the Liaison's post here."

"Doubtless it seems strange to you, from the
prudery of M'ksakka. And you may be correct: you
may *not* be suited for Arlet. I think you will have
to wait and see. Men change here—surely your
superiors on M'ksakka have warned you about that.
I can tell you irrefutably only that I know you are
suited for Astria." I took his hand. "M'lennin is
not. He is, however, a man who would be at home
in Arlet. Perhaps you and he could exchange posts.
I would relax the trade embargo for the right man.
You might find Astria profitable if such an arrangement were made."

Dellin, soon to be of Arlet, first whistled softly,
then dug in the dirt with a stick.

"If I'm not mistaken, that's a proposition—one
my 'superiors' have been longing to hear. But I'm
going to forget you made it." He looked up at me,
his face unreadable: "I'd think you'd want me less,
not more, after what happened. Your people set so
much store by physical prowess, and I couldn't
protect you, could hardly even control myself. As
you said, I might have got us both killed." Self-
recrimination was a cutting edge in his voice. The
torchlight flickered.

I shrugged. It had cost me to put that offer into
words. I was not used to being rejected; I was still
haughty and young. If I had made such an offer to
M'lennin, a star-flung celebration would have been
under way by now.

But Dellin had suffered a shock the effects of
which I only dimly understood, but which I could
still sense. So I said: "Perhaps I liked what I saw
in you when you bested yourself and endured them.
A boy would have died there, for his purity and
honor. M'lennin is such a boy. In Astria we are in
need of a man, sure enough of his strength to act

on his own standards. Would you trade Arlet for Astria, Khaf-Re Dellin?''

He stood abruptly and extended his hand to me.

"You speak of the Well but not the Well-Keepress. It's too soon Estri ... too soon for me to know what I'll want to do or need to do when I'm Liaison in Arlet. As you say, men change here. I don't think it would be Silistran of me to let you take advantage of me while I'm still a cultural virgin. And even if I wanted to switch Wells with M'lennin, it would be undiplomatic of me to suggest it, to say the least. If you were offering me the Well-Keepress, I'd move heaven and earth, but you're not, and these Wells, both of them, interest me less and less."

He stepped away from me and wandered among the bodies, stooping over the corpses, collecting weapons and leathers, bits of food, torch in hand. When he came back, I took the weapons and belts he gave me, while he gathered some coals and wood.

Then we carried our loot back to the hollow, made a fire, and cooked chunks of meat on sword points while Santh snored peacefully, stretched out with his belly to the flames. This was healthy: one does normal things, performs acts conservative of life, whenever one has nearly lost it. Dellin's instincts, I decided, were good.

So I brought up the matter of a couch-bond between us, which he had broached so obliquely, to clear the air between us: "I must dispose of this chaldra," I said, "and then, if you choose, we will discuss the disposition of the Well-Keepress." I had thought hard on how to answer without rejecting him. I did not entirely succeed.

"I see no way to dissuade you," he said.

"Would you like to have Santh with you in Arlet?" I asked.

"You think I need him?"

"*I* need him and cannot take him into the Well."

"If that great beast wants to come to Arlet," he said slowly, "I surely won't try to stop him. If he decides to take up residence at the Liaison's there, I won't argue. If you'd prefer a M'ksakkan embassy to the Arletian Well, I can safely extend our hospitality—no one's going to argue with me so early on in my residency."

"I must be in Well Arlet for Ristran's man to find me, when he comes."

He shook his head and puffed out his cheeks: "Inscrutable. I actually thought we were making some progress. All right, Well-Keepress, cozy up on your couch, or whatever you call it. At least I'll know where to find you, if I want to buy an hour or so of your time."

I threw my food and sword into the dirt and went to him, putting my head in his lap: "Do not be angry with me for the way I live, Khaf-Re," I pleaded. I found I truly cared.

He rubbed my shoulder and kissed me gently on the lips.

"Women are not so . . . free . . . on M'ksakka," he said gently.

"On Silistra," I whispered, "we are all bound."

When I awoke, Dellin was tending a fresh-made fire in the dim light. Beside the fire lay three fat black harths. He had hunted us breakfast with a longbow taken from the camp of the chaldless.

He had also appropriated for himself a vest of thick hide circles, linked together, such as is popular among the Slayers. It protects the vital organs, coming low over the hips, but leaves the wearer's arms and legs unencumbered. Beneath it he wore a short tas-leather breech. Around his waist was slung a Silistran pocket belt, so named because of its many compartments, from which hung a short sword in a tooled scabbard and a knife in sheath. He had a thong across his brow to keep his unruly hair back from his face as he poked the crackling logs and the sparks flew. In the light of sun's rising, he looked very Silistran, squatting before the fire in his leathers.

Going to the fire, I knelt beside him, fingering the harth carcasses.

"I found your viewer and holos among the loot from the hover," he said.

"Give them to me." I held out my hand.

"No, I will hold them until we reach Arlet." He took the birds and began to clean them. "They're safer with me." For the first time since we had left M'len's on our journey, he spoke to me in Silistran. "Where is Santh?"

"He was gone when I awoke. The hulion will find us if he so chooses." He met my eyes and his were hard. "We will strike out for the road, that way," he pointed, "as soon as we've eaten."

"I must wait for Santh."

"Estri, don't try my patience. I thought all night about what's happened since we met. I have paid for your use, in the requisite Silistran fashion, but it's you who've used me. I'm serving notice: I intend to get full value from you—you'll not make me the laughingstock of Arlet before I've even settled in there."

He reached into one of the pockets in his belt and drew forth a thong on which was strung perhaps two hundred gold dippars. He leaned to me and fastened the thong behind my neck. Then he leaned back and regarded me.

"Now you wear your Silistran worth. I was going to wait and pay you in Arlet, but I need to keep clear in my mind just who and what you are. And perhaps you, too, will find yourself better able to recollect your station."

I was angry. I reached up to remove the necklace of coins. He took my wrists and held them in one hand. His grip was not gentle. I had played the game of control and lost. One controls a man through his weakness, his self-image. Dellin had reassessed himself. He could not be handled now as easily as before. His mind, as well as his body, had come to Silistra.

Briefly, I struggled to free my hands, but he held me easily. I closed my eyes to read him, to find a reference point in him I could use, but he entwined his fingers in my hair and shook my head to and fro.

"No," he said. "Look at me."

I did so.

"Remove your chald." He let my hands go.

I shook my head, though his hand was still wound in my hair.

"Do it! Give me the respect you'd give one of your Silistran men. I could kill you here and now and blame it on the chaldless—nobody would doubt my word, and I wouldn't have to worry about you telling all your friends how I took it up the ass from a bunch of your woodsy degenerates! Be a good girl and I'll deliver you to Arlet. *Then* I'll give you back your chald and your artifacts. You don't have Santh to protect you now. You must depend on me. And I don't intend to be taken for a chaldless outlaw on the road to Arlet."

"You are unbalanced, from the shock!"

"On the contrary, I think I have, for the first time in my life, struck a tenable balance with myself. I don't want to bind you, Estri—you said yourself that it's too easy that way. By your chald and your father's ring shall I hold you. Give them to me!"

I did as he commanded. He was totally in control of the situation. For the first time, I feared him. To have a man come to the Well, money in hand, determined to take an evening's pleasure with a high-couch girl, is one thing. A woman has subtle but effective restraints upon his behavior. Here, alone, with Dellin, who had freed himself of those invisible bonds by which we bend men to our wills, I had no option. This was another thing entirely. I had put myself into his hands, when I thought those hands were weak. I had miscalculated. If I tried to escape him alone, my fate might be worse than any he'd mete out.

Taking my chald, he examined it, then removed my father's ring from the chald and slipped it on the middle finger of his left hand. The chald was too small for his waist. He draped it around his neck and lay down on the soft grass, pointing to the harths.

"Cook the meal." I did, and he ate his fill. Then he gave me the remains, and I devoured them. I read him, and what I saw confirmed what he had said.

So angry was he, deep within, that I didn't even dare comment that he would seem rather odd to any Silistran men he met, with a woman's chald draped round his neck and nothing at his waist. I thought to myself that he'd find out his errors soon enough. But then, I, too, was angry.

We struck out through the woods toward the road to Arlet. He moved quickly, said little, and I found myself half-running to match his pace. I called Santh, but got no response. I wondered if Dellin had somehow driven him away.

When we were in sight of the road, a wide stone-block thoroughfare, lightly traveled, we stopped to rest in a thicket. The road was below us; we could see a good distance in either direction without being observed.

I collapsed on the soft mossy ground, panting,

unmarked in body and mind, while they do not—I am supremely grateful for that, although my gratitude belongs to Santh, and not to you."

He touched my face. I could read the turmoil in him without trying.

"And though you could not protect me physically," I continued, as kindly as I could, "you trusted me, and for that I do thank you."

"You have no reason to thank me," he said sadly.

"Had your pride caused you to fight them, you would have lost. Perhaps your life, and certainly your maleness and your mind. What could I have salvaged of my own sanity had that been the case?" I hoped it would work. I could feel the degree to which he was shaken, almost to the very foundations of his being, and I did not like it.

Dellin made no reply.

"I think it is much harder for a man to be accosted than for a woman: for me it was an exaggeration of a normal experience. For a man, I would assume, there could be nothing but pain and humiliation in submission under duress." I looked at him questioningly, suddenly cold in a gusting breeze that blew down from the west and made me rub my arms.

"I, too, feel the chill," he admitted to one thing by acknowledging another.

I felt him relax, the whirling within him slow and cease.

"We will be," I quipped, "in fashion in Arlet."

"What?"

"M'lennin did not tell you, then, how Arlet differs from Astria?"

He rocked back on his heels, rubbing his eyes.

"Not so plainly as you just have, though I had heard . . . rumors. This is a strange world, Estri, especially for someone like me. Not your average

grateful for the respite. I had had much time to
think. I knew that my fear had triggered something else within me. I desperately wanted to please
Dellin, to reach the gentleness in him I had previously known, I told myself. For whatever reason, I
determined to do my best to placate him. His
rough, offhand treatment had me off-balance,
defensive, and much aroused.

When I was breathing easily, I crawled to where
he leaned against a needle-leaved evergreen. His
eyes were narrowed on the road. On my knees, I
put my cheek and arms against his thigh. He pushed
me roughly away.

"I will let you know when I want you," he said,
not taking his eyes from the horizon.

I lay where I had fallen. I wanted to cry but bit
my teeth into my wrist until the need had passed.
That much I would give no man who was only
playing at being Silistran, and succeeding only in
becoming a caricature. Whatever M'ksakka was
like, whatever its constraints, men slipped them
easily here, and all the wrath in them escaped in a
rush—sometimes, as with M'len, there was nothing left to take its place.

The part of me which can rise above paltry events
of the moment hoped that this would not be the
case with Dellin.

After a time he came to me and motioned me
up, pointing to a party of travellers just coming
into view below.

"That's a likely-looking group, there. They seem
headed in the right direction. I'm going to see if
we can join them. Whatever happens," he said,
loosening his sword in his scabbard, "keep silent
and do as you're told."

I trailed meekly behind him down the incline
and waited silently beside him at the road's edge
as a group of four men approached us.

When they were almost upon us, Dellin pointed to the ground. I sat. He went to meet them. I could see that they were Slayers, back from the hunt. They wore the slate-colored leather-and-metal armor of their profession, carried helmets crested with parr bristles and square shields emblazoned with the Slayers' device: sword and stones, in black upon silver. It must have been a successful hunt. Each man had his cape drawn up into a sling. Slayers hunt the chaldless outlaws for sport. In those capes would be trophies of their victories.

They were large, fierce, proud men. Dellin, I thought, did not look out of place among them. They circled around him; I heard laughter, then low exchanges, but could not catch the words. Dellin turned and pointed at me. One of the Slayers made a remark, and all laughed again. Dellin waved at me and then pointed to the ground in front of him.

I got up and ran to him, conscious of my ratted hair and filthy white s'kim.

"This," said Dellin when I stood before him, "is Estri. She has a speech impediment, but is otherwise sound." His eyes warned me. I flushed but said nothing.

"I have often thought," said a red-haired Slayer—their leader, from his belt devices—"that such is a glorious quality in a woman. You are very fortunate. I think life would be more pleasant if they were all born mute."

There was general laughter at that, and Dellin put his arms around my shoulder and kissed me for the first time that day. I melted against him, making it clear to the band of Slayers whose woman I was.

After some good-natured ribbing and the requisite manly posturing by all concerned, we moved

off in the direction of Arlet, safe in the center of
the red-haired Slayer's band.

"Where did you get her?" asked the red-haired
one, making small talk.

"I won her on a gamble, north of Astria."

"Umn," said the Slayer. "I wondered, until you
mentioned her muteness, why she wasn't in a Well.
Though she is, perhaps, too slim in the hips to
bear child, she is certainly better than what the
Wells customarily leave us."

"She is also very stupid," Dellin said, his hand
at my throat.

"That matters little when they are on their
backs."

"What about that necklace she wears?" asked
the red-haired Slayer. "That's a lot of money for a
woman to be carrying."

"She eats a great deal. I rent her out that she
may earn her keep," said Dellin. "She wears what
she has earned on the road from Astria."

I bit his hand. He jerked it back, into my hair,
grasping me tightly at the base on my skull.

"What is her price?" asked the red-haired one.

"Only one gold dippar, Ganrom. But for you I
will cut that in half."

I managed to step on Dellin's foot, but he didn't
stumble.

The red-haired Ganrom, leader of the Slayers,
grinned broadly. "I may take you up on your rea-
sonable offer, if you'll share our fire this night. I
think, too, some others of us are in need of release.
We are three days' march from Arlet, and we have
been on the hunt over a set."

He turned to his companions. There were guffaws,
and the heavyset, dark Slayer on my right reached
across me and pounded Dellin on the back.

"What say you, Idrer?" the leader asked of the
heavyset man.

"I say *I'd* have her if she were deaf, blind, *and* mute," answered the dark Slayer on my right.

"And you, Fen? And Mael, you also?" The two Slayers in the rear laughed their assent.

I heard little else that was said. My fury roared within me. One gold dippar indeed! If not for Dellin's restraining hand, and his possession of my chald and my father's ring, I would have run into the woods and taken my chances with the chaldless.

We proceeded at a good pace, faster than was comfortable for me, through the day. We overtook a party of merchants, with their large wagons pulled by plodding docile denters and, when the sun was low, we in turn were passed by two mounted runners, their red cloaks flying behind them, pushing their sleek threx at top speed, headed to Astria. Their four-footed threx showered us with clods of dirt and dust kicked up by their mighty hooves.

Soon after that, the Slayers turned off the road. The sun was sinking when we came to a clearing that showed traces of many previous camps. There the men set down their bulging capes and set about building a fire.

"Down the path," pointed Ganrom, "is a pool where the girl could wash. Let me send Idrer with her. I'd like to speak with you, Dellin, alone."

Dellin looked at me, then the red-haired Slayer. He raked his hand through his hair, then nodded and turned his back to me.

When I returned with Idrer from the pool, naked, carrying my hand-washed s'kim, the fire roared high and Dellin and Ganrom were huddled together like old friends, sharing a bladder of drink.

I was shivering in the cold night air, my hair wet, clammy, and dripping on my back. Hanging my s'kim to dry on a shrub, I sat close by the fire, hoping its heat would dry my hair and bake the chill from my bones. Idrer patted me on my damp head and went to Dellin.

"The moment took me," Idrer explained, handing Dellin a coin. "Your price," the heavyset Slayer continued, "is much too low. She is like a high-couch well woman."

Dellin snorted, looked down, then back up. "My appreciation, Slayer," he managed. "I taught her all she knows, but, like any other woman, she has her better times. Often I have to beat her to get her to perform. Perhaps she is taken with you." Dellin passed the bladder to Idrer.

"I was wondering," said Idrer slowly, "how she amassed so many coins at such a low price."

"We stopped in Port Astrin," bluffed Dellin airily.

"Ah," said Idrer. "That, then, explains it."

"Estri, come here," Dellin called. I went to him, managing to step on his foot in doing so. I was flushed, and not from the fire: I could play this game twice as well as he, and I was determined to teach him a lesson he desperately needed to learn— one must be *born* Silistran, one can't just play at it.

So I knelt before him docilely, and he pulled me to his lap and began caressing my breasts.

"I had a coin girl once," reminisced Ganrom. "I made much money on her, and she gave me great pleasure. She was comely for a Well reject, though not so beautiful as this one." I had never thought of the fate of the Well rejects. I was learning many things, with Dellin, not the least of these being that this game of his was becoming, moment by moment, as he fondled me, harder to win and harder to consider a game.

"What happened to her—your coin girl?" Dellin asked.

"I came upon hard times and traded her for a threx. Sometimes I wish I had not done so. The

Well women think themselves more than human. I
seldom use them."

"In Astria," said Dellin loyally, "they aim to
please."

"And they make sure you know it. I don't like
feeling as if I must thank a woman for pleasuring
her. I prefer to have the girl thank me." The red-
haired Slayer grinned.

Dellin's hands did their work. I knew he teased
me for the Slayers' benefit, but by that time I
could not help responding to him. He bent his
head to kiss my erect nipples, while I tried my
best not to put on a show for Ganrom and his men.
I heard meat sizzle on the fire and smelled the tas
as it cooked.

"I could tell them you are not what you pretend,"
I whispered in Dellin's ear. "They will kill you,
M'ksakkan Liaison or not, for hoodwinking them;
their honor will demand it. And I would still get to
Arlet—any of them would be glad to see me there
safely, once they know who I am."

"I wouldn't try it, if I were you," he whispered
thickly; "they'll never believe you, and you'll become what I have made you: a Well reject, a coin
girl. With a different master, perhaps Ganrom,
you'll play that role for the rest of your long life.
You're better off remaining a coin girl. You're right:
the Slayer would take great offense if he knew I
lied about you. He caught my accent, and called
me on it. It took me the whole time you were gone
to placate him. I didn't exactly lie, but I gave him
less than the truth. On Silistra, it seems, a man is
allowed some secrets."

His hand went to my belly, and I shivered
helplessly. The ring glinted in the firelight.

"What are you?" he hissed.

"A coin girl," I whispered, defeated, betrayed by
my body and my common sense.

"Will you eat, Dellin, or are you too full of love?" It was Mael's voice.

Dellin pushed me off his lap and I sprawled half on the ground, half on Ganrom's crossed legs.

"I was hoping you would be passed this way," said the red-haired Slayer through a mouthful of tender tas. He put a grease-slicked hand on my naked thigh. I looked up at Dellin beseechingly, but he had his hands on a tas chop and would not meet my eyes. I started to shift my hips off Ganrom's lap.

"No," he mumbled. A hot dribble of meat juice struck my thigh. "That is the part of you I will get to first. Let it be."

They did not offer me a piece of meat, though Dellin took a second chop, bit it once, and handed it to me. I gnawed it gratefully, trying to keep the grease from my face and hair and my attention on anything but my predicament.

The men passed the bladder, and Ganrom gave me a swallow when Dellin proffered it to him. It was crude kifra, but it warmed. I ached within. I wanted Dellin badly, but it was another who would have me. I hated him for arousing me, purposely, for Ganrom. Nor was I too pleased with myself: this was, after all, as much my fault as any trick of the time's.

After the third round of kifra, Ganrom's hands found me of interest.

Fen put another branch on the fire, that there would be sufficient light.

Dellin leaned down toward me where I lay, my head on the ground and my hips on the red-haired Slayer's lap.

"Estri"—his lips brushed my temple—"do use your skills. I would enjoy watching you. Give your best to Ganrom, and prettily. Perhaps, when you are done, I will reward you."

I would have in any case. I was beyond caring
where I was or who was who. But I moved for
Dellin, as seductively as possible, and with much
emotion. I was exquisite. I would make him sorry
he had given me to another man.

Ganrom did not believe it. I went for his inner
need and gave him such prolonged ecstasy that he
rolled and moaned and whimpered. The three
Slayers and Dellin got more than they bargained
for. One learns many dances in Astria.

Finally, I lay panting, sleek and glistening with
sweat in the fire's glow. Ganrom, beside me, took
a great breath of air. I bent one leg at the knee and
brought my foot near to my buttocks, rubbed my
inner thigh, and turned my face to Dellin, my lips
parted, chest heaving. I can't describe the look on
his face, but although it was his game, it was my
point.

Ganrom struggled to sit up. "Kifra," he croaked.
Someone handed him a wineskin. Then: "Dellin! I
will buy her from you. Name your price."

My heart stopped. Perhaps I had done too well.

Dellin started to laugh. He put his head in his
hands and shook with laughter. Uncertainly, the
others joined in.

Presently he looked up at the red-haired Slayer
who, to my amazement, was also consumed with
merriment. There were tears of mirth on his face.

"The reason you want her, Slayer, is the reason I
cannot part with her," Dellin chortled, short of
breath. "You know, as I, that we are all bound."

"Would that I were so bound." He was shaking
his head, back and forth, back and forth. "A coin
girl," said the Slayer in wonder. "A coin girl. How
may I convince you to allow us to accompany you
to Arlet—you and your coin girl, of course?"

Dellin, who had regained control of himself, inclined his head: "I'd be honored by your company,

as I am honored by your offer. So be it." Drunk, Dellin's Silistran was better, not worse; perhaps the hypno-tape he'd learned preempted his M'ksak-kan snytax more easily when he was inebriated. Whatever the reason, the Slayers around the camp-fire had truly accepted him—and me. I had no more doubts about getting safely to Arlet.

When Dellin passed the kifra bladder to me, I drank three swallows and handed it back. His fin-gers touched mine, and lingered. I caught his eye and enticed him without words. His lids half-closed, he looked coldly down upon me and signified his refusal. Then he gestured to Mael, the brown-skinned Slayer, to take his place next to me, and walked to the other side of the fire.

As Mael spoke gently to me, I glimpsed Dellin coming around to seat himself on Ganrom's far side. I rolled so that my back was to them, facing Mael. Mael was young and hesitant, for all his bravado earlier.

I touched him, and he was mine. I was glad, and I was faultless.

I rolled away from him and sat up, pawing the hair off my face and breasts. I shrugged and raised my hands, dropping them back in my lap: it was not my fault that this boy was not a man. I made sure to keep my head high and my back straight. I would not show Dellin that, among all these Slayers, it was him I yet hungered to touch.

Only one Slayer and I remained unacquainted: Fen, who had cooked the dinner, was blond and slighter than the others. He spoke quietly when he saw my eyes on him.

"I cannot," he declined. "Not like this, not now. Watching you was more than I needed, lady. I am not rejecting you. I will try tomorrow."

I tried to look disappointed.

Mael put his hands companionably around Fen's

shoulders, holding the wine to his lips. "I guess us boys have got to leave some things to the men." He was rueful about his own performance before his leader and the stranger, obviously relieved that Fen had fared as badly as, if not worse than, he.

Ganrom and Dellin were eyeing each other, making valiant efforts to remain upright and straight-faced. Idrer was lying on his side with a bladder pillowed on his arm, convulsing silently with laughter.

Dellin, I guessed, was less drunk than he appeared, though he seemed to match the Slayers' leader swallow for swallow. He caught my eyes and pointed to his lap. I nodded.

I stood, as languorously as I could manage, and walked my best toward him. Then I knelt beside him, and he pulled me against him. I had wanted his touch so desperately, tears squeezed from my eyes when I felt his arm around me. Tears of joy. I should have been anything but happy to be with the man who had done this to me.

He lay back and made me work, his heavy-lidded eyes on me. He took a long time with me, and I felt more with him in that awful place than I thought a woman could feel with a man in such circumstances. Yet he made no sound, nor did he once lose that distant look. I deep-read him: he had nothing more important within. He was engrossed in the act and in the context. But I could coax from him not a single moan of pleasure, even in the final moments.

I curled up on the ground beside him, my head at his calf and fell asleep to the sound of his voice, and Ganrom's, as they discussed hunting the chaldless.

The morning dawned bright and clear, and I found myself imprisoned within the circle of Dellin's arms. My back to his chest, he had held me through the night.

I lay unmoving, content, until the sounds of the Slayers rising woke him. He pushed back from me, stretching and yawning. We went together to the quiet pool and bathed; the warm muck on my feet and the cool waters on my flesh revived me, and by the time we had eaten, broken camp, and were on the road again, the morning sun had lost its ruddy glow. I labored, as before, to keep the pace. Even in such a simple thing as speed of stride is a woman at a disadvantage.

I thought, as we passed out of the wooded area into tilled land, about Arlet. It would be good to be within a Well once more, where men seek out a woman, pleasure with them, and depart. To spend long periods of time with a man, I concluded, is surely more difficult then having them come, high in expectation, to use one. The Well life allows a woman to maintain her dignity.

There were denter and woolly tas grazing in the rail-fenced pastures on both sides of the road. I could see farmers' keeps and animal barns in the distance. The green-and-gold binnirin waved high for miles in front of us, and the smell of newly turned earth came rich and moist to my nostrils. A yellow crier darted across the road, its wings invisible, screeching.

With Dellin's arm on mine, in the midst of the Slayers, I made my way toward Arlet. Only two more days, with luck, and I would see civilization again. I listened to the men jabber around me. Dellin concealed his ignorance of Silistra with masterful skills. And, listening, I realized he did this as a deep-reader does: by concentrating the men's attention to the subject he would study and drawing them out. I saw him make at least six intuitive jumps of understanding and began to wonder if perhaps he was not an undeveloped telepath, so smooth was his facade.

The road was becoming more traveled as we drew closer to Arlet. Often we passed traders, farmers, and carts.

We stopped and lunched in an unfenced field, under the shade of three huge wisper trees, a solitary stand in that wide expanse of woods and rocky ground.

When we had eaten, Mael drew out his sword and with its point made a large circle on a level stretch where no grass grew. This was the Slayers' circle.

He then, with decorum and attention to proper form, invited Fen to join him within its boundaries. The slight blond man accepted eagerly, and the two fell to swordplay with a will. They were well matched, and obviously familiar with each other's moves. They engaged and disengaged, laughing and cursing, neither able to score a hit, which would have been fatal had this not been play, or drive the other from the circle.

Finally, with more imagination than either had previously shown, Mael pretended to stumble, and rolled under Fen's guard, hoping to drive the point of his sword up to touch his opponent's breech. This he managed to do, but by that time Fen had his sword's point at Mael's throat.

"You are both dead," called Ganrom disgustedly. "My men have just slain each other, Dellin, with as much grace as a pair of three-legged threx." His voice turned soft, conspiratorial.

"Would you, my friend, like to join me in a little recreation?"

"Not with sword," Dellin declined. "I haven't the skill of you professionals."

Ganrom looked disappointed.

"I will, however—*if* and *only* if you insist, of

course—fight you hand-to-hand, no conventions. But I warn you, I learned what I know long ago, high in the north, and you shall surely make quick work of me. I have none of the refinements of you Slayers."

"I insist," said Ganrom happily, waving a bearlike paw at Dellin's disclaimers and stripping down to his breech eagerly. "I promise not to do you any permanent harm. If you would have quarter, just call out and it's yours."

Dellin freed himself of his garments and reached down, rubbing his hands in the dirt, a look of keen anticipation on his face. "Thanks," he replied, "and the same to you." I thought the Liaison Second badly underestimated his opponent.

Fen and Mael came and lay, one on each side of me, and flopped down on the grass, chins propped up on their elbows, to watch.

"Idrer, will you exercise the winner?" asked Ganrom as he and Dellin entered the empty circle.

The heavyset Idrer nodded but said nothing. The kifra had been drunk to the last drop the night before, and the big man had accounted for most of it. He had been taciturn and surly all morning.

Ganrom and Dellin were like two great tawny animals, circling each other in the midday sun, the red-haired and the black-haired heads weaving with concentration. They stalked, circled, feinted, each taking the other's measure. Dellin was on the defensive, dancing light to keep out of range of Ganrom's mighty arms. Ganrom dived for him, striking at Dellin's neck. Dellin ducked under him, fluid as running water, and his foot connected with the red-haired Slayer's belly.

Then Ganrom, with a howl of rage, launched himself upon the half-prostrate Dellin before he could regain his feet. They rolled in the dirt, grunting and growling. Suddenly, as if by magic, Dellin was out from under the Slayer, backing away, crouched low. Ganrom came at him again, trying for a shoulder hold. Dellin reached down and up under his opponent's arms, his hands at the other's throat. They rolled again in the dust. And disengaged. And engaged. They stood struggling, upright, their limbs tangled, each straining to throw the other, to break the hold, as still as living statues.

Abruptly, Dellin collapsed. Ganrom, startled, released his grip. On his knees in the dirt, Dellin reached up deftly and toppled the Slayer. They grappled once more, rolling.

Outside the circle, where rude comments and jibes had been flowing freely, everyone was very quiet.

The tangled bodies parted and both men staggered, begrimed and swaying, to opposite edges of the circle. Perspiration ran down them in rivulets, streaking their dusty limbs. Dellin was shaking his head back and forth, the red-haired Ganrom weaving.

Some Slayer whispered: "If one of them doesn't give, we'll be here until they both die of exhaustion."

Just at that moment, Dellin took a step forward, stopped, and rubbed his eyes: "I give you quarter, Slayer."

"And I you, Dellin. It's a long walk to Arlet. We shouldn't tire ourselves overmuch." Ganrom, his chest heaving, staggered to Dellin's side of the circle and clapped his arms about him.

"You ought to test for the Slayer's chain," advised Ganrom as the two men came to sit beside us in the shade. "With a little training, you might win one."

"Perhaps, but I would need a good teacher. You've seen my weakness at hand-to-hand, and that is my strongest skill."

"Ah, yes," commiserated the Slayer, "Hand-to-hand is my weakest skill, or I'd never have fought you, a civilian; you'd have no chance with me in any other contest. But keep in mind that the competition in that field is less than in the sword or stones. I myself have won the Golden Well in the Arlet hand-to-hand three passes running, there are so few who are even adequately trained in it. These young bucks want weapons, shiny metal, sharp edges; they forget that it's the hand that drives the blow home which matters. It's a sad situation, how poor our competitors are these days." The best compete in the pass games. Ganrom must have been skilled indeed to have triumphed three consecutive times.

Idrer waived his "exercise," as it was obvious neither man was in shape to fight again. He and Fen and Mael broke camp, and we took to the road once more.

Ganrom set a slower pace than previously, and for the first time I was able to pace them in comfort. We trekked long past sun's set, for the Slayers' leader sought a special place.

Little was different that night than the night before, save that we ate from a haunch of denter Mael bartered from a trader bound to Baniev, and Fen and Mael gave better accounts of themselves when dinner was done. We had also, at Idrer's insistence, purchased kifra of a better vintage than that the Slayers had supplied. There was some talk of the Day-Keepers calling a conclave of the forereaders and the Slayers, which struck me as strange, but I soon forgot it, at Dellin's hand.

He was, if possible, more distant than he had been the night before. He did not refuse me when I went to him, but he had no kindness for me, no intimacy in his lust. I would have given much for a gentle caress, an understanding smile. Neither was forthcoming.

I lay my head in his lap when the night was old and he had tired of me, not sleeping, just lying quietly, listening to his drink-muddled exchanges with Ganrom. His hand touched my hair; he stroked my head absently. I held my breath and then wondered what was happening to me: I, a woman of Astria, had lain still as stone on a man's lap as the night wasted away, hoping for such a touch, needing it, but unable to ask. I wished he would hold me, but he and Ganrom talked on.

Finally, I dozed, waking when he slid out from under me to strip off his gear. I feigned sleep when he lay down beside me, and rolled drowsily to him. He allowed me to rest my head on his shoulder, his arm went about me, and I slept.

The next day Detarsa first fifth, we made it to within sight of Arlet. The sky was gray and threatening, as it had been since sun's rise. When we came to the intersection where, from the road to Arlet, the thoroughfare that leads to Baniev and the sea branches right, and that which leads to Morrlta, where the trappers sell their pelts and buy their needs high in the foothills, branches left, Arlet crouched above us, only another half-day's journey, squat and angular on her craggy perch.

Arlet herself is built of dark blue gol-blocks, rather than the free-spiral gol-forms of Astria. The Well has been often expanded, and cube and tower jut out at odd angles, that they may find foothold on the rocky crag. She lies like a hulion sprawling on a log, dark and powerful. From where we were, I could not see the great wall of Arlet, which undulates about her like a tight-fitting chald, but I knew it was there, hidden in the shadows of the oncoming night. There is only one gate by which one may enter or leave Arlet, and the double doors of that gate stand thrice the height of a tall man; made of star-steel, when they were installed they were considered quite the scandal; now they are merely anachronistic, machine-powered and ponderous. Arlet is not an enticing sight, in the ominous dusk, from low on the road, but I was heartened to see her. Soon I would be free from Dellin and the Slayers, and in control of my destiny once more.

I would have gone on, having seen my destination, but no one asked my feelings.

The night wore away in its familiar pattern. This would be my last night with the Liaison Second of Arlet. I found that the thought upset me. I longed to speak to him, to advise him to take chaldra in Arlet, to find out if he would visit me in the Well, to test him out about the duty he had to the current Well-Keepress of Arlet, Celendra. I dared not.

He had said, I reminded myself, that he would give me what help he could. My inner self told me that it was a different man who had offered me the Liaison's house in Arlet, who had said he would buy my use in Arlet. I would, I told myself, be lucky to get my chald and my father's ring from him, and be quit of him forever. My inner self disagreed. I was perplexed and preoccupied. Dellin noticed, and took me away from the others, into the brush.

"Your heart," he chided, "is not in your work." A rain began to fall as we stood there, in the brush and the gloom, facing each other. Dellin's arms were folded across his chest, and the droplets glinted in his black hair.

"I would speak to you of Arlet," I said.

"When I seek you in Arlet, we will speak of Arlet."

"I cannot go into the Well looking like this." He had already told me what I wanted to know.

"I had not thought of that," he allowed. "Mael mentioned that tomorrow is market day in the Inner Well. I will buy you something with the dippars you made on the road. I will also give you your things. You deserve them."

He put his hand under my chin and tilted it up to look at my face.

I was glad it was raining.

"I love you," I whispered, unable to hold it back.

He raised an eyebrow and kissed me on the forehead. He did not reach out to hold me.

"I doubt it," he said finally.

"I have never said that to another man."

"That, I do believe."

"You wanted me before."

"I want you now. But on my terms. I only said that I doubted your love for me. I think, with all your experience, you know little of love." There was nothing I could say to that. I put my head against his chest.

He had me there, for I went on my knees to him and shamelessly begged, that he might recollect me the sooner in Arlet. The privacy of the scratchy, brittle brush was opulent luxury.

I remember little else of that night, for I was focused so on Dellin that I retained only the memory of his voice and his hands.

# IV.
## Well Arlet

It was close to mid-meal, bright and hot, when we neared the Arletian gate. The road was thronged with vendors, merchants and traders, for it was market day in the Inner Well. Arletians disdain uniformity of dress, and the crowd in the large U-shaped court of stalls was a riot of shifting, clashing primary colors. Laughter and hawkers' spiels drifted between the towering metal gates toward us as we threaded our way between riders and pedestrians, tourists and locals, star-traders and pelters down from the hills.

The feeling of holiday was strong around us, and the Slayers were much affected, fidgeting and joking, speculating on the delights they planned to purchase under the Well's copper-scaled roof.

"Will you sup with me tonight, Ganrom?" Dellin asked. "The hospitality of the Liaison Second's house can be stretched to include four more."

"You ought not to test your welcome there, my friend, by including Slayers in your party. There's little love lost between the M'ksakkan Second and the Slayers," Ganrom replied.

"Ah, but the old Second no longer holds court here, and the new, I hear, is determined to change all that," Dellin said as we were squeezed together by the unruly crowd that queued to pass under the scrutiny of the red-garbed guards lounging against Arlet's wide-swung metal gates and Dellin put the hand which bore my father's ring on my neck so we would not be separated by the crush of bodies.

"So be it then, Dellin," Ganrom said, accepting the invitation of the man who would soon be revealed to him as Arlet's new Liaison. "But if we're thrown out on our heads, then you must buy the dinner, at a place of our choosing."

"Done," the Liaison Second agreed. "At moon's rising, then?"

"At the Liaison Second's," Ganrom confirmed.

As we passed through the portal, two of the guards separated themselves from their fellows and blocked our path officiously.

"You cannot bring such a woman within the Well gates, Astrian," said the brown-skinned, portly guard to Dellin, who still wore my woven Astrian chald, though not so prominently that it would be easy to tell at a glance that the chald was a woman's.

As if they were one man, the Slayers around me loosened their swords in their scabbards.

The squat guard's hand was on his hilt.

Dellin looked him up and down slowly.

"Can you read, zealot?" he asked the guard.

In an eyeblink, the guard's sword cleared its scabbard; its naked blade gleamed in a steady hand as the brown-skinned one retorted, "Indeed I can, Astrian hayseed. And I'll be reading your name to the Day-Keepers this very evening if you don't get out of sight. Go on—and have your Slayer friends teach you some manners before you try to pass this gatepost again."

"I'm going to reach into my pocket and give you a thing to read," said Dellin, unperturbed. "You never know who may come walking through these gates to Arlet. If your literacy is an empty boast, you'd better find another who has the skill. Otherwise, it will not be my name that goes on the Day-Keepers' roll." As he spoke, he reached slowly into his pocketed parr belt and pulled forth a rolled sheet of orange fax.

The guard blanched when he saw it—fax is not common among Silistrans—but the matter had gone too far for him to back down. Taking the document Dellin held out, the gate guard awkwardly unrolled it, sword still in hand, his mate peering over his shoulder.

Behind him, I saw three other red-garbed guards sidling toward us through the crowd: we had blocked the entry, and the crowd was thickening behind us. The three came up alongside the guard who had spoken and his mate, ready to support them, if necessary, against the Slayers in our party.

The brown-skinned one's lips moved as he slowly and laboriously attempted to decode written B.F. Standard. Most of us speak at least a bit of M'ksakkan, but only the more literate can read their curious computer script.

"Give me that," snarled a florid-faced, middle-aged officer with golden squares at his shoulders. "What's the trouble here?" he snapped at Dellin as he snatched the fax from the semiliterate guard, who began trying to explain.

His superior silenced him with a wave. As the ranking guard's eyes flashed over the orange sheet, he let go of its lower edge and the fax rerolled itself. Then he handed the roll to Dellin, his face expressionless.

"Get back to work," he bawled at no one in particular.

Obediently, the knot of guards melted away. Behind me, the Slayers expelled their breath and shifted their hands from their weapons.

The gate-watch commander sighed in a long-suffering fashion: "Maybe I'd best escort you myself, sir—just to make sure none of my men bother your . . . ah . . . party further." He raised his right arm to his chest, forearm parallel to the ground in the Silistran gesture of respect and service.

Beside me, Ganrom muttered suspiciously to himself under his breath.

"Your name, Commander?" Dellin asked in a coldly officious voice.

"Tetrim, point leader, Liaison," answered the officer uncomfortably.

The Slayers around me whispered to each other. If they had previously suspected that Dellin might not be quite what he claimed or what he seemed, they knew now how completely they had been misled.

"That won't be necessary, Point Leader Tetrim. I'm content to make my own way for the nonce. But I suggest," Dellin said in a commanding tone that had no hint of suggestion about it, "that you send that man back to school. And any others here who cannot read Standard. Inform my house of my arrival, and tell them that there'll be five for evening's meal, at moon's rising."

Dismissed, the point leader, Tetrim, made haste to his fellows, to whom he spoke briefly, and then disappeared into the curious crowd of onlookers, taking the brown-skinned guard with him.

As we passed through the gate without further problem, Ganrom reached across me and, grinning, took Dellin's arm and pulled him roughly aside.

The two faced each other against the inside of Arlet's great wall, Ganrom with his brow furrowed in mock anger, Dellin with the look of a boy caught stealing brin.

"You lying outworlder!" Ganrom accused. "Liaison Second of Arlet, yet. Treacherous scumsucker!" And then he could restrain himself no longer. Peals of laughter rang from that mighty throat and broke Dellin's composure, and the two leaned against each other, pounding and poking.

"And do you know . . ." gasped Dellin, pointing his finger at me, shaking with mirth. "Can you guess who that . . . that girl is?"

"She is not, then, a coin girl?" wheezed Ganrom, leaning on Dellin. The other Slayers were also infected with mirth. They sat on the ground, their backs against the blue-gol blocks of Arlet, chuckling.

"Perhaps she is high-couch of Astria?" wisecracked Idrer, snorting in hilarity at his joke.

At that, Dellin sank back against the wall, rubbing his eyes with his hands.

I had hoped he would not tell them. I had also hoped he would include me in the guest list for his evening meal.

"Not possible, but funny, very funny," objected Ganrom.

"Why not possible, Ganrom?" said Dellin innocently, composed.

"She . . . she is mute, and agreeable, and . . . she obeys you," he trailed off.

"That she does. Here." Shaking with rage, I went to him. I considered strangling him with my chald, which he still wore around his neck.

"Magic," he said, putting his hand to my throat. "Speak. Tell them your name."

I did, and they fell silent. One does not so abuse a Well-Keepress.

"Give me my things, Dellin," I said, "and I will take my leave of you. Who knows what might befall me by way of your flapping tongue?"

"Soon enough, soon enough. Now be silent again,

or you'll not have them." He turned to the Slayers.
They looked, to a man, perturbed.

"At moon's rise, my friends. And don't look so
worried: isn't it a Silistran saying that one must
give a woman what she needs, no matter how high
her station?" and he turned me roughly around
and guided me through the crowd to an aisle of
stalls.

Through every stall in the Arletian market we
walked, until Dellin stopped me before a large
star-trader's booth filled with off-world fabrics and
crafts.

"Choose," he said, waving me inside, and struck
up a conversation with the clerk.

I was loath to touch the delicate gauzes and
silks with my filthy hands and the shopkeeper's
eyes followed me as if the same thought was in his
mind. Finally he suggested to Dellin that under
the circumstances I might use his shower stall in
the back room.

In the shopkeeper's portable shower, so narrow I
had barely enough space to turn about, I took my
time, luxuriating in a pleasure I had long taken for
granted.

Clean, I disdained my grimy s'kim, leaving it on
the dirt between shower and shop proper, and
went naked, covered with beaded drops of water,
to where Dellin lounged with the clerk. There was
a length of silvery silk and two silver clips, set
with white stones, and a bone comb backed with a
matching silver handle on the counter between them.

"I haven't much more time, Estri. These will
have to do." He gestured to me to dress.

I did so, slowly, before the popeyed clerk, taking
as much time before the mirror as I dared. Only
when the silvery silk was most artfully draped and
my hair sleek and shining did I leave the interior
of the star-trader's shop.

Dellin looked me up and down, nodded, and paid the bill. It was exorbitant. He steered me across the crowded Inner Well until we stood before three broad steps that led up to a massive thala door, upon which were carved many women.

"Turn for me." I did so. He took my chald from about his neck and with the tiny key unlocked it. He removed my father's ring from his middle finger and threaded the chald through its band, then fastened the chald around my waist and secured the key in its housing. He drew from his wide parr pocket belt a small tas bag and handed it to me. I could feel the viewer and slightly bigger holos through the buttery leather. He then reached behind my neck and removed the necklace of dippars he had put on me in the forest. He held it out to me.

"Take it. You earned them."

I shook my head. Again he tried to put the necklace of gold coins into my hands. I knew what he had paid at the star-trader's stall. He had not even haggled.

"I will not take payment from you, Dellin."

"But you'll lower your value!" he teased. "You cannot couch with me for nothing, like some binnirin farmer's daughter—not *you!*" He mocked me, but his tone was gentle.

I shook my head again and backed away from him.

Grinning broadly, he put the dippars, still threaded on the thong, in his belt: "If I contract for your services in the Arletian manner, you'll have no choice but to take my money," he reminded me.

"If you should," I allowed, "then I will have no choice." My voice trembled.

I found I had to get away from him: I ran quickly up the three steps to the Well and pushed through the carved thala door, closing it quickly behind me, leaning against it. Another moment, and he would have had me apologizing for my profession, of which I'd always been justifiably proud. I took deep breaths, counting, until my throat stopped aching. Then I opened my eyes.

A startled girl with a mop and bowl faced me, frozen where she'd been moist-dusting. She was a small girl with sturdy legs and pear-shaped breasts, a pleasant round face, large brown eyes, pale skin and a shaven head. She wore a mesh wisp of a breech, a metal triangle held over her crotch by a fine-linked brass chain, and nothing else. "High lady," she whispered, touching her forehead to the tiled blue floor, then looked up at me.

"Get up, girl. Is your mistress in?"

"She is in, if you are she whom we have been expecting." Her face was tense, her huge eyes luminous.

"I am Estri of Astria, Hadrath diet Estrazi. Will that do?"

"Oh, yes." She smiled, relief evident in her expression. "Mistress has been waiting for two days for you, high lady, and the Liaison's men have haunted us for word of you, and she hates waiting and she hates haunting and she is in a very bad temper." She stopped, put her hand to her mouth: she had said too much.

"Take me to her, then, and we will see if her mood brightens."

The shaven-headed girl dropped her bowl and rag on the deep-blue tiles and started down the dimly lit corridor. Her plump hips swung before me, the chain that came up between her buttocks, to split and encircle her loins, glittered as she moved.

The corridor gave way to the sunken, vaulted-ceilinged common room, with its inlaid floors of semiprecious-stone slabs. We walked past the entry desk, unattended at this early hour, down across the middle of the huge sunken, circular chamber, past low pillowed divans and furred cushions arranged in three seating sections. This evening those divans and cushions would seat the women of Arlet, each in her price section, and the men who would pleasure after buying a well token at the entry desk. The price of the token would determine the group from which each man could choose.

Now, in the afternoon, none reclined in the common room. My guide led me straight to the passageway opposite the entry. To my right were the open doors to the dining hall and baths, to my left the drink room, the drug chamber, and a narrow door leading to the staff quarters. The passage we entered, which led to the girls' keeps, branched right and left immediately under the lintel.

We took neither turn, but stopped before a starsteel panel, complete with red-glowing palm lock, directly in front of us. My guide touched the red oblong and the door slid soundlessly aside. Stepping inside, I saw Celendra Doried bast Aknet, Well-Keepress of Arlet, and her lair, for the first time.

Her room was warmly lit from a concealed source and hung with the rich, figured brocades from the desert tribes of the Parset barrens, barbaric and splendid. Not one surface of the large irregular keep was free from draperies of scarlets, umbers, and ochers. Hunting tapestries, geometrics, free-form swirls, all glowed forth in perpetual sunset hues, as if I had suddenly come into some magnificent apprei, the portable homes of the desert nomads. The ceiling was obscured with them, the floor strewn carelessly with priceless deep-pile Parset rugs whose psychotropic patterns dragged at the eye, teasing, confusing. Here and there, stout thala poles rose from the silky rugs, to disappear in the ceiling draperies. From these poles hung chains and lashes, daggers and cords.

In the midst of this rioting color, Celendra of Arlet reclined upon a great fall of cushions. The smell of narcotic danne was thick in the air as she rose like some sinuous dorkat, the wingless hulion of the desert, and moved noiselessly to take my hand. She was black as Santh, and as supple. Her hair was caught at the top of her head in a chased-silver cone, bursting from confinement at the nar-rowed opening of the cone's apex to flow blue-black and shining to her waist. She wore thick silver wristlets and anklets, and a band of the same chased metal at her regal throat. She was half again my weight, and this she carried on a massive lean frame with not a hint of fat, yet her breasts were great pointed pillows, and her lips full and inviting. Beside her I was but a stripling girl, not yet grown into my womanhood.

I thought of Dellin with this magnificent woman, and the image was a splinter in my heart.

She took my copper hand in her midnight one, and her silvered nails glittered: "Estri of Astria, you must be." She turned my hand over and exam-ined its palm as if it were my credentials.

"I am."

Then Celendra stood back, the better to appraise me. She wore an Arletian chald, loosely woven, hanging low over her navel, its chains separate and distinct between spaced knots against the dark of her skin. I picked out, among the chaldric chains, the golden links of birthing fulfilled, and the cop-per of the forereaders, and between them, like a dark shadow, the black-iron Slayer's chain, and felt a stab of jealousy. I'd tried my best for better than a century and never earned a birthing strand; the forereader's chain seemed, at that time, for-ever beyond my reach; and the black-iron Slayer's strand was one I'd never seen a woman boast—later, I'd understand too well how she'd come by it. Then, I could only envy her fifteen-strand chald that spoke so eloquently of her accomplishments.

"Perhaps you are truly daughter of chaos," she spoke again in a husky voice slurred with danne. "Come sit with me, and we shall test the time." Forereaders use danne to dive deep in the time flow. Celendra was still half-tranced. She smiled, and her white teeth flashed.

Seated among the cushions, she prepared the smoke, and I partook of it with her, trying to ignore the way she peered at me over the smoldering bowl of her gem-encrusted pipe through gold-green eyes whose whites were reddened from the drug.

But soon enough the danne began to take effect: I felt my muscles relax and my mind slow in its whirling as we smoked the yellow herb. My emotions receded, leaving me clear and calm: danne gives one distance from one's situation.

"I knew you would come today," said the Keepress of Arlet. "All the forereaders leave for conclave with the Day-Keepers, but I think what they seek might be here in Arlet." She spoke as if to herself, but her eyes lay heavy on me.

"I encountered some . . . delays . . . on the way here," I apologized. "I'm sorry if I kept you from your call to conclave. You needn't have waited on my—"

"No matter." She waved her hand. "All right with me. That impotent M'ksakkan First rousted out all the Liaison's men. *Where* is she? Where are *they?* They have not let us *live.* I *told* them, but they believe only what their eyes can see, ears can hear, hands can touch. *I* saw you, and the winds from the abyss blew around you. Your feet were imprisoned in the weave of the time-flow, and your hands bound behind. The current dragged you off at right angles to your chosen path, and the life spirits warred over you. Then, slowly, the branch rejoined the time-flow, and that flow drew you here. Almost, you were lost to the call of the crux time, but in the end, it triumphed. The Day-Keepers sense a great crux, and they call us together to prepare. Even the haughty dhareners are blinded by the mists such time throws out, so we may not avoid our destiny. But *I* see. And, of course, that I might not lead them, the flow bound me here." She stared at me, leaning forward, her eyes narrowed, her red tongue darting out to moisten her lips, awaiting some sort of response.

"I see," I said and nodded sagely; I had no idea what to make of so much forereader's talk.

"What's that?" The danne was making her querulous. "What say you, pawn of power?" she demanded. "What sense do you make of my reading?"

I decided that Celendra smoked much too much danne; drugs, in excess, can blunt even a forereader's talent; my deep-reading of her produced only confusion.

But I still had to respond in some inoffensive manner: "I say that I, too, am blinded by the mists such time throws out."

She nodded. I wondered how much true knowledge she had, how much was seeress drug babble.

"This is very lovely." I flicked my hand, indicating the keep about us, hoping to change the subject.

"Yes, yes. I try to keep my father's heritage around—to remind me of what I am and how I came to be. Do you not, also, in Astria?"

"I would, if I had access to it."

She looked at me questioningly. It seemed she knew less than she pretended.

The moment was opportune. I took one of the holos from the tas bag and handed it to her.

She peered at it, blinking, struggling for focus.

"My father," I explained. "I seek him. Have you serviced such a man in Arlet?"

"No." She handed it back, and I replaced it carefully in the tas bag. "If I had, I would remember. I, too, might be tempted to seek such a one. If you find him, invite him for me to Arlet." She grinned, chiaroscuro.

"How did you fare with the Liaison Second?" she asked.

"Not as well as I would have wished. He is overly muscled and sadistic." I shrugged. "I do not envy you, Celendra. M'lennin is bad enough. Dellin is an exceedingly difficult man." Half a truth is better than none.

"M'ksakkan, isn't he? He will mellow, as M'lennin did. When M'glarenn couched the Keepress Astria, the story goes, he used four additional women a day for a thousand days. When the restraints of M'ksakka are thrown off, much comes bubbling to the surface that has been long festering in them."

"Perhaps," I allowed. "Perhaps not, though. If you think M'lennin mellow," I said slyly, remembering my conversation with Dellin, "I will be glad to exchange Liaisons with you. M'lennin and I have come to . . . dislike . . . each other."

"But if this Dellin is so difficult, where is the advantage in having him instead?"

"I have a revenge to work on that man," I said coldly.

"That I understand."

I had thought she would.

"How would you enjoy my hospitality, Estri of Astria? You need not work in Arlet. We are not so light in our touch as you in Astria. You might find our couch overly taxing, and so much has been made of your arrival that continuing subterfuge is out of the question. If you couch here, you will have to do it as Estri of Astria."

I dreaded the thought of inactivity. My feelings for Dellin would only grow stronger should I not work at my craft.

"I need a change. I would work until the Day-Keepers' envoy finds me. Under the circumstances, I will take whatever your couch-price is as my own." I knew her price was somewhat less than mine; I had no wish to offend her by demanding more.

"My thought, exactly," Celendra fairly purred.

"I see you wear the Slayers' chain," I observed. "I have some small skill, imparted to me by Rin diet Tron. At your convenience, perhaps we could work out together."

Celendra reached out and squeezed my arm, then sank back into the cushions. "But you do not wear the black chain?"

"As you said, in Astria we keep our touch light."

The Well-Keepress laughed, low and throatily: "I had thought you much less than you are, Keepress," she said.

"And I you."

Celendra reached behind her and threw aside a small Parset rug. Beneath it was a square of star-steel. Disapprovingly, I realized it was a communicator. She pushed a button, then replaced the rug. Someday, as had happened long ago in Astria, she would have need of the device, and it would malfunction. Dependence on the star-folk's toys always leads to harm.

"First let one of my girls show you your keep, then meet me for a meal in the dining hall at the fourth bell. Then we will go to the circle." She leaned over and kissed me on the lips.

The same shaven-headed girl appeared at the door and took me to my Arletian keep.

At its door, she turned to me.

"Should I stay, high lady?" said she, wetting her lips.

I was puzzled: "I can find my way about, I think."

The girl flushed, wheeled, and ran lightly down the hall.

Shrugging to myself, I palmed the lock and the door drew back to admit me to my new quarters. The keep was much the same as Celendra's, but in pale blues and golds. No dark blue gol-work was visible behind the layers of fabric and drapes. The couch was wide and its wood frame gold-leafed. I was glad to see a window, large and overlooking the craggy drop to the road. The window, however, did not open. I peered behind the curtains of pale blue that framed it and saw two small grilles set neatly into the ceiling high above my head. Temperature control, another star trick. I would never allow such dependency on machines in Astria. I was beginning to understand why Arlet, although second among the Wells, was such a rich post for the Liaison, and why M'lennin carped so at Astria's low import policy.

I explored further, poking into chests full of fabric, boxes of jewelry and chains. The posts in the rooms bore lashes and gaudy dirks, manacles and rings, as had Celendra's. I took the key ring that hung on the post nearest the couch and buried it beneath a length of Koster silk in the largest of the three carved chests. None would put such chains upon me, be it the couching style of Arlet or not.

Then I stripped off the silvery garment Dellin had given me, and the clips and comb, and carefully folded the material around them. These, with the tas pouch, I buried also in the great thala chest. In the washroom there were combs aplenty; and brushes; and thick, absorbent, sky-colored toweling.

Although I was bone-tired, when I threw myself on the couch and tried to nap, I found I could not. My mind chased itself in circles. Finally I gave up.

I would need something to wear to the circle. From the chest full of textiles, I took a length of plain white tas wool and cut it to shape with a gol-knife, fashioning a breech out of one half and breast band of the other, fastening them with bronze clips I found among the jewelry.

When I had finished, second bell had just rung.

I did an hour of dhara-san, that exercise system which welds mind to body, clears the soul, and releases repressed energy for constructive use. I stretched long in warm-ups, the back of my legs informing me it had been too long since I had practiced my routine. By third bell I had a good sweat and was in the dhar, the contortions of great skill. I took a long headstand, letting my mind roll free. Thoughts of Dellin and my father, Celendra's obscurity and my great-grandmother's warning passed through me and away, joining the dreams of seven glowing-skinned men and hand-held stars which had preceded them in a place my mind had made for questions that have no answers and riddles that cannot be solved. I regained my perspective, remembering that it is best to do what can be done and to leave the insoluble to the dhareners and the forereaders.

My mind, clear, considered more immediate concerns from a fresh perspective. Perhaps Dellin *was* the "one who is not as he seems" of whom my great-grandmother had warned me, for he had almost lured me from my quest. And then again, perhaps not: my great-grandmother was a forereader also, and their pronouncements have a way of making themselves true by the efforts of those who have heard them. I would not be a party to fulfilling Hadrath's prophesies: they would have to come true without my help.

I thought of the time around me, and pinpointed the feel. Silistrans learn to identify four major subdivisions of time, and sixteen minor ones. Though no forereader, I had not needed Celendra to tell me that I was in draw, to crux, and had little choice but to follow where the time currents led. I would, I decided, control my destiny as best I could. It occurred to me that the decision was probably preordained, and I came out of my head-stand into a crouch. I could carry that line of reasoning no further. But I felt fine, tingling, whole again. My equilibrium had returned to me.

Thus I made my way to the common room, and through it to the dining hall, in good spirits. I took a table in the hall's far corner, from which I could observe the entire room. There were only four girls eating, sitting together at one of the glass-and-gol trestle tables. They whispered to each other when I passed them and took my seat. A staffer in gray came to me to take my order.

"I wait for your mistress," I said to the middle-aged, nondescript man in staffer's garb. "Bring me rana and honey, and fruit juice."

He scurried off.

By the time the stimulating hot drink was cooled enough to drink, Celendra sat opposite me. She wore a leather breech and band, studded with brass, and bands on her throat and wrists to match. Her silken hair was caught at the back of her neck in a thick knot fastened with a brass clip.

The staffer hovered over her. She ordered juice and rana for herself. One does not take intoxicating beverage before entering the circle, if one is wise.

As we ate, we discussed the passes' take, which always increases in the spring, and the quality of our respective clientele.

I had a question strong in my mind, and when the opportunity arose, I asked it: "How," I queried, "does the Well-Keepress of Arlet avoid being abused by her clients? The chains I saw in your keep are not just for show?"

"What makes you think I would avoid the chains? Not many men could conquer me, even for an evening, without them. One must not make value judgements, Estri, about primal needs. One had the needs before one learned the values. And it is not always the men who wield the lash and hold the leash. One must give to get. I find it easier, bound. If one cannot respect the man, one can at least respect the chains. And they allow us to extend our experience beyond the limits of play-acting, into totality. A taste of reality is welcome, every once in a while."

I recalled all too well my "taste of reality" with the chaldless in the forest, but I didn't interrupt her to argue. I was a guest in her keep, in a foreign Well. It was my duty to be polite and to adapt. If I could not, I would leave, take commercial lodgings, or prevail upon the Liaison Second to accommodate me. At this thought, I smiled slightly.

At that, Celendra's eyebrows raised and she proceeded to further instruct me: "It is the nature of men to conquer, and of woman to fight being conquered. Surely you yourself have at times wished for bonds against which to struggle, bonds more physical, hence less demanding, than the bonds of chaldra?"

I looked into my cup. I knew she was right about the basic nature of the sexes, but I didn't entirely agree with the conclusions she drew from those truths: "And yet there is the matter of pride," I objected.

"Do I seem to you lacking in pride? One often wins by losing."

"I shall see for myself." I grinned at her, letting my curiosity show. "There is much food for thought here in Arlet." I pushed away my cup.

"Shall we?" Celendra invited. I rose, and we walked the halls of Arlet, coming at last to a large turfed outdoor practice area, behind the Well proper but within the outer wall. There was a number of Arletian guards, a half-dozen Slayers, and some twenty well women sitting on the tiered gol seats backed up against the outer wall. Two men fought hand-to-hand within one circle; two worked at stones, the five-lashed weighted whip, in another. The three outer circles were empty.

Racked against the wall of the Well itself, next to the door through which we had come, were weapons of every conceivable variety.

Celendra gestured to them.

"Your choice, Estri." I had hoped she would cede me the option. With her greater size and weight I would have been hopelessly outclassed at stones or hand-to-hand. I went to the rack. There I found what I wanted: gol-knives, forearm-length straight blades, with one edge serrated. The points were guarded a finger's width down the blade, that one might strike with force and not puncture one's opponent too deeply. I tried several until I found one with a balance I liked.

Some of the men had left their ladies and were milling about the area. The stone-fighters had finished and walked toward us to replace their weapons in the rack.

As they approached, Celendra spoke to the larger, a dark-tanned man in leather breech.

"Will you call for us, Jerin?" Jerin grinned as he racked his stones. Wiping the sweat from his eyes, he walked to the nearest circle, bounded in low gol-blocks, where he hunkered down, waiting.

Celendra tossed her head. She took a gol-knife without testing. She knew which she wanted.

We stepped within the circle.

She opposite me, we both took time, eyes closed, to ready ourselves.

I would be the slitsa, the deadly serpent. Like the slitsa, I would hypnotize, striking and gone, deadly. I went through the ritual, feeling the knife as my head, my eyes, my fangs. My hand was one with my weapon, my eyes were in the blade, I was what the knife was. I was ready before Jerin called us out.

I faced my quarry, crouched, swaying. The gol-knife writhed back and forth in my grasp. Her eyes followed. I kept my eyes from focusing on her blade as she leaped toward me. When she reached my position, I was not there, but behind her. As she whirled to meet me, I slashed out, and the teeth of the gol's serrated edge raked her dark shoulder. I had first blood. She cursed, leaped, and struck down. I felt the wind from her thrust, but the slitsa, ever moving, remained untouched. Some had come to the edge of the circle. I heard rather than saw them. My eyes were for Celendra's face, reading. She stood, legs planted wide apart, tossing the knife from hand to hand. I waited.

When she thought she had my attention diverted, she struck. Whirling not quite fast enough, I felt the gol-teeth on my arm. Infuriated, I ducked under her slash and felt the gol-point connect with her rib cage. No longer were we playing at battle. Before I could withdraw, her blade came up, for my throat.

Beyond thought, uncaring of consequences, I met her blade with mine, so close to my face I could see the sweat on her black hand. Blood trickled down my arm from her shoulder, from her ribs. But she was stronger than I. Slowly my blade was pushed up by hers. I disengaged, rolling. I heard shouts. She landed where I had just been. I scrambled to my knees. She was on her feet. I tossed my head to clear the hair from my face. In that moment, while she waited, tossing her blade, crouched, I knew I could take her. She should have come in and downed me then, but she did not. Celendra, too, knew that I was more than her match. I struck up at her, launching myself at the hand that would hold the blade when I reached her, and connected. My fanged gol-knife bit hers from her hand, and it flew from the circle. So does the tiny slitsa down the mighty dorkat.

I threw my blade after hers, and, slicked and panting, reached out to her, my hand wet with blood from my gol-bitten arm. She looked at me, did Celendra, and took it slowly, struggling with her feelings as I would have, had she bested me.

Then her arm went around my waist and she ruffled my hair: "Not bad, little high-couch girl. In fact, respectable." She led me from the circle.

Jerin, who had called for us, already had our knives back on the rack. The other Slayers and the house guards regarded us with amused respect, standing in small knots around the circle. I saw coins change hands. So they had bet on us. I wondered what my odds had been.

Putting my scraped arm to my mouth, I began sucking the blood just as a girl appeared with water and clean cloths. Taking a cloth, I turned to Celendra, who allowed me to clean and dress her scrapes. It was the least I could do, though none were deep, nor would they scar noticeably.

Some of the Slayers hung about; no doubt they would have approached us, had they dared. We sat together on the ground and watched the men practice until the sixth bell, at which time Celendra arose, thanking me for the match.

"My honor," I said.

"Next time, Estri, I will be ready for you."

"The element of surprise does have its limitations," I agreed.

She would probably beat me badly the next time, if I were fool enough to use the same technique.

"Take a meal with me in my keep?"

I nodded. "I would be much pleased to do so."

"Eighth bell," she said, disappearing through the door near the racked weapons.

As she entered the doorway, two of the Slayers I had seen watching us earlier made their way toward me.

"Would you go again, lady?" asked one of the pair hovering over me where I sat with my rear on the low gol-bricks.

"Thanks, no." I smiled up at them. The sun was at their backs. "Celendra gave me all the exercise I needed—almost more than I bargained for."

"We won a set's pay on you," said the other, whose voice was quiet, almost gentle.

"You have excellent judgment," I congratulated them.

The one who had spoken last knelt down before me, casting a long shadow: "Be careful of her, lady. She does *not* like to lose. She's slit throats for less."

So Celendra had enemies among the Slayers—or at least critics. "No one likes to lose," I answered him.

This Slayer was lithe and well set-up, his dark hair shorter than the Arletian fashion, his skin deeply tanned and scored around his calm brown eyes. He might have been handsome but for a scar that ran the length of his face, following his swooping cheekbone down to his jaw.

His mouth twitched, he started to say more, and stopped.

"Yes?" I prompted. It was getting chilly as I sat there with the sweat drying on me.

"Are you of this Well? Had I seen you before, I would remember. If you are . . ." his slight pause had a half-smile in it, not lascivious, almost shy, "I'll give back some of what I won on you."

"I am new here." I told him my name. He raised an eyebrow but did not withdraw.

"And your price?" he asked.

Putting on my best smile, I named it, then got to my feet. I find it hard to feel feminine directly after an encounter in the circle.

"I will see you later," he said to me as I headed for the door to the Well.

"Tasa," I replied.

As I made my way back to my blue-and-gold hung keep, the Slayer's words rang in my ears. Perhaps I should not have scored Celendra. The fight had taken me; I had barely even considered the politics of beating one's hostess before her own people one day in that stranger's hospitality. I had been going since sun's rising without food, and little drink, and under much pressure. Determined to get some rest before the evening's activities, I headed for my new keep, wondering whether Dellin would couch Celendra this night, and then whether that possibility had had anything to do with my precipitation of our sojourn to the Slayer's circle.

When at last I lay down on the blue-spread couch, I went within myself to that place which is neither sleep nor waking, where time slows down, and one can crowd an evening's rest into the space of two bells.

"Before the eighth bell," I told myself aloud, "you will awaken."

I opened my eyes to see the fattening crescent of moon peak above the crags through the window to my left. For a moment the scene flickered, and it was as if I stood high on the gleaming towers of Astria, with the crescent moon shining on the Litess River as it wound toward Port Astrin and the sea. Then, again, it was the barren crags of Arlet before me, and I rose, stretched, wet-clothed my body clean, and went, naked but for my chald, to dinner in Celendra's keep.

As I turned the corner and slapped the palm-lock, the eighth bell chimed. Celendra sat before a low table set with covered dishes. She rose to greet me, and the chains she wore rustled softly as she moved. Her body was a chalder's dream. From a wide silver collar, fine chain dipped and looped down her breasts, nipped in by a metal waist cinch, from which more woven chain depended to the tops of her thighs. She wore arm bracelets and wristlets. Her hair was loose and as long as mine, blue-black silk on silver on midnight.

She greeted me and guided me to the table, where we sat, legs crossed, on low cushions.

"Your fitters here in Arlet are to be commended for their originality." I was feeling parochial and underdressed. "While I'm here, perhaps you'll arrange a fitting for me? I'd especially like a breech and band like the one you wore this afternoon," I said.

"Thank you," acknowledged Celendra. "I will have one made for you by our rematch, tomorrow, fourth bell." She seemed the same; I could detect no hostility, by ear or reading.

"Fourth bell, then. I have a feeling it will be your score. If you have fought as few women as I, you will understand when I say that I enjoyed that match as much as any I have had an occasion to fight." I prodded her a little more.

"Indeed," said Celendra, serving me fried harth and mashed tuns, fruit and drink. "I have had little experience with women opponents. I find I rather like it. There are many things that two women can experience together that a woman and a man cannot." She looked at me keenly.

I had prodded too hard.

I let her innuendo pass, studying my plate instead, searching for a choice bit of meat.

"You have been reserved for the evening, you know."

I looked at her from behind my kifra goblet of M'ksakkan crystal.

"No, I did not know. Who has done me the honor?" I said, sounding cooler than I felt. "Dellin?"

"Sereth crill Tyris, of the Arletian Slayers' Seven."

"Oh," I said, hiding my disappointment.

"Certainly," she said as if I'd insulted her personally, "even in Astria folk have heard of Sereth, who was the overall champion at the last Slayers' conclave, who slew the outlaw band of Gershom at the falls of Santha, who subdued the renegade Slayer Ferin?" She was grinning, now, wickedly.

I had heard of him. He had been brought before the Slayers' Council to justify his excessive kill record. It was said that in his keep beyond Arlet he had three well women whom he had got with child. Three is very many on Silistra.

"The same Sereth of Arlet about whom the song 'Sweeper of the Mountains' was written?" I asked. We keep far more musicians in Astria than Arlet, and I remembered the tune clearly, for it had been in an experimental scale composed of the overtones contained within A440.

"The same," she confirmed. "If I had chosen a man for you, one to teach you the ways of Arlet, I could not have done better."

"Then I am doubly honored," I said without enthusiasm. "Why is he not in conclave with the forereaders and Day-Keepers, along with the other high six of the Arletian Slayers?"

"One had to stay behind to greet the new Liaison. Sereth is not a man to sit and talk, days on end, as they do in conclave. And I think he will attempt to make a more satisfactory arrangement with the new Liaison than was between the Slayers and the old Liaison. I would do such a thing, if I were he," Celendra speculated.

I was not listening. Sereth of Arlet was a man one heard about in songs, not a man one expected to couch. He was the kind of man about whom women talk. And the women's talk said he was excessively discerning and difficult to please; worse, that he had been known to leave before sun's rising should a woman not prove sufficiently interesting. Although I was not much in the mood for an arrogant Arletian connoisseur, if I thoroughly pleased him, it would be a poultice to my bruised ego, perhaps even an antidote for the fever Dellin had infected me with, a fever which still coursed my blood. And I *would* please him. More, I would astound him; my reputation was at stake. After all, was I not Estri of Astria? I, also, have had songs written about me that are widely sung. Sereth had never been to Astria; therefore, he had never been with a good deep-reader.

For some time, I had been inattentive to Celendra's prattle, I realized. Now I listened sharply: her last word had been "Liaison."

"Have you been approached by the new Liaison Second?" I asked.

"He sent a message informing us he would honor the Well with his presence." I caught the hostility in Celendra's voice. He had not, then, "reserved" the Well-Keepress.

But someone had reserved me, and he would know that. Perhaps he would do his duty by the Well-Keepress. I had my own chaldra to fulfill.

"May I go as I am?" I asked Celendra over a

final sip of kifra. I had been to Dritira and Stra,
Galesh and Torwin, Baniev and Port Astrin, but
never before this day had I been within a rival
Well. Arlet was as different from Astria as the
Sabembe range from the Parset barrens.

"You had better, or lose whatever you wear to
Sereth's hand." Celendra's leer reiterated her
intimations: that I was in for an awakening of
sorts with this much-vaunted Sereth.

I stood up. I wanted to hear no more about
Sereth of Arlet, of the Slayers' Seven. I would see
what developed.

The common room was transformed at night
into a dreamland. Its M'ksakkan chandeliers, hung
on long chains from the vaulted copper ceiling,
gleamed and twinkled. Musicians played cadenced
Silistran music from their box against the far wall.
As we entered from Celendra's keep, the milling
mass of well women and customers enveloped us.
The air was heavy with the sweet smell of danne
and the acrid tang of distrit, the bar-pressed danne
resin, and the women's perfume and the close smell
of perhaps five hundred bodies in a small space. I
was jostled by a trader from Kost, blue-white skin
and silver hair set off by a knit-silk navy jumper,
embroidered in metallic thread. An Iartex noble,
with bells and bars of his rank, pinched my naked
copper rump. Celendra was grabbed up by a pair
of twins from Katir, with tufted ears and slit-
pupiled eyes who pulled her away in the crowd. A
well woman, laughing, caught up in the arms of a
M'ksakkan, floated past me on her way to her
keep. I made for the crowd's edge and found sanc-
tuary against the wall that separated the doors to
the Well's drink and drug rooms.

The wall against my back gave me courage: in
this strange place where no one knew me and I
knew no one, I was feeling a new emotion: shyness.

Scanning the throng, I saw no one familiar except the small shaven-headed girl who had guided me to Celendra upon my arrival. She looked lovely, dressed in scarlet web-worked pants, though she was in the lowest-price section.

My hostess, Celendra, seemed to have disappeared altogether. Once I thought I saw her, but the black figure turned, and I saw it to be a man of Hertekiea, his silky hair down on his hips. The Hertekiens count a man's hair length as we do high-chaldra. The dark one must have been an influential personage indeed on his home planet.

The drink room was dark and full of men's rumbling voices; when I ventured in, I discovered that it served not only kifra, brin, and fruited jeri, but the drinks of a hundred worlds. The decor, I noticed disapprovingly, was Bipedal Standard Modern. I slipped through the crowd and sidled my way to the server, ordered narne, and took my glass to an alcove from where I could see not only the whole drink chamber, but the entry desk and most of the common room as well. There were only a dozen females in the drink room, women who had already gotten a mate for the night and were, at their customer's bidding, awaiting his readiness there.

Hands reached around from behind me and cupped my breasts. Resisting the impulse to throw my drink, I turned to face the man to whom those hands belonged.

It was the scarred Slayer who had warned me about Celendra at the circle. He was larger than he had seemed earlier when he was squatting before me with the sun at his back.

"Tenist dast-ei," I greeted him, as a well woman.

"Tenist mist-as," he replied solemnly, as a customer.

"I have been reserved for this evening by one

Sereth crill Tyris. I am indescribably downcast that I will not be able to serve you," I said with ritual decorum.

"Sereth crill Tyris. I know him intimately. Come upstairs with me for a brief time. The Seven will take no offense."

"Though you are all brothers, beneath the Seven, I think in this case I must decline." I backed away from him, into a Koster, spilling that one's drink over his front and my rear. "It is my first evening here, and I have no wish to make an enemy. Another time, approach me." I smiled at him.

The scar-faced, dark-tanned Slayer still had his hands on my waist. He pulled me against him in the midst of the crowded drinking chamber.

"So you're afraid of offending the Seven, is that it?" he asked me, his lips at my ear.

"One would be a fool not to fear the wrath of such a man. It is said he kills for sport more than duty. If I were you, I would not tempt him."

"Now we have each warned the other once," he said. "You must at least allow me to buy you a drink."

If he would let me go, he could buy me anything.

"I have had enough drink, I think." I still held my empty glass of narne. "But you may, if you wish, get me some distrit, for I have had a long and tiring day, and expect a longer night."

"Your pleasure, Estri," he said, his arm around my waist, threading me through the crowd and around the corner into the drug chamber, where seats appeared as if by magic before us in the crowded room. I leaned back against the cushions while the Slayer snapped a server to us with a raised hand.

I decided I rather liked this easy, confident man. The scar on his face, once one got used to it, set off his angular features. He would have been unbearably pretty without it.

When the tray of distrit was set before us on its spindly legs, he loaded the pipe and held it to my lips. I took a long puff and held it. He, also, sucked in the smoke, but very little. I could feel the stimulant working within me.

I looked up, toward the door, in time to see Dellin, resplendent in his black-and-gold formal Liaison's garb, with Ganrom at his side, heading toward us.

I looked quickly away. The last thing I wanted was an encounter with Dellin, and certainly not now, while I was in the company of a man whose name I did not even know. It would have suited me much better if Dellin had not seen me here at all, had asked after me only to find that I was busy couching Sereth of Arlet.

"Trouble?" the Slayer said, watching my face with eyes gone glittery and cold. "Whatever it is, I assure you, we'll handle it."

I had not realized my emotion showed so. But I had no time to explain or make excuses—Dellin and Ganrom were upon us.

"Just the man I was looking for," Ganrom said jovially, reaching toward the seated Slayer, who did not rise but put out his hand laconically.

"Ganrom," the seated Slayer said, a greeting that was neutral in tone; he was still watching me, sidelong. "How was the hunting in the forests? How many teeth did you take?"

When he gestured for them to sit, Ganrom pulled an unwary out-worlder roughly from his seat. The small Iartex hissed his anger and scuttled away. Dellin put his hand over his eyes, a pained expression on his face. When Ganrom eyed a second Iartex, on the other side of the closest tray, the man hastily rose and departed.

The two seated themselves. Dellin stared into

my eyes until I looked away. When I looked up, I could see the muscles twitch in his jaw.

"Ganrom, if you would stay gainfully in my employ," Dellin said, "you must learn to be a little softer with the people whose rights I must protect."

"Agrh," snarled Ganrom, so that I realized he was more than a little drunk. "When the Liaison Second needs seating, the star-slimies ought to have sense enough to jump up and move."

The scarred Slayer picked up the pipe and passed it to Dellin without a word.

Dellin took a very cautious taste.

Then the Slayer who was my companion spoke to his bond-brother: "Ganrom," he said, "why were you looking for me, and how come you're so destitute that you've got to take star-money? Worse, M'ksakkan money—the Liaison Second's, you said? Time was when no self-respecting Slayer would spit on that door." His voice was very soft. It sent chills up me.

"Introductions. You must forgive me, brother. Khaf-Re Dellin, Liaison Second of Arlet." He waved his hands about. "Sereth crill Tyris, of the Slayers' Seven."

I pulled away from the scarred Slayer, Sereth of Arlet, on pretense of refilling the pipe. So this was he. His amusement with me in the drinking chamber now made sense.

"I'm determined to change all that, Sereth crill Tyris, if you and your bond-brothers give me half a chance," Dellin was saying politically. "As I told Ganrom and his men, any Slayer who will work with the Liaisons on wiping out the chaldless and making the roads safe for off-world shipping will be handsomely rewarded. Such a thing could be arranged without decreasing the mobility of the Slayers or interfering with private projects or Day-Keepers' tasks. I ask no loyalty that would interfere with chaldra. You would do what you do now, and get tithe from the Liaisons, whether or not you get tithe from your private clients. We could back you up with more than money. Think about it: the technology of the Liaisons at your disposal. And another thing: I will test for the Slayers chain, under Ganrom's tutelage. I think, when I wear it, things will be easier for my embassy with both the Slayers and the Day-Keepers."

I sucked in my breath in surprise. Dellin had recovered from what could have been a disastrous first encounter brilliantly, assessed the situation and calculated his moves. A Liaison with chaldra would be a formidable figure in Silistran politics. A Slayer in the Liaisons would be able to command a virtual army, should the need arise, of fierce guerrilla fighters. I wondered what the Day-Keepers would think of Dellin's ideas.

Sereth slipped down on his spine, looking at Dellin pensively. He pulled at my hair.

"What do you think, lady? Is this a change for the better, or just some sly off-world trick?"

"I am not the one to ask."

"But what if it were Astria?" By the hair he pulled me to his chest. I felt Dellin's eyes on me. I stretched against Sereth's hard body and wiggled closer.

"If it were Astria? In Astria, it could not happen. M'lennin would no more take chaldra than sleep with the slitsa in his burrow. But, if somehow such a proposal were made in Astria . . ." Dellin's eyes pleaded. That pleased me. ". . . I think I would give it a try. If, as the Liaison said, his house and the hostel could work together without conflict, and profitably, both would benefit. If the Liaison took the black chain, he would learn much of Silistra by his studies. Of course, he would then be bound to Arlet, and Arlet to him. Like any long-term partnership, the thing must be delicately done. If it does not serve the Slayers, they can always revert to their former status." If my endorsement mattered, I had given Dellin his chance.

Sereth reached forward, as he had not done before, and extended his hand, palm up, to Dellin, who took it, grinning.

"We will try. I promise only that," Sereth warned. "Tomorrow we will discuss it further. Ganrom, how many teeth *did* you take?"

"Forty between us." The Slayers took one tooth from each corpse.

"So the hunting was adequate. Was it profitable?"

Ganrom shrugged. Then he brightened, licked his lips, and reached for the pipe. "You are really going to enjoy that one," said Ganrom, pointing at me.

"I hope so," Sereth replied. "I paid an exorbitant price. I like to get my money's worth."

Dellin got up abruptly.

"I must go see to the Well-Keepress," he said casually. "Make a time with Ganrom. I will be at your convenience. Tasa." He waved, disappearing in the crowded common room beyond.

I could feel both Slayers relax.

Sereth whistled softly through his teeth. "Things," he said to Ganrom, "may well *be* changing in Arlet—but not necessarily for the better. My foresight tells me that all the men better stay within a day's trek of the hostel for a pass, at least, until we see where the flow is taking us." He and Ganrom exchanged a look full of significance.

I felt the wind from the abyss chill me, and then it was gone.

I shivered against Sereth crill Tyris's chest and he twined his fingers in my hair as he spoke to his lieutenant of Slayers' business—quotas and politics and security on the open road.

As they talked, I puffed on the pipe, and I, on

little food and rest, got very high. The drug precipitated my talent, and the presence of Sereth of
Arlet came flooding into me. His brown eyes that
sparkled as if at some private joke were unguarded
now, as he talked with a man he trusted, and he
was as relaxed that evening as I've ever seen him,
yet always conscious of himself as what the Slayers
had made him: precise, tenacious, sure in his power
and his skill. My deep-reading showed me only
one thing about this man that he hid inside: Sereth
wanted to stop time's very passing; having come
up through the ranks to his position, he relished it,
yet he was still hungry. His appetite for life was
staggering.

It was well I had some warning before Sereth
crill Tyris set about teaching me the difference
between Astria and Arlet. In Astria the woman
gives the man what he wants; in Arlet, he takes it.
What had been fetish to Dellin was foreplay to
Sereth. Considering his size and strength, bonds
were superfluous; considering his predilictions, they
were a joke. But he was fond of jokes and more
fond of taking from a woman whatever she chose
to withhold. By hiding the standard trappings of
Arletian sex, I had sealed my own fate. Eventually,
weeping, I brought him the key ring that I had
hidden earlier, that no man might bind me. With
the ring in my hand I went to him, that he might
put the chains of Arlet on me and teach me their
meaning. This he was willing to do, until the sun
peaked the crags of Arlet.

"So," he grunted, "you think you know, now,
the ways of Arlet?"

"Unchain me," I suggested.

"No."

"It is morning," I protested.

"I will pay the overage. Perhaps I will stay until

tomorrow morning. I have to be here for the set games."

"Then I am truly lost," I groaned.

"Lost? I've just found you. More, you may have found yourself," he teased.

"Here I am, in chains, with a maniac, in Arlet." I giggled. "If my girls could see me now, I would be much diminished."

"If anyone could see you now, you would be much diminished. In fact, you *are* much diminished. I diminished you. I ought to know." His tongue licked at my navel.

I shivered. "You cannot be serious. *I* cannot spend the day bound up like some threx in heat."

"I'm deadly serious. It's serious business, making a woman out of a spoiled high-couch brat who's never done an honest stitch of work or had her bottom spanked."

"You would not *dare!*" I said through clenched teeth which threatened to chatter.

"Are you frightened?" he asked hopefully.

"No. Nothing would bother me now. You are right, my diminishment is complete." I moved my wrists, and the chain clinked. "Eventually you will leave, and I will hide these keys and get me from Arlet."

"Do not be too sure that there's nothing that would bother you now. After all, I have been doing this a long time. I can teach you more of Arlet yet. What if you are pregnant?"

I rolled away from him as best I could. "*I* am Well-Keepress," I reminded him, but he wasn't listening.

His hands were in my chald. "Where did you get this?" he said in a strained voice.

"What? Get what? What is wrong?"

"This ring on your chald—where did you get it?"

I tried to sit up, but I was well-restrained.

"Why?" I asked, my throat closing up suddenly, as much from that deadly quiet tone of his as from his question.

"When I was up at the Falls of Santha, I found a cave behind the falls and, within it, a very similar design on a slab of metal. I thought it was something left from before the rebuilding, and reported it to the dhareners as such. How did you come by this ring?"

I realized that Sereth crill Tyris had interrogated many folk in less pleasant circumstances than these; the habitual tone he used and the changes in his attitude toward me were truly frightening. So I told him only that it had been my father's, and that I would like very much to see the cave at the Falls of Santha.

"We both get consideration for our services, Estri. Who pays whom if we go joint venturing up to the Falls of Santha?"

"What if I get the Liaison to pay for it, as a joint project of his and mine? Then you can do what you will with the money."

He looked at me very solemnly for a moment. Then he pulled me to him, and we missed sun's meal, and at mid-meal Celendra sent the shaven-headed girl to check on us, and Sereth had food sent up, which I ate in the jewelry-like chains of Arlet. In the late day, just after fourth bell, the girl returned and announced that the Liaison Second was awaiting Sereth crill Tyris in the dining room. He left me there, helpless, to await his return.

I had missed my match with Celendra. I hoped she would understand.

With my hands braceleted to a ring sunk in the floor above my head, and my ankles to one of the posts, I was well-secured, among the parset rugs and silken cushions of my blue-hung keep. Sereth did not return until after the fifth bell, by which time my muscles ached from inactivity and I knew I would kill Sereth of Arlet if given half a chance.

When the door slid aside to admit him, Sereth of the Slayers' Seven was not alone. Craning my neck, I saw Dellin push Celendra, looking somewhat diminished herself, in bracelets and leashed, across the threshold. She was pale under her dark skin. Dellin pulled her to where I lay bound on the rugs and chained her by the neck to the ring that secured my wrists. He gave her a long tether. Her hands were bound in front of her. Dellin, before he rose from securing her, reached across and touched my face.

"You look well-used, Estri. The Seven must suit you."

I did not answer, but turned my head away. This was more than I could stand, Dellin seeing me thus. I fought back the tears.

Sereth stood staring pensively down at us, Celendra and myself, chained to the same ring, his arms folded across his chest.

As unpredictably as a gust of wind, his emotion reached me, and I realized I was in the middle of a situation not of my making, one of old hostility and highly-charged grudges well and carefully kept. I looked from Sereth to Celendra, and back again, not understanding why, but knowing who: between Celendra and Sereth crill Tyris, there could never be peace.

Then the Seven of Arlet said: "What do you think, Dellin? They look good together, do they not?"

I turned to Celendra for comfort, for she was more experienced than I, but her face was drawn and tight, and a more than a little fearful.

"They do complement each other," Dellin agreed.

"Shall we make them work? They are good for little else." Sereth prodded Celendra with his foot. "Long ago, when I brought child on this one, she

invoked the Well-Keepress's immunity against me."
He had that quiet tone that had chilled me in the
drug chamber.

"This one," said Dellin, his foot at my neck,
"rejected my offer of shelter and protection, in
favor of well work and chaldra."

"So they both would rather be bought and paid
for, at the command of any master, than trust
themselves to a single man."

"We have bought them, for the time."

"And paid dearly for their use. And there are two
of us, which should please them," mused Sereth.
"But they're still too full of themselves for my taste."

"Well-Keepresses," reminded Dellin. "Maybe it's
an occupational hazard. If you are as tired as I,
then let's do what we discussed. I think it would
put the situation in perspective for them." I did
not believe what I read in him.

Sereth took a lash from the post, and without
warning brought it down upon us, my stomach
and Celendra's hip, for she was on her side. The
thonged lash bit, and I gasped in pain. He raised
the whip to strike again.

"What do you want from us?" I pleaded, but his
arm came down. Celendra struggled to her knees
and put a leg over me. She knelt over me. I could
see the long slitsa-shaped welts rising on her skin.

"I would have done this another way, Estri, on
my own accord," she said, leaning close to my
face, her lips against my neck.

"Sereth! This has gone altogether too far!" I
protested, straining at my bonds, pulling away.

"Move away from her," Sereth commanded of
Celendra.

Relief flooded me.

"Invite her," he ordered me, bringing the thronged
lash down hard on my stomach. I bit my lip.
Celendra knelt at my side, shaking her head.

There was nothing for it but to obey him. Later, I promised myself, he would pay for his entertainment. But I never thought either of us would pay so much for the games we played in Arlet then.

They sat on either side of us, and we followed their instructions until their voices faded. Then there were only Celendra and I, prisoners of mutual need that was, in the end, only partially fulfilled.

When, in the tangle of bodies that followed, I was once again servicing Sereth, my emotion got the better of me.

"I hate you," I told him.

"Good," he grunted. "You can feel something, then. There's hope for you yet. Hate and love are like pain and pleasure, lady, at times one and the same. Between now and the Falls of Santha, you'll learn still more about yourself, I promise you."

"Our bargain is void. I will choose another to escort me."

"Dellin."

The Liaison looked up from Celendra when Sereth called his name.

"Estri no longer wants me to take her to Santha."

"I can't spare anyone from my staff, and we have an agreement Sereth," Dellin objected. "Besides, from what she's told me, she must go—to fulfill her blasted chaldra. Or does chaldra mean less today than yesterday, Estri?"

He would not get that from me. I would not abrogate my chaldra.

"Then," I said, defeated, "after I see the Day-Keeper, you will have your way with me, as you have had all along." I myself did not know to which of them I spoke.

The sun sank, the moon rose, and the four of us together spent the night. Toward sun's rising we slept, and I awakened at seventh bell, mid-meal hour, in Celendra's arms, still chained with her to the ring set into the floor. I moaned and turned, and she pulled me close, nuzzling my hair. The key ring was between us, that we might free ourselves, and Sereth and Dellin were nowhere in sight. They had gone, I realized, to the pass games, for this was Detarsa first seventh. I had been absent a set from Astria, sun's rising tomorrow. I roused Celendra, whose hands freed us from our bracelets.

"Shall we go to the games?" I asked her, sitting cross-legged, facing her, as I unlocked the leashed metal band from her throat.

"It would be foolish to so encourage them," she replied, fingering the swollen welts on her belly and hips.

"Perhaps their events are ended."

"And perhaps not. I have a Well to run." She looked at me critically, eyeing my marked flesh. "I shall tender the Liaison a bill for this," she said as she rose awkwardly and stretched. I too was stiff and sore in every muscle.

We bathed together, I washing her hair and she mine, soaking a long while in the steaming water, fragrant with soothing oils. My welts smarted and burned.

"If I could"—Celendra winced as I applied salve to her belly—"I would have them both castrated. When men interfere between two women, they overstep their authority."

"They paid for us," I reminded her. I had little interest in Celendra's advances, no matter what the circumstances. I did not tell her that, nor that I had never been with a woman before, nor that I had gotten great pleasure from her touch. I handed the salve to her, and she dressed my lesions, and my eyes watered with the pain.

"Tonight," she said, "you will not know these

marks existed." I thought I would know, for the rest of my life, marks from the last evening's couching.

We went to her keep, where she had food brought to us, and went over the night's take, and did her paperwork. I dozed on her couch.

"Estri . . ." She shook me awake.

"What?"

"Ginisha was settled by Jerin, while we were with Sereth and Dellin."

I groaned. That meant Feast of Conception. When a well woman is impregnated, all men who were that night in the Well are given free access the following evening, for they are considered talismans to the lucky well woman. The Well is closed to business from any others, and a great feast and debauch is put on for the lucky couple at the Well's expense. Each man receives a special token, which has no denomination, and is free to use it any way he sees fit.

"And another thing: your Day-Keeper has arrived, and awaits your pleasure. He is quartered in their offices across the court. Shall I send him your regrets at being indisposed, or can you face him today?"

"Can I get him into the feast? Or plead exhaustion, and not attend myself? I must see him and get on with my search. I cannot stay much longer in Arlet. I am not suited to this life."

"It is not always like this," she said softly, running her hand over my back. "I will get you a token for him for this evening, but I would not tempt the fates by having you absent from the Feast of Conception." It would be a bad omen if all who had taken part in the eve of conception were not present for the celebration.

"I'll go now then, first to my keep and dress, then to the Well physician to make sure that the small pain of ovulation has not been smothered by the larger pains. Directly from there I will go to the Day-Keepers' offices."

"It would take a magician, not a physician, to figure out whose child it was if you caught last night. Here," she said, handing me a tas-wrapped bundle.

I unwrapped the breech and band, black with chased-silver studs and buckles, that Celendra had promised to have made for me.

"It is superb," I said softly, kissing her on the top of her harth-black head.

I put it on. The leather was soft and supple, the lining web-cloth. I looked at myself in the mirror behind Celendra's couch. In the breech and band, with the scarlet-hung keep of the Keepress for backdrop, I looked, with my copper skin and damp-darkened hair, like some parset warrior woman.

"It suits you," Celendra commented. "May the flow guide you. I will leave instructions for you to get the token for your Day-Keeper at the entry desk."

I nodded as I made for the door: "My thanks again, Celendra. Tasa."

In the physician's keep I got, from a kindly old man in the cerise of his calling, a shot of time-release stimulant. He gave me the usual warnings about perspective and possible drug psychosis. I had no alternative other than stimulants, or I would not have used them. He checked me, and my cervix showed not even a hint of blue, nor were any of the other tests positive. Wide-awake and trembling from the drug, sure that I was not pregnant, I made my way past the entry desk, where I picked up the token, and across the Inner Well to the Day-Keepers' offices.

My mind blithered information at me. I recalled all I had ever known of the Day-Keepers. I recalled how, thousands of years ago, when Silistra's great

machines warred with each other, releasing holo-
causts of bacteria and flame upon the planet, the
high Day-Keepers, our dhareners, and our forereaders, under the direction and tutelage of our
first dhare, Khys, had been ready. In seven subterranean labyrinths, the two groups secreted themselves, living underground for more than a thousand years. During that time had the Day-Keepers
and forereaders developed the system of chaldra,
which allows an individual to feed his need for
crisis and problem on a physical level, rather than
internalizing his struggles. There, too, had the
Slayers been envisioned, and the Well system begun.
We are, all of us on Silistra, descended from the
seven groups of Day-Keepers and forereaders, the
bast, the crill, the diet, the stoen, the aniet, the
rendi, and the gaesh. There, too, had the Day-
Keepers and forereaders begun the temporal selec-
tion process that was their major function. Out of
all possibilities inherent in time, they choose that
most compatible with their long-range objectives,
and through the arm of the Slayers implement
their desires. Time charting is a difficult under-
taking. The measure of their success is that Silistra
lives without great machines of wars, without op-
pressive government, and that we are repopulating
our decimated planet.

I wondered what this dharener would look like.
Each, when he takes his majority, chooses a period
of Silistran culture, a particular civilization, and
becomes, out of time, its representative. Their specialty they wear about them, dressing, speaking,
thinking their choice. I had seen Day-Keepers tat-
tooed from head to foot, in the manner of the
Gristasha tribes who preceded the Parsets, fur-
clad and matted as our most ancient prehistoric
ancestors would have been, even knit-suited and

painted about the eyes as we were in the late machine age.

I was before the door to the Day-Keepers' offices without remembering how I had come there. It was unmistakable. A heavy Silistran steel slab propped up by thick gol-blocks, and that was all. The door led deep into the ground, I knew, into the labyrinth where our forebears had lived so long away from the sun and wind. Each Well is built over a portion of the old hides, as they are called. In Astria the door to the Day-Keepers' offices are not within the Well, for the hides extend for miles underground, but otherwise it was identical to this door within the gates of Arlet.

As I reached out to pull the ring that would inform those within that someone desired entrance, the door swung back. The man who stepped blinking into the sun to greet me with outstretched hand could only have been my dharener: he wore a plumed headdress and brocaded robe, heavy with gems and metallic thread. His hair was drawn back into a club and sheened with oil. He carried the curved sword of the ancient Stoth priests, with gem-encrusted hilt. On his feet were bejeweled sandals. I breathed a sigh of relief. Stothric is one of my better ancient dialects. I would not have to shame myself by conversing with this high one in modern Silistran.

"Presti m'it ci Vedrev bast Iradea," he said.

"Prest m'it, may the sun shine in your soul, dharener Vedrev," I replied. "Ci Estri Hadrath diet Estrazi."

# V.
## The Feast of Conception

When the dharener Vedrev's hand touched mine, a great peace came over me. I was at one with time, sure of my position in the process we know as reality. I jerked my hand away. I had seen as the forereaders see. This was indeed an accomplished Day-Keeper! I had never met a Day-Keeper who could not influence one's thinking, but I did not remember one so forceful as this man Vedrev bast Iradea.

"Will you please shield?" I asked him as he motioned me into the dark passageway and the closing door cut out the afternoon light: his touch in my mind was like nothing so much as a narcotic tranquilizer, glossing my very thoughts with a false security and unwarranted comfort.

The emotions in my mind became once more my own as the robed dharener guided me into a thala-paneled room filled with scrolls, fax, and sheaves of bookworks in their tas envelopes, and dominated by a huge desk littered with rolls and spools and loose sheets.

Motioning me into a high-backed stuffed chair,

Vedrev took one identical to it behind the desk, where long shadows cast by fish-oil lamps on the wall made him look like something escaped from one of my more primal nightmares.

Even as I wrinkled my nose at the smell from the oil lamps, I realized that, through the very floor of the high Day-Keeper's office, I could feel the heart of the hide, beating. These old machines, which had kept us alive a thousand years beneath the earth, still survived, preserving the hides themselves and the treasures of antiquity they contained in case they were ever needed again.

I saw this as necessary and natural, and dissimilar from the useless star-machines. When my forebears returned to the surface they had been determined to live independently of the technology which, after nearly destroying us, had become our only method of survival for so long. They also determined that the machines that had so well serviced them should continue to exist. After all, they were Silistran machines, they had served us faithfully, and a wise man never cuts off his only avenue of retreat. Deep within the hides were even preserved the terrible instruments of destruction that had almost annihilated us. But only the highest Day-Keeper of all, Silistra's dharen, knew exactly where.

"And how fared you on the road to Arlet, Estri?" Vedrev bast Iradea asked me softly over steepled fingers. His eyes were the palest of blues, ringed with black; his hair white as ice at the temples, graying black where it was clubbed at the base of the neck of this imposing, large-headed man in his middle years, who had a stare like the great beaked ebvrasea, those giant cousins of the harth who soar high in the Sabembe.

"Not as well as I might have. However, I did manage to do Dellin, the new Liaison Second of

Arlet, some good in his relationships with the Slayers. He's decided to test for the Slayers' chaldra, and has even secured Sereth of Arlet as his sponsor. What think you?"

Never before had a Liaison for the Bipedal Federate Trade Union been willing to test for any chain, let alone the Slayers'. They were merely the B.F. representatives on Silistra, interested in their quotas and profits.

"I think the time is right," Vedrev was nodding his head slowly. "Do not be so foolish as to ignore the pull to crux, for it affects us all, Estri. In all likelihood, this is no disconnected event nor discrete coincidence. The time pulls us toward a mighty change, so great that I have not been able to find a single forereader who is unaffected by it, and therefore can read the flow." Now he shook his head. "I left early from conclave. They get nowhere. All are blinded by the mists of the crux. The abyss may call us all if this change cannot be charted, and we are all blind." His expression was sour and frustrated and for an instant he glared at me as if these matters were in some way my fault.

I shifted in my chair but said nothing.

"I tell you this for a reason." His hands went to the pile of information beside him. They sought and found a thick bound sheaf. "I have your records, Well-Keepress. Your forebears all were forereaders with an index of nine or better. You could, in your testing, equal them in objective tests but were totally unable to function in life situations involving animate objects. Thus your rating is only a four. Have you ever given this any thought?"

I wanted to find my father, not discuss my mental deficiencies.

"As little as possible, dharener: if Day-Keepers could not suggest a cure, how might I? My own life is, to me, and to any I have yet encountered, unreadable. Even Celendra, who tells me she is an accomplished forereader, could ascertain only what *had* happened to me—not what *will* happen. When forereaders cannot see, they predict all manner of catastrophe, on the assumption that if they cannot see it, it must be high crux. No one's whole life can be draw for crux; therefore, they are wrong. Presently, I am concerned only with fulfilling this chaldra and getting back to Astria while I still have my sanity." I was brusque because I was walking the drug-tightrope between despair and exhilaration, and though I knew it, I could do little about it.

Vedrev scowled briefly, then sighed as if saying, "Well, what can you do with such a one?" Out loud, he said only, "I think you should reexamine your data." Then: "I do not want to frighten you but it is my feeling that you are deeply involved in the change we sense. So do be careful, Estri. When you are ready to think in more impersonal terms, we will discuss this matter further. Now, let me see what you have for me." His rebuke stung.

"I have this," I said, disengaging my father's ring from my chald and putting it into his brown, sinewy hand. "Sereth of Arlet says that he has seen a similar sign behind the Falls of Santha."

"And that you should have stumbled upon that information, heard it from the mouth of the only man who has seen what lies behind the falls—this, also, you would count as coincidence?" He sucked his teeth, holding the ring close to his face as he got a glass from his desk and fitted it to his eye. Through the jeweler's eyepiece, he peered long at my father's ring, then shuffled through his mounds of paper and fax. A scroll dropped to the floor, clattering loudly on the black gol. I retrieved it. He had not heard or, hearing, had not deigned to notice.

At length he raised his head, and his face was suffused with excitement as he said, "It is certainly genuine. And it bears both the sign and script attributed to the seed-sowers. That script, the first ever written, is unmistakable. I would say it is an artifact of the seed-sowers, and yet it is not more than a few hundred years old. If this truly matches with what the Seven found at Santha—which he only recently reported to us—then it would be safe to say that both are of seed-sowers."

"There is no such thing as 'seed-sowers,'" I protested, growing uneasy. "It is an old legend, a fright-restraint invented by primitive priests to keep the populace under control!"

"And the same legend was invented by every early Silistran culture, even those so isolated that they could have had no contact with one another, and by more than half of the other planets of the B.F., also isolated from each other?" He bared his teeth. "Come, now, Estri, open your mind."

"All primitives need a spiritual archetype outside themselves, until they can deal with the spirit within," I said from rote. I once calculated that I had, at the time of my graduation from Day-Keeper's school, spent forty-five years in academic situations.

Now I rose to my feet.

"I do not *want* to be part of some higher-plan function, some whirlpool in temporal events! I am not *interested* in ancient legends. I need to know," I enunciated slowly and distinctly, my temper barely under wraps, "where to look for my father. Ristran sent me to you for help. Before I set off for the Falls of Santha, will you come into Arlet and examine the artifacts I have with me? It is Feast of Conception, but I have a token for you." I wanted, most of all at that moment, to get out of there: the smell of the oil lamps and the vibration of the

floor and the drug and the lack of sleep were con-
spiring against me. I badly needed fresh air.

He looked at me queerly, then rose and put his
arm around my shoulder. When we stood in the
open air, he returned to me my father's ring.

"I accept your invitation—I shall go with you to
the feast, Estri; I'll help you however I can—we all
feel, including those of us at the Lake of Horns,
where my brother dhareners are not unaware of
your situation, that it is very important that you
remain strong. If you fail, none of us can help you,
and it might affect the crux adversely. Consider,
however, that if I am right, you will need a man of
your father's race to get you with child, and all
that is done other than that coupling is simply
going through the motions."

High dhareners at the Lake of Horns, aware of
me? My situation—whatever it was—being discussed in the fabled city of the dhareners? The
comment shocked me into silence. Now, from my
distant vantage, I can only wonder what sort of
help they thought they could give me. We are all
arrogant fools, who understand nothing and are
categorically unable to admit it. Every forereader
and dharener, every M'ksakkan and starchild, every human who strives to codify a superlogical
universe by means of categorization, logic, and the
supernumeraries of conscious thought has forgotten that thought is a byproduct of the universal
process, not the other way around. Thought must
occur in time; it is depended on sequence and
duration; it can never pierce beyond the temporal
limit to understand what motivates creation and
models time itself.

What the time demanded then was that Vedrev
and I walk together through the gathering shadows,
across the court where the shopkeepers were lock-
ing their stalls for the night, and into the common

room of Well Arlet, where servers were removing the customary Well seating and replacing it with long planked tables of half wisper logs and benches, so that all might be seated together for the feast.

In my keep I retrieved from the thala chest the silvery material Dellin had given me, in which I had wrapped the viewer and fax letter, and handed them to Vedrev.

The Day-Keeper sat cross-legged before the window, amid the blue cushions, and viewed the oblong. When he was finished, he replaced it carefully in the tas pouch. He looked at me, where I lay propped on one elbow staring at the crags below.

"I thought I could not be more sure," he said softly, "about your destiny—and all of ours. But this . . . When you find Him, give Him our regards."

His inflection made me stare: my father was impressive, true, but no man deserves to be spoken of in such a fashion, I thought then.

Meanwhile, Vedrev was reading the letter. He scowled and ground his teeth and must have read it more than once, for it was a long time before he put it away: the moon was above the crags when he next spoke to me:

"Have you heeded these warnings?"

"To the best of my ability. Secrecy was impossible. It is common knowledge that I am in Arlet."

"And Baniev?"

"I have managed to avoid it."

"Perhaps there is something that may be searched from this. If Astria had access to information, I might match her channels and pick up what she learned." I knew what he meant: time search. Vedrev proposed to connect with Astria, at the moment she received the pertinent information, and experience it with her. It is a scarce skill, the ability to send the mind to where time has no density and directly experience the long-dead past.

So I dozed in my keep while the Day-Keeper tranced, and at eighth bell Celendra herself came to escort us to the Feast of Conception. I had no time to ask him what he had accomplished, only time to give him his token, that he might use the woman of his choice at the feast, and make my body ready. Since it was handy, I wore the silvery draped sheath that Dellin had bought me, and fastened it again with the silver clips set with white stones, then followed Celendra and Vedrev to the common room.

One thing the dharener had said came back to me, though I hadn't marked it at the time: Going through the motions indeed! If Vedrev was right, and I could bear child only by one of my father's race, where did that leave me?

The thought obsessed me while I watched Celendra, who was doing her act for the Day-Keeper, as we all tend to do with such a man, though the dharener certainly saw right through her facade into the less pleasant deeps beneath.

After much fussing about, Celendra finally seated us, putting me on her left, Vedrev on her right, and herself between us at the head of the central table. On my other side sat Sereth, and Dellin opposite him; then Genisha and Jerin, the guests of honor. Genisha, the small shaven-headed girl who had been the first I had met in Arlet seemed quite pleased with her body's choice of Jerin, the Arletian Slayer who had called my bout with Celendra. But then, girls, at times, have been known to stretch the rules. Perhaps Jerin could not be proved the sperm-father of the child. He was, however, the announced father, which would suffice, since there were no challengers.

The musicians were pounding out a pulsing dance rhythm and the cleared center of the common room filled with writhing figures. Feast of Conception has its own style, its own formula, its own music and dance. It is the oldest performed ceremony on Silistra—perhaps the most important one: there had not been such a feast in Astria for over two years.

I watched the dancers in silence, refusing both Dellin and Sereth with a shake of my head. I was flashing and dizzy; sound and sight receded and sharpened around me. My hands shook and my legs also, and I clasped my fingers together in my lap and concentrated upon maintaining consciousness. I saw the man of Hertekiea, whom I had mistaken the night before for Celendra, whirl by me with a blond well woman in his arms. Also I recognized that Koster whose drink I had spilled in my first meeting with Sereth, and the Iartex whom Ganrom had so rudely unseated. The air around me was already thick with danne and distrit and I rested my cold forehead on a sweating palm.

Sereth of the Slayers' Seven touched my arm and peered into my face, offering a lit pipe to me. Wordlessly, I refused it: I was descending fast from the stimulant; another, similar drug would only make matters worse.

Having been effectively separated from the Day-Keeper by Celendra, when I began weaving in my chair I could not turn elsewhere but to Sereth: I put a hand on his shoulder as if we were on a ship and I had to steady myself against the pitching of its decks.

"Not doing too well, Estri? Here, try this." Solicitous, he handed me a goblet of kifra. I used both hands to take it from him, but it fell from my grasp, spilling its contents over my lap, his thigh, and my plate on its way to the floor.

"I am *so* tired," I whispered, leaning against him, trembling, as the servers cleaned the mess from the table and our laps. I was lonely in this strange place, disoriented and suddenly afraid. And I wanted Santh. I had not seen my black friend for a set's time. I tried to call him, but all I got was hazy hulion close-ups, in which Santh nuzzled a sandy female. I did, however, see great falls at their backs. Perhaps spring and its call had drawn Santh home. Dimly I realized that I would see him soon, if such was the case.

Sereth was speaking to me, but I could hear only the growl of his voice, not the words. When I looked him in the face, it was as if he were at one end of a long black tunnel, and I at the other.

"I cannot hear you," I said. I hoped he could hear me. I had no way of judging the loudness of my voice, or even whether I had really spoken or only thought I had. Then even the black tunnel down which I squinted at the world began to close, the light at its end in which Sereth's face was limned began to spin. I gripped the tabletop with both hands and for a time knew nothing describable.

The next thing I knew was the feel of something touching my lips: a hard something, then a cold liquid something, spilling into my mouth between my teeth. This I swallowed, choking and spitting. Slowly, as the bitter drink flooded my mouth and throat, I realized that a cerise-clad physician with a five-strand chald was standing over me. I could see his chald very clearly: Arletian. Others, too, leaned over me. If I could have moved my body I would have pushed away from the crowd. It was hard to breathe and they seemed to be stealing all my air.

Slowly, under the physician's ministrations, the room focused and my body returned to my control. I could hear and had an awareness of the placement of my extremities.

"I am almost fine," I said to him, and waved more bitter drink away. I had had enough drugs. Sereth's hand was on my shoulder; his arm held me upright. Dellin looked strained and white under his dark skin. Vedrev the Day-Keeper was gesturing to him and leaning confidentially close. I realized that I *was* recovering as I found myself wondering if Dellin would learn tonight what chaldra entailed.

"Shall I take you upstairs?" Sereth offered.

"Not until I've eaten and had some rana—with you, I'll need all my strength," I declined.

"Food it is, then," he said cheerfully, slipping from his seat beside me to hunt up a server, that I might have some solid nourishment in my stomach, and rana, as I had asked him, to wash it down. I leaned my head in my hands, my elbows steadied on the trestle table. The meal would not be served for another bell.

I caught myself listening attentively to Dellin and Vedrev and that made me angry: I told myself that I no longer cared whether Dellin acquired chaldra or not. What matter his problems, when I had so many of my own? How could I feel so strongly about a man who had so viciously used me? Sereth was a violent man by nature, and he did only what was natural to him—barring the incident with Celendra, when his fury was aroused, he had been merely playful in our couching, displaying no malice aforethought. Dellin, on the other hand, seemed to do everything with ulterior motives. An opportunist and a plotter, he now used his moments with the dharener, as he had used me to his advantage with Ganrom and Sereth, to further his position in Arlet.

A shadow fell across me, and I looked up to see a trader in pelts and leather towering over me. Brown eyes under prominent brows, a flattish nose, and petulant lower lip were all that were visible of his features, save for a mass of unkempt dark beard that rested on his chest. He had his well token in his hand, and I was about to explain my indisposition when I realized I could not read him. I could get nothing from his mind! The burly man stood staring down at me. I raised my hand and pulled hair from my face.

As I opened my mouth to speak, a well token landed with a crack in my empty plate, where it rolled on its edge in ever smaller circles until, finally, it fell quivering to its side and lay still.

It was not the trader's token, for he still held his in his hand. I looked around. The Day-Keeper's eyes smiled at me and he turned back to Dellin.

Celendra, however, was quick to intervene in my behalf, putting her arms around the trader's massive neck soothingly.

"We will find you another girl," she said as she led the flushed, grumbling man toward the second table. "One with more strength and stamina. That one will be of little use to any man tonight. She is worn and weak. We will find you a nice fresh girl who can do justice to a Morrltan's needs."

I saw Sereth making his way cautiously through the crowd with a tray on which were covered dishes and a steaming pot. He placed the tray between his place and mine and reached for my plate.

"Whose?" he asked me, referring to the well token. He slid it off the plate onto the wisper-log table.

I gestured to the Day-Keeper. He had presented me with an easy out from the hoary trader, and I had thought no more about it.

"What do you want with her, Vedrev?" said Sereth crill Tyris in his deadly quiet voice. "She's in no shape for anything but sleep. And that ought to be beside the point—you dhareners have already got the best of our women, and you don't share them: stay away from our well women, or we lesser mortals might begin to resent you high-handed spiritual types." There was no mistaking the threat there, although Sereth spoke as low as a man whispering to his lover.

Perhaps I had waxed hysterical, but I had to jam my hand into my mouth to keep from laughing: Sereth of the Slayers' Seven, a killer by profession and one so good at it he'd risen to a position of ultimate power among ranks of killers, was going to protect me from Vedrev, the dharener, a man whose weapons were only words and whose dedication was to the preservation of life, not the eradication of it.

Vedrev said flatly: "While you were gone to the kitchen, a trader came to take her. But you are precisely right: I have no need of a well woman, especially one who has been so badly mistreated." Vedrev stared at Sereth as if at a melon full of maggots, his mouth an angry white line.

Sereth's hand went to his hilt, and then to the table. Gripping the thick edge so hard with one hand that his knuckles paled, he stared at the well token in the other.

Then he took a deep breath and tossed the well token that had been on my plate to Vedrev, who did not deign to glance at it, but held the Slayer's gaze until Sereth looked away.

"I'm seeing that she eats, aren't I? I'll see that she sleeps," Sereth muttered, "and is not disturbed." He seemed to want to say more. Instead, he shook his head and took his seat abruptly.

I was then served my early dinner by Sereth of Arlet, who said not a word to anyone until I was finished, but sat with his arms folded across his chest, slid down on his spine. His face was tightly drawn. One does not gainsay a high Day-Keeper.

They are categorically above reproach. He had already said too much, perhaps risked too much: Vedrev's anger could cost Sereth his appointment, the rank it had taken him years to earn.

I brushed his thigh with my palm under the table and turned my attention to the meal he'd brought me. Soon the food stopped my head from spinning and brought strength back into my limbs.

I was even able to sort the sounds of Dellin and Celendra and the Day-Keeper from the noise around us: the subject of the conversation was the legend of the seed-sowers. Dellin recalled similar M'ksakkan legends. Celendra was intrigued. I thought that the dharener Vedrev must be very sure to sow his own seed so early.

Sereth leaned close to me, as if to pick at the remains on my plate.

"What did you tell Vedrev, that he's holding me responsible for your condition? I have my differences with the Day-Keepers. I don't need you to make it worse."

"I told him nothing except that I had been with you, and you had told me of the artifact at the Falls of Santha." I apologized sincerely. "I think he simply assumed it, because of the seating and your reaction to his token. That man, the trader who would have couched me—I could not read him. Nothing. That has never happened to me before."

"I want you to make the matter of who did how much to whom clear with that dharener before we go to Santha. I can do without another call to stand judgment before that pack of old ladies. What is this deep-reading? All I know is what's commonly said: that the forereaders and the girls of Astria do it. Can you tell me what I'm thinking?"

"Not exactly—not conscious words you are framing for communication. But deep-seated emotion, underlying motivation, primal drives ... these I can read with clarity—when I am myself. At this moment I doubt if I could read you the alphabet."

"What, then, is the import of your inability to read the trader?" His eyes were narrowed quizzically on me.

"Perhaps you are right; perhaps it is just that I am so very tired."

"Let me take you upstairs. You have done your duty to the Well, little Keepress, and more."

"You are my will," I sighed, an old phrase for acquiescence I had not used since my training years. "Just let's watch Genisha dance first."

So we sat in the common room while the Feast of Conception roared around us, and on that most joyous occasion I struggled to keep my eyelids from closing of their own accord. By the time the six courses had been served and cleared and the great dessert tray was making its way up and down the aisles between the trestle tables, I was dozing for sweet instants, catching myself and starting back to consciousness, then fading again. Thus I missed Genisha's dance to Jerin, that which is the most beautiful of Silistran dances, where the elements of submission and free will, sex and love, swirl around the dancers like sheer silks. I drifted off to sleep with my head on Sereth's shoulder and did not awaken until I found myself in his arms at the door to my keep.

Once within, in the soft-lit blue-and-gold chamber, he stripped from me the silvery silk Dellin had given me and laid me on the couch, pulling the covers up around me almost tenderly. Some while later I was again awakened, to take the bath he had drawn for me. He bathed with me, but not with the intent other than helpful. So I did let Sereth of Arlet, of the Slayer's Seven, wash and bathe me like a child and dry me in the soft toweling and put me again in my couch.

I told him drowsily to go back downstairs and enjoy the feast, but he refused.

"I," he said, "am also tired. I've had a trying few days and Vedrev's being here is not the least of it. I should have had more sense . . . at least, I ought to keep clear of him for the rest of the evening. If you have no objection, I'll rest here with you. Trouble seeks you, lady, like the ebvrasea the mountain taslings, and it might be better if you are not alone, lest it strike when we least expect it."

"Lest the days all slip away." I smiled at him, quoting from the beautiful old song about two lovers who pegged every moment of their time, so that they might spend eternity together. Sereth pegged this time that I might survive it.

"Lest Vedrev blame it on me if some ill befalls you because I wasn't around to prevent it," he said sardonically. "Doubtless," he added, pulling the cover up around him and settling on his side, "the days will all slip away regardless. But I have gotten into a habit, and it is a hard one to break." He leaned over and kissed me on the lips, so lightly, and the hair of his thick-matted chest tickled me.

I wonder whether he meant the habit of me, or the habit of pegging time, or the habit of circumventing trouble with the dhareners, but I was too sleepy to ask.

We were awakened by the four bells of Arlet, tolling stridently together. Each bell, on a normal day, has seven enths to toll, but when all bells ring together, twelve soundings, it is said they weep for a soul. Someone was dead in Arlet. It is not often that such sounds are heard, for death is long coming to take us on Silistra. But come it does. I shivered and pressed closed to Sereth.

He was frowning. As the only member of the

Slayers' Seven in Arlet, if the passing was other than natural, it was his duty to make an inquiry. If natural, he must still take a hand. The bearers would have to be chosen from the ranks of the Slayers. The family, if they were not aware, informed, the deceased one's goods apportioned fairly. The ceremony and the writing of the name in the Day-Keeper's roll were the responsibility of the Slayers' Seven.

Sereth slid out from between the couch covers and began to dress.

"May I join you?" I asked.

"If you wish, Estri, but whatever's going on, it won't be pleasant, coming completely unexpected."

Then the death was no timely one of old age's infirmity.

I threw back the silken couch spread and the web-cloth undercover and went to retrieve the breech and band Celendra had given me from the smaller thala chest.

"How do you feel?" asked Sereth, watching me as, bent over from the waist, I untangled my hair with rapid strokes of the bone comb, holding high the ends which brushed my toes.

"Fine." I straightened up, throwing back my head, feeling the strands around me crackle with static. "I needed the rest badly, I guess. However . . . I do feel a trifle foolish for causing so much trouble last night."

He shrugged and guided me out the door, saying, "I must change into more suitable clothing. Will you eat with me in my hostel?"

I agreed. I was curious to see how the Slayers lived in Arlet, and what Sereth of the Slayers' Seven chose to keep around him.

We were halfway across the Inner Well when Celendra caught up with us. I thought it was the first time I had seen that woman hurry.

When she reached us, she was gasping for breath: "Do you need me for the inquiry, Sereth?" Familiarly, she put her hand on the Slayer's arm.

"I haven't decided yet if there will be one."

"There will doubtless be one."

"Then you know more than I."

"I know that Fressa had nothing to do with it."

"With *what*, woman?" demanded the Slayer. "If you have something to say, say it. I belong at the hostel, sorting this thing out, not prattling gossip with women in a Well court." He took hold of her shoulders, his hands digging into her flesh, and lifted her so that her feet barely touched the ground.

"Put me down—dear one—and I will walk you there," Celendra retorted in a fashion which said clearly that these two often behaved so with one another. "*And* tell you," she added cattily, "what you need to know, as usual."

As we walked across the Inner Well, me in my band and breech, studded with silver, Celendra clothed in her dusky skin, and Sereth in his worn slate Slayer's garb, she told us what had happened:

"Remember that trader that wanted you last night, Estri? He was found this morning, after leaving Fressa's couch before sun's rising, wandering mindless in the Inner Well. He died within a bell of being discovered. He could neither see nor hear, nor did he respond to touch. The physicians say his mind was totally isolated, cut off from all sensory input. He died horribly, degenerating before the healers' eyes. There is no known poison that could do such a thing. No traces of foreign chemicals in the blood. But every sensory path to the brain was destroyed."

"If there is no poison, and no marks of violence on the body, why are you worried about your girl? Why would we blame her, or anyone, for the

inexplicable?" Sereth asked her, hands on his hips
and one foot on the lowest step leading up to the
Slayers' hostel, an imposing structure of silvery
gol, with thala door and lintel. The hostel had no
windows, but narrow open slits through which a
man could aim a weapon. It had been long since
those slits had been needed in Arlet, but the Slayers
stand ever ready to defend her.

Celendra hesitated on the staircase: "I must get
back to my Well. I just wanted you to know what I
knew, lest the physicians, having no answer to
your questions, use Fressa to take the blame. They
seldom admit to ignorance."

"I appreciate it. Tasa," said Sereth without a
hint of emotion, as if he did not appreciate it at all
and knew she knew it, but was being polite in
front of me.

We passed many men in the winding passages of
the hostel, hurrying through the corridors, metal
clanking, gathered in small knots of subdued
conversation. In the kitchen, where the serving
alcove was filled with men in slate and black
leathers, the talk was louder, a maddening rumble.
And yet there was little laughter.

A table of light needle-wood was clear in a corner of the high-ceilinged gray alcove; above it,
swords and shields were racked upon the walls,
many ancient beyond description, jewel-hilted, and
with precious-metal inlay. Other than weapons,
the severity of the man-height gray gol-blocks
around us was unbroken; beneath my feet, the
floor was planked thala, the southern variety, with
brown over-grain.

Sereth steered me toward the empty table. Men
got up from their grilled parr and eggs to query
him.

"What rises, Seven?" asked one, a large man
who stepped directly into our path.

"What indeed? There's nothing I like less than an unclear enemy," said another, joining the first before Sereth could answer.

"He's right," said a third. "Give me something I can see to fight, and I'll bring you its teeth. But this . . . Poison? What?"

"Could it be some new disease—something the Day-Keepers and the physicians can't handle?" asked a fourth with a worried expression and an accent I did not recognize.

Virulent disease had long ago been conquered on Silistra. These men were much shaken by the thought of a microscopic enemy against whom there was no defense.

Finally, when the men had all voiced their fears, Sereth said: "I think nothing yet. I have to find out. Should I tell you my guess, perhaps a wrong one, just to tell you something? Are you a clutch of old ladies, that I have to comfort you in your fears? Leave me be. When I have something to say, I'll say it." Angry, the Seven pushed his way through the men that had encircled us.

One of them, more persistent than the others, followed us to the table and then stood by, saying nothing and glancing covertly at me until Sereth looked up at him.

"Tyith, I hate it when you hover over me," Sereth sighed. "If you want to help, then bring us a meal. And lots of rana. I need a clear head."

The young, red-haired Slayer, whose skin was darker than tan and who wore the red knotted cord of a Slayer's apprentice at his waist, hurried to obey.

When the boy had disappeared around the corner to the kitchen proper, Sereth of Arlet put his head in his hands, rubbing his eyes: "I have never *seen* such a time," he said. "It whirls and blows around us, and my guess is that it's blowing us

something we could as well do without. You haven't
been here; you don't realize . . . it's been one irregu-
larity after another: the death of the old Liaison,
you, Dellin, Vedrev, so many new variables. Now,
this. Those old women must be gnashing their
teeth and pulling their hair out by handfuls over
this one." The thought seemed to cheer him, that
the Day-Keepers would be adversely affected.

He pulled a knife from its sheath, a small dagger,
and began cleaning his nails.

"All things," I said, "will come clear when the
draw to crux is complete, when the time reaches its
fullness," I told him.

He made a sour face at me: "Now you sound like
one of them—you're not a secret agent of the
dhareners, by any chance, come here to spy on
me? Or a thrice-damned forereader in disguise?"

I assured him I was neither.

"Then don't philosophize at me. There is no use
discussing the undiscussable, no sense in speculating with no information," he said to me as the
food came. Filling a bowl with rana, he handed it
to me: "Tell me what you read from Dellin, our
new Second, with your Astrian skills."

I had wondered when it would come up: I had
seen the canny look on Sereth's face when he asked
me about deep-reading; I was not the Day-Keepers'
spy, but he would make me his, if he could.

But I owed Dellin nothing, so I said: "He is an
intelligent and devious man, though it may be
that I am not objective—I thought for a while that
I cared for him, but I think now that I do not."

Sereth leaned back in his chair, his long legs
crossed, looking up at me intently from beneath
the shadow his dark hair cast, falling over his
forehead, listening as if it were his sole purpose in
life.

"Dellin is much taken with Silistra; he wishes to

make himself as Silistran as he can. That can serve you to your advantage if you play him right. He is, however," I cautioned, "a M'ksakkan, and profit and quota are to them as chaldra is to us. He will have difficulty, living as he wishes, with a foot in both worlds. Eventually, there will come a situation in which the need of Arlet and those of the M'ksakkan Bipedal Federate are in conflict. One cannot trust him until that time has come and gone. But he thinks himself sincere, and thusly may be used, perhaps, to advantage by one subtle enough in his approach. Remember, a Liaison with Slayer's chaldra is a bridge between worlds, a bridge that has never been trod."

"And a bridge provides access from both sides of the abyss it spans, eh?"

"Such is the nature of a bridge," I affirmed.

"Could you read this Fressa for me, and tell me if she is innocent of whatever Celendra tried to cover?"

"Perhaps. Let me see." I closed my eyes and got her easily: "She did not service that trader properly, Sereth," I told him, surprised. "He acted very strangely with her, and spilled his seed on her breasts and spoke to her in an unknown tongue. She should have reported it right away. It bothers her, or I would not be getting such detail."

"But she did nothing to him—nothing that might have killed him?"

"She is guilty of not calling a physician as soon as he left her, for he seemed to her deranged, but of no more than that."

Sereth stabbed a parr strip, still bubbly with juice, with the dagger. Such niceties as cutlery were not favored by the Slayers. The apprentice had brought us no utensils with our meal. I picked up a strip in my fingers. Sereth, grinning, reached back, and, the chair tilted back on two legs, took a gold-hilted knife from its sheath on the wall and handed it to me.

"How will this affect our journey to the Falls of Santha?" I asked him, spearing a strip of parr.

"I have to see. Since the physicians have already given their opinion, then the papers are most likely done. Today is Detarsa second first, and the rest of the Seven will not be in Arlet until second seventh. If the arrangements for the funeral and disposition can be made within that time, I have to be on hand for the occasion. If they take longer, then I may be able to leave by the fifth. I can check with the writer before I go to the Day-Keepers and find out for certain—see how many blanks on the poor bastard's paperwork are filled in, and how many are still open. A man cannot go to rest in Arlet with unfilled blanks on his papers." Sereth's rueful tone told me he was not fond of this part of his job.

"I am ready to leave when you are," I said, draining my rana bowl, whose contents had gone from steaming to tepid while we talked, then peered into the dark, bitter sediment.

As he refilled my bowl from a metal pot, Vedrev and another Day-Keeper, whose head was shaven in lateral strips in the manner of the Darsti builders, swept toward us through a rapidly thinning crowd of Slayers.

Vedrev made a striking figure in his Stothric priest's robe and plumes, and he knew it: With a dramatic flourish he slammed three sheets of parchment, and one of orange fax, down hard on the table.

Sereth of Arlet looked up at him with narrowed eyes, tense in his seat: "Sit down, Day-Keepers. I would have been with you presently, after I was done here. Thanks for saving me the walk."

Ignoring Sereth's barely-veiled truculence, Vedrev patted my hand: "How are you, Estri?"

"Much rested, thank you. Tell us about the trader's death. It is the subject of the moment." I smiled at him.

"This *looks* to be in order, anyway," Sereth said grudgingly, scanning the papers the Day-Keepers had brought for his approval. With a marker the other Day-Keeper produced, Sereth signed the three white sheets, then pressed his index finger to the fax. "Except for the cause of death—you've left that blank. What are you calling it?"

"Natural causes. It is no disease, and how anything living could have done that to another being is beyond my comprehension. How should I write it? Mind-burn? Should I give them my suppositions? If it happens again, however, we are in for trouble. I sent a messenger to Baniev to inform his family. There is little enough wealth to distribute. I think the Day-Keepers might gift the widow, since there is no one to take up her couch-mate's chaldra."

If the man had been killed by another, the killer would have had either to take up the man's chaldra—his responsibilities—or gift his house so that it might survive. In a case like this, where there was no one responsible, the Day-Keepers did as they saw fit.

"Baniev," I repeated what the dharener had said in disbelief. "Vedrev, I thought he was from Morrlta?"

"No, although that was the natural assumption, for he wore Morrltan clothes. So I, unwittingly, kept you from a man of Baniev. Another coincidence, Estri? And that that man died in such an unusual fashion? This, too, a coincidence?"

"What are you two talking about?" Sereth interrupted.

"And I *could not* read him. I told Sereth at the

time—nothing: I got nothing from him! I would have told you, but I had no chance. Sereth, tell him I told you."

"Someone tell *me* what is going on! Yes, you told me. But you were so tired, you could not keep your eyes open. What difference does it make?"

"I could get nothing from him either, Estri," said Vedrev to me, as if the Slayer were not present. "I thought it some trick of paranoia in my own mind. I had such a strong feeling of impending disaster, I was seeing potential culprits all around me. I am glad I picked the right one." He looked meaningfully at Sereth.

The Slayer, however, did not realize that in his own way Vedrev was apologizing. He had his arms folded and was slid deep in the chair, his most hostile position.

"Day-Keeper, inform a poor ignorant Slayer. What *shall* I do, O high one? Shall I take this lady to Santha, or tend to the funerary rites?" Sereth was being savagely polite. "What does Baniev mean to both of you that it doesn't to me? Come on, Vedrev, enlighten me—I've had enough of your games to last me three lifetimes in the last day. You owe me *some* kind of explanation."

The other, silent Day-Keeper scowled as if at some terrible impropriety while Vedrev, in a low, clipped voice, told Sereth of my great-grandmother's letter.

"Is there anything *else* I must keep her away from? Harths, perhaps, or taslings? Or perhaps a strong wind?"

"This is a serious matter, Slayer. If it is beyond your abilities, I can surely find another to take Estri to the Falls of Santha; someone who will follow directions. But go she must. And soon. So make haste, if you will take her. Pick the funeral bearers and set the disposition of his goods in motion, and depart as soon as that is done—or say you decline, and you're free to find someone more . . . suitable."

"The day hasn't dawned on which I'd ask you to excuse me from the performance of my duties. If you've decided, in your finite wisdom, that she's—" he flicked his head toward me "—one of them, than I'm not going to argue," said Sereth coldly.

"Seven, I would much rather you take Estri home to Astria, where she is safe. If anything happens to her, much feeling will arise between Ristran and myself because of it. But it is to the Falls of Santh she must go."

"As luck will have it, I've made an arrangement with the Liaison Second to take her there—and his is a prior commitment. So where does that leave us?"

Vedrev stood abruptly, departing in a swirl of robes without another word to the Slayer as, behind him, the bench on which he'd sat tumbled to the floor, clattering, and the other Day-Keeper gathered up the papers hastily and trotted after his master, who was already striding out the door.

"He was trying to be nice to you, Sereth. You seemed determined not to let him. He would have relieved you from your other burdens so that we could leave immediately, but you made it impossible. Why did you bait him so? Now we will have to wait until the fifth, at least."

"Maybe I don't want Vedrev unilaterally deciding to relieve me of any of my 'burdens.' And maybe the additional rest will do you good. It *is* a long and difficult trail," said the Slayer icily, rising.

He led me through the winding dark halls of the hostel, to his chamber, small and severe, which had that smell a place has when seldom used. I sat on the narrow, pelt-covered gol slab as he discarded his worn vest of circlets, tunic, and breech.

Before the crossed spear and shield, racked blades and the tas-wrapped, seven-lashed stones, naked, his chald glittering in the meager light from the wall slits, he seemed to be the archetypal Silistran—formidable, stern, the killer by whose sword Silistra had been raised from ashes.

I had expected some grand keep, but now I realized that such would have been out of character for this man. Also, I reminded myself, he did not live here, but somewhere out of Arlet, with his prized threx herd.

He turned from me and stooped to open the single wisper chest, drawing out a tooled and armored vest, circlets overlaid with steel at breast and back, and took from the wall a silver-hilted sword in figured scabbard.

I leaned over on impulse and took the worn common leathers into my lap: "May I take this, Sereth?" I fingered a place under the armhole where the color was gone from the hide and the soldered links thinned to the breaking point. "It could do with some oil and polish, and the chalder should check these links." It smelled strong, of sweat and trail use.

He looked up from buckling the black sword belt, with the Seven's mark worked on it, around his waist. He looked regal and imposing, quite different from the dusty Slayer who had offered to try me the day I had fought Celendra.

"That's work for an apprentice, not a well woman."

"I would enjoy it."

"Then do as you please." He was still angry with me for speaking my mind at table.

The plain wooden door swung slowly open, and the red-haired, rana-skinned youth who served us in the dining alcove peered around it.

"What is it, Tyith? Come in and close it."

The youth did as he was bid, squatting in the corner. His eyes were yellow-brown, wide, and clear. He stared at me solemnly.

"Estri, this is my son, Tyith bast Sereth."

The boy jumped to his feet, wiping his hand on his rump, then outthrust it in greeting. Sereth's son had his father's lithe body, but otherwise little favored him.

"Out of Celendra?" I guessed.

Sereth nodded. A man-child takes the mother's hide-name and the father's first; a girl-child, the mother's first and hide, and the father's first. It had been an easy guess, given the bast hide-name, Tyith's dusk-dark skin and sensuous features. The flaming hair, however, fit neither parent's stamp.

The boy's hand was cold, moist, and hard with callus.

"I am done with my duties," he said to his father. "I beat Uther soundly at stones, and got a nod from the master with short-sword." His pride was ill-concealed. "I wondered if you had anything for me to do, for I have won the rest of the day free."

"What of maintenance?" said Sereth sternly.

"That was the prize I won from Uther."

"Only a fool lets another tend his gear, when his life depends on it. Who knows how deeply your victory rankled your opponent? When you beat a man, even in fun, he is half an enemy. You may take this lady, since you have so much free time, back to the Well. Keep out of your mother's clutches and come straight back, and I will take you with me to find bearers for the funeral."

Sereth rose and came to me and whispered in my ear. I nodded, realizing for the first time, with his request, how deeply the trader's strange death had worried him.

"And bring Uther and another with you," he told Tyith, "*and* your gear. I want to check its condition personally before I send the three of you to the farm to bring back Issa and Krist, and another mount of your choice—one you would like under you on the trail to Santha."

The boy's eyes fairly shone. "Issa and Krist?" he asked wonderingly.

"What good is a first string, except to use when one needs a threx?" Sereth queried his son with a fond gruffness.

"Can I take *Wirin?*"

"You will need a special threx for such a long trek. Wirin is a judicious choice. now, move. I want them here by sun's rising tomorrow."

The boy was halfway down the hall before Sereth waved me after him.

"Wait," I called after Tyith, running to catch up.

He waited, shifting from foot to foot, his face screwed up.

"You must be very proud of your father," I said to him as we crossed the threshold into the blinding bright of the Inner Well.

"Pride is the cloak of fools. It has no place in a Slayer's heart," the boy quoted. "I try to live up to his expectations, which are often beyond me. My mother wanted me to go to the Day-Keepers' school, but I have only sisters . . . and anyway, my call is as his."

"In such matters," I reminded him gently, "it is the individual's chaldra to please his inner self, the wishes of the mother, the father, or the teacher notwithstanding. Who brought you up?" When Tyith spoke of his father, it was as if he spoke of a hero; when he mentioned his mother, it was as if he spoke of a mystery he'd given up trying to comprehend.

"I spent equal time at my father's farm, where there are well women, and with Vistri bast Fevnell, who raised up Celendra." There was just a hint of defensiveness in his tone.

I was about to comment when Dellin came tearing down the Well steps and stopped dead in his tracks, watching us approach him. I still carried Sereth's common leathers.

"What is it?" I said when he made no move to greet me or step from my path. Suddenly I realized how bright and hot it was that midday, with the sun beating down on our heads from a cloudless sky.

"I have been looking for you since mid-meal, Estri," Dellin said as if it were my fault that he hadn't found me. "Where were you? Who is this? Have you taken to couching children? What is that on your arm? Are you up for the Slayer's chain?"

Khaf-Re Dellin was more angry than I had ever seen him.

"Tyith, take this to the chalder, tell him to check it and do as he sees fit, and that I will come for it this evening. And do not forget about taking your own gear to your father for his inspection."

"I wouldn't have forgotten," Tyith called back over his shoulder, already running.

Dellin shook my arm urgently. "Where *were* you?" he demanded again.

"With Sereth, in the hostel."

"Perhaps if I chain and whip you, you will follow me around, also?"

"You have no right to pass judgment on whom I see, or why. I did not initiate this relationship with the Slayer; it just . . . happened. And furthermore," I said defensively, "unless I am mistaken, you and Sereth between you have apportioned a great deal of my time, both past and future, *and* without my consent. Now, what troubles you?"

"Vedrev has been to see me." Dellin announced.

"And what does the Day-Keeper want with you?"

"What he wants is that I keep my hand out of his affairs. You should know, you and Sereth. I need that witchman's goodwill, and with you and the Slayer pulling power plays, I've nearly lost it already. How was I to know that you're some sort of Day-Keeper's project? He informed me that the Falls of Santha are sacrosanct, and by involving myself in your problems, I was tipping some infernal balance. Crux, he called it. I'd like to crux him! He backed me into a corner and peeled back the layers of my mind like diseased fruit, to see if it's rotten through and through. Then he changed his tune and began going on about the seed-sowers, as if nothing had happened. I'll need the gods of my mother to protect me when the rest of his rank return from conclave! He mentioned that there was no record at any port on Silistra of the arrival of your father, Estrazi; not a ship, not an ID, nothing. If your father came here, which he obviously did, he had either an undetectable space craft, which is impossible, or some way of traveling without spacecraft, which is also impossible."

Three or four knots of people had gathered in the shade near us. I cautioned Dellin to lower his voice.

"That," Dellin continued, "is what triggered my memory. I showed him a map I got just before I left M'ksakka. It's the newest survey ship's work, the first accurate holo of this cluster of stars, taken from a probe on its way to Grieodsa nebula. He agrees with me that it has an uncanny resemblance to the design on your ring. Remember the red stone? There's a red giant in exactly that position. We faxed M'lennin, and he checked the copies he had of your tape against the recording made on the B.F.'s visit to the one inhabitable planet of that system. The syntax and phonemes showed significant similarities to the voice sample we had from you. The reason the first search came up with nothing is that the planet is proscribed, and proscribed data are under a special code. Do you know what it means when a planet is proscribed?"

I shook my head mutely. The hairs stood up all over my body in the hot sun.

"It means that, for one reason or another, a planet is unsuitable for contact. I remember seeing the tapes of first contact with the planet of the red star, which is called Zredori. I'll never forget it: its inhabitants are cannibals, barbarians, and before the eyes of the transmitting camera, disemboweled every member of the first contact party, with great relish. Then we lost the picture. They probably smashed the ship to pieces. They are, truly, animals. Copper-skinned animals. No ship will take you there. Proscription is permanent, not some warning to be ignored at will. There is little resemblance between those savages, shambling about on four limbs with human bones in their ears, and the man I saw, your father, on the tape. Now, what say you?"

*Copper-skinned?* "What did Vedrev say?"

"Nothing fazes that man. His answer was that perhaps two races live on Zredori, and that we met the primitives only, or that they wanted no uninvited guests and chose that manner to so inform us. But he has never seen the contact tape. He still holds to his seed-sower theory. If those are the seed-sowers, senility has come upon them, and they have greatly degenerated. He sent me to tell you, to see what you want to do."

"I will think about it," I said, "on the way to Santha. If there is no way to reach Zredori by starship, if it is indeed the right place, then another way will surely be provided me. My father told me to seek him. I am no uninvited guest."

"If, as Vedrev thinks, these are more than men,

this race from which you sprung, then what are
you?" His finger dug painfully into my arm. "If
you can't conceive with any but your father's
people, and they are degenerate barbarians, then
will you go and live among them? If they are
near-gods, what will you do? You said once you
cared for me. . . ."

He stopped and looked at me, then pulled me
close: "I do not want you to go, Estri. Give up this
quest. It's not worth dying like the trader from
Baniev . . . nothing is. Maybe your father's changed
his mind, and is trying to tell you. If he *is* all-
powerful, he could simply have come here and
taken you. He didn't. Don't go. Please. I can't give
you a logical reason, but you people put a lot of
store in gut instinct, and my gut instinct is telling
me you're walking into something that's a whole
lot more than you're prepared to deal with. Stay
here. Move in with me. . . . We'll work it out."

I experienced no sense of triumph as he pled
with me to stay. I could hardly breathe, so tight
did Dellin hold me there in the Inner Well, with
the growing number of curious onlookers staring
at us.

"Let us go to my keep and talk this thing out
privately. I want to see the star picture."

"I have it with me," Dellin said as we mounted
the steps to the Well.

# VI.
## The Cowled One

When Celendra heard that Sereth intended to take Tyith to Santha, she locked herself in her keep, refusing to eat or to speak, not even to the Slayer himself.

On the second fifth, the day we left Arlet, she had still not broken her fast and her silence. The day dawned bright and humid, a continuation of the unseasonably warm spell that had persisted through the whole set previous.

I met Sereth and Tyith in the Inner Well at first light, wearing the tas jerkin and boots I had brought from Astria and carrying both hunting knife and straight sword, for Dellin had insisted I be fully armed. With me I also had a thick brist-fur pelt for the cold nights to come: high in the Sabembe range, spring would be barely started.

When I first glimpsed the three threx Tyith had brought from Sereth's string, I gasped in admiration: never had I seen such depth of chest, thick-muscled quarters, symmetry of line. From tri-part steel-shod hooves to bristled manes and tiny pointed ears, they were flawless. Their iridescent hides gleamed in the early light as they ate, their wedge-shaped heads thrust deep in buckets of eggs and chunked bondrex. Threx are omnivorous but prefer meat, fresh and raw. One among the three was female, and she shone fire-gold in the early light like a precious stone in between the setting of her large, darker companions. They switched their bristled tails and blew softly through distended nostrils as Tyith fussed over them, rubbing the biggest male, whose steel-blue body already shone like a mirror, with astringent about the pasterns.

With nothing better to do while waiting for his father, I helped Tyith, taking a rag to the black's long legs while Tyith sung the threx's praises and tried to pretend he was not excited.

Sereth did not appear until we had them saddled and the wire-banded bitless headstalls latched around their graceful throats. Issa, the female, had given us a hard time, throwing her head into the air when the harness was presented; I had to hold her by her sensitive ears while Tyith slipped the strap over them and she rolled her huge brown eyes, snorting spray and froth.

"I have never seen their equal," I said to Sereth as he checked the girths to see that they were tight but not binding, and the tailpieces to make certain no bristles were caught in the loops, and the breastplates to make sure that they would keep the saddles of parr-covered wood lined with tas fleece from slipping back as we rode.

"I thought Issa would suit you," he commented as he gave me a leg up and adjusted my stirrups. The threx danced in place when she felt my weight on her, plunging and snuffling until Sereth hit her smartly across the muzzle.

"Quiet down," he said to her. "You'll get all the run you can use, soon enough." Then, to me: "I raced her last year and she still thinks 'ride' means 'run.' But she was unbeaten the entire season." I stroked Issa's twitching neck, already slick with moisture as Sereth stepped back from us for one final, critical scrutiny and then went to his own mount.

When Sereth swung up on Krist, the gigantic black, and wound his reins once around the saddle grip, the black threx stood stock-still for a moment, sniffing the breeze, his head high and ears turned behind, as if to make sure the weight on his back was truly his master, and then, without apparent guidance, ambled toward the Arletian gates, head low to the ground and snaking back and forth, ears flicking.

Issa leaped after him, almost unseating me. I jerked hard back on her, but by that time she was abreast of Krist and content to pace him. I gave her rein, for she pulled fiercely, and when she had it, she settled into a swinging walk.

Sereth nodded. "They both work better with knee than rein. I like a short handle on a threx—keeps them from losing their spirit through overtraining."

I could hear Tyith's mount, Wirin, blowing and jiggling behind us.

The sleepy gatekeeper, near the end of his shift, yawned and stretched as he let us through. Immediately outside the walls of Arlet, Wirin came up on my threx's right-hand side: he did not like going last any more than Issa had.

It was a marvelous morning to set about doing anything; a perfect one for trekking deep into the country in good company on threx as fine as these from Sereth's string. I kept casting sidelong glances at the Slayer easy on his mount beside me: I had not seen Sereth since that day in the hostel, he being busy with the funeral and I with Dellin and Vedrev; I had forgotten how much I liked this calm and competent murderer, how easy it was to feel safe—even optimistic—with him as my body-guard.

It wasn't long until the refreshing morning breezes dissipated and I began looking forward to the cooler air of the mountains, yet I felt happier than I had since I left Astria with Santh. The threx under me was easy-gaited and even, and I exulted in the feel of her muscles between my legs. It would take us about a set to reach the falls, a distance of five hundred neras, more or less: about twice the distance of Arlet from Astria. A threx can easily do eighty neras a day, while a man at a grueling pace might make thirty.

We stopped for a meal in a field of knee-high grass, where a rocky-bottomed stream muttered its way down the gentle slope. Sereth sent the boy to hunt for our food, and Tyith was puffed up with pride as he slunk through the grass with his longbow. Nearby, our threx grazed, hobbled, content with the fresh sweet spring grass.

Though our saddle pouches were filled with dried fruit, pounded denter, and waterskins, we would, whenever possible, eat what the area provided, Sereth explained before he took a strip of denter to Krist; and the big black nuzzled his master's shoulder, dribbling green froth all over the leather I had spent a whole day conditioning.

I stood well back from Krist and his master, watching from a safe distance—threx are unpredictable at best, have been known to turn on their riders, drag them from the saddle, and trample them to death; and Krist was an unaltered male—until Sereth motioned to me to join them.

Standing by Sereth's side and a little behind him, I gingerly scratched the threx's black pointed ears, and the giant beast stretched his neck out and opened his mouth wide, tongue lolling.

"See?" Sereth's sidelong squint was full of

amusement. "Nothing to be afraid of. Krist would never hurt you. My girls rode him when they were the height of his knee. He just makes a great show."

The black threx flattened his ears and nipped lightning fast at his master, as if to prove him wrong. Those mighty teeth snapped together with an audible click, a hair's breadth from the Slayer's arm.

Sereth grabbed him where the nerve endings are exposed on the muzzle, pressing cruelly. The animal closed his eyes and stood shivering until the Slayer released him. With a disapproving snort, Krist dropped his head to the grass. I heard his teeth grinding the tender shoots.

"We will make Morrlta by nightfall," Sereth said, turning from the threx to face me.

"Right now, if the trip took forever, I would not be sorry." I grinned at him and stretched. Here in the rolling field under the midday sun with this man and those incredibly fine threx and the Falls of Santha ahead, I felt reborn. There is nothing like the mountains in spring, with the world waking all around, singing, to give one perspective.

"I have never seen you so relaxed," he said, pulling me toward him.

At that moment, Tyith appeared with a young bondrex, a male with curled horns, over his shoulder. I jumped away from Sereth, smoothing my jerkin.

"Do not be foolish," Sereth said, putting his arm ostentatiously around my waist. "Tyith could not care less where my hand lies at a given moment. He knows me and he knows his mother—perhaps too well. He was point between us, growing up, passed from hand to hand as our tempers and convenience dictated." His stare was brutal. "It was no easy childhood, but an instructive one. And now that he's old enough to couch whoever he chooses without my approval, I certainly do not need his."

That was the first he had ever spoken to me of
his relationship, or lack of one, with Celendra,
mother of his only son. I had wondered, when the
boy had mentioned his upbringing, why the Day-
Keepers had allowed it. It is a Silistran rule never
to suffer the child to become a focus for parental
manipulation. If Sereth and Celendra had not been
so high in Arlet, the disposition of the child would
have been different, I mused as we walked back to
the stream to help Tyith prepare the meat.

And yet Tyith seemed unscarred by his unusual
upbringing; the boy beamed at Sereth's praise over
his hunting prowess, his large eyes dancing with
satisfaction he wasn't concerned to hide—a far cry
from the overly controlled, solemn lad I had first
met in the common room of the Slayers' hostel. It
was obvious to me, if not to his father, that this
boy was allowed to spend much too little time
with his father, whom he so obviously worshipped.

The bondrex was unusually tasty and, at Sereth's
suggestion, young Tyith hacked off the spiraled
horns and packed them carefully in his saddlebag.
Then, as Sereth's son doused the fire and cleaned
the leftovers from the bones for the threx, his father and I collected large stones.

There in the high grassed field we made a circle
of rocks, and Sereth crill Tyris schooled me at
knife and sword in turn. I could not, trying with
all my skill, get through his guard, so I had no
need to pull my stroke. Finally, my right arm aching so I could scarce keep my numbed fingers
around the hilt, I threw the sword to the grass, and
gave him point.

Then I rested while he worked briefly with Tyith.
With the boy, he was very hard, sending the knife
flying from the youth's hand with his second stroke.
With sword, also, he made short work of him. I
thought it cruel, unworthy of the Seven of Arlet, to

deal so ruthlessly with his son's barely emergent skill.

"Perhaps tomorrow you will be able to keep a better hold on your weapons."

Tyith said nothing and turned to fetch the threx.

"He loves you so," I objected when Tyith was out of earshot. "You could have given him, fairly, the courtesy you showed me."

"Do you plan to make your living by the sword and your fitness to bear it? He does. There will always be somebody to fight for you, lady. Tyith will have only the help he can draw from within— and perhaps a lesson or two I can teach him. With you it's play; I like to watch you move. With him it is chaldra. Never will I be easy on him. Easy is not what a Slayer's life is about. One day, he may be able to knock the knife from my hand on the second stroke. When and if he can, he will. I can only hope I'll live to see it—and that he will. Until then, it is necessary for both of us to know that he cannot." His eyes were hard. Sereth of Arlet did not like criticism.

I shrugged and turned from him to help Tyith with the threx, reminding myself of the low worth of words: I had often found it served me better to keep silent. Especially with this man, I had been foolish to break my custom.

We harnessed and mounted and returned to the Morrltan road in silence. Issa, as usual, could not suffer being second, so Sereth and I rode abreast, with Wirin and Tyith bringing up the rear. The road became dirt-and-stone path, the fields scarce; forest thickened. We began to climb, the threx scrambling up what was now only rocky trail. Once, Wirin stumbled and almost fell. Both Tyith and Sereth dismounted to check Wirin's tri-shod front foot and determined that the mid-shoe was loose, and so we walked them slowly toward Morrlta proper, where we could perhaps have the nails redriven. We arrived, well past dusk, under a rising gibbous moon, at the outskirts of Morrlta, the pelter town that has its few crude log buildings at the Sabembe's very feet.

We did not venture into Morrlta proper, but stopped at a group of four low wooden shacks perhaps five neras from town. Sereth felt that we would be safer in the tiny, ill-lit room he bought from the grizzled innkeeper than in the Morrltan town, where one could have found at least indoor plumbing.

We ate greasy overcooked stew sopped up with binnirin bread and drank the poor vintage of kifra served to us by one of the innkeeper's coin girls. There were perhaps a dozen others present in the roadhouse: pelters and mountain men, loud and drunken, who were drinking much more than they ate at one of the other hand-hewn tables. One grabbed the coin girl who served us—a light-haired, fair-skinned girl with four digits on each hand—as she came toward us to serve kifra. The pitcher dropped from her grasp and smashed on the dirt floor.

Tyith was on his feet, sword drawn, before Sereth could stop him. The Seven slid from his seat and touched the boy's shoulder. Tyith shook him off.

"Let her go, slime," young Tyith said forcefully in a fair imitation of his father.

I saw Sereth's eyes flick around the room and his hand go to his hilt. He did not, however, draw his blade.

One could have sliced the silence. The bearded pelter who had the blond coin girl on his lap looked Tyith slowly up and down, then his father, a pace behind.

"Did you want her for the night, Slayer?" The pelter grimaced, revealing broken teeth.

Sereth had his knife in hand now, cleaning his nails.

"If it's any of your business, pelt-monger, yes, maybe I do want her. But what I want more is for you to take your grimy hands off her, and pay for that pitcher you just broke—you just bought it. And now the girl has to go fetch us another. We get angry when we're thirsty."

The bearded, swarthy pelter stared hard at Sereth and cast a quizzical look at me as I came up beside Tyith. Then he grumbled something, shrugged, and released the girl, who darted back toward the bar.

The pelter was now leaning on the table with both hands in plain sight, elaborately picking his teeth with a pottery shard: "I need no trouble with Slayers this early in the season," he said in a placatory way. I could feel the tension ease. "She is bony, anyhow." He turned his back to us. He had not acceded to Tyith's demand that he pay for the kifra. Chairs scraped as his companions relaxed, and they bent their heads over their drinks.

Tyith bristled and took a step forward, as if he might push the matter. Sereth put his arm around the boy's shoulders and said quietly, as he took a pair of gold dippars from his pouch, "Use these on that girl, since you fancy her enough to risk all our lives for her," then turned toward me:

"We'll want an early start. And I have to see the smith an hour before first light." As we left, Sereth tossed a half-dippar amid the remains of the meal. He had well-tipped the four-fingered girl.

"Try to stay out of trouble, and be at the stall before the shoer, with Wirin in good order," he said to Tyith, his hand on the back of his son's neck, before we went upstairs.

Thus Sereth and I spent the night alone together in our filthy, ill-lit room, on a feather-stuffed pallet set on a web-cloth grill which sank toward the middle and creaked when one moved with the strain of web against the wooden frame.

"There are bugs in this place," I complained. "I can feel them. I cannot sleep here." I twitched and itched, just thinking about it.

"There are bugs in the open, also. They do not bother you unduly there. What difference a bug on the ground, or a bug on the couch? Take off your clothes."

I did, and climbed with much distaste between the damp-smelling covers. Sereth brought my knife and his with him, sliding his by the blade between pallet and frame. He handed me mine, and I did the same.

Sometime later, when I lay, unable to move, drained in mind and body, panting and sweat-dampened atop the rumpled and wadded covers, Sereth rose and slapped my rump smartly, going with blade in hand to check the door. Whatever he had heard, I had not.

"Bounce," he hissed. As I obediently bounced and thrashed, he jerked the door violently open.

But there was no one there. Watching Sereth put his free hand on the doorjamb, then lean his hand on it and peer in both directions, I lay silent, listening.

When he left the room, I closed my eyes to listen harder. All I heard were Sereth's footsteps up and down the hall.

When he came back, he was shaking his head as if in disgust: "Nothing," he said, closing the door and throwing the bolt. "But either I heard footsteps, or my ears are lying to me."

Instead of coming directly back to bed, he went to the shuttered window and opened it, letting in the risen moon's light and the clear, starry night, and stood there relieving himself.

When he had finished at the window, he left it

open and, roughly pulling the covers aside, climbed under them with me. I took no notice: when he had opened the shutters, I had seen, clear and sharp, hovering in the moonlight, a cowled figure wrapped in shadow, peering in at me from its perch in midair. Within the shadow I could see only eyes, burning, pulsing bronze. But Sereth had not seen. He had calmly relieved himself at the window and come to couch. It had been so real that the reality of the room within which I lay had become dwarfed, overshadowed by the cowled one's presence.

I said nothing about it to Sereth, but it was long before I slept, before my heavy lids closed of their own accord, blocking the peaceful night sky from my view.

And in my dreams, the apparition reappeared amid a sliding time-scape, calling out to me from an ice-silvered peak. I tried to resist, but the ground under my feet turned to a rushing river which carried me, its current running backward, closer and closer to that beckoning shape. I woke before I reached it, dry-mouthed, shaking.

The sky, predawn soft and colorless, greeted me, whispering windsong. I lay a long while staring at the clouds. Sereth was, I assumed, with the shoer. I dressed quickly and went to meet him, disdaining another meal from the innkeeper's squalid kitchen.

"I was just coming to rouse you," said the Slayer as I descended the steps to the yard. Wirin, Issa, and Krist were harnessed and ready, Tyith already mounted.

I avoided the Slayer's hand and went to Issa, swinging up on her back without assistance. She sidestepped, jiggling. Sereth took her head, stroking her, looking up at me. A wild wind blew moist and cold, promising a storm soon to come.

"What troubles you, lady?" he asked me, while

Tyith looked on with an expression that said: I knew it; women are all alike.

I had no answer which would make any sense, so perhaps Tyith was right; telling Sereth about a dream even I could not fathom certainly was wrong. So I said: "I am only anxious to be away from here."

"That is easily done." He let go Issa and mounted Krist, who stamped and blew his impatience, and we left Morrlta at a lope, heading due north, toward Santha.

Before long, all semblance of trail had disappeared and the rain and wind down from the north beat the air from my lungs. Our threx steamed as the cold wet hit their hot, straining bodies. Issa's muzzle seemed to drag along the rocky ground as she picked her way up the treacherous slope. I could see Krist's hindquarters ahead, bunching, sweat and rain running in rivulets down his legs as he hazarded the steep climb, Sereth bent over his withers.

In no time, I was wet and miserable, shivering, muddy, and cold. The sun had made no appearance by midday, nor did we stop to eat, and it was all I could do, leaning forward with my chest against the threx's plunging neck, to keep my seat as she scrambled and hopped her way along a treacherous streambed coursing runoff that seemed to go on forever.

When I was sure I would fall from the saddle numb with exhaustion, Krist's rear, in front of me, finally halted. I had seen nothing but his flanks for neras. The black stood, head low, heaving. His legs were widespread and he trembled. Issa laid her muzzle on his rump. Krist did not even twitch his bristled tail.

Sereth turned in his saddle, his face begrimed, pointed off to the right, and kicked Krist into motion. Speech would have been a gift to the howling wind, which already begrudged us breath.

We trudged through trailless forest, branches snapping against us, for what seemed another day, finally emerging into a clearing where a building of calked stones had once stood. Now it was crumbling and roofless, but its standing walls still offered some shelter from the storm.

Dismounting, we led the threx through the stone-littered yard and the open space that had once been a door. The punishing wind and much of the rain excluded by the high walls, we huddled together and ate dried fruit and meat from our stores. There was no way to walk out the threx, so they stood, steaming, shifting their weight from foot to foot.

"Are you still in love, Tyith?" Sereth asked when we had eaten our fill and were resting, steaming a bit ourselves with our backs to one cold stone wall. The wind's howl had diminished to a whine; the storm seemed to be abating.

"I am," said Tyith in a husky voice.

"He thinks he got the coin girl with child," Sereth explained to me. "That is truly what I need—two more mouths to feed. Tyith, if you still want her on the way home, and if she *is* pregnant and has not told her master, you might bid for her."

If she *had* told her master, the chance of fulfilling chaldra would not be easily bought. Even to the rightful father, the price would be high. If a man owns a coin girl, any issue from that girl is considered his. This is an incentive to the master to keep his girls in good condition. Tyith would be stealing the child from under the rightful legal guardian if the girl was pregnant and he succeeded in purchasing her.

"Bid for her?" Tyith repeated, grinning widely.

"If you want her," Sereth amended.

"Of *course* I do," said the youth, scrambling to his feet, taking the pelt that had covered the three of us with him.

"Give that back, you dorkat whelp!" Sereth of Arlet scrambled after his son. He caught and downed the lad, and the two wrestled playfully, twisted in the brist pelt.

Something in me was pleased that Sereth had not discouraged Tyith from involving himself with the four-fingered coin girl. Or perhaps it was just that, for the first time that day, the sun broke through the overcast, showing the time to be around third second, or fifth bell in Arlet. Our twenty-eight-enth day is divided into four sevens. Midday is second seventh, midnight is fourth seventh. The bells have so rung since hide days.

The warmth of the sun called me. I stretched and stood, wishing the dampness out of my aching muscles. It felt as if my back and bottom bore the imprint of every stone in the wall. Such a change had the sunlight wrought that, as I looked around me where monochrome had become stone and grass, clover and mud, and the dark rich forest beyond the clearing enticing rather than forbidding, it was as if I were in a place entirely new. Such weight we put upon what our eyes see and body feels. This had been a distressing, ugly place in the storm-gray cold. It was now pleasant, perhaps even picturesque, with the red-gold light and warmth upon it—or upon me.

I went to Issa, while Sereth and Tyith were sorting the harness, and picked out the stones from between shoes and inner hooves before I went to get my gear. The threx and I were beginning to develop a rapport, and I wanted to encourage her. She stood easily for me as I slipped the headstall over her ears and looped the girths that held the saddle tight.

Soon we were mounted and cutting back through dense trees the way we had come, but the spray from the dripping needled branches glittering in the sun was far preferable to the gloom and wind and rain that had driven us before it to the crumbled shelter.

Once on the almost invisible trail, however, the mud proved increasingly difficult. The threx floundered and skidded, and only their mountain ancestry saved them, a dozen times, from nasty falls as we picked our way up one of the unnamed foothills of the Sambembe range.

Toward dusk we gained the rounded plateau, heavily forested, that would host us for the night. Ahead for the morrow was harder going, and well into twilight we loped among trees that were so high-branched we had no need to crouch down to avoid low limbs, in order to make what time we could in the last light and get an edge on the morning's climb.

Suddenly I heard a sharp crack and Issa leaped high into the air. Thrown forward onto her neck, I grabbed with both hands in her bristled crest just as, in two jumps, she passed Krist and, head held high, plunged ahead at breakneck speed with her reins dangling loose around her legs. Foolishly, I was leaning over to grab one instead of looking where we were going when she bunched under me and launched herself into the air. I did not make the jump with her. I was first aware of the rope stretched between the trees when I landed on it. It wrenched my back badly, but broke my fall, which nonetheless knocked the wind from my lungs and the sight from my eyes.

When the pulse pounding red before my eyes and loud in my ears receded and, painfully, my burning lungs drew in air once more, I struggled to lift myself onto hands and knees.

Still I could not hear clearly, but my lifted eyes saw in slow motion, dreamlike, Krist's belly above me as he leaped to avoid trampling me.

Wirin was riderless, a knot of men about him. I saw Tyith, his blade flashing. Then the lad was down in the midst of them, and Krist's hoofbeats shook the ground as Sereth and his threx plunged into the middle of the men who had his son trapped between them.

Krist squealed and thrashed in rage, great-toothed jaws snapping at the men gathered around him. Sereth hacked at them from the bloody-mouthed beast's back. Gore flew in chunks. The ground was slippery, covered with it. I saw a head, severed, roll under the savage threx's legs and be crushed gray and pulpy. I saw Sereth's sword cleave a man from shoulder to breastbone, where it lodged. He was drenched red, his arms dripping.

I tried to rise, to help, for there were many hands at him, trying to drag him from the saddle, and he with only knife to keep them back, but my legs wouldn't obey me. I was rooted from the knees to the earth—and not by fear or some consequence of the spill I had taken. The first time one's limbs are found to be under another's control is a terrifying moment.

I struggled, tossing my head wildly. Then I saw it, from the corner of my eye.

It hovered at the edge of my vision so that I could not turn to face it, that cowled figure, from dream and vision spawned, and it spoke echoing words in my mind while the wind blew at its cowl, whipping and snapping.

The voice I heard was wind, also; wind from the chasm at the edge of the world: *"Give up,"* it demanded. *"Turn back and forget. Leave this mystery unsolved forever, these stones you seek unturned, and save what days you may."*

My heart convulsed in fear, yet my body did not tremble, nor my mind run in circles like the caged beast who sees its death approaching. Instead, from deep behind my awareness, that which guides me spoke, void-toned and ringing. The fear of me listened numbly to its nonverbal counsel, and then I knew what I must say.

"You cannot deny me my birthright," I told it. "You cannot stop me by your own hand. This thing will be, and you cannot block it."

"I will." This time its voice did not thunder, but whispered in my head, a promise given with a glee I was not wise enough then to understand. "I have. Those who aid you—will you give them death as a fit price for this 'birthright' of yours? This world—will you give it up? If you open the way beyond, who will use it? You cannot say, you do not know, you will never be strong enough to control what now you think you want."

"Do speak more," I said to it, "that I may know you when we meet again." My terrified self crouched scrabbling at the edge of sanity. The power within me took no notice.

"Dissolution will certainly accompany you." The bronze fires from my dreams burned inside my mind as his voice like smelting bronze seemed to issue from it. "Blood and death mark your path."

"In flesh or spirit, I will find you, when I am strong. You cannot harm me—you are forbidden." I didn't know how I knew this; the words just came but I did not doubt their truth. "I, on the other hand, am bound by no such injunction. Let his will be done." And then that power which possessed me from without receded, leaving me with my terror, kneeling, trembling violently on the ground. Its image, too, was gone from where I'd seen it. Everything was as it had been before—almost.

There was no cowled one among the trees any longer. There was no sound but the blowing and stamping of threx. There were no men fighting, oblivious to another battle I had fought.

Freed from my paralysis, I rose unsteadily. Behind me was Krist, knee-deep in gory corpses, his muzzle bloodied almost to the eye sockets. He seemed unhurt, munching there among the dead, but very much alone.

Sereth was my only thought as I ran among the corpses and the carnage, backed the threx and pulled at the mangled bodies; but of the seven I turned, none was the man I sought, and none lived.

Tearing my hair away from my face with bloody hands, I peered into the twilight and the trees, searching for some sign of Sereth. Perhaps he had dragged himself, wounded, to hiding. I saw nothing that would indicate a wounded man had dragged himself or crashed into the brush.

Slowly, my eyes on the ground looking for discrete signs in the chaotic mud, I made my way under the rope stretched between the trees, to Wirin and the second clump of still forms beyond. I felt no pain, no emotion, just empty cold.

I found them both there, in the fading light, beyond the steel-blue threx. Four motionless bodies lay on their backs, turning blind eyes to the sky. A fifth form squatted over the last, still as death.

Sereth, expressionless, stared down into the smiling face of his only son. I remember thinking it odd that Tyith smiled, as I bent to close his sightless eyes and noticed the deep chest wound, pulled back in rictus, wide as my hand, that had killed him.

Then I sat by the boy's shoulder, facing Sereth, who ignored me, as darkness fell and the moon rose. Twice I spoke to the Slayer, but he did not seem to hear. I cried a long while.

Much later, I heard Krist's trumpeting bellow, and an answer, and I knew Issa was back. I thought I should feed them, but then I remembered the grisly feast at Krist's feet. When I felt able, I went to Wirin and got the tools and gathered wood and made a fire. It was a cold night in the foothills of the Sabembe.

When I had the blaze crackling steady, I caught the threx and hobbled them, took the brist pelt from Issa's cantle, and went to rouse Sereth: there are limits to grief, to what is healthy for the living.

I had had long enough to think about the day's tragedy, what might have been, what had to be. I had wrestled with my guilt by the dead boy's side. My help, had the cowled thing not interposed itself so that I was unable to give it, would have done Tyith little good. He had died before my eyes in those first moments, while I grasped at consciousness under the rope and Krist's belly. That I was guilty as a catalyst was a certainty: if not involved with me, the boy would have lived. So the cowled one had not lied to me, although its warning had come too late for Tyith, even if I had heeded it. But I was not willing to take the weight for that burden, nor to let the cowled one claim Tyith's death as both his prophesy and his doing. Crux calls its children home, all of us, sometime, and it chooses who and when, according to a rhythm we cannot perceive.

"Sereth . . ." I leaned between him and the body, to cover the corpse with the brist pelt. Putting both hands on his shoulders, I touched my cheek to his.

"Sereth," I whispered, "please talk to me," I shook him.

Finally his gaze turned outward in his set face, flicker-lit by the fire. He shrugged my hands off and stood awkwardly. He had been crouched too long in the same position.

His voice when he spoke was rough and thick; his stare struck me like a physical blow: "I knew it. I could feel it coming. But what can a man say to his son about groundless fears until they're not groundless? . . ." He broke off, spread his hands, then continued: "I knew it then, and I *tried* to protect him, thought I could do it if I kept him with me. . . . I *led* him to his death by trying to stave it off. . . . But Celendra knew exactly what I was doing. Mourning him that way, before we even left . . ." His eyes cut into me with every question I could not answer, and he cursed and sank back down by the brist-fur-covered corpse, and his shoulders shook, and I left him and tended the fire until he came and held me.

I held back my own tears for his sake, as he had held back his wrath for mine, and eventually he released me and sat staring into the fire, red-eyed, swollen-faced, silent.

When I could face it, I offered him dried meat, but he shook his head, and after the first salty, stringy bite, I put it down. My mouth was too dry to make eating more than a chore.

We sat there together all night long, huddled against each other close to the fire. When the jitkaws took rhythm song and the black sky above us steeled, he put his arm around me.

"We will give him to the falls," he said. I had wondered what to do with the body. We could not fire him, here in the forests, as was proper, and we could not bury the body on this rocky shelf or leave it in the open. But if he were wrapped in the brist pelt and thrown from the Falls of Santha, his spirit would certainly find its destined rest.

"What happened to you when you fell?" he asked suddenly.

I told him. He had a right to know. And finally I told him about the dreams and the apparition at

the window at Morrlta, and the demands the cowled
one had made of me while he and Tyith had bat-
tled for our lives. I told him also what I had
realized, and experienced, in those moments: that
the cowled one could not touch me himself; only
through others could he harm me. When he asked
me why I thought that was, I couldn't answer
either of us satisfactorily.

I did advise him to take Tyith's body back to
Arlet, and let me continue on my own, but both of
us knew he would not do so.

"He died well, and I would not belittle him by
leaving the task we took up unfulfilled." He had
control, save that his tone was that cold, flat quiet
that chilled me. "Anyway, I gave my word to Vedrev
and his lot that I'd see you up to Santha and back
safely. I have to do that."

"I grieve with you," I said softly, as he rose and
damped the fire, "but I need you, and my need
makes me selfish—I am glad we will go the rest of
the way together. I shall say the words for Tyith
with you at Santha." I knew nothing else to do.

We took sword belts from the dead men and
with them bound the brist pelt tight around Tyith's
body. He seemed smaller, somehow, in death, and
light. Some of the men were chalded, some chaldless, and it was odd that they should have banded
together. By rights we should have taken the
chalded, or their belts at least, to the Day-Keepers,
but we left them, instead, for the forest scavengers.
Tyith we hoisted across Wirin's quivering back.

The smell of death was on his master and the
steel-gray threx did not like it. When he turned his
head and sniffed at the brist-wrapped bundle slung
across his back, Wirin's ears went back; he lifted
his head and uttered an awful trumpeted wail,
and then stood, head between his knees, quiet, while
we tied Tyith's body firmly to saddle and girth.

As the day unfolded, Sereth and I explored what I soon came to realize was an altered relationship. The pace he set was difficult both for me and the threx, with short stops but no real rest, but that was only the first sign of the change between us—or inside him.

All too soon I realized that I was now just another commission to him, another woman. He was no harder on me than he had been the day we met, but the softenings, the little considerations, the wordless gestures that had been between us affirmation of a growing empathy, were conspicuously absent. Once, I had wanted desperately to please the discriminating Sereth of Arlet, larger-than-life legend. When he had denigrated me, I had implemented a plan to make him court me at the very level he had chosen to put me, and I had succeeded. Until Tyith. Now I had lost all the ground I had gained with him. It was a measure of his strength that he did not openly blame me, for he would have been within his rights.

He merely retreated into himself, becoming once again that distant, intense, time-hoarding Slayer who had fancied me in Arlet. And the further he pushed me from him, the more I craved our former intimacy. I would have gladly borne him a son to replace the one I had helped him lose, if only I could have so commanded my self-willed reproductive system. That I could not do. Nothing less, I was sure, would suffice.

My musings were interrupted around sun's set, when we came upon a wild golachit who had somehow fallen from the ledge above to land on his back wedged between two large angular boulders. The giant insect's strident high-octave whine had attracted perhaps a dozen of his fellows, from threx length to thrice that long, who clustered together below the giant lying with its legs waving, wedged between the rocks.

The other golachits of his nest were keening. But no golachit will move to help another right itself, for such a death is common to them, natural, and right—or so Sereth said, rejecting my hypothesis that they simply had no idea how to do it.

Dismounting and scrambling to its side, we could see the softer underbelly, already cracked, and the bubbling blue froth on its perpendicular excrescence tube. Its great recessed eyes followed us. The chitinous shell seemed undamaged. Another day of exposure to the sun would surely finish it, if the night-hunting ebvrasea did not plunge their cruel beaks deep in its belly. An ebvrasea could not kill a golachit with its eight legs under it, but an overturned one is helpless.

Sereth walked quickly back to the threx, returning with a long, soft web-fiber rope. This he looped around the golachit's body, wedging it between thorax and head. The giant amber golachit clicked its mandibles weakly.

Sereth handed me a section of the long line and I kept it tight around the golachit while the Slayer played the coil to its end. He backed Wirin carefully up the rocky incline, until he could run the slack through the breast band around the steed's chest, then mounted and urged the threx forward.

The big threx's muscles bunched as he strained against the rope until he was sitting on his hind legs in his effort, but the overturned golachit did not budge. The web-rope hummed with strain until Sereth called to the threx to stop pulling.

My heart sank. I knew it was just a life-affirming gesture, a balm to our own hearts and nothing more, but I wanted to save that golachit and I knew he did too.

First the Slayer checked the threx's saddle, every girth and buckle, then the rope; then he went hand-over-hand down the rope to the golachit, fiddled around it, and came slowly back as the other golachits clicked their mandibles and watched him with their weird insect eyes.

Sereth hunkered down, arms crossed over his knees and just stared at the situation pensively—the golachit, the rocks, the played line. Then he got up, went back down the rope to the insect, and pushed at its shell while its legs waved in the air.

No matter what success he'd had in loosening the golachit wedged in the rocks, as Sereth came back up the slope, I realized he was going to try once more. Foam flecked Wirin's chest as he gamely struggled to move the wedged weight. Stones flew under his hooves, but to no avail.

This time, when he yelled to the threx to cease pulling, I was sure he would retrieve his line and leave the insect to its fate.

But instead, leaving Wirin harnessed, he brought Krist carefully beside him, backing the second threx cautiously through the jumbled rocks. There was barely room for the two threx to stand abreast with level footing under them, but finally he had them positioned and then backed them in unison so that he could get the rope around both their mighty chests.

That done, he stood before them, retreating slowly, calling. A good distance in front of them, he stopped, raised both hands, and whistled shrilly.

Grunting, the threx threw themselves against the rope, determined to get to their master. The golachit's hard shell grated against the rocks, and it was free.

The threx's lunging carried them thundering forward, and Sereth, running, narrowly escaped being trampled.

The golachit lay on its side, stunned for a moment. The keening of its fellows abruptly stopped. All that could be heard was rock settling, pebbles rolling, and the snorts of hard-breathing threx. Then, with a hissing squeak, the golachit righted itself, rocking on outstretched legs, until its teetering bulk fell heavily on its belly. It still wore the rope around it.

Sereth, coiling the slack in his hand, went slowly toward it, then paused directly in front of it, showing no fear, before he walked up to its head and disengaged the loop.

Only when he had retreated out of reach of those deadly mandibles did I dare breathe. A golachit is an intelligent being, but this one had lain in torture under the sun for long hours.

Cocking its head at him, the golachit stood quietly, weaving on its eight legs, its excrescence tube stretched out before it, and from that tube came two tiny drops of fire-red gol. Then the golachit, with amazing agility for a creature of such great size, turned on its back legs and scrabbled across the rocks to join its fellows, who twittered and chittered at each other as their number closed around the amber giant protectively, and the whole herd moved off into the rocks, shadow on shadow in the failing light.

I scrambled down from my perch against the boulders. Sereth had picked up the gol drops by the time I reached him. They were blood-pulse in his palm. Red gol material is secreted only at times of great joy or crisis, and is priced higher among us than any precious stone. The golachit had amply thanked us for aiding it.

Sereth did not offer me the drops, even to hold, but put them in his belt. I went silently to Issa and stroked her tender nose, where the skin is bare near the nostrils. I felt very lonely, and I was glad to have the threx's head rubbing against my shoulder. She closed her eyes, her jaw resting on my neck, and sighed heavily. Issa was tired. It had been a grueling day on this rugged path. The trees had dwindled and shrunken, and soon we would not even have their meager shelter, for the Falls of Santha, birthplace of the mighty Litess River, lie almost at the snow line.

Sereth checked both threx's legs and quarters in turn, running his hands over first Krist and then Wirin. He then examined their shoes and cleaned the gravel from their inner hooves. When he was satisfied that both were sound, he used some of the coiled rope to attach Wirin's halter to the cantle of Krist's saddle, and mounted the black.

I thought, as my threx followed Wirin up the tas trail, that it was a wonder Tyith's body had not come loose from its bonds. But it bobbled, brist-wrapped, in front of me along the trail until my eyes could not distinguish it any longer in the dark and Sereth was forced to call a halt for the day, lest one of the threx lame itself in a crevice in the dark.

There was no place suitable for a camp, but we found a level stretch wide enough for the animals to stand abreast, with some scrawny needle trees and sparse grass. We used our waterskins that night, mostly for the threx, and our stored foods. The moon was coming up, the night dry and clear. It seemed much quieter here in the mountains. My breathing sounded loud in my ears; the threx's teeth ground and grated rhythmically. Sereth disdained a fire, though the night was chill, and I huddled against him for warmth, glad for such physical contact in the wake of death and anxious for his more intimate touch, but nothing came of it.

When he lay down to sleep with me, I felt even colder, more alone, than before. It seemed to me then that it was I who had been hurt deeply by Tyith's death and he who had recovered unscathed.

Resentful in my isolation, I felt the need to hurt back.

"What will you do about your son's child?" I said to Sereth when I was sure he was almost asleep.

"What?" He rolled to face me, eyes heavy-lidded

in the moonlight and all of his bones casting black shadows that made him look like a granite statue in one of my schoolhalls.

"I said, what will you do about your son's child? Though she is a coin girl, by her grace, Tyith has begotten a child—fulfilled his chaldra. Surely you won't consider leaving the spawn of your own blood to grow up in a Morrltan tavern?"

Sereth of Arlet made a rude noise and turned his back to me. But I was awake long into the evening while he tossed and turned and occasionally muttered or clenched his fists beside me. Finally, my satisfaction lulled me and I slept, mercifully dreamlessly, until he woke me before the sun's rise:

"Get up." He shook me so that the back of my head bounced against the hard ground.

I pushed peace away, slipping back into my stiff body like a rider long away from the saddle. I managed to get my elbows under me, and felt the Slayer's hands leave my shoulders, and the shaking cease.

"What do *you* think I should do, Estri?"

"About what?" I asked innocently.

"About the coin girl." He threw a strip of dried meat in my lap.

I threw it back. I would do without rather than eat that foul stuff another day.

"Take her home, Sereth, and have your well women raise her child. She is not so badly deformed that you cannot find some use for her. What the child will be like," I said wickedly, "is anyone's guess. You may try a physician, but even if the child is deformed, or an idiot, it is still the only issue of your dead son. What else can you do but take the girl and provide her and your grandson the best possible home?" I tried not to let my pleasure show. The last thing Sereth crill Tyris would want is a child of the type that so often results from such a union. But I had spoken truly—there was no fit thing to do but take the pregnant mother in.

And he knew it.

"Are you so sure there will be a child?" He stood over me, hands on his hips, his fists clenched, no smile in his deep brown eyes now, his face showing the strain of his loss in every muscle and the very tone of his skin so that it seemed he had aged a year in the night.

"Are you so unsure that you will ignore Tyith's wishes? When he was alive, you gave him permission—even advised him—to make her a member of your family. I saw how those words of yours pleased him. In death, can you possibly owe him less than in life?"

The Slayer turned from me, mute, and went to harness the threx.

I smiled to myself and followed. Such verbal swordplay is woman's game, and in it I can usually count point. And I *was* sure that the coin girl had conceived: I looked at her when the question first arose, and I had seen the egg in the womb, silver on red, and the sperm swim, and their ultimate connection. The sharpness and self-mobility of the image denoted truth. In such simple psychic function, I am as good as any.

Issa was cranky, twitching her ears and snapping the air, but no real trouble. I wondered, as I fitted her gear, what had made her bolt that afternoon. I remembered the cracking sound I had heard. And those thoughts led me to wonder how extensive the cowled one's ability to control material reality truly was.

I was soon to find out.

By the time the sun, directly overhead, cast no shadow, we had gained the plateau of Santha and turned due east, and were making our way across the relatively flat rocky ground with ease. To our left, the Sabémes towered, ice caps glittering, and the wind that swept down upon us from those heights was dry and chill.

The air up here was noticeably thinner, so that my lungs seemed ever-hungry and my pulse was continually thumping in my ears and, though I was grateful when Sereth called a halt, I couldn't seem to regain my former vigor.

Though the view to our right—of the foothills we had climbed, and Morrlta and Arlet spread out below, mantled in mist—was magnificent, I found I wasn't enjoying it: the apprehension I felt all morning had consolidated into precognition, an impossible vision of a future to come in which I seemed to be finding and losing everything at once in a chaotic universe full of stars and days to come. My body was chilled with the distress that came with this forereading which, unbidden and unwelcome, now plagued me, my stomach aching and cramping. Yet the vision was unclear and the apprehensive feeling seemed unnatural, even ungrateful—I was forereading, wasn't I? I should have been glad. And yet I knew, somehow, that what I was experiencing was not forereading as Celendra or some other seeress might do it, and I was not glad at all to be feeling such inexpressable dread.

For something to occupy my mind, I explored the rocks, looking for something I could not find, and came away dissatisfied.

Sereth, lounging with his back to a large boulder, watched me, unspeaking, the drawn look that had taken his angular features and made them harsh gone now, as if he had found comfort in the mountains and sustenance for his spirit somewhere along the trail.

I envied him his quick recovery—I was not so resilient. I still saw Tyith's shock of auburn hair and his sloe-eyed face—saw that face unnaturally pale and smiling up at the sky, while in his chest a gaping hole smiled also. It seemed impossible to me that a man, even a man whose profession was killing, could be so quickly healed from such a loss. He was not healed, of course; but I did not understand Sereth, nor even how men deal with death, and one is always hostile to what one does not understand.

I collapsed beside him, content to let my pumping lungs rest and my lungs stop burning.

"What did you see?" The unspoken laughter was again in his brown eyes and he spoke as casually as if we were once again in the drink room in Arlet.

"Nothing. I saw nothing—would that I had. We'll need shelter tonight—safe shelter, if such a thing exists here. I have a feeling, and I dare not ignore it this time."

His eyes searched mine, the glint in them no longer a smile, but some sharper, professional light. I had thought he would dismiss my fears out of hand.

"I know a place," he said slowly. "A cave, with good cover, easy to defend. Will that do? What do you sense?"

Defend from what? I could not say, but the weight I felt lightened: he hadn't mocked me, but believed me and took me seriously.

"How far?" I asked.

"We could make it before sun's set. The cowled man—thing, spirit, whatever it is—is that what you fear?"

I nodded.

Sereth shifted against the rocks, his hand unconsciously going to his sword hilt, loosening it in its scabbard, his eyes flicking over the shadows around us. "I wish this were over and done with, and you safely back in Arlet," he said with a deep exhalation.

Touching his shoulder, I told him: "You and I

will part at the Falls of Santha. I won't burden your return—you will be able to set your own pace." I had known since my confrontation with the cowled one but I hadn't faced it—watching him there, realizing how dear his quiet competence and the steel beneath it had become, how much I would miss his sidelong, appreciative glances, his offhanded touch, the surety in his face and body that calmed me and made me notice the color of the sky and the tenor of the wind in a way I'd never known before. I admitted it now, aloud, and became deeply and inexpressably sad—and not only over his loss, on my account, of his son.

And he, understanding nothing of what I felt, said in that pragmatic way of his: "You are no burden that I didn't willingly take up. Remember that day out behind the Well in Arlet? I started this thing with you, and I'll finish it. What happens, happens. No well woman of my acquaintance is going to face that . . . thing . . . or these mountains alone. And that has nothing to do with Vedrev, or Dellin, or your hunger for chaldra—it's got to do with me . . . my sense of fitness. I finish what I start."

"I will find my way from Santha, and it is a path for one person only." I tried again to make it clear. "If we make it there, you will have discharged your duty. The rest has nothing to do with what I want, or what you want, or what Dellin or Vedrev wants. It is fixed—ineluctable. I will go on and you will stay behind."

I did not underestimate the cowled one. Within the available probabilities, it seemed to me that I would make it to Santha. I was not so sure about the Slayer. But my recently surfaced scanning skill was adamant. To discuss it further would solidify a time line unacceptable to me.

"Women! Nothing is 'fixed,' except that in order

to fulfill my commitment to Dellin, I must return you in good shape to Arlet. At least, I hope not. If your inner voice is whispering secrets in your ear again, I suggest you share your information with me. If you had done so before, we might have fared better." That was the first time he had spoken of my complicity in Tyith's death.

Yet I could not tell him more than I had.

"I have no specifics, just a feeling," I lied, to protect him. "But give me some time, and I will go and see what I can see."

He nodded, and I lay back against the rocks and prepared my body for trance. Not, as I had said, to clarify my feeling, but to do what I might to shift and solidify the time flow as best I could. I could not alter the draw to crux, but perhaps I could designate which approach we would take.

I made my heartbeat and respiration slow, which left my limbs cold and tingling. Sounds around me became magnified, then faded, leaving me floating, with unfeeling flesh, in the red-dark where the time tracks meet. Into the ball of writhing color I went, instinctively, for I had never been taught to do so, finding my branching line and Sereth's, luminous and intertwined amid countless unborn tomorrows.

I did what was needed. My own line, before me, twisting mist of unsolidified reality, ceased to branch and became clear. Like a great pulsing ball, the crux sucked all the alternatives within itself. I could not seen beyond. Not one twisting path toward the crux failed to enter it. I wanted no more foreknowledge; my mind reeled. Yet I found the strength to enter Sereth's flow, to disentangle his from mine just before the great ball devoured it, and to cause the sharp cessation of his line to fold back upon itself and become absorbed. As I watched, new branches sprouted from that spot, so close to crux, and drifted away tangentially. It was enough. I saw the main path firm and take color, and I knew I had done all I could. I pushed back from the flickering probabilities, and floated free until my body claimed me.

I found my eyes and caused the lids to open. The numbness drained slowly from my limbs, and I felt the wind tickle my face with strands of hair, and my ears again sorted sound. I saw the sun, still high, and Sereth, his position unchanged. What had been done had taken only moments.

When the tingling was gone, I sat up and met his questioning gaze. I shook my head as if nothing had been accomplished.

Sereth got to his feet and extended his hand to me. I took it and rose, and he put his arms around me, holding me close, stroking my back.

"You lie to me, lady," he said softly in my ear. "But I will not press you. I, too, sometimes see."

Eventually he released me, that we might make the cave before dark.

Not long afterward, as we rode three abreast along the wide rocky shelf, we heard a thunderous noise that shook the ground under the threx's feet and made them snort and dance in fear. I could feel Issa tremble between my legs. There was not a cloud in the sky, yet it was as if lightning had struck uncomfortably close. The air was charged, the silence deafening in its wake.

I looked at Sereth, and he at me, but Krist plunged and reared under him, and I had my hands full with Issa's fear, and Wirin's ears were flat to his head, and it was perhaps five neras later that we found the source of the ear-splitting crack:

Our threx balked and reared at the edge of a wide crevice, perhaps two threx-lengths across, that extended, barring our path, as far as the eye could see in both directions.

The threx sidled back from the abyss, from which steam hissed, blowing toward us on the west wind.

"This wasn't here the last time I came this way," Sereth said needlessly, dismounting and squatting uncomfortably close to the edge. He picked up a fist-sized rock and tossed it into the maw that had opened in the ground. Beside him, I waited to hear it land, but no sound came out of the crevice.

"Shall we chance it?" he asked me. "It will take us a set to retrace our path and come up again from the south."

"Let it be your decision."

He squinted at the far side, where a luckless tree dangled by its scrawny roots, top downward, over endless descent. The mist curled around its tortured limbs, and the smell of rock dust and warm earth belly was acrid in my nostrils.

"We will try it," he said finally. He went to Wirin and began loosening the straps that bound Tyith's body, gamy now from so long in the brist pelt. Taking a deep breath, I went to him. When we had it free, the Slayer picked the corpse up in his arms and carried it to the abyss, where he uncovered his dead son's face and kissed Tyith's forehead before he let the body fall.

Again I listened for the sound of a weight striking bottom and again I heard nothing.

So much for all the fine words we might have said over Tyith at the Falls of Santha.

Sereth stripped Wirin totally, while the steel threx stood, eyes rolling, then sniffed his tack, discarded on the ground. Stroking his neck, Sereth told the big threx: "That's a good fellow. Stay, now. Stay," almost tenderly.

Then the Slayer went to Krist and mounted, trotting the big black threx another few lengths back from the crevice and, wheeling him, launched the black threx at full speed toward the gaping split.

Almost at its edge, when Krist should have bunched for the jump, the black slid down on his haunches, shying right, foam flying in gobs from his mouth. Again Sereth tried him, and again the threx refused.

The Slayer, angry and tense, walked him a third time back from the crevice. He dismounted and took one of the discarded sword belts from the ground, and stood with it in his hand as he spoke reassuringly to the agitated animal, then mounted, sword belt in his left hand, to try once again.

On this third try, at a dead run, goaded by the strap stinging his rump, the black launched himself, stones flying from beneath his hooves, across the gap. It seemed that they hovered there unreasonably long, over beckoning eternity, and then Krist's front hooves were on the far side. He scrambled for footing, his rear feet pounding the air, and he was over, on his knees, safe on solid ground. Sereth vaulted from his back, taking his head, urging him up. Heaving, the black got his feet under him and stood, legs spread, his huge head pressed against Sereth's chest, his whole body slick with froth and sweat.

Issa turned her head and rubbed it against my knee as if trying to cajole me out of following suit. I walked her slowly until we were twice as far back as Sereth had gone for a start on the leap, and turned her about—and froze with fear, facing the crevice with the trembling threx under me. For some time I sat her there, stroking her neck, until her trembling ceased.

Taking a deep breath, I dug both heels into her side and leaned low on her, against the bristles of her neck, my weight on her forequarters as we sped toward our fate. My eyes were on Sereth, safe on the other side, waiting. I expected her to refuse the leap, was prepared for an abrupt halt as we pounded close to the edge, but she bunched under me and leaped with such force that I had all I could do to stay steady on her withers. My head pressed to her neck, I could see with clarity the mist and steam below us. My heart sank with Issa's bulk, and my stomach rose in my throat as we passed the apex of our arc. I thought us far too short, but her front legs hit the ground and her rear the half-rooted tree, and she lunged, scrabbling, her belly scraping the edge, the tree under her rear hooves cracking beneath her weight. Her left rear gained solid footing just as the tree, ripped away from the edge by her struggles, plunged into the gap.

I was off her, pulling at her head, without knowing how I had gotten there. Her knees were cut and bleeding, but she had made the jump. I stroked her where she lay, sucking wind and trembling, until I had my own legs under control. Then, Sereth at her other side, we urged her to her feet. The threx would not put her left rear on the ground, but held it gingerly high.

Sereth, kneeling beside Issa's injured leg, cursed softly. Her pastern was ripped open to the tendon, the blood flowing down her tri-part hoof and puddling on the rocky ground.

Cutting two long strips from my tas jerkin, I got the salve Celendra had given me in Arlet from my belt and Sereth held Issa's head still while I spread the yellow gel thick over the cut and bound it. The threx almost jerked Sereth off his feet in her attempts to rip the foreign object from her leg, but he managed to hold her.

When I took her head, he went to the edge of the crevice and picked up two good-sized rocks. Wirin, on the other side, his nose high in the air, whickered questioningly and paced back and forth along the abyss.

"Wirin, *home! Go home!*" he shouted, throwing

the rocks for emphasis. Both hit the ground short of the steel-gray threx, who snorted and backed uncertainly away.

"Go on! Home!"

Trumpeting, pawing the ground, Wirin regarded us. Then, with a final shake of his head, he turned tail and loped away.

"Do you think he will?" I said to Sereth's back, watching the retreating threx.

Sereth shrugged and turned from the crevice, going to Krist, who was sniffing Issa's bandaged leg.

"No matter. He will survive in the mountains, surely, if he does not choose to return to the farm. I caught him, perhaps eighty neras from here, the year Tyith was born. His mother, whom I was hunting, was dead when I found them. He was born in this range, still suckling when I took him."

I was surprised. There are few threx herds left in the mountains. They are too tempting a prize, too valuable. I wondered if Wirin would go to the farm or become another loss I had caused Sereth of Arlet.

We led our two remaining threx, with Issa hobbling and snorting every time she tried to put weight on her left hind leg, until dusk came upon us. I was desperate to reach shelter before night, but complaining about it or reminding Sereth served no purpose: I had warned him. He had listened. Now, with an injured threx who should be resting, we were making the best time we could.

I looked up into the darkening sky and my nervousness got the better of me: "Will we make it to the cave before dark?" I asked him, trying to hide my agitation.

"Must we?"

"It would be wise."

Sereth, his eyes on his wounded threx, quickened the pace. Issa struggled bravely to keep going.

Dark was falling fast around us. I found myself sweating, grinding my teeth together so hard my jaws ached, and cursing the brave beast silently for something that was not her fault, but mine.

As the first star appeared overhead, uncannily bright in the thin air, we began to climb from the shelf up the slope. High above us, a rustling as if of many wings could be heard as the night came to life around us.

"Almost there," said Sereth just before the first ebvrasea, shrieking, dived at us out of the gloom.

Krist trumpeted before me, but I could not see him clearly—he was a black on black shadow in the mountain night that fell on us like a flung cloak.

Out of that darkness, wings brushed my head, and the wind from their passage was a fierce gust. I hurried Issa up the rocky incline, the ebvrasea all around me. Beaks ripped at my clothing, my hair. I tried, with my knife, to fend them off. I heard Issa squeal in pain as I collided with a rock in front of me.

"Here," said Sereth urgently, his voice coming from my right, mixed with the snap of wings and the unmistakable kill cry of the mountain ebvrasea.

Those unseen beaks tore at me and I lost my hold on Issa's reins and sank to the ground, protecting my face with my arms as vicious claws dug into my back.

Of the rest of that interval, I remember only that I was screaming when I felt Sereth's hand on me and heard the sing of his sword, the thunking sound it made as it bit into feathered flesh and severed wing and bone.

Somehow he dragged me and Issa, whom he had by the reins, into the cave's mouth. Outside, I heard the angry cries of the ebvrasea, whose twice-man-length wingspread would not allow them access. There must have been a great number of them, by the wind sound and the numberless screechings.

The Seven stared at the night full of wings: "Ebvrasea *never* hunt in flocks."

Crumpled where Sereth had dropped me against the cave wall, I realized that there was blood trickling down my back, along my arm, across my side. There had been no pain when I was struck by beaks and raked by claws, but now my wounds burned unbearably. I heard Sereth moving around. I tried to rise, to see to Issa, but my legs and arms would not obey me.

The last thing I remember, before unconsciousness took me, was silence, as if the birds, as a group, had given us up as a bad job.

# VII.
## Beneath the Falls of Santha

I woke to the smell of roasting ebvrasea, from a dream of seven glowing men in a seven-cornered room who sat in judgement upon me before an audience of shapeless, glowing forms, just as sentence was about to be passed.

Daylight streamed in the open cave mouth and from where I lay I could see the remains of what must have been a night-long battle. At least a score of huge ebvrasea carcasses littered the ground directly before the cave.

Several more of the birds lay inside, on the cave's floor, dressed and plucked. Sereth had his back to me as he squatted tending the ebvrasea he turned on a spit.

Looking around me to see where he might have gotten the wood, I realized that this cave was well-used: there were stacked kindling and waterskins against the rear wall.

I tried to sit up but fell back, dizzy, on my stomach. My back and left shoulder throbbed in their tas bandages, my arm in front of me bore a deep open slash the length of my hand, white and swollen at the edges, angry red in the middle. It had truly happened, then; the solitary predators of the mountains had gone against their nature and attacked us. I shivered and tried to rise again, but the requisite strength was lacking. I cursed the cowled one, yet envied his skill.

I could see Issa and Krist, heads on each other's rumps, dozing to my left. Issa had a badly gashed shoulder, but she stood squarely on her injured rear foot, thanks to Celendra's salve.

When Sereth rose from the fire, he came and knelt beside me. I put my hand out to him, smiled my best, and saw his face relax.

"Lie still," he warned as he began loosening the bandage and removing it from my back. I moaned when he pulled the clotted leather, stuck fast to my flesh, away from the wound and redressed it.

"Do I need another bandage?" I managed.

"Not if you remember not to roll on it. I wanted to keep it clean." I felt the cooling yellow salve ease the throb.

"Can you sit? You should eat. You lost a good deal of blood." He eased me up and I crossed my legs under me, leaning against him until the result-ant attack of dizziness faded and sight returned to my eyes.

"Good enough," Sereth said, peering into my eyes, then left me to return with a steaming, black-crisped ebvrasea slice, and watch while I ate it.

"You had me worried but I should have known better," he admitted, getting me another chunk of the dark meat and sitting beside me then with an ebvrasea's leg for himself. It was a huge leg, from that mighty beast, the size of my own arm.

When my stomach would hold no more, I put the meat aside and leaned against his shoulder. My muscles trembled uncontrollably, and my eye-lids seemed to have a mind of their own.

"Do you think they will return?" he asked me, his eyes on the sky.

"I doubt it. He has yet to try the same stroke twice."

The Slayer squinted into the sun. I could see the muscles twitch in his jaw.

"You know, I did not truly believe you until last night. Now ... well—" He broke off, then began again: "I ought to take you back to Arlet, even if I have to sling you over my saddle. I, if not you, should have enough sense to realize that someone is suggesting in no uncertain terms that we forget this thing." He frowned. "I never thought I'd hear myself say it—I *don't* run ... not from anything mortal, anyway. But this is some supernatural enemy; if my pride can bow before expediency, yours can. You are out of your depth, and I even more so. I can*not* fight this spirit *and* the whole of nature, which it seems to command. Let it go, Estri. No man is worth this."

It must have cost him to admit his fear and his willingness to give up. *No man is worth this*, he had said. He, then, held the same attitude as Dellin, that I searched for a man to get me with child, more than release from the chaldra of the mother. I wondered what else Dellin had told him.

But what he said gave me cause to reflect: if Sereth, who lived forever on the edge of the abyss, found himself unnerved by what had happened, who was I to insist that we proceed? But I was as loath to face the crevice and the long arduous trek to Arlet as the unknown ahead. And might not the cowled one, seeing us routed, redouble his efforts? I thought so. As long as I proceeded on my father's business, I had some little protection—the cowled one had as much as admitted that it could not touch me directly. If I turned back, perhaps the cowled being would be satisfied, perhaps not.

"If we turn back now, he will surely kill us," I said slowly.

"Is it a he?" Sereth said with a trace of suspicion—he was no fool; he was bound to suspect that I knew more than I was telling.

"I think so. And I think I know the rules of this game. But I cannot be sure. If we wait here a day and nothing more happens, will you trust me and go on?"

"Even if something does happen, and you still want it, I will take you. I *said* I would. I will not go back on my word. But I do not like it."

I could feel him tense, but he did not draw away from me.

"Sereth, let me sleep. I will think on what you have said."

"Sleep sitting up, then. I don't want you rolling that wound in the dirt."

So I did, fitfully, waking often, through that whole day, and then deeply through the night.

In the early morning, when I woke, Sereth was not in the cave. Neither was Issa. Krist dozed contentedly, leaning against the cave wall. I felt reasonably healthy; the salve had done its work on my arm. There was only a tiny dark line where the nasty gash had been. My back, when I rose and stretched, did not pain me. I picked up a quarter-full waterskin and drained it, and was starting toward the kindling when I heard Issa enter the cave. She was saddled, walking easily on her feet. Sereth led her and from the look on his face I could tell that the threx's condition pleased him.

He dropped her reins near the opening, and while she sniffed hungrily at the carcasses piled there, the Slayer picked up one plucked winged corpse and lugged its considerable weight to Krist, where the black stood dozing.

Slapping the threx resoundingly on the neck, he

dropped the bloodied bird in front of him. Issa followed of her own accord, sniffing. The two fell to their feeding with relish.

Although we had plenty of wood, Sereth hacked cooked meat off the previous evening's meal and handed it to me.

I ate it greedily, with my fingers, licking the grease from them hungrily. He threw me the knife he had used, and I went and cut another.

"Your back looks fine." He was leaning over me as I squatted above the bird. "You heal quickly."

"It is Celendra's salve that heals quickly."

"You don't have it in Astria?"

"I never needed it in Astria. I suppose we must."

"It is from the caocu root."

"Then we certainly have it." I could hear his unasked question. "There has been no further trouble? While I slept, were you bothered?"

"Nothing untoward," he admitted.

"Then we will try it?"

"If you wish."

"But you think me foolish." I turned, still on my knees, and looked up at him.

"I think you're too stubborn for your own good. But we will try it." He put his hand on my face, tracing the line of my cheek with a callused finger. The look he gave me spoke for itself.

Sometime later, near midday, we left the cave. Sereth of Arlet would not, at least, face the trail unsated.

Issa was sound under me, fresh and saucy from her rest. We made good speed that afternoon and slept in the open that evening without problem.

On the morning of the third fourth, the day we had expected to reach the falls, we turned southeast and began descending. Trees became more common, though still small and scrubby, and often we had grassed ground under us instead of sheet rock. By that evening, we could hear the Falls of Santha roaring in the distance. The night was misted and cloudy, and the moon wore gauzy rings around her three-quarters-full girth. I woke near dawn, weeping, with no recollection of the reason for my tears. Sereth held me until I fell back to sleep, but we were both drawn and troubled in the morning. My dreams had proved too accurate to discount, and though neither of us mentioned it, we both held those tears to be an evil omen.

As I got myself dressed in the tatters and strips of what had once been my tas jerkin, now bloodied and stiff and barely enough for breech and band, Krist let out an ear-shattering trumpet and skittered in his hobbles. Sereth shot me a look that said "Get ready," and went to calm him. I dived for my sword belt and knife and was just buckling them around me when Santh ambled into the clearing, a tawny and obviously pregnant female a pace behind.

"Santh," I called delightedly, running to embrace him, regardless of Sereth's drawn sword and the threx's agitation at being so close to their hereditary enemy.

The Slayer, his hands full with the two plunging, rearing beasts, looked on in wonder as the giant hulion licked my face and arms and extended his head that I might scratch behind his ears.

"Get him *out* of here, Estri. Now!"

I looked up at Sereth, holding tight to Krist's headstall. The threx was wide-eyed and foam-flecked, his teeth snapping the air.

"Where were you when I needed you?" I chided the hulion softly.

He purred and followed me down an incline, his huge feet padding silently behind me.

"Who is your lady friend?" I asked him, when

we were some distance from Sereth and the threx, but Santh only licked his tawny mate with his huge red tongue, his golden eyes glowing with pride.

I spent a long time with the hulion, petting and scratching, and getting acquainted with the sand-colored mother-to-be, and would have stayed longer, but Sereth called down an ultimatum: Leave now, or turn back.

I made the quickest farewell I could, and turned to depart. Santh bounded in front of me, blocking my path.

"Not you, too," I said to him.

His tail lashed angrily; he growled as if to a cub.

"I *must* do this thing. Never fear—I will be back to see your babies," I promised.

The hulion growled again but did not move out of the way. I sighed and put my hands on his head, one each in front of his ears, where the hair grows thin and swirls, and we considered each other's feelings for a time. Eventually, not convinced, snuffling, the great beast, with a snap of his mighty wings, let me pass. It disturbed his sense of rightness, I knew, and he was concerned. His non-verbal thought pattern was clearer than words could ever be, and more frightening. Santh had given me a farewell full of finality, and his sense of loss was so strong that I was much shaken when I climbed out of the depression to rejoin Sereth and the threx.

"If you can summon hulions, you should have done it when the ebvrasea attacked us," Sereth observed. His tone was cold and his eyes distrustful, as if I had somehow betrayed him.

"It is only that one hulion whom I can summon, and only sometimes—when *he* chooses. As it happens, I did not summon him. He chanced upon us. As it was with you and Wirin, so was it with Santh and M'lennin: the First gave him to me as a couch-gift long ago. But one cannot own such a creature." My voice sounded sharp and weary. "He thinks we will never see each other again."

"I was not aware that hulions thought at all," he said, jerking tight Krist's girth so that the threx started in surprise. "I have had more than enough of this whole business, preternatural, supernatural, and downright unnatural. I just want to get it over with."

"Why are you so angry?"

He turned from the threx and faced me, one hand on his hilt, the other on the threx's headstall.

"Angry. Let's see: perhaps because of Tyith, per-haps Issa, perhaps Wirin, perhaps the cowled one, or Dellin, or the trouble you caused me with the Day-Keepers. Perhaps because I think, as does your winged friend, that we will never see each other again, or even because if that is so, and you do find your way alone from Santha, I will have trou-ble convincing our dear dharener Vedrev and your friend Dellin that I have properly discharged my duty—that you aren't lying dead somewhere along the trail. Or perhaps," he grinned without humor, "it's only that without you beside me when I ride into Arlet I may have trouble collecting my money." Then he stopped grinning. "I have a choice of reasons. Any one will do. Now, shall we go?" And he swung up into Krist's saddle.

Well-chastised, I went to Issa and mounted, lop-ing her to catch up with him. I had left myself wide open, and I could not blame him for taking the opportunity. But I never expected him to consider our imminent parting as one of his reasons. In spite of everything, this pleased me.

As we rode abreast at a gentle, ground-eating lope, I snuck covert glances at him, slouched effort-lessly in his saddle, his body moving with Krist, one with his mount while the roaring of the falls grew louder and louder, until it drowned out the threx's hoofbeats.

We topped a rise, and I saw it: the magnificence of the Falls of Santha. The entire cataract was the height of fifteen men, rainbow-crowned and mist-robed, its white water pounded, plunging to the rocks below, rising there in perpetual rain before it submitted to the call of the Litess and started its journey to the sea. Out of solid rock the torrent roared, from some underground source never determined.

Sereth signaled me to follow behind and Krist picked his way fastidiously down the slope between the boulders scattered at random as if by some giant hand, that littered our path. It took us as long to negotiate those scant two neras as it would have forty on level ground.

We left the threx unharnessed at the foot of the falls themselves and began to climb the rocks up the western side.

Within moments I was soaked to the skin, as wet as the slippery boulders we scaled so slowly and carefully as we inched our way along.

Speech was out of the question, so loudly did Santha roar around us. I followed in Sereth's footsteps until there was nothing in the world but slick wet rock and the Slayer's agile form in front of me. After what seemed like days, he veered away from fallside and slithered down into a crevice in the rock, mercifully dry.

I lowered myself gingerly after him, hanging by my hands until I felt him take hold of my waist. He set me on the ground beside him, where the roar of the falls was much diminished, and I looked about me.

We were in a strangely regular passage hewn

out of solid rock that glowed with a green lumi-
nescence.

Taking my hand, Sereth led me deep into the
stone corridor, past many turnings. Once he stopped
and fingered a section high on the wall, where two
passages intersected with the one we were following, and then took the middle one. The deeper we
went within the mountain, the quieter it became.
Soon I could hear nothing but the sounds of our
footfalls on the rock floor.

The eerie green light steadily brightened until I
could see the thick layer of dust on the passage
floor eddying and puffing with our steps. It filled
my mouth and nose, and my eyes stung and watered from the airborne grit. I pushed back my
matted hair from my face with my free hand, feeling the painful twisted clots of it stiff and scratchy
against my skin as we came to another intersection,
and Sereth again reached high on the right-hand
wall.

"These chips cost me a good steel sword," he
said, taking my hand, that I might feel the blazes
he had made. By standing on my toes I could just
reach them with my fingertips: three parallel
gouges, shallow but easily read against the slick,
smooth-surfaced rock.

"Three for straight. Two for left. One for right. If
you and I truly part company here, you would do
well to go by them. One could be long lost in this
maze." His voice sounded dull, without inflection,
as if the walls sucked up the intruding noise. "One
more turning," he continued, "and we are there."

He took my left hand in his right. I gripped it
tightly and tried to follow, but my legs would not
obey me. My teeth chattered and my skin crawled.

When he had spoken, I had gotten nothing from
him but the sound of his voice. And I *knew*: there
was no draw-feel to the time, none of that vague

excitement that had been with me the whole of my life. I had somehow, in this underground labyrinth, entered into the circle of crux. And I could sense nothing.

Sereth pulled at my arm but it happened far from me. It was as if I had suddenly gone blind. All the tiny bits of direct information with which my mind skills had been providing me all my life were gone. I could sort no probabilities, for there were none. From this point in time, dependent upon what occurred, a whole new set of alternatives would be born. And I could not weigh them, not hedge my bet. Terrified, I begged him to hold me. He did so.

"Tighter," I whispered. "Tighter still," as if the pain as he crushed me to him would somehow anchor me to life.

"Any tighter and your ribs will crack," he said, amused, his lips against my neck. "Surely you are not so deep in your need that you must have it now, here, in this place?" he asked, misreading my trembling.

"No," I moaned, my head against his chest. "Just hold me. Please."

He did, and I searched within me for that inner strength that had always in the past come to aid me. When I found it, weak and shrunken, I went about driving the debilitating fear from my mind. When that was done, and my body's reaction calmed, I raised my lips to his and kissed him, long and hard. In that kiss were all the thanks and affection I was too proud to speak, and he too much a Slayer to hear.

He pulled back from me, tossing his head. A smile touched the corners of his mouth. The green glow on his scarred face distorted his features, caused his skin to take on a darker hue.

Hands on my shoulders, he looked down into my

face: "No one would blame you if you left here with me." His voice was gentle. "You have given this chaldra of the mother more than any mother has a right to ask."

"It is too late," I heard myself say.

Sereth crill Tyris didn't argue; he just blew out a deep breath through clenched teeth and took my hand in his, and we walked down the corridor until it ended, then took its final turning to the right.

The spirit, as Sereth had called it—or him—was standing there in the eerie green glow, all cowled and pulsing bronze and massive, barring our path. Beyond, I could see the passage open into a huge cavern.

But I could not move.

"Go back," the cowled one commanded. "Go back and await him. He will come to you in Arlet when the time is right."

Out of the corner of my eye I could see Sereth, still as stone, frozen in mid-stride.

I struggled for my voice, which by his power the cowled one had taken from me: I *would* speak! My tongue felt huge and swollen in my dry mouth.

But I took control of that tongue: "If such were true, you would have saved us all much trouble, and told me before. Nothing but evil has come from you in the past. I am not such a fool as to believe you. Get from my path. Cease to obstruct me. By my father's will, I command you."

"Are you so selfish as to be willing to pay your passage with yet another life?" the cowled apparition boomed, and raised his hand toward Sereth.

And the Slayer fell to his hands and knees, then crumpled to the ground. By my peripheral vision, I watched him fall, for I could not turn my head. I thought of the Baniese trader, and that horrible death he had died. My stomach churned.

"Gladly will I bargain his life to you, child of Estrazi. There is still time—and hope for a man who has shown more courage that I'd thought the entire race had in its collective craw. Turn from this path and he is yours. Continue, selfish, selfish child, and your selfishness will destroy him. Surely you care for something besides yourself?" The voice was full of sibilances that scraped my spine.

"No!" I said. I honestly thought it was too late for Sereth: he was motionless and, knowing him, I assumed that life had already fled him, for if he could have risen, he would have, to fight for me if he could have crawled, he would have crawled, to defend me.

"Horrid thing," I spat at the cowled one before me. "You will not trick me. And you will not stop me." I tried to see the face within the shadowed cowl. I could not.

"There are already enough of the children gathered. You are not needed," he said, voice slick and oily, and the image before me pulsed and wavered. "But go on, if you insist." It seemed to shrug. "I have done my best to stop you. You will wish, very soon, that you had listened. But since I am neither so young nor so greedy as you, I will do you a service—I will give you his life. In exchange, you will serve me equal value when we meet again."

It was a thread of hope I was eager to grasp. I wanted no more death on my account. If it were true, if life could be brought back to the still man I could barely see out of the corner of my eye . . . . Sereth's loss was a gaping hole within me, already. And now the cowled thing was saying I could save the Slayer who so redundantly saved me from every misfortune thrown in my path.

The price, at the time, seemed little enough to pay.

I said, "All right. I agree."

At my words, the cowled one waved his hand and the force that had held me prisoner was gone so abruptly that I staggered and stumbled as the impetus of my interrupted stride carried me forward.

I went to my knees by Sereth, not daring to believe, but desperate with hope.

He was on his belly, his head turned away from me. I remember the feel of his silky, thick brown hair under my anxious hands as I turned his head toward me. His face was peaceful and composed, as if in sleep, and with my hands at his temples, I could feel, clearly and distinctly, the blood pounding there. He lived! But the Baniese had lived awhile, cut off from all sensory reality. His eyeballs moved, as if he were dreaming, under closed lids.

With difficulty I turned him over and then sat quietly and quite helplessly beside him, watching the slow rise and fall of his chest, covered with the dust of the passage floor.

The cowled one was gone when I first had the wit to look about for him. His physical presence, or the absence of it, mattered little at that moment: he had won. I could never leave Sereth, alive but unconscious—perhaps in coma, a sleep from which he might never wake—alone in the passage under Santha.

The cowled one's bargain, his offer of Sereth's life, had been but a final gloating goad. What semblance of life was this? I said softly to the man who could not hear me, "I did my best. I could not know for certain ... Sereth? Can you hear me?" And I said other things, for I thought my heart would break. I had been selfish, been what he'd called me long ago—a spoiled high couch brat. And this was the result of it.

I stared at the once-mighty Slayer for a long

time, wondering how I could have gone so wrong. I had seen Sereth's timeline fold back upon itself and branch: I had stayed in that nether-world until I was sure I had done it, and done it right. Was all I had learned, all my blood proclaimed, useless? Was I merely conjuring visions to amuse myself, an addled well woman with no purpose other than the begetting of offspring? I still could not believe it, even there and then.

But the reality was clear and overpowering: my constricted, dust-filled throat burned and ached as I watched the sleeping man before me, a man any other woman of Silistra would have been content to couch, without seeking bronze people who might or might not exist, and a father who had deserted me before I was born and who also might no longer exist.

I lay my head on Sereth's chest and wept quietly. Spiritual doubts, ethical doubts, and intellectual doubts receded before a looming physical doubt, brought forward by the fact that, for the first time in my life, I had truly failed, ringingly and completely, at something: I now doubted myself in my totality.

I especially doubted my ability to drag that large, powerful man back along the passage, up out of the crevice, down the fallside jumble of rocks to where the threx grazed, waiting.

And then Sereth groaned and his arm went about me. I cried his name.

His eyes opened and focused. I was limp with relief.

"Let me sit up." Slowly he struggled to a sitting position, crossing his legs under him hesitantly, as if relearning their control. He swayed and I put my arm about his shoulders to steady him but he shook me off, supporting himself with stiffened arms, his head bowed low.

"Dizzy," he mumbled, one hand to his brow. He

sat very still, breathing deeply, for a long while.

"Your friend has a heavy stroke," he said finally, raising his eyes to my face. It was as if he would smile but had forgotten how.

"I thought I had lost you," I said.

"You lost me long ago, Estri. Nor would you have had it otherwise," he said flatly.

I sat back from him; he had misconstrued everything . . . there was no time to explain, to make him understand what I hardly understood myself. "Did . . ." I tried again: "Did it hurt?"

"No. Just nothing. Floating nothing. My mind still reels. That was one very lonely place, where he sent me."

I knelt before him in the dust of the corridor. I wondered if he knew how he had regained his life.

"What of . . . of what he said?" I asked.

"I heard none of it." I could see his body steadying under him. He no longer needed the support of his stiffened arms to keep him erect.

And I had very little time. I leaned forward and kissed him gently, then rose to my feet. I was glad he had no remembrance of my meeting with the cowled one, of the bargain I had made.

"Estri, wait." But I was already running toward that chamber I had given so much to reach.

I looked back and saw him leaning unsteadily against the passage wall, watching me. I could not wait until he was fully recovered—then, with his soft voice and his hard ways, he might be able to stop me.

The great cavern was not natural in its form. It was smooth and regular, as had been the passages, and brightly green-lit. The floor was unseamed, through the expanse of it was as great as Arlet's Inner Well.

In its center, I saw what I had sought so long.

It sat waiting, twice my body's length, the height

of my knee: a platform made of the same material as my father's ring.

I knelt before it. Emblazoned upon the side of the oblong platform, magnified perhaps a thousand times, so that it covered the whole middle of the longitudinal side, was the pattern that the ring bore, fashioned just the same, from scintillating inset stones. Only these stones were not white, save for one, but every shade imaginable. A fortune beyond comprehension glittered here in the green-lit cavern below the Falls of Santha and Sereth, the only person beside myself ever to see it, had not even mentioned the fact.

The blood-red stone in the upper-right arm of the spiral was the size of my fist. I ran my dust-covered hand over it. There was no doubt in my mind as to what to do.

I got to my feet and regarded the couch-sized upper side. There were two sets of gleaming golden rungs recessed deep in the black stone, perhaps one-fifth distance from either end.

I lay belly-down between them, hooking my feet under one pair of rungs, my fingers around the other. My hair, falling over my face, obscured my vision but the stone was warm against my belly, my legs, my arms.

I heard Sereth's voice dimly. Then I heard a great rushing, and my consciousness blew apart screaming, every molecule straining to retain its relationship to its fellows. And we were lost, all the billions of fragments of me, among polarized entities of undulating colored light, each atom distinct, forming great serpents who wound the centers of the gravity circuits that join all matter— synchronism preexisting. Pulling reality constantly within, ever devouring the now, they whirled and spun in nontime.

Then I lay on my stomach with the warmth of

the black stone once again against my flesh, exhaling the breath I had drawn on Silistra into an alien air, content to lie there with my eyes closed, savoring my body, once again whole, though I had no idea where I might be.

The air in my nostrils was thick and syrupy, full of almost-tastes and nameless smells. It was rich and intoxicating and brought to me a sense of fullness.

In a few breaths, I had had enough of it: its heaviness sickened. But there was nothing else to breathe. And it was uncomfortably warm. Perspiration trickled down between my breasts.

Lossening my fingers from their aching grip upon the golden rungs, I rolled quickly to my back, as one dives into mysterious waters—then sucked in another breath involuntarily as the reality of the place crashed in upon me:

I was in a small crystal chamber. Through the walls I could see another chamber, and another, and another. In each was a similar platform. Far down the prismatic row, I could see shapes moving among the crystals. Above me I could see the sky. It was a blue sky, where it was not green or gray or white or gold or black or red. The cubes of storm became summer's day, became twilight, and morn and snow's fall, and lightning flash.

This panorama overhead melted and reformed before me, ever-changing, yet each segment of it remaining distinctly enclosed by some invisible geometric barrier. My eyes ached from it. I turned my head to the left, expecting to see again only the ever-receding crystalline partitions. . . .

Instead, I saw two lithe yet powerful bronze figures who had not been there before. One was a female. She was molten, brazen perfection, that reality of which I was only a shadow. Her companion was a head taller, and twice her girth, as perfectly formed and primally male as she was female, and a shade darker of hair and eye. He had a haughty, angular face, with a high forehead and prominent brows. It was not the face of my father. Otherwise they might have been brothers.

I thought to rise to greet them, but the female put forth her hand and I was paralyzed.

She came forward, on her face an expression of infinite compassion, and leaned over me where I lay helpless. In her hand was a band of metal on which were glyphs unfamiliar to me, and this she snapped closed around my neck. It was a tight fit; I could feel the restraining snugness when I swallowed. The metal was cold and unyielding.

I tried to speak, and the woman brought her lips close to mine and kissed me. Then her cool hand was on my brow, and sleep rushed upon me, and I saw nothing.

# VIII.
## My Father's Daughter's Brother

I leaned back against the crystal-clear wall of
my prison and tried to comb the snarls from my
hair with my fingers. It was very difficult work,
painful, frustrating. When I had regained consciousness, I had been alone in the crystal cube, under
that alien jumble of tiny chunks of sky. I had felt
every reachable inch of my prison in the hysteria
that followed my reawakening. There was no seam
or joint in the cube's construction. It had no door.
It adjoined the other crystal cubes on the bottom,
and the two sides parallel with the long end of the
platform. Above us was the sky. I had tried to
determine the number of cubes, and the height to
which we were stacked, but I could not tell it.
There were more than four cubes under me, or just
that number. Between the cubes were white walkways, on the side parallel with the short end of the
platform, and these made perspective impossible.
Eventually I had given up trying to determine my
surroundings. I was on an unknown world, held by
an unknown race, for an unknown reason. That I
should be so desperately concerned with ascertain-

ing the exact nature of my prison seemed finally ludicrous.

I do not know what I expected to find on the other side of the black platform on Silistra. I think I expected my father to greet me like some treasured, long-lost love, and escort me through a land of story-book marvels. I had not expected, certainly, to be stripped and imprisoned by strangers without so much as the courtesy to inquire as to my reason for being here.

Disgusted, I ripped the snarl out in a clump and straightened up. My shoulders were sore from too long spent tensed in one position. I stared again at the walls that bound me in. Only one cube directly adjoining held an occupant, and this was the cube I had arbitrarily dubbed north. In it was a black couch or platform, with no identifying device—identical, as far as I could see, to mine. Recessed into the north wall was an oblong about the height of the lower part of my body, but an arm's length off the floor. Set beneath this box, sunken into the clear floor, were what could only have been, as in my cube, a bowl and plate. Within the clear oblong box, the length of my lower body, an arm's length wide, and that high off the ground, writhed an unpleasant-looking, thick, roiling brown mass. Half between gas and liquid, it was ever in motion, and tiny sparks of colored light chased each other sporadically across the restless surface. I was glad it was enclosed.

I had tried to remember the details of my awakening on the platform when the bronze man and woman found me. I wanted to know if this was indeed the cube into which I had arrived, or another. I did not remember the brown-filled container, and likewise I did not remember the dark-brown Hertekiean-looking man who inhabited the cage adjoining north.

My hands went to my neck. I tried, once again, to get my fingers under the metal band that encircled my throat. But I could not ease the unyielding pressure. It fit so snugly I found it uncomfortable, irritating. I ran blind fingertips over the alien engraved script, as I had a hundred times since my awakening. The glyphs did not give up their message. I wondered what information was written there. And why.

I had not had anything to eat. There had been no food presented me. I thought I had been up perhaps eight bells, for my stomach rumbled angrily. The sky was all times, nonsequentially. Some of it was always any time of day or night one could choose. I would have to see whether or not a pattern emerged in the sky's movements. The level of light had so far stayed the same. There was no glare, nor shadow, nor bright or dim. It was actually very good light, but unnerving. If there was no pattern in the sky, I would have to rely upon my internal clock.

I had seen the dark man, who seemed very bronzed for a Hertekiean, go to his plate and bowl under the brown mass and proceed to eat and drink. I had gone to my bowl, hungrily, thinking it was feeding time, but no food or drink had appeared.

Across the walkways I could see others in their cubes. Behind them, on the western side, a volcano belched and fumed. On the eastern side, a great ice floe dipped and rose. To the north and south, I could see nothing but the top row of the seemingly endless stacked cubes. I remembered the dream I had had in the hover the day Dellin and I had left the Liaison First's for Arlet; that dream of time-space jammed together in a checkerboard land where an expanse of winter laid half-atop a chunk of primal sea, bubbling over an unseen edge into a volcano vomiting fire and ash onto a plain fluid with waving grain. This was surely that place. I recollected that in that dream I had seen a huge bronze figure, and that figure had worn my father's ring. I had thought the dream allegorical. I now knew better. But my father's ring was still safe, bound to my waist by my eighteen-strand chald.

When I saw the Hertekiean again rise and go to his box of brown swirl, I rose myself and went and pressed my body against the wall we shared in common. He took up his bowl and plate, and I motioned him to me. He came up to the wall, and I could see the steam rising from the large chunk of black seared meat, running with bloody juice, upon his plate. My mouth watered.

I pointed to my open mouth, then my stomach, rubbing it, then his plate. Then I shrugged and opened my arms wide. I hoped my signing made sense to him. The dark eyes followed me; his brow furrowed. He pointed to my bowl and plate. I shrugged again. My dark neighbor put down his plate and bowl. He pointed to his temple, then to the brown roiling mass enclosed in the clear oblong, then to his plate.

I shook my head. The Hertekiean tossed his tangled mane of waist-length hair and folded himself into a cross-legged sitting position, facing me. I pressed my face against the partition that separated us and spoke to him slowly in Standard, then Hertekiean. He put his hand to his ear, then signed no. He could not hear me. His eyes met mine for a moment; then he dropped his gaze and picked up his plate. He took the chunk of meat, with its delicate pink-red center, and tore at it with teeth and fingers. The bloody juice ran down his chin and arms. He pointed once again to the brown oblong within my cube. I went to it, turning my back to him. I could not bear to watch him eat.

I squatted before my bowl and plate. Nothing appeared upon the plate, nothing within the bowl. My mouth watered uncontrollably, and every time I swallowed I was reminded of the unpleasantly tight band around my neck.

I felt of the band again, and again failed to find lock or seam, clasp or closure. My stomach seemed intent upon devouring itself in lieu of food. The thick air, with its strange odors, only aggravated my hunger. I could feel rivulets of sweat running down my back, over my buttocks. I put my head in my hands and fought the hysteria rising in me.

Eventually the call of my hunger and the trembling of my limbs faded. Hopefully, my captors would, at their leisure, provide me with food. I ran my hands once again over the oblong container that held the brown mass, then about the floor around the recessed bowl and cup. There was no way I could find to precipitate a meal—no button, no lever, no dial or bar to be turned or pressed. I sighed and rose. Through the floor I could see below me the white-blond head of the female occupant of the cube beneath. She, also, had fed.

I did a full dhara-san routine, the first I had done since arriving long ago in Arlet. My body was stiff and angry with neglect. The contortions and twists and stretches of physical discipline calmed my mind and restored my equilibrium. I stood on my head and counted two thousand, and when I came down, soaked with sweat, I lay for a time looking up at the sky, letting my mind roam at will.

I thought of Silistra. I wondered with much concern about Sereth—if he would make it safely to Arlet, if he would acquire the coin girl who nurtured Tyith's child, his grandson. Dellin, I was sure, would not be easily convinced that the Slayer had properly discharged his commission. The Day-

Keepers, also, would be little pleased. I hoped that those farsighted ones, with their insightful awareness, would be easy on the Slayer. Although, in my service, he had acted often in ways unacceptable by tradition, he had had little choice. If the Day-Keepers were aware, by their devious methods, that he had left chalded corpses on the road to Santha, without any attempt to ascertain their identity or take up their chalds, his very livelihood, his position among the Slayers, would be in jeopardy. Though he and I knew he had done no wrong, given the circumstances and the pressures upon us, none not cognizant of the situation would agree. And I was not there to uphold him. It was at that moment I conceived this accounting, that I might testify on his behalf, though I was worlds away. How I expected to get my writing to those I would inform was not clear to me. Now that I am almost finished, it is still unclear.

I sat up in time to see the Hertekiean relieving himself in the southwest corner of his cube. I followed suit, finding by example the area of my own prison designed for that purpose. My water drained into the floor through some method I could not apprehend, since that area, as the rest of the cube floor, seemed solid to the touch. But I was much relaxed when I had finished.

My mind returned to Silistra like metal to a magnet. I wondered whether Dellin would risk his relationship with Sereth and let his loss show. The Liaison Second's face was often in my mind in those first days, as was Sereth's, and those of the others who had been involved with my journey. Celendra would be much trouble to Sereth, who had lost, on my account, her only child. I did not envy him, though he was free and I a prisoner, for she would be formidable in her rage.

I slept and awoke. Remembrance of my dream,

one of a long luxurious shower, was so strong I could smell the water. My throat was parched and dry and my tongue furred in my mouth. I sat up and rubbed the sleep from my eyes. I got to my feet and walked listlessly to my bowl and plate. Water covered the floor of the whole northern end of the cube. I went to my knees before the bowl and plate and found them overflowing with blessed wetness. The water I had smelled upon awakening overflowed the bowl. I drank thirstily, kneeling in the puddle. Then I rolled my body around in it, rubbing the moisture over my skin, my hair, my face. Only when I had soaked myself, naked but in chald and collar, did I sit back and try to make sense out of what had happened.

I saw my neighbor peering at me. He nodded his head encouragingly and rubbed his stomach. I had dreamed of water, of shower, of infinite wetness. Either my awareness of available water had precipitated the dream, or the dream the available water. I was inclined to think the latter. My stomach was swollen with air, gurgling loudly. The water had lubricated my thinking, as well as my parched innards. It had had a strange taste, metallic, gritty, but it had been water.

I tried visualizing a thick parr steak. I saw it in my mind, charred black on the outside, barely warmed in the middle. Nothing happened. I opened my eyes and regarded the Hertekiean, squatting by our shared wall, staring at me intensely. He put his finger to his temple, pointed to the brown roiling mass above my plate and bowl, closed his eyes, squeezing them dramatically together, rubbing his stomach. It could mean no other thing.

I sat myself a hand's breadth in front of the oblong brown mass and tried again. This time I brought to bear every scrap of information I had about parr steak. I tasted it. I felt the juice, hot

and steamy, run down my throat. I conceived the
texture of it, how many teeth would tear a bite
from the larger chunk, what mastication of that
bite involved, muscularly and tactilely. I went
through chewing and swallowing motions with my
throat and tongue, all the while seeing in my mind's
eye with three-dimensional clarity that which I
wanted to eat. Every time I swallowed, I was reminded of the metal collar around my neck. I
envisioned as well as I could the molecular structure of the cooked parr. My stomach cried out in
desperation. I heard a soft thudding sound with
my straining ears.

Cautiously I opened my eyes. On the plate, within
its recess, was a shapeless brown mass, gelatinous
and oozing. It steamed and quivered there. It was
not parr steak, by any means, but the smell that
came to me on the steam convinced me it was
food.

As I leaned forward and took the plate upon my
lap, I saw the Hertekiean, his arms raised wide
above his head, applauding me in the fashion of
his homeland.

I stuck my finger into the oozing, unappetizing
mass and put that finger in my mouth. It was not
any food I had ever tasted, but it resembled, in its
tang and saltiness, parr meat. I picked the plate up
and devoured the gooey, warm, semi-solid mass.
When I had licked the plate clean and with my
fingers wiped every smear from my face, I carefully replaced the plate in its recess.

So I began to learn to feed myself. I had said
once to Dellin, long ago, that it was a wonder that
I could do so. Now, such was truly the case. I
worked long on my visualization of parr steak, and
on the fourth try I had something that resembled,
in taste and texture, that food. The Hertekiean had
tried to sign me some obscure message, pointing

to the brown mass and shaking his head, circling his hands and then lowering them slowly to the ground, but I was too concerned with the mechanics of feeding myself to pay him more than token attention. My second try at the parr had given me mediocre results, soft and claylike in texture. That I had thrown to the part of the cube where I had relieved myself, and it had been absorbed by that self-cleaning section of floor. The third I had partaken of briefly, also. Its color and texture were better, but the taste was not right. The fourth I enjoyed mightily, tearing at the firm-textured, juicy flesh. Then, my hunger sated, I sat myself on the black platform which served me as couch and considered my surroundings again, greatly cheered. At least I would not starve.

From that greater distance I conceived my water. Evidently distance from the brown oblong made no difference. When I had filled my bowl with water that I had visualized from clear bubbling brook, icy and cold, I went and tasted it. I nodded approvingly as the chill liquid spread inside me, pure and refreshing. If one could get a little water, I reasoned, conscious suddenly of my begrimed state, one could get a lot. I lay myself over the recessed depression that held bowl and plate and created for myself a sporadic lateral shower. First I managed to wet my body above the waist; then I moved up and soaked my hips and legs. Finally I laid my head between bowl and plate and washed, soapless, the filth from my hair. The water ran dark a long time, with Silistran dirt and dust.

I took up my position against the south wall and began combing my hair with my fingers. I smiled, for the first time since my arrival—clean, and with a full stomach. My situation took on a different light. Doubtless this was some simple mistake, soon to be remedied by my father. Surely he would not allow me to be treated so. I felt a sudden superiority to my cube-mates. They would stay forever in this dismal place, while I, certainly, would be soon rescued by my father and treated regally, as befitted my station as daughter of one of the lords of this world. My former psychic blindness was beginning to lift: I could feel the timelines regrouping. Soon, I was sure, I would be able to see, to ascertain the probabilities inherent in this time, and guide my own among them.

The Hertekiean was at our shared wall, trying to attract my attention. Poor thing. I wondered how long he had been here. I owed him something for trying to help me divine the function of the brown sludge within the oblong container. Perhaps when I was freed I would ask my father to release him. I got up and went and sat opposite him, the clear crystal wall a sound barrier between us. He kept shaking his head, pointing to my food box and his own. They were identical, as far as I could tell, save that his brown mass seemed a few shades lighter, and the texture not so dense. I signed my puzzlement. He again brought his hands slowly down until they rested on the floor. Then he raised them above his head, fingers wiggling, and brought them down, splayed, to the floor. I wondered what he was trying to say.

After a time, disgusted, I went to my black couch and lay with my back to him. I had much better things to do than watch him sign. I would have read him, but for some reason I was not able. I wondered if the crystal was barrier to thought and emotion as well as sound. I could not, though I tried and tried, make connection mentally with any of my cube-mates. Nor could I sense any mind anywhere. I decided that it must be that the substance in which I was enclosed acted as a damper, for all my other psychic functions had returned to me, although they were of little use in this altered reality.

I cannot say how much time passed before I slept, for I spent much of it within, trying to integrate my ego with my situation and those strengthened skills I felt within me. I seemed different in some subtle way and went deeper and deeper within, to attempt to assess that difference and familiarize myself with it. Yet I could find no specific area or understanding to which I had not had previous access. I was altered, but I couldn't say how, or ever how I knew I was.

Upon awakening I conjured my food, drink, and shower, as I had done before. I worked hard at my dhara-san. It was painful, for I stretched muscles long ignored.

Then I turned to what I now fondly regarded as my food box, and began experimenting. I created much food that I did not eat before I had managed a narne fruit. When I had it, crisp and tart and red in my hand, I turned to materializing a strachy tun. I became absorbed and obsessed with the brown roiling mass that created at my bidding the desires of my mind. I settled into a routine of exercise and meditation, creation and thought, and I did not notice that the brown mass grew ever more tenuous, and the spark lights that had once chased each other in profusion grew fewer and fewer.

When I had slept six times, it seemed to me that I was having more trouble than I had come to expect with the food production. I found myself straining harder and harder, and getting less satisfactory results. My parr was again claylike, my narne soft and pulpy. I thought long on this. I had not had sign contact with the Hertekiean for three sleeps, since he had thrown up his hands disgustedly one morning when I emerged from under my makeshift shower, and turned his back. With this deteriorating of the level of my objective success, the well-being I had experienced began also to fade. Perhaps my father was dead, in truth, and I would stay here until I died, half-starved and surely insane from boredom. I found it difficult to keep my mind on any one object; it jumped and rambled and would not respond to my demands for silence and concentration.

At the eighth waking period, I could get little but unrecognizable white sludge from my food box, and the brown mass seemed absolutely tenuous. It was then that I went to the wall I shared with my dark neighbor, with the plate of unpalatable lumpy gruel in my hands. It was a long while before he noticed me and came to stand there. I signed my plight by pointing to the plate and my much-diminished stock of brown foodstuff.

He nodded and pointed to his own. When I had first compared the two oblongs, mine had been the darker, the thicker. Now his was noticeably more solid, though I thought it less dense than it had been when I first saw it.

He held up eight fingers, then pointed to where I had discarded my rejected efforts and let the floor absorb them. Then he gestured again, his hands high over his head, fingers wriggling, bringing them down over his body, then shaking them, as if to rid them of excess liquid. With a sinking stomach I realized what he had been trying to tell me all along. There was a finite amount of brown semiliquid provided, and I had squandered most of mine. It was my own stupidity that had brought this about.

The dark man shrugged his shoulders and spread his hands wide. There was nothing he could do for me. He wandered to his black couch and lay down upon it.

I regarded the brown semiliquid left in my oblong food box. The less dense the brown stuff, the more difficult it was to control. I thought of my daily showers, and groaned out loud. I wondered what would happen when the wispy remains of the brown stuff were gone. If my father had intended to come for me, certainly he would have done so by now. Disconsolately, I ate the unappetizing white gruel. I dared not try for a better meal. The stiffness from resumed daily dhara-san had faded, and I threw myself into the postures with all my strength.

When I was done, I was physically exhausted, but my mental state was no better. I lay on my black hard couch and wept. My stomach cramped and my breasts felt exceptionally sensitive. My erect nipples burned when I touched them. When my hunger drove me again to seek to create a meal, my back pained me terribly, my intestines were constricted, and upon rising I became so dizzy that I staggered and would have fallen but for the wall of my prison against which I stumbled. I thought dimly, through a haze of pain, that I must have made some mistake in creating the white gruel. I dry-heaved on my hands and knees, but I had nothing to give up. When that was done, I crawled weakly back to the couch and dragged myself up upon it. I slept fitfully, and when I awakened, the couch was slick with blood. My thighs were covered in it, and it poured forth from me in a steady stream. Fear formed a cold knot in my aching belly. I examined my red-covered hand. The blood was fresh and new. I thought it ironic that my mistake with the food source had caused me to hemorrhage, and what a foolish reason that was to die, here on some nameless world so far from home.

I prepared myself, as we of Silistra are taught, to let go the things of flesh and substance, to embrace that existence of mind that is after death. But death did not come for me, as I lay waiting for it, but sleep instead.

When I awoke, I found the bleeding somewhat abated, though still occurring. I had thought never to awaken, and I was not much pleased. My breasts no longer pained me, nor my intestines nor groin. I sat up cautiously and waited until the dizziness receded. There was much dried blood, dark and caked on my body. I realized, finally, what significance my bleeding bore. And I mourned. I mourned a long time that never-to-be born egg that had somehow made its way to my womb, only to languish and die there unfertilized. On Silistra, I must have produced it. When? I thought perhaps somewhere along the trail with Sereth. I remembered the time it could have been, when we came upon the crevice we had jumped with the threx. Not after that had Sereth put seed within me, but had used me otherwise. So I had my chance, and had not made use of it. I wondered, as I keened the child-death chant, if ever another egg would be granted me, ever in my life. I prayed to the old gods, in my bereavement, that such would not be the case.

I wondered how long I had truly been in my cube. Long enough for the egg to die and be expelled. Longer than I had reckoned it.

Uncaring of my food supply, I filled my bowl with water and rubbed the blood from my hips and legs. Then again, and cleaned the rest of me as best I could. Having been denied my child, I cared not at that moment if I lived. I made no attempt to produce food for myself, but lay where I was before the north wall and slept.

When I next awoke, the bleeding was truly stopped, and I needed only half a bowl to clean the streaks and clots from my upper thighs. I had just finished doing this, and was about to drink the remainder, when a noise behind me made me turn.

They were standing there, on the other side of the black platform, that spectacular bronze woman and man who had first met me with collar and kiss when I arrived. The man's haughty, angular face bore a suppressed smile; his eyes were calm and wise, glowing with internal fire. She beside him was symmetrical perfection, with round full breasts and generous hips. Her face was the most beautiful I had ever seen; her dark hair glowed with a life of its own.

"Welcome to Mi'ysten, which you have called Zredori, little sister," said the woman in a voice musical in both ear and mind. She spoke to me in archaic Silistran, a Stoth dialect, and spoke it with no hint of accent or flaw.

I got slowly to my feet and regarded them, the black platform between us. I was still deep in my grief, weaving on my feet, unsteady.

The bronze man came around the couch and took me by the arm. His hand was cool on my skin, his flesh smooth. I looked at his hand on my arm, bronze on copper, at the perfection of its form, at the ring he wore on his middle finger, the ring that was identical to the one I wore threaded through the chald at my waist.

"You are not he," I said, looking up into those flickering fire-eyes. My eyes were level with the nipples on his thick-haired chest.

"No." He smiled and spoke for the first time. "I am not. I am Raet." But I knew who he was. I knew that voice, and the accompanying mind-touch. I was not mistaken.

I struggled to pull my arm from his grasp, but it was as iron. I tried to claw his face, mindless with fear and rage, but he caught my hand.

"Would you prefer that I bound you, or removed your body from your control?" he queried me calmly, holding me now by both wrists. I shook my head mutely. I was not willing to experience again the paralysis I had undergone by his will under the Falls of Santha.

The woman was beside us, peering anxiously into my face. She touched my hair, then my brow, with her cool hand. I felt my hate and fear receding, replaced by a passive calm. I had no choice but to do as they bid. I felt, for the first time, an anxious desire to please them, these beings who held my life in their hands.

"You have been long enough here, Estri," the woman said. "I would take you to my tridoe—my keep—but you must behave like an intelligent, civilized being." She looked around at the cube that had been my home. "And yet . . ." She hesitated. "And yet, that may be too much to ask." She brought from nowhere a pair of metal bracelets, joined by a short length of chain, and a longer chain of the same whitish metal. The chain she clipped to the band around my neck, the bracelets she snapped shut upon my wrists, held by Raet in front of me. But I did not struggle. In the end, they would have their way with me. I had no defense, no escape.

Leashed and braceleted, I was led through a door that opened magically before us, out of the cube and onto the white walkways. Raet held the leash attached to my collar loosely in his left hand, and the woman, still unnamed, she who had called me "little sister," held my right arm. She was a head taller than I. I saw the Hertekiean, his face pressed to the wall of his cube, staring after us. If my hands were free, I would have waved him tasa.

We walked along the white way, between the rows of cubes with their isolated occupants, under the shifting sky. My lost child was strong in my mind, and the question of who had precipitated the egg into my womb; and my body, long celibate, was burning, aware of the bronze Raet on my left.

"I would have given you that child, there at the Feast of Conception, but your guardians were too close around you, and kept me from you." I threw up all my mind shields. I was humiliated that he had caught my errant body's need.

"The Baniese!" I accused. He smiled. I tightened my block.

"That will do you little good," he said. So his reading was such that my shield was useless. I let it drop.

"And if you had succeeded, Raet?" said the woman. "She would have been triply admixed, and so disqualified from the tests. And you would have won. It must rankle you that you did not." I could feel her grip tighten on my arm. The wave of hostility that came from her toward the bronze Raet made my head spin.

"Little sister"—the superb woman spoke to me—"your scores were the highest of any of the children. Our father, in his choice of your mother, was well-vindicated."

"Our father?" I asked. The rest of what she said was too obscure.

"Estrazi had me by Tyiana. I am Esyia, your half-sister. And Raet, whom you have evidently met, is also my mother's son." Then Astria had been right. My father's daughter's brother had sought me. A strong wind buffeted me. We were

coming to the end of the stacked cubes. The view
between the stacks wrenched at my sanity.

"What tests?" I asked her. She and Raet exchanged glances.

"I think it makes little difference now," he said
to her.

"It is still not within our function to discuss it
with her," she said.

"You brought it up," he reminded her.

As they wrangled, we came to a place where the
stacked cubes abruptly ended. The panorama before me strained my cognizance of reality. From a
central point, triangular spokes of terrain radiated.
Lush forest, shimmering with mist, great barren
steppe, ice waste, rolling sea. My body felt their
pull. I was glad for the bronzes' grasp upon me. I
was drawn like metal scraps to a strong magnet.

"Now you know part of the reason for the collar
you wear," Raet said in my ear. "These are departure points"—he waved his hand at the spectacle
before us—"for experimental climes, tangential
realities. Within these areas do we refine our
prototypes, before seating them in space-time. Their
sequentiality is greatly quickened, hence the pull
you feel. The molecules of your body, linear-
conditioned, feel it. If we were not with you, nor
the collar you wear upon your neck, you would be
drawn into the closest of them, probably that
rainforest there, to live out your span triple-timed.
Once you became so entrapped, it is doubtful even
we could find you before dissolution overtook your
body."

I shivered. Vaguely, I apprehended what he was
saying. I could not, alone, walk safely upon the
face of this world. I began to realize just how far
advanced the bronzes were. And with that realiza-
tion, my assessment of myself and reality as I had
known it began to crack and crumble.

Esyia waved her hand, and a section of the white way rolled back, revealing steps descending steeply into darkness. We made our way down them, and onto a landing before which were double doors. The doors opened at our approach. We stepped within the cubicle so revealed, and my stomach came up in my throat as I felt the floor moving down under me.

"We could have come a quicker way, but for you," Raet said. "Did you find transition to Mi'ysten uncomfortable?"

I shuddered in remembrance of the agony I had experienced on the black platform. I nodded.

"You see, Esyia? There is a flaw in their basic structure that no amount of admixing or evolution will cure. They remain locked in space-time because it is impossible for them to function out of it. Even this one, doubtless the best of the lot, cannot make even such a simple adjustment. I submit to you that such deficiencies are irreparable." His tone said he had won some great, long-standing battle, using me as example. I felt a great unease, as if by my reaction I had put myself in danger.

"Do not worry, little one." Esyia's hand was on my temple, and peace returned to me. "They will never be able to sway the assessors now, not with your performance taken into account." The doors slid soundlessly open, and I did not find out who "they" were, or what assessors she meant. The scene revealed by the open doors was unremarkable, and I breathed a sigh of relief. A long corridor stretched before us, white and solid, with doors at regular intervals down its length. The floor was of some rusty stonelike material solid and warm under my bare feet. We made our way along it.

"Where is my father?" I asked.

"At the star nurseries," Raet explained, as if

such an answer made it all clear. "He is at a critical stage in his shaping, and will return when he has his project stabilized. You will stay with us, your choice of Esyia's tridoe or mine, until he does. That is, unless you would return to the cubes."

That was no choice at all. Raet's hand was on the small of my back. I tried to ignore my body, surging at his touch. I had much reason to hate him, but I could find no hate in me. My mind raged at my weakness, but my body would not listen. What he had said—that he would have given me a child in Arlet—rang in my head. I longed to fill that void within me. I wondered if he might not be able to do so here, despite the fact that I had so recently lost one.

"No," he said. I winced and concentrated upon keeping my thoughts under control. But they would not obey me. No he could not? Or no he would not? My mind demanded an answer.

"No I cannot, but not for the reason you think." I caught his amused expression out of the corner of my eye. My skin felt hot and flushed.

"Estrazi would doubtless reduce him to component atoms," Eysia put in. "Such a child, so admixed in but two generations, would upset his plans. If it had been done before the testing, the constants would have fallen out differently. There would have been no need to worry what effect such a child would have upon the future of your planet."

Certainly they felt my confusion, but neither deigned to enlighten me.

We stopped before a door, identical in my sight to dozens we had passed, and it opened obediently. Within, I saw sculptured gardens, under a summer sky. We walked between fancifully trimmed hedges of flowering bush, gold and pearl and green. The walk was flagged with slabs of iridescent stone, the air cool and clean, with pungent aliveness that tickled my nostrils. At the end of the long straight path, I could see an arabesqued, towered building, of some gold-veined white stone.

Up the tiered steps we went, and into a mosaicked hall of breathtaking beauty. Esyia's tridoe made Astria seem some peasant hovel. Precious metals filigreed the door lintels, the walls were covered with hangings of vibrant intricate silks. They showed me through the tridoe: the kitchen, where a great table of some golden material was laid with platters of the same; the sleeping rooms, each more wonderful than the one preceding it; the large chamber that could seat three hundred. In the kitchen were no stoves, no stores, no plumbing. In the sleeping rooms were no facilities for grooming or toilet. I had been here long enough not to need to ask why.

In that sleeping room of umber and ocher, which Esyia assigned to me, was a great couch of intaglioed sienna metal. I sat upon it, on the spread that bore the same pattern as my father's ring. Raet removed the leash from my collar. My hands were still bound in front of me. He looked down upon me.

"Will you behave yourself?" he said severely.

"It seems I have little choice."

He looked at me with that expression of distrust I have come to expect from him, and touched the metal bracelets at my wrists. They fell away and hit the brightly patterned thick-piled earth-tone rug and were gone. He stood, muscles tensed, regarding me like the dorkat one finds in the parrhouse among its slaughter: one can never tell what the wild and dangerous beast will do.

"Are these quarters satisfactory?" Esyia asked softly, stepping between us.

I nodded, but my mind knew my body's need, and spoke its message.

"Oh," she said, and circuited the large room. "How about here?" And where the keep narrowed into an alcove, a wall came into being. Since the retarded child could not dispose of her own waste or attend to her own cleanliness, mechanical means had been provided.

I put my recently freed hands in my lap. I wished they would remove my collar.

"That we will not do, for your sake as much as ours," said Esyia, coming to sit beside me. "We will come for you later, and share a meal," she said, and her body was gone from the room. I looked dumbly at the wrinkled depression where her bottom had indented the coverlet with her weight. Raet leaned against one of the chased bronze posts that rose from the couch to meet the muraled ceiling high above our heads.

What can I say about him? That he was his father's son seemed a certainty. That I was so aroused by him as to make the misery he had caused me on Silistra inconsequential? That even Tyith's death was not meaningful enough to stem my need for him? All of that and more. That I cared not that he considered me at best a wild animal, incapable of rational thought? Doubtless. Trembling with eagerness, I went to him, honored beyond comprehension that he would deign to use me. That no child could come from this union, I had previously ascertained. But I wanted that meaningless couching more than I had wanted any other, and I despised myself for the need. Perhaps he used me out of pity, perhaps curiosity, perhaps to further put me in my place. That last he truly accomplished. I, so skilled in the needs of men, found myself barely able to satisfy him. His vitality was such that when I lay finally exhausted from my efforts, I understood why my mother had given up her life to bear a child to such a one. But I would not be allowed that sense of purpose, that rationalization, that Estrazi had permitted my mother. With this couching, I had met my own lust head-on for the first time in my life. To do so is a shattering experience for a woman. To do so with a creature as superior to oneself as one is to the bondrex on the plain rubs salt into the open wound.

When he had gone from the keep, by that instant exit the Mi'ysten prefer, I thought long upon what had occurred. Full of self-recrimination, I paced off my assigned quarters. There were no windows in the ocher keep, nor would the door open for me. I was as much a prisoner as I had been in the crystal cube, but in a more urbane setting. I cannot blame them for being loath to let the beast roam their keep at will. I would not set a dorkat loose in the halls of Astria.

"Flesh toy," he had called me, "come here."

"We are all flesh," I had replied.

"Ah, but we by choice, and you by design. There in is a great difference." His voice had been husky, his eyes half-closed. God-man or not, the man in him knew and desired me.

I held onto that one shred of comfort. For whatever reason, I excited him. When he was gone, I was consumed with fear that I could not do so again, that he might never again use me. I found myself desperate for his acknowledgment. I doubted I would ever have his respect, but how he regarded me seemed more important than the next breath I would take—out of proportion to what had occurred. I was more right than I knew.

I determined to ask Esyia if she could teach me a mind shield effective against him. I could not bear the thought that Raet had access to the emotional maelstrom whirling within me.

We were in the kitchen, Esyia and I. She had
come for me while I lay, drained and dozing, on
the black couch-spread that bore my father's mark,
and escorted me through the corridors into the
kitchen with the great golden table. The walls,
which had been sculptured winy rock when I had
first seen them, were covered so thickly by green-
leaved plants that the rock was merely the pattern
in which the creeping shiny-leaved mat had conceived to grow. That any plants could have grown
up along the walls in such profusion in the short
time since I had been in that room was impossible.

I went and ran my hand along their slick-smooth
leaves. Up to my wrist I buried it in new green.
The smell of growth was tangy in my nostrils.

"Do you like it?" Esyia asked, pride in her voice.
"I thought it a nice change."

I nodded, running my hand through my tangled
hair. She had suggested that I help her with the
meal. There was little chance that I could help this
woman with anything. When she had arrived to
bring me to this greened kitchen, I had been dreaming of Sereth crill Tyris. I could not put the dream
from my mind. In it he had been called to task, at
Celendra's bidding, by the Day-Keepers, for not
returning Tyith's body, nor mine, to Arlet, nor
having proof that I still lived. I was greatly troubled,
for in the dream the council had stripped from the
Seven all his rank and privilege and turned him,
chaldless and outlaw, out from Arlet. If it had not
been for Sereth, and what he had taught me about
myself, I surely would not have survived my couching with Raet with my mind intact.

Esyia came to me where I stood against the
living tapestry that covered the walls of the lofty-
ceilinged hall. She took my hand from my neck
where I worried a thick knot of hair. Then she put
both hands to the crown of my head and slowly

brought them down. My scalp tingled, and every hair on my head raised itself away from its fellows and settled, tangle-free and shining, down against my back. I could feel the electricity dissipate, crackling around me.

Esyia smiled at me. I took up a handful of my long bronze mane and stared at it incredulously. I shook my head, unbelieving.

"Could you teach me that?" I asked her.

"Is that really what you want to learn?" she said, and led me to sit at the great golden table, she at its head and I beside her, on her right. The cushioned, carved chair was warm and yielding against my naked flesh. I leaned back gingerly, for the work that Raet's hands had done upon me was beginning to bear fruit. I could see the bruises darkening on my thighs, feel them tender on my back and rump. On my breasts the marks his teeth had made were raised and purple.

"I would learn a way to keep Raet out of my mind," I said.

"If you had such a skill, it would be a blessing to all of us. Everyone in a sereel radius must know of your coupling. You are a very strong sender."

I wondered what a sereel was. I noticed that Esyia's face seemed pinched and drawn. I could feel the flush of embarrassment creep across my skin. I saw again that moment in the couching when, on my hands and knees, I had kissed his feet, laid my cheek against them. Dismally I remembered that I had begged to be allowed to do so.

"He is very difficult Mi'yst." Esyia commiserated.

"I meant a block, a screen, to keep him from reading my thoughts," I explained.

She spread her hands wide.

"I will submit your request to one of the fathers," she said, "but we must make the meal. Let us have

it typically Silistran." She smiled comfortingly. "I
have not been there since the shaping, and I must
have the exactness of the meal—the components
and their preparation—from your mind."

I obediently visualized the most sumptuous and
delectable Astrian feast I could conceive: jellied
harth, golden-fried grinta, denter with a danne-
flavored sauce, cheesed tuns, narne wine, kifra,
fresh greens, and fruit I arrayed before my mind's
eye. Homesickness swelled and drowned me in a
great wave.

With no more effort from Esyia than it would
have cost me to raise a fork to my mouth, the
dishes I had pictured appeared before us, covering
the length of the golden table, steaming hot and
frosty cold, sliced and glazed and sauced, perfect. I
reached to the fresh fruit and picked from its stalk
a fat gul, purple-blue-skinned and juicy. The juice
was tart and sweet and achingly familiar. I crunched
the seed within it. My throat convulsed, and I
lowered my head to hide my tears.

There was enough food upon that long table to
feed a hundred. I was about to comment upon this
to Elsyia when they started appearing. The air
would shimmer and spark, and one would be where
none had been before. I wondered how they kept
from colliding with one another. Soon the room
was filled with naked bronze forms. I had not
realized there could be such variety within perfection. Esyia introduced me to so many, so fast, I
despaired at divining one from the other. Could
they all know what Raet had done to me? Their
amused faces, smiling, seemed to say that they
did.

Esyia was speaking to me, her hand upon the
arm of a Mi'ysten who could have been my father's
brother. He carried more mass than Raet, seemed
more mature. The bronze face was unlined, but

the eyes, fire-gleam that held mine steadily, were wise beyond compassion.

"This is Kystrai, one of the fathers," Esyia had said. I could feel his delicate probe, and yet I felt calmed under his scrutiny.

"So this is Estri, daughter of Estrazi by a space-time woman. You are she who would learn to shield?" His questioning seemed rhetorical.

I nodded.

"Teach her, Esyia," he said slowly, never taking his eyes from me. "It will be instructive to see how far she can progress." He chuckled. My confusion must have been a screeching wail in their minds. He had not been present when I had asked Esyia to do me that service.

"But—" Esyia protested. Seating himself between us, he raised a hand and cut her off.

I hardly noticed. Raet had arrived, simultaneous with a lithe, copper-skinned woman whose bronze hip-length hair was streaked with gold. Her whole body shimmered with tiny points of light. She took Raet's hand, laughing, and the sparks flowed from her hand to his, up his arm, into his mouth. I felt as if I had been cruelly struck in the solar plexus. Such love-play was, for me, unattainable. I could not compete with such a woman, against whose beauty I was merely plain. I felt again the animal, the retarded alien. By escorting such a creature into my sight, Raet had made my diminishment complete. I wondered if she, too, knew from my mind what had occurred with him; if he would treat her, his equal, as he had treated me. I hunched over in my seat, my arms crossed over my breasts to hide, some way, the marks he had left upon me. I tried desperately to control my agonized thoughts.

As I had known he would, his hand on her high, gilded rump, Raet guided her toward us. I did not bother to remember her name. I saw only the smile that flickered at the corners of Raet's mouth, and Kystrai's hand on my arm.

Raet leaned his weight upon the table, between me and Kystrai. His elbow brushed my breast and started it burning. He spoke low in Kystrai's ear, then took his hand from the table and laid it on the back of my neck, massaging gently, while he spoke in a tongue I did not know to Kystrai, whom Esyia had called a father. I almost cried out for joy that his touch was upon me. I let my eyes roam from the muscles of his back to the sparkling girl's face. It was a face full of impatient disdain, and that disdain held more than a trace of annoyance.

"Your bodies sing well together, yet you hear only your preconceptions," said Kystrai to Raet in Silistran. Raet did not answer, but his hand kneading the back of my neck tensed and stopped. I leaned back in my chair and again regarded the gold-bronze girl, whose hostility came to me strong and clear. When her eyes met mine, I stuck out my tongue at her.

Almost instantaneous with her angry flush, a blast of force came roaring toward me, rocking me back. And Kystrai's hand was before my face, the fingers spread, I was dimly aware of Raet picking himself up from the floor, but my attention was on the girl whom he had brought to the feast. Paled under her glowing skin, she staggered backward as if struck until she fell into two Mi'ysten, who supported her, or she would have fallen. Her eyes rolled in her head, and she gasped for breath.

Kystrai, his hand now on my shoulder, stood by my chair. In the sudden silence, all eyes were on him.

"Retire, Geselle, and contemplate your lamentably short temper. To strike so at one unable to defend herself is surely no act of a daughter of mine."

The weaving girl looked up at Kystai. For a moment I thought she would speak. The next moment, she was gone.

"I had better see to her," Raet said from behind me, and he also was gone.

"And I, find another to help serve," murmured Esyia as she dissappeared into the crowd of bronze bodies.

"Let me apologize to you, in order, for my flesh son and daughter," said Kystrai as he took his seat beside me. "You creatures of time and space must go beyond your natural abilities to fulfill your destiny; the Mi'ysten children must simply grow into theirs."

"I had thought Raet to be Estrazi's son," I managed. "Are they full brother and sister?"

"Their mothers are not the same," Kystrai answered me, "but all of them, as your people, are truly brother and sister."

"What did you do to her?"

"I simply turned back her own sending upon her."

I wondered what would have happened if the full force of that sending had struck me. I saw, at the far end of the long table, Esyia and three other women serving the Silistran meal.

"What did you mean," I asked Kystrai, "when you said that Raet hears only his preconceptions, but our bodies sing well?"

Kystrai smiled and reached out his right hand to my arm. I saw upon the middle finger of that hand the same ring I still wore threaded through my chald.

"Raet and some of the other children have long agitated to wipe clean the time-space worlds and start anew. He argues that useless pain and turmoil are all that have come from the old experiments, most of which were long ago abandoned.

You have proved him false. He has not the grace to admit his mistake. You are its symbol. And yet his flesh knows yours, and calls it equal. His passion frightens you; your awe of him sustains his position. Do not let it be so. In him, the creative surges. Never mistake him for being of lesser appetites than yourself. Or than your father's. In our image, complete, were you all made. The beast creates. The beast is preexisting. Drive out the beast, and you have driven out your divinity." Kystrai's hand on my arm caused a strange coolness to flow over my flesh, and the bruises on my body tingled. As I watched, the raised marks upon my breasts faded and were gone. What he had said echoed in my mind.

"I see," I said. "I can understand his point of view. Upon this world, I am as the most deformed chaldless, unable to feed myself, unable to walk alone in the open, unable to perform the most basic functions without special help. By my own standards I am unfit to live among you. Once I agitated, upon Silistra, for the euthanasia of the chaldless. I cannot condemn him for doing the same. How can I expect him to desire me, if I could not desire the twisted-limbed chaldless on his wheeled cart, propelling himself through the squalid streets of Port Astrin by his callused, stumped wrists? Next to Mi'ysten, Silistra is a planet of chaldless."

Esyia leaned down and took the plate from in front of me, and filled it with Silistran food. The smells of home assailed me.

"Surely the old legends of your people retain the primal command—that you experience creation and return it to us?" Kystrai said gently.

I nodded. My homesickness would not let me speak. Kystrai's plate was full, and Esyia moved to take her own seat on his other side. The father leaned back in his carved chair, his eyes probing.

"At one time, I had thought Raet right, that perhaps it would be kinder to free the flawed creatures from their struggles. Your appearance here, in spite of Raet's efforts, and your test scores and adjustments, have convinced me that I was wrong. You are the first of the time-space worlds who had managed to do so. It is a great accomplishment, greater than you presently understand. You have done your planet a service. Do not be so harsh in your reassessment of yourself and your world. If your testing has found you acceptable in my sight, surely you can be acceptable in your own."

My shredded ego, long comatose in its cave within myself, stirred and began to lick its wounds. I watched Kystrai's right hand as he forked sauced denter into his mouth.

"What is the significance of the ring?" I asked him. "I had thought it my father's crest, but you wear it, and Raet, and the same sign is worked into the spread of my couch."

"It is the sign of the Shapers, the blueprint of the projected extent of the worlds of time and space. Not all of us shape. Among the Shapers, Estrazi is surely the greatest. He would be here now, but for his work." He waved a hand at the ceiling, and it became a star-filled evening sky.

"Look there," he said. My eyes followed his pointing finger, to a spot empty of light. "When you see a flash, there, when the new star is born, he will return. And that star will truly be most perfect." His voice had an odd tone, his face a look of dreamlike ecstasy.

"Perhaps it is born now, and the light has not yet reached us." I hoped it would not be hundreds of years, or thousands, I would spend here until Estrazi returned.

"Such thinking is a constant of space-time, not

Mi'ysten. You will see it when it occurs, if you look, and within the moment of flashing birth, he will be here."

The ceiling became again opaque, and Kystrai turned to his plate. Esyia's eyes caught mine, and the almost imperceptible shake of her head warned me to silence. I felt a hand on my back, and Raet slid into the chair on my left. The now-familiar warmth kindled in my body.

I wondered how long he had been here, what part of Kystrai's conversation with me he had heard.

I turned to my plate and tasted the cheesed tuns. Raet's presence beside me, and the Silistran food in my mouth, reminded me of all that he had done upon Silistra; of Sereth crill Tyris and the attacks of the chalded and chaldless, of the ebvrasea, and of the great crack that had opened to obstruct us in the very earth itself.

"Kystrai," I said softly. He turned those molten eyes upon me. "When your daughter threatened me with a simple sending, you protected me and chastised her. And yet Raet is allowed to do as he pleases with man and beast upon Silistra. Even the earth itself obeys him. Why rebuke the one and not the other? What rules are there, and what name has this game?" My fingers in my lap were shaking. But that power within me knew no fear, not even of Raet's stiffened body upon my left, still but for the rubbing together of forefinger and thumb.

Long moments Kystrai looked at me without speaking, and then at Raet.

"Will you not speak for yourself, created son?" said Kystrai at length.

The son, before the father, lowered his eyes. "Though it is my right," he growled, "I will not debate matters of fitness with a time-space creature.

Nor do I feel the need to justify my actions. What I do in my realm is my own affair. Unless, of course, the daughter of Estrazi chooses to contest with me. . . ." And with only a raised eyebrow and the most gently supercilious smile, he fell silent.

"It is a thought," said Kystrai solemnly, taking my hand in his, which did not shake, and squeezing. "Within the broader mandate, what he says is true: we do not interfere between the Mi'ysten children and the time-space spawn, nor in the administration of such worlds by those who claim the Shaper heritage. It is that heritage which has brought you here, and which has entitled you to those exemptions you now enjoy."

Once more he squeezed my hand, clasping it between both of his. Then he released it, and turned to Esyia, speaking with her in the sibilant language of Mi'ysten. I toyed with my food, disquieted, not daring even to raise my eyes to Raet. As I sat there, his hand touched my thigh under the table. An audible sigh came from me, as the breath I had held in expectation of his displeasure fled my lungs. My disquiet flowed after it. I wondered if somehow Raet could control my body's reaction, as Esyia had been able to bring peace to me with a touch of her hand, if spirit and emotion were as much "his realm" as the earth that parted to serve him upon the plateau of Santha. I shook the thought away. My need was strong upon me from that simple touch, and I ate without tasting, until my plate was cleaned. When I looked up from it, Kystrai was no longer in the chair upon my right. I was sorry. I would have wished him tasa.

"The food was the best thing about Silistra," Raet said. His tone was intimate, as if my audacious queries had never been spoken. He leaned close.

"I wish I were there now," I said.

"What? And not discharge the chaldra of the mother? After all you have gone through to get here, you would leave without ever meeting your father? Is the Shapers' heritage so paltry that you would not tarry here long enough to claim it?" He laughed.

"When will I see him? What is a star nursery? What of the others in the cubes? Kystrai said I was the first to arrive here of my own accord. How did they get here? What will happen to them? And to me?" Bereft of breath and composure, I pressed my palms to my eyes, to ease the blurring that threatened any moment to overflow into tears.

"All those things you should have asked Kystrai. I cannot tell you. But you may learn it." His eyes made me forget my questions. His hand tracing my spine brought the blood surging to my skin. "You may learn it, though I have my doubts as to what he will accomplish by schooling you. The fathers know what they do, but the presence of the lame and halt of time and space proves them not infallible."

"Schooling me!" I repeated dumbly.

"You did not understand him, then? Your Shapers' heritage—they would see you claim it."

Unable to restrain myself, I leaned my shoulder against him. The coolness of his flesh soothed my heat. Doubtless he heard my thoughts, though I tried to keep them from him, for his tone was much softened, and his arm went around my waist.

"And perhaps you will find the learning easy. It is not a thing to await with such trepidation. The rewards are bountiful for one who shapes." His mouth was close to my ear. I did not mistake the irony, nor the sarcasm upon which his words rode.

"What do you mean?" I asked. Seemingly, he ignored my question.

"I had thought you not strong enough to have

come so far with mind intact. I was mistaken in that. Perhaps I will, through you, come to look upon Silistra with different eyes."

I remembered what Kystrai had said, reminding myself that my personal worth, and, through me, that of Silistra, were still being assessed. I began to have some sense of the reason I had felt Raet's opinion of me to be so important. And he was intimating that he would, for the time, suspend judgment. With a shiver, I wondered what would attend that judgment, what kind of forces were being held in abeyance. I turned to him, announced ruler of the realm that included Silistra. I must please him. I recollected the power he had demonstrated over my world. I shuddered. Fear and desire admixed in me, each upstepping the other's intensity. I felt my skin dampen and my heart begin a thudding, syncopated pound.

"Let us begin our farewells, and then I will show you my tridoe," Raet said in my ear, and rose from the table. Gratefully, I followed after him.

# IX.
## To Stand Among the Shapers

He with whom I studied was called Teris. He resembled Esyia in skin tone and Kystrai in build and mind-touch. His patience seemed infinite, his insight awe-inspiring. It was he who gave me, in that first consummate instruction, the weapons I needed to break through the psychological barriers my upbringing had created. Often I have recollected Teris's teaching, and each time I am reminded of a story I once heard concerning an infant who was raised by dorkats. The child, past puberty when discovered by the Day-Keepers, had been to all intents and purposes a dorkat. As the Day-Keepers struggled with that child, to teach him to walk erect and speak and use his hands for more than tearing meat from a fresh kill, so did Teris struggle with me, to teach me to shape.

It was Raet who delivered me to him, and he was not pleased to do so. Sullenly, he led me along the walkway through the time-fields of the tangential climes. Somehow I tripped over my own feet and fell onto the lush greenery of the rainforest's edge. A great whirlpool sucked at me. My hands gripped the walkway, and my body was stretched so tight from the pull that I thought my arms would be torn from their sockets. Raet, legs spread wide, still holding the leash attached to my collar, looked pensively down at me. It flashed into my mind that he would rather lose his new toy than give it up to another.

"Help me," I gasped. My fingers were numb. I could not hold on much longer.

"Climb back on the walkway," he suggested, a smile playing at the corners of his mouth.

"I haven't the strength," I pleaded.

He squatted down, his feet inches from my white-knuckled, aching hands. "If I let you slip away, things would become suddenly very simple," he said softly. His eyes stared into mine steadily.

"Raet, please!"

"Once before I gifted you with life."

"I beg you, do not do this," I moaned, my arms and shoulders aflame with strain.

"You do recollect it, then? And acknowledge that with this service I do you, you stand twice in my debt?"

"Yes, oh, yes."

He smiled, then, and languorously extended his hand. When his fingertips touched me, the pull fell away from my limbs and I was able to crawl onto the slightly raised walk. I crouched there and stared into the dappled rainforest that had nearly claimed me, my arms clutched around my trembling body.

"What seek you from me? What threat could I possibly be to you?" I whispered, my eyes imploring. I had seen, in his tridoe, the measure of his detachment and the cruelty of which he was capable. Raet played with animal life as a child might with those blocks which interlock, from which structures may be made in accordance with the child's imagination. Some of his experiments had been so ill-fit to walk, hop, or fly that I had still not shaken the horror from me. "Please," I enjoined him, when he did not answer, "what service may I do you, you who claim dominion over the world of my origin?"

"Well spoken," he said gravely, extending his hand to me. "You are your father's daughter. For now, I will ask no more than that; cede me your recognition of my mandate."

"I do so vow," I mumbled, staring into his narrowed eyes, filled with consternation, that such a one would seek to bind me. And he had, thusly, my word from me before I had any inkling of what kills I had so imbound.

We made our way to Teris without further incident, but nowhere along the walkway did I see any sign of the multitude of cubes that had once lined the white walk. It was as if the cube in which I had been imprisoned, and the hundreds of others exactly like it, had never been.

I did not ask Raet. Doubtless he had my questions from my mind. He did not choose to enlighten me.

The classes were held in a large open field, where the walkway abruptly ended, under the multicolored sky. I saw perhaps a hundred Mi'ysten children with a handful of adults, sitting scattered on the saw-toothed grass.

Raet threaded me through the groups of youngsters, ranging from crawlers to postpubescent youths. I was very conscious of the leash in his hand and the band at my throat. Where could I run, I thought bitterly, where the Mi'ysten could not find me?

The grass was cool under my feet, the earth carpeted warm and yielding. For the first time since my arrival, I trod Mi'ysten soil.

Raet jerked me to a stop by a group of six bronzed

toddlers overseen by a sharp-featured, stock Mi'y-sten who wore a blue circlet about his head. He was the first Mi'ysten I had seen who wore any-thing upon his person but an occasional Shaper's ring. Looking about me, I realized that all the adults in the field had so bound their heads.

"Teris," said Raet, handing him the chain leash dangling from the band around my neck, "Estri. I do not envy you your task." And he was gone from my side.

Teris smiled at me kindly. "I think we will not need this, you and I," he said, and snapped the leash from my collar. It dropped to the ground. Not since then have I worn one.

His voice was low, modulated, suited to his easy manner. The laughter in his pale amber eyes had no cruelty in it. I found myself much reassured by him, in those first few moments of our acquaint-ance. He greeted me in Silistran, not the archaic Stoth dialect that the Mi'ysten favored, but mod-ern Silistran, as it is spoken in Astria.

Greatly eased, I sat at his bidding on the grass, and watched the children at their lessons. They were shaping fruit.

After a time, he spoke to me. "We will begin where you left off," said my teacher. Between us appeared a roiling ball of thick brown substance, over which fiery sparks chased frantically.

"Make the fruit of your choice," he directed.

My stomach curled back upon itself. My palms wept, and I could not steady my breathing. I was nervous before my teacher. He raised both brows. I sighed and closed my eyes, repeating the ritual I had developed while in my cube.

I reopened them only when I heard a distinct thud. As I had conceived it, the narne fruit lay upon its side, red and shiny in the serrated grass.

I regarded Teris.

He picked it up and examined its form, then bit into it, then caused it to halve itself in his hands.

"Good," he pronounced. "Now, make another."

I waited for the ball of brown matter. Nothing appeared in the space between us. Teris stared at me intently. I held his gaze as long as I could. With dropped eyes I considered.

"I cannot," I burst out. "I need the brown matter."

"Make it," he commanded.

"Out of the air? I cannot."

"Why not? All you need is present in the air you breathe. Remember, you are no longer on Silistra."

I remembered. And I recalled how thick and filling this Mi'ysten air had seemed when I first breathed it.

I raised my head to him. It could not be.

He nodded encouragingly.

I closed my eyes and attempted to conceive the brown matter in the space between us, just as I had seen it. I could not hold the image. I was ignorant of the brown material. Knowledge of its consistency, temperature, qualities, and properties—all were lacking. I had never studied the brown matter, nor used it in its raw form. I had been foolish. I realized it was not the first time I had been impeded by my own superficiality.

Once more I met the eyes of my teacher. Patient Teris, how infantile I must have seemed to him.

"Demand to know," he advised. "Demand to see. You can get the information you need."

"From where?"

"From within. You have access to direct information. You have interacted with the brown mass. Somewhere you know it. One does not have to know why one knows a thing in order to benefit from the knowing."

I did as he commanded. After long failing, long

refusing, long pretending, anguished, I shaped another red, juicy narne from the air of Mi'ysten. I had not wanted to. I had not wanted to learn the truth—that the Mi'ysten could shape fruit, trees, skies, mountains, worlds, stars. Nor that they had, in some distant time and from some unknown space, shaped even my world, even my ancestors. I had shaped. Truly, I did not want to know it, or accept it and my half-breed status and the ramifications of my father's nature.

In that first shock, I did not want to be as they. I coveted not at all the power over life and death and the control of reality I saw around me, that omnipotence within which they lived, free from all that could threaten them. Eternally. How quickly would I be consumed by boredom if such a life were mine? It would not be so. I was not as they. I would not, could not be. Nor would they ever accept me among them.

That thought comforted me, momentarily.

"What you fear is the loss of relevance," Teris chided me softly. I had forgotten. On Mi'ysten there was for me no privacy.

"Relevance," he continued, "is in itself a construct superimposed upon reality, upon the universe, by your limited brains and linear thought processes. It stands like a stenciled no-trespassing sign nailed askew upon the first tree of the last forest at the edge of your world, where no eye will ever pass that can read the language in which it was written. Yet truth proclaims itself." He hested the second narne fruit into the air, where it spun between us, unsupported. Teris's eyes sucked my feelings from me.

I had shaped.

Oh, barely, perhaps, but enough to taste the burden, enough to know what question might be asked.

"Teris," I said to him, "Raet exacted from me an acknowledgement of his sovereignity, but over *what*, I am not sure. Nor do I have the 'why' of it."

The narne fruit plummeted to the ground, rolled thrice, lay against its twin near my foot. Teris considered it. When he raised his countenance to me, I could not name his expression.

"I am a Mi'ysten child—a created son, as is he. Those of us who seek shaping skills are not many, nor are we as successful as our fathers. I can see no resolution, in the long run, of the struggle between the children for the father's heritage. But I am not among those who favor such drastic steps as Raet and some others have proposed. If, between you two, some grounds for converse could be found, it would be a union whose fruit would be prized highly by many of us."

"I do not understand."

"None of the Mi'ysten children have been successful in creating a stable world. If the space-time children were no more, there would be many new theaters upon which experimental dramas might be staged."

I merely stared at him.

"Among our assigned labors is the caretaking of creation. Raet and his followers tread the thin line between self-aggrandizement and iniquity, between innovation and insurrection. If the assessors vote as I belive they·will, it may be a rebuke sufficient of itself to remind them of their place. You will have influence upon your father, in whose hands all of creation truly rests. Do you see?"

"If Raet comes upon the need, he will call on me to stand for him?"

"At least. Your expressed word has done that much, already. By accepting his mandate in the worlds of time and space, you have gainsaid aforehand any objection you might have justly entered, should you claim your full blood-right."

I did not tell him that I would not have gainsaid Raet, regardless. I asked, instead, of those others who had been in the cubes, and was told that all but three were returned to their homes without the lapse of any subjective time. Their loved ones did not miss them, for they were never gone. Nor did they recollect Mi'ysten, not even the cubes in which they had lived. Of the three, I was one. The other two, Teris assured me, I would see in good time. And upon that subject he would speak no more.

The Mi'ysten guard their privacy. I questioned him about what Dellin had told me: of the contact team that had landed on Zredori, and their horrible demise. He answered that the ship had landed in a tangential clime where primitives were developing. When I only regarded him, he added that they had been unexpected. I answered him that it was unlike the Mi'ysten to make such an oversight. Surely the crude creatures of time and space could not so surprise their creators. He looked at me very keenly, dismissed his other students, and escorted me to Esyia's tridoe. He never taught me again.

What other instruction I received, she imparted to me. I learned from her that shaping on Mi'ysten is not the toil of shaping in the worlds of time and space, where entropy reigns. She could give me no more than the most elementary of mind shields, nor dared she instruct me in the obviation of space, that mode of travel most favored by Mi'ystens. The first, I attempted on my own with partially satisfactory results, building upon the infant's shield whose workings Esyia was qualified to teach. The second was a skill about which I would have been content to remain ignorant, but that I felt so keenly my immurement, made ever sharper by the freedom Esyia and her siblings enjoyed.

It became Raet's habit to come and take me, occasionally. And when he did not, the feelings I had for him—the raging, halting love—caused me great pain. As it was then, so is it still, between us. When I am with him, I despise myself for my weakness—that I can never be more than flesh toy to him; that I cannot even refuse to love him. These conflicting emotions, Esyia assures me, will pass; eventually I will either love or hate him, destroy or be destroyed by him: so she has told me. But so far I have come to no decision. When I am with him, I regret my limitations, my Silistran blood, with all my heart. And when he does not seek me, when that pain recedes, the constrictive chill of loneliness and longing takes its place. I have a thousand times cursed him, and as many times traded off in fantasy all that I might ever become for revenge upon his supernal flesh. I would, at those moments, be gone from this place, away from him, home on Silistra, and be there gladly, with no remembrance of what has here occurred. Or would have, until this day just passed, if one may give names like "day" and "night" to time as it is experienced here.

Just after my rising meal, he came to see me. I can recognize that in his own way he gets value from me, else he would not do so. We went together to his tridoe, and he made for me a night sky like the one Kystrai had made in the dining hall. I look forward to that the most, out of all that transpires when I couch him—seeing the evening sky. So much do I crave it that the fact that such a sky might be made for my view directly following sleep and sun's meal no longer troubles me. One never knows how one would miss the night until it is taken away.

"Do you like it?" he asked, nuzzling my ear as I lay on my back in his feather-edged, cerise grass, looking up at the stars.

"It is very beautiful," I allowed. I tried in vain to pick constellations I knew from the blazing myriad points of light.

"It is more than that," he said, his lips in my hair. "It is the night sky you have been awaiting. Look there. . . . I may not see you after this," Raet said, and put his arms around me. I turned my face to him, to protest. The afterimage of the explosion danced upon his forehead, new star glowing bold between his eyes.

"And I am certain that such will be the case," came the voice from above me, where I lay beneath Raet on the cool grass.

Raet rolled from me, and Estrazi was all that my mother had promised, and more. I rose to my knees, struck dumb and witless. The recording of my conception had not prepared me for him. Ah, father, before whom the morning star pales insignificant, and all that I have borne to kneel before thy brightness becomes too meager to speak, I have no question for you who have labored in the lands of life interminably. I have in me no single query in the babbling tongues of creation. No supplication, not from me, not when the torrent of the grace and compassion inundates my soul.

Through my tears, I saw him reach out to me. How did he appear, most supernal of masters? In a flesh form so magnificent that his brightness illuminated the air around. I saw myself then, in that glow; myself as he saw me, a triumph of life, a wonder so great that a song might be made for my singularity. I, his creation, beheld him.

Our fingers touched.

He smiled, not with mouth, but with those eyes like universes forming.

I sensed rather than saw his attention shift. Before me that superb form disintegrated and reformed into a writhing slitsa of light. It pulsed a moment, dancing upon the grass. Then it shot into the air, to be met there by another. And, clawing hair back from my face, turning round and round in vain for sight of Raet, I knew what I had seen. Raet! It was up, then, I looked, into the night sky, where he pulsed in his light form. Bright against the dark firmament, the two spun and closed. I crammed my knuckles into my mouth and sank down upon the grass, craning my neck to see them. They became one, flared unbearably, disengaged, and melded again. The pulsating glare grew in intensity until I threw my arm over my face and huddled, sobbing, my head turned away.

When I lowered my arm from my face, Estrazi sat upon the ground before me. Raet was nowhere to be seen. My father's countenance bore a contemplative smile. His glowing eyes caressed me.

Still upon my knees, I sat back on my heels.

"Raet?" I whispered. "Surely you did not destroy him? I am deep in his debt. I . . ." I could not further speak of him. His dissolution upon my account was more than I could bear.

"He is not for you," Estrazi said sternly. "But I did not destroy him. I merely chastised him. When Raet comes to an accounting, it will be to all of us. If he does. As for debts owing, between you two there are none. You should have come here bearing the child of one I had chosen for that honor, one equal to you in all things. It was Raet's hand that stayed that life from forming in you, and his hand also that caused you to expel an egg unquickened. So you stand even with him; his takings and givings sum the same. That brilliance of his may yet end much fallen." He paused, inclining his magnificent head.

I shifted my knees from the pebbles that jabbed up through the grass. I said nothing.

"Daughter," he said slowly, "I will rescind my injunction. I would not constrain you unduly on this our first meeting. Do as you will with him. Only, remember that you owe him no allegiance, and remember what I have said."

I went to him and sat by his side. He took my hand in his. I could not speak. I merely leaned my head upon his shoulder, watching the light dance out from his skin.

"You are much like your mother," he remarked. "Out of all the women of time and space, I had the most hope for her. She, among all of them, was the only one who knew me. She had no fear, no superstition. If I had not needed you so desperately, I would have brought her here. I have often thought of her. It gives me great pleasure that you have so much of her strength, her fitness, her beauty."

"For what did you need me so desperately? Are you not omnipotent, omniscient?"

"For what, you will summarily apprehend." Estrazi smiled, and a warm breeze came out of nowhere and fondled my skin. His arm went round my back and I leaned my weight against his cool flesh. "As for omniscience, upon such a tiny scale, none can claim it. The interruption of probability by a Mi'ysten is not foreseeable, since they are not creatures of time."

And summarily, I did apprehend Estrazi's purpose, for I was thereupon lifted up in my father's arms, and when he set me again upon the ground, we stood in a vast natural amphitheater, wherein all the legions of creation had convened to hear the assessors render judgment upon the worlds of time and space.

My father, as Architect of Days, presided. Beside him were arrayed the six other fathers, Kystrai directly upon his right. Upon his left sat the assessors themselves, each of whom wore the aspect of a silhouette before flame, and those flames that came out from each dark man-form melded into one another in one great conflagration. All around that central circle were gathered the factions who would this day hold forth. At the forefront of one group was Teris, and of the other, Raet. Directly opposed to the assessors stood the Hertekiean, myself, and the blond girl who had been beneath me in the cubes. The Hertekiean took my left hand in his right and held it. It was good. I reached with my right and clasped the hand of the blond girl.

Long did Teris hold forth in his impassioned plea for the flawed creatures of time and space, while the winged and the mist-formed and those whose feet were golden talons hovered and stood and sat, each in his circle, ranged around the central pit. And even longer did Raet deliver his diatribe. With implacable logic he submitted his appeal to reason and order. Striding to and fro before the assessors (upon whom it was difficult to look for more than a moment), he stated his case for the purging from all the worlds of creation those children hopelessly enfleshed.

The Hertekiean's grip upon my hand became painful. It seemed to me, staring around at the convoked host, that many leaned forward, that many nodded heads.

Upon his conclusion, Teris made rebuttal, using, as had Raet, myself and the Hertekiean and the blond girl as examples.

Once more, and briefly, did Raet speak. Not once in the final speech did he even look upon me, but faced the assessors the whole time.

When that was done, my father directed the general vote. Both he and Kystrai, and Raet and

Teris, abstained, as concerned parties whose judgment could not be unbiased.

There was no word spoken nor ballot passed, only a long silence, broken at last by the assessors. As one being, they rose up. From seven throats came their decision: "There will be no cleansing of the time-space worlds. In all their imperfection, they must remain. It is Time itself that will remake the inhabitants thereof." And they were gone.

Pandemonium broke loose then in the great amphitheater. The Hertekiean lifted me bodily into the air and swung me around. When he released me, it was into Estrazi's arms.

"Take a loan from me, little one," he whispered into my hair, "against that wealth you hold still buried within." And from him, into me came a flood of strength and knowing that spread out through my form like the first sip of water slaking a long-borne thirst, and like that water, brought to my awareness, by its easing, every cranny of what had lain long parched within. The power which had aided me on occasion in the past seemed to rise up and out, until it looked through my eyes. And when Estrazi released me, though I staggered briefly, I had no need of question, but met his gentle smile.

We parted, then; he to join Kystrai and the other fathers, and I to do what had long cried out for the doing, what the power within me demanded, and what Estrazi's gift had made it impossible for me to avoid.

I sought Raet. I sought him through the crowded confusion of the convoked host, with Estrazi's words reverberating in my mind: *Do as you will with him. I rescind my injunction. Do . . .*

I found him, near the lowest of the grassed ledges that encircled the pit like so many concentric bangles, amid a score of his followers. His face was terrible to look upon, his eyes glowing slits of flame, as if by their heat alone he could char his defeat to ashes. How long had he labored, how painstaking had been his preparation for this, the moment of his defaming and mortification?

The stiffening of his frame, his countenance, suffused with rage, and the grim line of his mouth as he threaded his way toward me through his allies spoke most eloquently. It was I, in his sight, and I alone who had brought his plans to ruin. Ambition, thwarted, is the bitterrest of poisons.

What might I have said to him, had he not so menacingly, so inexorably approached? I know not; only do I recollect his contorted face and the wrath and animosity that issued therefrom, and the answer his fury called forth from me.

"Cousin ..." I greeted him coldly, the power within me parrying the projectile of his rage as if it were never launched.

He halted, at arm's length. All emotion drained from his face, and the assessing calm so revealed was more chilling than the wind from the abyss.

"When you are possessed of those skills to which you now only aspire," he spat, "and only then, will I hear from you a claim of propinquity. Claim kinship with great care, Estri, for when you do so, you will have gainsaid the immunity your ineptitude demands." His hands, at his sides, were balled into fists.

"I will waive it," hissed the power within me, while my heart longed to ease him in his distress. "Too long have you obstructed me. Even with guile and dishonor did you exact from me a vow in reparation for a debt nonexistent. Release me, by word or contest!"

"I release you," he said almost inaudibly. "I would not have it said that I am so lacking in fitness as to destroy a creature inarguably my inferior." And he wheeled and strode away into the midst of his minions.

I watched him through a comber of ambivalence that threatened to throw me to my knees. My love decried my heartlessness, my hate reviled me, that I dealt so lightly with my enemy.

When at last I could no longer see him, I turned, and found my father smiling down upon me.

"Come, little one," he said, encircling my shoulders with his arm. "I will show you an end worthy of the most arduous labors, and what triumph you may one day enjoy."

He took me, then, to view his most recent creation, and it was truly perfect. We floated there unscathed in the void before that raging newborn, supported and surrounded by the imperviousness of Estrazi's skills. My lungs did not gasp upon the vacuum, nor did my blood become crystals of ice. I but stood at his side, upon the platform of realized will, and beheld what heritage might someday be mine.

Raet has bespoken it: I could not have survived a moment of that experience upon the strength of my barely emergent skills.

But I am learning.

I have showered in star's breath.

# Glossary

**aniet:** One of the seven interconnected underground life-support complexes that housed refugee Silistrans during the thousand year period known as hide-days. The hide aniet lies under the Dead Sea in the Parset Desert; or the hide-name aniet, as Aknet aniet Beshost. Of all the hides of Silistra, the blood of aniet is the least common, being confined almost exclusively to the Parset Lands by an insular confederation of tribes who maintain there a strict autonomy. Almost one-half of aniet's survivors were of Gristasha tribesmen, and this strong infusion makes "aniet's stamp" an easily recognizable Silistran type.

**apprei:** The tapestried, pyramidal tents of the nomadic desert cities of the Parset tribes.

**Arlet:** Well Arlet. Also, the lands controlled by her.

**Arletian:** Of or pertaining to Well Arlet. In couching, any coupling attended by bondage or containing elements of submission; as criticism, excessive vehemence, or roughness.

**Astria:** Well Astria. The lands controlled by Well Astria, including Port Astrin, her dependent city. Sometimes, in colloquial speech, it may denote the Well Foundress: "By Astria!"

**Astria Barina diet Hadrath:** The Foundress of Well Astria, great-grandam of Estri Hadrath diet Estrazi. It is legend that Astria was born in hide-year sixty-three. This cannot presently be authenticated due to the unavailability of hide records. Astria died Cai first fifth, 24,833 of the Silistran calendar.

**Baniese:** Of or pertaining to Baniev.

**Baniev:** Silistra's most northern coast port. Baniev's

major exports are: the famed northern thala; danne, the yellow herb that grows high in the Sabembes; and the tri-sailed long ship whose fleetness has no equal even in the quays of Dritira.

bast: The hide bast, which lies under the Well Arlet and is said to extend under the Sabembe range. The hide name "bast."

Beten: The planet Beten twins Katrii around the G-star Cerioles. Famed for her mathematicians and her astrogators, it was Betenese minds which first solved the congruence problem and put such outlying worlds as Silistra upon the interstellar trade routes, previously restricted to those worlds in the Inner Stars and Central Clusters.

Betenese: Having origin on the planet Beten.

binnirin: A high-protein, high-fat grain that grows in numerous varieties all over Silistra. Binnirin proliferates with little urging, and is the hardiest and most nutritious of Silistra's grains. Kernel size varies with region and variety, but is generally bifurcated, with twinned germs. The plant, when mature, may reach the height of a man, and the ripe grain is a tannish-brown. Anything tannish-brown may be called binnirin. From the grain comes flour and the fermented beverage brin, as well as oil and stalk fodder for denter and parr.

Bipedal Federate Standard Time: (BFST) Measured in hours, minutes, and seconds; an hour being equal to twenty-one twenty-seconds of an enth.

Bipedal Federation: (B.F.) The M'kssakkan confederacy of worlds as a whole, including both the Bipedal Federate Trade Union (merchant arm), and the Bipedal Federate Group (the original fifty-five worlds, commonly referred to as the Inner Stars).

Bipedal Standard: (B.S.) Universal mean weights and measures.

birth-price: The fee paid to a man by the Well for impregnating a woman in exchange for waiving his right to her baby, generally in the area of a thousand gold dippars and never more than ten thousand.

bondrex: A class of horned herbivores; any undomesticated grazer whose milk and meat are not coveted by man (except the steppe bondrex, prized and raised for its long, silky hair). There are nineteen species of bondrex cataloged on Silistra, requirements for inclusion into this group being a split or cloven hoof, three stomachs, horned males (both branching and curled), a height no more than five B.S. feet at shoulder, and an average weight of no more than eight hundred B.S. pounds.

brin: A mind intoxicant drink fermented from the binnirin grain, most commonly in wisper-wood casks.

brist: A large and ferocious Silistran carnivore, hunted both for pelt and meat. Brist have a standing height of up to sixteen B.S. feet, a weight of up to twenty-five hundred pounds. Unless ill or frightened, brist walk upright. Their appearance is generally manlike. The head is round, the jaw slung under and hinged below side-set ears. The whole body is covered with a thick coat, generally brown, much prized for its warmth and durability. The brist has six clawed digits on hands and feet, and opposing thumbs. Their cry is high and shrill, almost a bark.

caocu: A yellowish, lanceolate-leaved plant from the swamps of Galesh. This phototropic plant unfurls its leaves only at night, at which time they emit a phosphorescent glow. Although attempts have been made to cultivate the caocu, the medicinal value of the cultivated plant is markedly reduced as compared to the wild plant hunted in its riparian habitat of choice. The caocu's root, and to a lesser extent its stalk and leaves, contain a benign acid of phosphorus not found in any other Silistran plant (the "fourth" phosphor), which accelerates localized cell reparation and retards the formation of scar tissue; the reagent caophosphor; the yellow salve extracted from the root.

Centaus: The planet Centaus is an airless sphere composed almost exclusively of heavy metals; the single satellite of the yellow dwarf Artersh.

chald: (Stothric: spirit-bond.) A belt of chains commonly soldered around the waist.

chalded: Possessed of or wearing a chald.

Chaldless: Possessing no chald; one who has been either unwilling or unable to acquire chaldra; an outlaw; one who has been stripped of his chald for iniquitous behavior, and so disbarred from Silistran society.

chaldra: Numerous volumes exist upon the subject of chaldra, first and foremost *Ors Chaldra* (the dharen Khys, hide-year sixty-three); Khys's postulates of self-rule; the goal-seeking morality of Silistra in general, including both high-chaldra (tasks and responsibilities undertaken to strengthen the spirit form and increase survival potential of the eternal particle, the individual consciousness, or the flesh race as a whole) and low-chaldra (pertaining to the survival and betterment of the mundane individual, the acquiring of life skills of material import only); a trade of craft chain.

chaldric: Demanded by chaldra; the "chaldric strands" that make up a chald; duties or labors determined by the Laws of Chaldra.

chan-tera: (chan: will of; tera: life.) Avowed life dedication; that toward which the life labors, any ongoing struggle to perfect.

chit-guard: Caretakers and handlers of golachits, most often an apprentice position.

coin girl: A girl who couches for pay outside the

Well system. Most often such girls sell themselves into long-term servitude contracts as a last resort when the alternatives to such work are meager. Coin girls are sometimes purchased as children from chaldless, and in this fashion a comely chaldless girl may better her estate. Coin girls, though generally chaldless, are not considered outlaw, nor are they disbarred from acquiring chaldra, should they choose to labor toward that end.

couch: (n.) A sleeping platform, any surface used for coupling.

couch: (v.t.) To copulate.

couchbond: A companionship agreement between two consenting adults. (Low-chaldra.) The titrium couchbond strand is issued to the male at puberty after potency has been determined. No Day-Keeper need officiate at such an enchalding, nor is a chalder demanded by custom. The titrium chain may be inwoven or removed from a chald at the discretion of the two parties involved. There is no minimum or maximum time of couchbond.

couch-gift: The tokens exchanged upon the assumption of couchbond, forever after the property of the individual in receipt. Also, any gift of sentiment.

couching: (n.) Any single coupling; a style, as "an Astrian couching."

couch-mate: Persons bound together by love and/or issue; in usage, those in extended couchbond, those who consider their relationship more binding than simple couchbond. Couch-mate denotes responsibility of a high moral order between two people. Gifting between couch-mates is traditionally regulated; one gives either the gift of life (progeny, animal, or human) or the gift of death (knife or sword).

couch-met: Met while performing well work; couching partners who have no previous acquaintance.

couch-price: The fee a woman demands for her sexual services. Fees may range from as low as a titrium half-well for a coin girl to as high as fifty gold dippers for a *high-couch* girl.

couch-sisters: Well women; those of the same Well.

crill: The hide crill, under the city Nin Sihaen across the Karir-Thoss River, is the most westerly of all Silistran hides; the hide-name crill, as: Sereth crill Tyris.

crux: One of the major Weathers of Life; time within which only that preordained may be done. Time so obscured that no foreknowledge may be gathered of what will occur therein. Colloquially, the abyss. Any time that spawns far-reaching changes whose effects and purposes are supernal in nature. Events that precipitate numinosity or nympholeptic response in the superconscious.

danne: Psychotropic yellow herb that grows best at high altitudes in stony soil. The strength and efficacy of danne vary greatly from area to area. The best danne grown high in the Sabembe range. Danne lowers both blood pressure and brainwave frequency and is mildly hallucinogenic. It is removed from the human system neither by the kidneys nor liver, but goes directly to the brain and seems to be absorbed by the hypothalamus. It was once thought to be a "brain food" and sympathetic nervous-system revivifier with cumulative effects, but no empirical experiments have proved this out. Danne neither prolongs life nor increases intelligence; it simply alters consciousness with no long-term effects whatsoever.

Day-Keepers: The guardians of Silistran history, past, present, and future. The Day-Keeper hierarchy as a whole is referred to as the Dharendiil, a High Day-Keeper as dharener. Over these presides the dharen, the spiritual guide of Silistra.

It is said that when Khys conceived the Dharendiil, he directed that Day-Keeper always be capitalized as a reminder to those who bear the title of the humbleness of their function. The forereaders, however, were given no such injunction, and maintain the lower-case honors.

Day-Keepers' Clock: A mythical gnomon upon whose face all that ever was, is, and will be is enscribed. Usually an oath, as "By the Day-Keepers' Clock."

Day-Keepers' Roll: The records of the dead, the archives into which name and history are entered upon an individual's death.

deep-reader: One whose skills allow access to the deeper consciousness of another, exempting thoughts framed for communication. The value of deep-reading is considered by many to be greater than that of surface reading, for thoughts upon the surface, like the tip of an iceberg, give little and often faulty enlightenment as to what lurks beneath.

denter: A large-humped, nub-horned animal, passive and tractable, raised for meat and dairy, and often used as a draft beast. This single-hoofed animal ranges from ten to fourteen hands and may reach a weight of thirteen hundred B.S. pounds.

Detarsa: Fifth pass of the Silistran calendar.

dhara-san: (Stothric: homage to the day.) A system of mental and physical discipline said to align the sevenfold spirit with the human form. The physical and mental exercises are divided into eleven degrees, each of which has subdivisions, or embrasures, of sufficient diversity to allow the student to tailor his routine to his specific goals.

dharen: (ST) The spiritual ruler of Silistra; the supreme authority of the Day-Keeper hierarchy.

dharener: (ST) A high Day-Keeper; one who holds the administrative rank of dharen; a hide council member. (In the Parset Lands, where the dhareners posture at autonomy, the hide council seeks no higher authority.)

diet: The hide diet, which extends under Well Astria, has her entrance on the banks of the Litess River, within the walls of the Day-Keepers' School; the hide name diet.

dippar: Silistran coinage. One gold dippar is equaled by fifty copper dippars. Dippars are minted only in independent cities, as opposed to titrium and gold half-wells and wells, minted by the Well system. They are round with octagonal holes punched in mid-disk, and are intaglioed with a representation of the city in which they were struck.

distrit: A bar-pressed, resinous stimulant rendered from danne and the gum of the fulchra tree, in itself a stimulant. The gum and danne powder are boiled until a thick yellow infusion the consistency of honey is produced. This is poured into oblong molds to set and cure. Although danne by itself may have soporific effects, when ingested in distrit form, its effects are nearly opposite—a raising of blood pressure with contraction of blood vessels and capillaries. Classified as a revivifier, distrit in excessive amounts may cause insomnia.

dorkat: Wingless cousin of the hulion, the dorkat has the same wedge-shaped head and pointed ears. The hind musculature tends to be lighter, but the forequarters are as heavily developed. Although the cranial capacity is identical with the hulion's, dorkats do not demonstrate more than half the intelligence of their winged brethren. The nocturnal dorkat is prevalent in all the wilderness areas of Silistra, and its prey is thusly varied, dependent upon what the area will provide. They are exclusively carnivores, with protruding incisors. Dorkats, unlike hulions, have been known to turn man-eater, and are often troublesome raiders to herders of domesticated beasts.

draw: Draw time, one of the Weathers of Life, recognizable by the acceleration of the procession of events, and to the individual by an increased sensitivity and awareness of proximity to crux. Draw time, when properly exploited, is said to be the most fruitful of all the Weathers.

Dritira: Fifth-largest Silistran city, largest southern port. Dritira receives goods overland from Stra and Galesh, and ships from every city with merchant fleets. The Embrodming Inlet, which she shares with the city of the written word, Yardum-Or, is the most trafficked harbor upon Silistra. Dritira, as Yardum-Or, is a dependent city to Well Oppiri, third most prestigious of the Silistran Wells.

ebvrasea: The largest of Silistra's omnivorous birds. Ebvraseas have been known to achieve a wingspread of sixteen feet or more. They are night hunters and seldom venture out of their craggy realms. Ebvraseas mate for life. They live isolated by the pair, and even mates do not hunt together. The average clutch of eggs is three, with seldom more than one reaching maturity. An adult ebvrasea will eat egg or young of another, even sometimes devouring their own offspring. Ebvraseas are most often black, brown, or white. The average lifespan of the mountain ebvrasea is forty Silistran years.

enth: One twenty-eighth of the Silistran day; each enth contains seventh-five *iths*.

Falls of Santha: The great cascades at the source

of the Litess River, high on the Plateau of Santha
in the Sabembe range.

fax: An orangy elastic material common to M'ksakkans and other B.F. races. Fax does not burn;
neither can it be torn or denuded of its message
by any means known upon Silistra.

Feast of Conception: The oldest performed ceremony upon Silistra, dating back into prehistory.
Before Haroun-Vhass, the Fall of Man, Silistrans
observed Feast of Conception.

forereaders: Those females who have received training in the sorting of probability. Forereaders are
the most powerful and prestigious women on
Silistra, those whom the Day-Keepers have chosen to share their work, those whose innate foreseeing ability is .88999 or better.

forereading: Stochastic processing, the sorting of
probability.

gaesh: The hide gaesh, beneath the jungle city of
Galesh on the Karir-Thoss River. The hide name
gaesh.

Galesh: The city that feeds Silistra, Galesh lies in
the most fertile Karir-Thoss Valley. The Galeshir
swamps yield a number of medicinal herbs that
cannot be found elsewhere, as well as the swamp
kepher from whose scent glands come the base
fixatives for the much-sought Galeshir perfumes.
In this tropical climate the Silistran silkworm
thrives; Galeshir carpets are second only to Parset
rugs in their beauty and durability.

gol: The excrescence of the golachit of Silistra. Gol
comes naturally in five colors: blue, amber, white,
silver, and red. Black or other adulterated colors
are produced by feeding the golachit the proper
melanis (harmless chemically treated fungi). Gol
is considered superior as a building material
because of its permanence; gol might last a man
a lifetime, while iron, brick, and wood seem to

wear away visibly under the Silistran eye. Gol hardens upon exposure to air, the mean time being one-quarter ith. Gol may be seen in Silistran buildings as sheet gol, gol-bricks, or gol-forms, the natural mode of golachit building, and also in smaller molded shapes such as tables, pedestals, or even the serrated blade of the gol-knife.

golachit: The great builder beetle of Silistra thrives both in a wild state in the gollands at the feet of the Sabembes, and in a mutually beneficial symbiosis with man. As with web-weaver and webber, so do golachit and golmaster blend minds and create together such beauty as would have remained unrealizable dream for either alone. The golachit is a scavenger by nature and finds both food and stimulation in this community with man. Golachits are fascinated by human children, and wild ones have often come into the human-golachit fraternity by following some hill-roaming child. Once in converse with a human mind, the golachit becomes fiercely protective of its humans and patrols the borders of their joint estate ceaselessly, marking off its territory with periodic excrescences. The golachit often travels in bands of up to a score, and many has been the man who has befriended one golachit and found, next morning, his good luck much multiplied. Golachits have been known to live a thousand years.

golmaster: One who enters into community of minds with a golachit; a golarchitect.

grinta: The most common flatfish on Silistra, recognized by its rusty brown dorsal scales and pale white ventral.

gristasha: The dark-skinned primitives who formed one-half of the hide aniet, precursors to the Parsets, who still tattoo themselves as did their fierce progenitors. The Parset culture, in language and custom, bears heavily this **gristasha** influence.

gul: The ovoid, juicy fruit from which Kifra is obtained; any of the three varieties of gul, the yellow, the orange, the purple-blue.

half-dippar: Silistran coinage; half-dippars, whether gold or copper, have no holes.

half-well: (titrium.) Silistran coinage, Well-minted, of the pink metal titrium. Two titrium half-wells equal one gold half-well. The titrium half-well still bears the profile of M'glarren, first Liaison to Silistra and couch-mate of the Foundress Astria, the only Well coin of any denomination ever to be struck with a male image. All other well coins bear the countenances of distinguished Well-Keepresses.

harth: (n.) A common and tasty bird whose feathers are black and iridescent. The harth thrives in city and town, as well as plain and forest. He is a migrating bird, preferring warm weather. In the northern regions at harvest past, the sky is indeed "harth-black" with their numbers, screeching their distinctive "Hareee, haree" cry.

harth: (adj.) Anything black and shining, especially black with blue or purple overtones.

Hertekiea: A planet in the Wingtip Cluster, the inhabitants of which have achieved homogeneity of race. The typical Hertekiean has darker skin than one might expect for a world in which the yellow, green, red, and violet races were absorbed by the blue race, but her proximity to the ever-flaring star Bnien is said to account for the increased melanin production of the last ten generations. The dark lords of Hertekiea, otherwise, are in size and build much like Silistrans, and ideologically compatible as well. The Hertekiean men and women display by hair length and intricate braiding patterns thereof those motives and bindings that are known on Silistra as chaldra.

hest: To bend or twist natural law to serve the will; to command by mind; to cause a probability not inherent in the time to manifest. (The line between hesting and shaping *is* somewhat difficult to define when highly skilled individuals are concerned. The rule of thumb is held to be thus: if natural law must be remade or totally superseded, as in creating a permanent object such as fruit or a star, one is shaping. If one is simply controlling an already existing object or event, as would be the case if one caused a fruit or star already in existence to alter its behavior but not its structure, one is hesting. The fruit or star one moves to the right or the left or higher in the sky by will would not have behaved in that fashion, but is still the same star or fruit as was a natural inhabitant of the time before the hest was applied. If one, on the other hand, creates fruit or star, one has brought into the time, by a suspension of natural law, that which heretofore did not exist. (One shapes matter. One hests time.) In usage, bringing in a hest, affecting probability.

hide: The seven hides of Silistra: aniet, bast, crill, diet, gaesh, rendi, and stoen. Each hide supported a thousand survivors and their progeny through the long years of waiting until the planet's surface was again habitable. Under the aegis of the dharen's Day-Keepers and forereaders, the hides were built and operating sixty years before the projected disaster. But few believed, and thus only in hide aniet were there other than Day-Keepers and forereaders when the world exploded into war. It is said that the word "hide" derived from the scoffing and mocking of pre-hide Silistra at the project. "Khys's burrows" was another early name for the interconnected life-support complexes that saved what little of Silistra that was desirous of survival.

hide-days: The thousand years of subterranean living, accounted hide-year one through one thousand. Our present calendar date of 25,693 is counted from the first year spent above the ground. All that occurred before hide-year one is termed pre-hide, or prehistoric.

hide-name: Any of the seven hide-names: aniet, bast, crill, diet, gaesh, rendi, and stoen. Hide descent is always carried through the mother. The hide-name is second in the male, third in the female, and always takes lower-case honors.

high-couch: Formally, the Well-Keepress; also any woman able to demand over thirty gold dippars per couching.

hulion: The most intelligent animal on explored Silistra. The hulion—winged, furred carnivore of the Sabembe range—shuns civilization. They are known to have mind skills and a complex language, but are not symbolizers such as man. The hulion does as he wills upon Silistra, and none obstruct him. The high Sabembes and the unnamed western mountains are their domain of choice. There is no beast, including man, that can stand before a hulion's onslaught—up to twenty-three hundred B.S. pounds of sinew and tooth and claw. Hulions have been seen with wingspreads four times the height of a man, beasts so large that their jaws could snap a man in half. Disregarding the wings, a hulion much resembles a large dorkat, even to the slit-pupiled eyes and the silk-tufted tail.

Iartex: One from the planet Iarte. The small stature and scuttling gait of these off-worlders is attributed to their planet's half-again B.S. gravity. The Itabe colonized Iartex six thousand, three hundred years ago, and (other than the physical alteration their adopted homeland made upon them) seem to all intents and purposes culturally identical with their mother world, although each decries the other for its moral decay, and both sight unresolvable differences in their life-views.

Inner Well: The great central court within a Well's walls.

Itabe: A .99998 planet which revolves around the star Eeia, closest neighbor to M'ksakka's system; Dellin's birthplace.

Itabic: One of Itabe, the race from which Dellin's mother sprang. The Itabic peoples have made numerous contributions to society, the most notable being their Multilingual Cipher system, which lay bare the logics of language common to all cultures and has been of inestimable aid to Liaison missions and contact teams alike.

ith: One-seventy-fifth of an enth.

jeri: A costly and exotic M'ksakkan drink which mixes seven fruits with a char-filtered grain beverage; a sweet drink much favored by women.

jitkaw: Named for its cry, the jitkaw is a brightly crest-headed bird, usually tri-toned, with a curving beak and red eyes. The males have tails twice the length of the females, on which flames of light color scallop each feather's tip. A red-yellow-amber jitkaw is held to be a harbinger of glad tidings, while a green-yellow-blue is the worst of signs.

Katrir: An off-world race characterized by tufted ears, split-pupiled eyes, and multiple birthings; from the planet Katrii, the gemstone center of the civilized worlds, and twin to the planet Beten.

kifra: A Silistran drink made from crushed guls, a live fruit wine.

Koster: Having origin upon the planet Kost, famous for her silks. The inhabitants of Kost, at least the ruling class, have a bluish, pale cast to their skin, and silvery hair, even in youth.

Liaison: The contact officers installed as semipermanent officials on Bipedal Federate Trade Union worlds. The designation "First," "Second," etc., is Silistran, but indicative of the local M'ksakkan hierarchy.

Liaison's Port: Foundress Astria's couch-gift to the M'ksakkan M'glarren; Silistra's single space port.

Litess: The Litess River.

Macara: The fourth pass of the Silistran calendar.

M'glarren: Couch-mate of Well Foundress Astria, first M'ksakkan to set foot upon Silistran soil.

Mi'ysten: True name for both the planet and people of the world the M'ksakkans call Zredori; experimental sphere of the Shapers.

M'ksakka: The administrative planet of the B.F. Group and Bipedal Federate Trade Union. M'ksakka is highly industrialized world that exports all types of leisure and convenience machinery, a superior solar sail, and a synthetic shatterproof crystal.

M'ksakkan: Originating upon M'ksakka. All M'ksakkans, unless very high or very low in their society, bear the M' before their name; as M'lennin, or, converserly, Khaf-Re Dellin.

Morrlta: The pelter town nestled in the foothills of the Sabembes.

narne: A red, round fruit with crisp white pulp and a distinctly salty aftertaste; the tree, which bears red leaves and fruits eight passes out of the year; the drink made from pulping the fruit.

nera: 1.2 B.S. miles; Silistran measure of distance.

Oguast: A provisionally entered B.F. planet in Silistra's own sector. Oguast's surface is eighty-

two percent water, her main exports are wistwa
ivory and articles of superior ceramic process.

parr: The small, wiry-haired food beast of Silistra.
Parr seldom reach more than six hands in height,
but may carry up to four hundred B.S. pounds.
The snub-nosed, flop-eared parr provides Silistra
with meats, hide, fertilizer, and glue. It is said of
a parr that only its hair does man no service.

parr-breeder: One who raises parr; one who wears
the low-chaldric brown strand.

parr-hide: The sturdiest leather available on Silistra,
parr-hide is thicker and less pliable than either
tas or denter. Its main uses are in harnesses,
footwear, armor, and weapon-related leathers.

Parset: (adj.) Having origin in the Parset Lands.

Parset: (n.) An individual of any one of the five
Parset tribes.

Parset Lands: The Parset Desert; the Parset barrens;
the territories of the five tribes—Coseve, Dordassa,
Itophe, Menetph (under which lies hide aniet),
and Nemar. The Parset Lands lie at the bottom
of Skirr Valley. They are bounded on the north-
east by the tail of the Sabembes, on the east and
south by the Embrodming Sea, and on the west
by the southern Yaica range and the river Oppi.

pass: One-fourteenth of the Silistran year; the
Silistran lunation. Each pass is composed of four
sets.

peg: (v., to peg time.) To scale down one's time
sense, to become concerned with the moment, to
expand the moment. Pegging time is a prerequi-
site to all temporal skills. More formally referred
to as "taking stance in the now," this process is
the Silistran weapon against idleness and apathy,
as well as the first step in sorting: discerning the
probabilities available from the moment. The
moment is infinitely fruitful; it is the mind's
apprehension of it that is subject to famine and

drought. If a man, at the end of the day, recollects only a blur of similitude, it is then incumbent upon him to redouble his efforts to "take stance," lest he come to the end of his life and find, in truth, that the days have all slipped away.

**pelter:** Trapper, one who hunts for fur beasts.

**Pleiatu:** The inhabitants of the planet Pliatus; master weavers of the known stars whose dyes make even Parset colors drab by comparison.

**point-leader:** Rank designation; officer over twenty in any private mercenary force, such as the Well guards.

**Port Astrin:** Well Astria's dependent city. Port Astrin, adjoining the Liaison's Port, caters more than any other Silistran city to off-worlders. "If a man itches for the stars, send him to Port Astrin. If Astrin does not sate, buy him passage, for where spirit goes, flesh must sometimes follow."—Astrian proverb. In Port Astrin may be found all manner of off-world recreation and necessity. She is the only authorized embarkation/debarkation center, housing both M'ksakkan and Silistran Port Authorities.

**presti m'it:** (Stothric: Presti, let us be of; m'it, one flesh; thus, let us be of one flesh. Prest m'it: we be of one flesh.) Traditional Day-Keeper greeting.

**ragony:** Tan-and-black-striped hardwood from the deciduous ragony tree. Ragony is used where a decorative wood is desired. It is not uncommon, nor so costly as thala, and is often used as a substitute for thala where price is a concern.

**rana:** A hot, stimulating drink, rusty-brown in color, from the steppe-grown berried plant of the same name.

**rana:** (adj.) Being of the color rana, rusty-brown.

**rendi:** The hide rendi, under the city of Stra, which

lies on the most western shores of the inland
Opirian Sea; the hide-name rendi.

Sabembes: The Sabembe range, sometimes called
the Eastern Crags.

Santha: The Plateau of Santha; the Falls of Santha.

seed-sowers: Variously known as the Lawgivers,
Lords of Form, Creator Sons, System Suzerains,
Pantheon of Gods, etc.; any postulated supernal
hierarchy that aids, guides, judges, or in any way
concerns itself with the lives of men; the doc-
trines of supernormal paternity and judgment.
In specific, as it is known upon Silistra: In the
beginning, there was the differentiation of One
into the Sevenfold, and the resulting Interchange
begat Time, and into Time was birthed Matter
out of the Universe Mother by God the Absolute.
Then began Dispensation of Labors and the creation of the Master Circuits, upon which were
laid the superuniverses in plan and potential,
that creation be ongoing. Into being came then
the Hierarachy in its multitudinous Corps. These
began instantly upon their functions; creation
by differentation and the Ordering of Time and
Space. Under the guidance of the Creator Spirit
was undertaken the design and implementation
of the personalizable minuscule, diversely known
as the Mirror of Creation, the Eyes of God, and
Mortal Man. So great were the hopes of the
Source Indivisible for Man that the command
came down the hierarchal circuits: In your own
image, let them be made. And even did the Father Indissoluble send out fragments of himself
to partake of the Apprehension of Creation from
within as full partners with mortals of Silistra,
and upon this decision came into being the seed-
sowers, that the divinity-destined minuscules receive the aid and comfort due these flesh-children
of God the Sevenfold. Into seed-sower care were

placed the worlds of man, and even did they come upon Silistra and give instruction and guidance to the seven root-races. These Created Sons and Daughters lived side by side with primitives of Silistra, giving fire and language and in some cases admixing with mortals until the races of Man were secure. At that time, their mandate ended, they retired from the planet to the Magisterial Plane to take up the increasingly complex duties of caring for all that they had wrought, and to await reassignment in the worlds of ongoing creation.

**sereel:** A Mi'ysten measure of mental broadcast range.

**set:** Seven days; one quarter of the Silistra pass. Sets in a pass are reckoned first through fourth. "First third" would be the third day of the first set in a given Silistran pass.

**Seven:** A man who has attained the rank of seventh in the council of seven Slayers that oversees the Slayers of a given hostel; in addressing one of that rank: "Seven"; in speaking of him, "the Seven" of a given hostel.

**Shaper:** One who can control the constituents of matter and form them to this will.

**Silistra:** The third planet of the star Veriti; in usage, the inhabited continent, exempting the Polar Wastes and those shores of which none are empowered to speak.

**Silistran:** (adj.) Of Silistra.

**Silistran:** (language.) Often called modern or New Silistran, the planetary tongue. Although some may not speak Darsti, the language of science, nor Stothric, the language of metaphysics, nor Parset, the tongue of the desert dwellers, all speak Silistran.

**s'kim:** An unrestricting short garment worn by women, often white. A s'kim may be tied in

numerous ways, and is differentiated from a
short-length wrap by its strings at neck, waist,
and hip.

Slayers: The enforcement arm of the Day-Keepers,
those who have tested for and been awarded the
black-iron chain, chaldric strand of the Slayers.
Slayers are an authority as accessible to one
man as any other, and there is no man who is
denied the strength of a Slayer's arm, be his
need just and true, and his waist chalded. A
Slayer is responsible to his Slayers' Seven and
ultimately to the Day-Keepers for his actions,
but in practice he is usually his own authority,
responsible to the Law Within. The limit of fourteen Slayers upon any one commission, however,
is strictly enforced. The Slayer's device is the
crossed sword and stones in black, upon a silver
ground. Their leather colors are slate and black.
Sub-ranks are indicated by belt colors and cords.

Slayers' Seven: The top-ranking Slayers in a given
hostel; the seven officials directly responsible to
the Day-Keepers for the comportment of their
hostel. Each is addressed by his rank number,
"One" through "Seven."

slitsa: Any legless reptile; of the class "slitsa." There
are one hundred and five species of slitsa.

stoen: The hide stoen, under the Lake of Horns,
that Day-Keepers' city west of the Yaica mountains and east of the Karir-Thoss River; the hide-
name stoen.

stones: The weighted whip of the Slayers. All
"stones" are five-lashed except within the Slayers'
Seven itself, where the number of lashes corres-
ponds to the rank of the official concerned.

Stoth: The Stoth disciplines; the prehistoric philos-
ophy and religion that were precursors to the
Day-Keepers and the Weathers of Life.

Stothric: An archaic Silistran language; the language of methaphysics; the traditional garb of the Stoth priesthood.

Stra: The city of Stra, upon the most westerly shore of the inland Opirian Sea. Stra is the mining capital of Silistra, the home of famed stra-metal, whose secret is considered Stra's greatest treasure. Stra also refines copper, bauxite, iron, and gold, all of which they mine in the rich Yaica range. Within Stra's gates are Well Frenya, and beneath her, the hide rendi.

stra: That greenish metal refined in the city of Stra, whose resistance to corrosion and tensile strength are greater than that of Silistran steel.

tas: The woolly hill grazer whose flesh is most highly prized of all Silistran meats. Tas graze well on most Silistran forage, the only exception being climatic—a hot tas will not eat. Even in the north it is customary to shear tas thrice yearly, that the spring and summer heat not kill them in large numbers.

tas-skin: Often referred to simply as tas, or tas-suede. The hide of the tas may be split very thin, and even in splits rivals the durability of leathers thrice as thick. Tas is often used in clothing or to line coarser leathers. Tas is recommended for use in any case where softness and pliability are a main concern.

Tasa: (Stothric: be blessed.) The common Silistran farewell.

tasling: A tas under six years of age.

"Tenist dast-ei": "May your unions be fruitful." Traditional well woman's greeting to a customer.

"Tenist mist-as": "May your womb bear my fruit." Traditional customer's response.

thala: The most costly hardwood upon Silistra. Northern thala, the preferred variety, is black with a blue cast. Southern thala, substantially less expensive, is black with brown overgrain. It lacks the sheen and depth of northern thala, but shares its near-imperviousness to weather.

Thrah: Iridescent long-haired pelts from the planet Torth; the animal from which the Thrah pelt comes is about the same size as a brist and might be mistaken for one, but for the long, multicolored coat and the fact that the thrah walks on all fours and is mute.

threx: The preferred riding beast of Silistra. The threx may range from fifteen to twenty hands in height, from one to two thousand B.S. pounds. It prefers meat but can subsist upon almost anything. It is readily domesticated up to a point, but remains a moderately dangerous animal at all times. Threx can reach a speed of up to forty neras an enth for short periods, and in endurance races have been known to make as much as six hundred neras in four days. Threx are readily trained and often war-trained. Threx-men are fond of saying that there is no weapon but man more dangerous than threx. The threx of the north and the Parset threx, who has two vertebrae fewer than his northern cousin, are in some other ways dissimilar: the Parset threx has a more efficient metabolism, nictitating membranes, nostrils that can be closed at will, and greater strength and stamina than the common Silistran threx.

titrium: A pinkish metal similar to gold but less costly. Titrium is the metal of the couchbond strand, and the half-well titrium coin. Titrium is a product of the city Torwin.

Torth: The planet Torth, from which Silistra buys more goods than from all the other star-worlds combined. Torth sculpture, whether out of metal or stone, or in the form of "Torth sculptured hangings" is much sought upon Silistra. A Torth sculptured hanging is basically a thick-piled tapestry worked upon a very fine grid with threads woven from the Thrah-hair, and then carved to various depths, revealing at each level different tones of color.

Torwin: The city Torwin, from which comes titrium. Torwin is sometimes called the musicians' city. Both players and makers of instruments throng Torwin from elsewhere on Silistra, to study the aural arts. Torwin, upon the Karir river delta, has both a sea and river port, and from it ships tropical fruits and certain crustaceous delicacies north.

tridoe: A Mi'ysten holding or keep.

tun: A starchy, black-skinned tuber with yellow pulp that grows in stony, sandy, or even poor soil.

web-cloth: A nearly indestructible material made in collaboration by web-weavers and webbers, Silistra's largest arachnids.

web-fiber: The web-strands used for ropemaking when optimum strength is required and the fact that web-fiber rope cannot be cut is no deterrent. Web-fiber is produced only by training webber-weaver pairs, and is much less common than hemp rope.

web-work: Open-weave, diaphanous body dressing, usually geometric in pattern; more than lace and less than cloth, very similar to the unguided work of webber alone.

Well Arlet: The second most prestigious Well on Silistra lies on the elbow of the Sabembe range, above the hide bast.

Well Astria: The most venerated Well on Silistra, Astria bears the name of the Well Foundress Astria Barina diet Hadrath, author of the Well Woman's Ors (Stothric: book). Astria was the premier Well, and although different in trappings and style, in substance every Well upon Silistra is patterned after the Astrian form. Well Astria lies upon the plain of Astria, fifty-eight neras from hide diet and the Day-Keepers' School.

well tokens: (gold and silver.) Must be purchased with regular coinage or won in the pass and set games. Well tokens from one well may not be used in another, nor are they considered coinage per se. The nondenominational well token used at Feast of Conception and other ceremonial fetes never leaves the well, but it collected with great attention and reverence and stored until fortune dictates they be used again. The same nondenominational tokens have been used in Well Astria since the Well's founding, were in fact used at that first well feast.

wind from the abyss: In the *Ors Yris-tera* (Book of the Weathers of Life), written by the dharen Khys, is the first known reference to the wind from the abyss, and it is from this book of divination that the term came into general usage. Who of Silistra has not at one time or another thrown the bone yris-tera pieces onto the three level board and found himself delineated as the "ebvrasea upon the square of overriding purpose"? Says the Ors: "His wings beat upon the wind from the abyss." And: "Stalking is assiduous; Stalking culls the weak from the strong; in both the hunters and the hunted does it perform this function." (Khys, from the divination "Stalking.") In common usage, the chill of premonition, the physical forewarning of danger that may not be avoided. "Before Stalking, who can stand but those who also stalk?"

wisper: Wisper tree, a fan-leaved evergreen whose bark is smooth and velvety; the soft, resinous wood of the wisper tree.

wistwa: The great sea beast of Oguast. It is maintained by Oguasti that two tall men, one upon the other's shoulders, could stand within the rib cage of the wistwa, and that the top man might then stretch his arms upward in vain to touch the backbone of the great sea beast of Oguast; the ivory of such a beast.

yellow crier: A bright yellow bird that might lie in the palm of a hand. In flight the yellow crier's wings are invisible. It darts at great speed and low altitude after the insects that are its prey. Its beak is as long again as its head, and from its mouth comes a sound like a screaming child's.

Zredori: The M'ksakkan misnomer for Mi'ysten.

# Silistran Calendar

pass of winter solstice

Orsai
Tisera
Cai
Macara
Detarsa
Jicar
Finara

pass of summer solstice

Amarsa
Cetet
Enar
Brinar
Decra
Sisaen
Laoral

# FREE!!
# BOOKS BY MAIL
# CATALOGUE

BOOKS BY MAIL will share with you our current bestselling books as well as hard to find specialty titles in areas that will match your interests. You will be updated on what's new from Pocket Books at no cost to you. Just fill in the coupon below and discover the convenience of having books delivered to your home.

---

**BOOKS BY MAIL**
**320 Steelcase Rd. E.**
**Markham, Ont. L3R 2M1**

Please send Books By Mail catalogue to:

Name_____
                    (please print)
Address_____

City_____

Prov._____ Postal Code _____
                                        (BBM2)